RESISTANCE™
A HOLE IN THE SKY

By William C. Dietz

Resistance: The Gathering Storm

RESISTANCE™
A HOLE IN THE SKY

Withdrawn/ABCL

William C. Dietz

BALLANTINE BOOKS • NEW YORK

Resistance: A Hole in the Sky is a work of fiction. Names, characters, places, and incidents are the products of the author's imagination or are used fictitiously. Any resemblance to actual events, locales, or persons, living or dead, is entirely coincidental.

A Del Rey Mass Market Original

Copyright © 2011 by Sony Computer Entertainment America LLC.

Published in the United States by Del Rey Books, an imprint of The Random House Publishing Group, a division of Random House, Inc., New York.

DEL REY is a registered trademark and the Del Rey colophon is a trademark of Random House, Inc.

Resistance is a trademark of Sony Computer Entertainment America LLC.

ISBN 978-0-345-50843-0

Printed in the United States of America

www.delreybooks.com
www.bioware.com

9 8 7 6 5 4 3 2 1

Del Rey mass market edition August 2011

For Marjorie with all my love

ACKNOWLEDGMENTS

I would like to thank President and CEO of Insomniac Games Ted Price, as well as Chief Creative Officer Brian Hastings, Creative Director Marcus Smith, Writer Jon Paquette, and all the rest of the folks at Insomniac Games for their help and support.

Thanks also go to Sony Computer Entertainment America Senior Producer Frank Simon and my editor, Tricia Pasternak.

CHAPTER ONE
BACK ATCHA

It was 0836 in the morning, but so dark it might have been evening. Purplish clouds hung low over the snow-shrouded city as if to smother it. And when they parted, it was to allow the upper reaches of an alien structure to pass through a black-rimmed hole and touch the sky beyond. At its base, the tower wasn't so much a symmetrical obelisk as a muscular tree trunk that had driven its angular roots down through New York's outer crust into the subterranean flesh below.

The very sight of the brooding tower and the dim lights that glowed within served to reignite President Thomas Voss's hatred for the Chimera. He was lying prone on the roof of a half-gutted warehouse, looking across the half-frozen Hudson River through a pair of powerful binoculars.

The top third of the Empire State Building had been sheared off, leaving an ice-encrusted stump to poke up out of the hills of drifted snow surrounding the tower. Voss knew that thousands of such structures had been excavated across the surface of the planet. All working in concert to cool Earth's atmosphere and make it comfortable for the Chimera.

The rotten bastards, Voss thought to himself. *Damn them to hell!*

Although the truth was that the Chimeran forms weren't so much individuals as functionaries. All controlled by a hive-mind that was better described as an "it" rather than a "them."

But the hive-mind could manifest itself in more than a dozen different forms. It landed in Russia, and then exploded out of that country in 1949 and overran Europe. The luckiest humans died. The less fortunate succumbed to the alien virus and were transformed into Chimera.

Within a year most of Europe had fallen, leaving only Great Britain to carry on. But after a desperate struggle, England fell as well, and the Chimera attacked America in 1952. American towns and cities were overrun, and millions of citizens were transformed into monstrosities. And, with the exception of a top-secret organization called SRPA (Special Research Projects Administration), the government had been slow to react. Voss, then Assistant Secretary of the Interior, admitted as much. The result was a vast Chimeran-dominated wasteland that stretched from coast to coast and from Canada to Mexico.

They could not conduct a census, or do any of the other things governments were supposed to do, but Voss and his staff estimated that most of the country's 160 million citizens had been killed by the Chimera, rampant disease, or starvation. The 10 million or so people who remained were hiding from alien hunter-killer teams and trying to eke out whatever sort of living they could.

But if Voss and a force of volunteers could enter New York and destroy the Chimeran tower, the victory would not only slow the systematic effort to cool the planet's atmosphere, it would send a message of hope to the citizens of the United States. *And* cement his position as President, a responsibility Voss had assumed after the VTOL (vertical takeoff and landing aircraft) carrying

President McCullen and the surviving members of his cabinet had been shot down.

An Army general assumed the presidency after that. He was subsequently killed by a Titan at the battle of Phoenix, leaving the nation rudderless until Voss stepped forward. "So, Marvin," Voss said as he lowered his glasses. "What do you think?"

Rather than scan the New York skyline, Captain Marvin Kawecki's binoculars were focused on the problem immediately in front of them and off to the left. And that was the approach to the Holland Tunnel. Kawecki had a shock of dark hair, squinty eyes, and a weather-seamed face. "I can see half a dozen Hybrids. All of them are inside the central toll station. I think Chu could nail half of them—but we'll need a second sniper to get all six. Can you handle that, Mr. President?"

"I'll sure as hell try," Voss said as he secured his binoculars. "Let's go down and take them out."

Kawecki thumbed his mike. Like most members of the team, he wore fingerless knit gloves. "We're pulling out. Lang, find a path to the brick building that fronts the toll plaza. We'll clear the center booth from there. Over."

The other soldiers, all of whom had been providing security up until then, seemed to materialize out of nowhere. All were veterans, experts at urban warfare, and had accompanied Voss on the long three-month journey from Freedom Base in the Ozark National Forest.

There had once been sixteen troopers, but a long series of battles had taken their toll. The remaining soldiers were dressed in whatever manner they preferred and armed with a wild variety of human and Chimeran weaponry. No orders were given, nor were any required as a man named Lang took the point position. He had a long, lugubrious face and the manner of an undertaker. Kawecki was next, followed by Voss, Private Mason,

Corporal Rigg, Private Venley, Private Chu, and Sergeant Alvarez, the last having been promoted to second-in-command when Lieutenant Hopper took a projectile between the eyes just east of Louisville.

Lang led them around a large hole and down three flights of switchbacking stairs to the ground floor, where he paused just inside a shattered doorway. The Chimera were called "stinks" for a reason, and Lang had an extremely acute sense of smell. Just one of the reasons why he was on point.

Once he was sure it was safe, Lang slipped out through the door, took a left, and made his way down a sloping passageway. From there he led them through a half-burned factory to a door on the north side. Waving the rest of the men into cover, he went forward alone.

Voss and the others could do nothing but wait as Lang crossed an alley and disappeared into the one-story brick building fronting the toll plaza. Finally, his voice hushed, the scout invited the snipers to join him.

Chu had the sharpest eye on the team. But Voss was pretty good too, and proud to have been chosen for such an important task. Because he knew that the title "President" didn't mean very much to the men around him. Not anymore. Their respect had to be earned.

After entering through the back door, the men made their way past a row of looted offices and into the lobby beyond. Lang was waiting for them. He pointed to the shattered windows that bracketed the front door and looked out onto the toll plaza. Voss chose the window on the left, Chu took the right, and Lang turned his back on both of them in order to watch the back entrance.

Chu was armed with a scope-mounted government-issue L23 Fareye. Without a sniper's rifle of his own, Voss had to rely on his carbine. Though equipped with an open sight, in the right hands the weapon was very accurate and capable of firing a lot of rounds in a short period of time. Voss thumbed the safety off, eyed the toll booth, and saw the stinks lurking inside. In a perverse sort of way, their presence was a good sign. Because there was no reason to guard a tunnel that was closed. Voss kept his voice low. "I'll break the glass and wait for you to take two of them out. Then I'll hose the rest of the bastards down."

Chu kept his eye glued to the scope as he spoke. "Sounds good. I'll start with the stink on the far right."

Voss chose a target of his own. Even though his task was to break the glass, he hoped to nail one of the aliens at the same time. His right index finger tightened, the rifle jerked, and the bullet made a flat cracking sound as it passed through the air. Glass exploded, and the stink spun halfway around as half of its head disappeared in a cloud of blood. Then Chu fired. Both of his shots found their targets—they dropped as if they had been poleaxed.

But by then the toll booth's front door had flown open, and in typical Chimeran fashion, the surviving stinks charged straight into the human guns. They were horrible-looking things with no hair, low foreheads, and needle-sharp fangs.

Chu dropped one of them. But since the Fareye's rate of fire was relatively slow, it was up to Voss to put the rest of them down. The Hybrids were not only fast, but firing Bullseyes as they came. Voss had good reason to be concerned as a volley of homing tags stuttered past his head. Because if one of the tags hit, *all* of the subsequent projectiles would strike him too, no matter where the stink aimed its weapon.

So Voss forced himself to concentrate as he put two rounds into the first 'brid and saw patches of blood appear on its chest. The Chimera staggered, but still managed to take three more steps, before a final bullet took the top of its head off.

But precious seconds had been lost. The next alien was only ten feet away and closing fast when Voss pulled the trigger and held it back. Brass shell casings arced away and a row of bloody divots appeared across the stink's muscular chest. Such was the creature's momentum, however, that it slammed into the window frame before it finally came to a halt. Then, like a just-cut tree, the six-eyed monstrosity toppled over. Voss reflexively jerked on the carbine's trigger, heard his weapon click empty, and hoped his fear didn't show.

The sound of sustained gunfire brought Kawecki and the rest of the team forward. "Good work," the officer said approvingly as puffs of lung-warmed air drifted away from his lips. "Maybe some of the other stinks will hear the shooting and come running or maybe they won't. Let's enter the tunnel as quickly as we can. At least they won't be able to nail us from above."

Voss nodded, released his empty magazine, and caught it. Clips, like everything else, were hard to come by. Stowing the empty in a pouch, he pushed a spare up into the well and pumped a shell into the weapon's chamber.

Then it was time to follow Kawecki past a shot-up delivery truck. A bright red, yellow, and blue "Wonder Bread" logo was painted on its side. A frozen mummy could be seen sitting behind the wheel, forever eyeing the traffic ahead.

Darkness closed around them as they entered the two-lane-wide eastbound tube. Voss knew the tunnel was a little more than a mile and a half long, and about ninety-three feet deep at its lowest point. Reaching the other side would be a challenge—but it had to be done if they were going to attack the tower.

Inside the tunnel, the only lights were the beams from their weapons. And if it was frigid outside, it was even more so beneath the river, where the cold air had a tendency to collect. The pale beams played across the tiled ceiling, filthy walls, and cars that had been caught in the tunnel on the day New York was overwhelmed.

Voss couldn't help but think about the people who had been in the vehicles all around him. It seemed reasonable to assume that at least some of them had been able to walk out. But what then? Had they been able to reach their homes? Or had they been slaughtered from above?

He pushed the questions away. His job was to focus on the present and the people who were still alive. "I have a pod farm on the right," Lang commented from up ahead. "Stay left. Over."

The fleshy structures stood about seven feet tall, and Voss knew the ones in front of him had been created by one or more Spinners. The ugly, blunt-headed creatures had razor-sharp teeth, sickle-shaped claws, and a ridge that ran all the way to the end of their pointy tails. So it was important to keep a sharp eye out.

Under normal circumstances, the team simply went around the cocoons, and the Grims "cooking" inside them, even if there weren't any stinks around. It was nice to burn them out when they could spare an air-fuel grenade. But as tempting as the opportunity was, they couldn't spare any ordnance. They left the pod farm untouched.

The side-wash from his light illuminated the cocoons as Voss walked past. The pods were pulsating, as if synched to a heartbeat deep within, and he was glad to put the groaning sounds behind him.

After fifteen minutes or so, the ice began to crackle and water splashed away from Voss's boots. "It's getting deeper," Lang warned over the radio. "We'd better climb up onto the walkway. Over."

Pedestrians weren't allowed in the tunnel, but a raised walkway had been provided in case there was a need to evacuate the tube, so it was a simple matter to climb up onto it. However, as the team continued downwards, it wasn't long before the thick green-gray slush was sloshing over the platform as well. "We can use the cars as stepping stones," Lang suggested, as he jumped onto the roof of a taxi. "But they're slippery, so watch your step. Over."

The pace slowed considerably as the team was forced to leap from roof to roof while battling to stay upright. But worst of all was the occasional need to jump into the ice-cold water and wade with weapons held high.

Voss had just completed such a journey, and was standing on the trunk of a '52 Chevy, when he heard a scream and turned to see a series of muzzle flashes.

"It's Venley!" Rigg shouted in between short bursts from Mason's Wraith. "He was wading across a gap when something took him!"

"It was a Fury," Chu added grimly. "The damned thing was hiding behind a truck. Over."

"Cease fire!" Kawecki ordered sternly. "Save your ammo. You could pour bullets into that Fury all day long without giving it a headache. Close the gap and keep moving. That's all we can do."

Voss knew Kawecki was correct, but that didn't make him feel any better. Why had the Chimera allowed five people to pass before attacking Venley? Why not kill Lang, Kawecki, or himself? There was no way to know as they plowed ahead, careful to take even the most circuitous routes, rather than enter the water again.

It was tedious work, but gradually the water level began to fall, and they could climb up onto the elevated walkway once more. That was when Voss saw a message scrawled on the wall and paused to read it. "Watch out!" the block letters said. "Furies in the water."

Now you tell us, Voss thought bitterly. *Now you fucking tell us*. It wasn't the anonymous author's fault, of course—but it felt good to vent some of his anger.

Kawecki called a halt so the men could change into mostly dry clothing and brew some coffee. Then, with something warm in their stomachs, it was time to go.

The next fifteen minutes were spent climbing a gradual slope until they could see a half-circle of gray light. Snow was falling beyond. The lacy curtain billowed occasionally when the breeze hit. Then the snowfall steadied again, as if determined to throw a new shroud over the city.

"There were guards at the west end," Kawecki observed evenly. "So it would make sense if there were guards at *this* end as well. Take it slow. Over."

But, logical or not, there weren't any Chimera waiting outside the tunnel. There *had* been, however, judging from the maze of half-filled tracks, which meant the stinks might return at any moment. Still, Voss and Kawecki knew that all sorts of dangers could be lying in wait, so they paused to study the area through their binoculars before proceeding.

Some of the surrounding buildings were still reasonably intact. But one of them appeared to have been stomped by a gigantic foot, suggesting that a three hundred-foot-tall Leviathan might have passed through the area at some point, leaving a path of destruction in its wake. As Voss scanned the cityscape from left to right he saw the tail end of a SRPA VTOL sticking out of the side of a skyscraper. One of hundreds that had been shot down trying to defend the city.

A frayed banner, with the words "GIGANTIC SALE" emblazoned across it, hung from the building next to it. And a barely visible flagpole could be seen jutting out from the second floor of the high-rise on the opposite side of the street. "There it is," he said. "At two o'clock."

Kawecki turned slightly and made a minute adjustment to his glasses. "Check! There's Old Glory! Right where she's supposed to be. It looks like Lucy is still alive. Thank God for that."

Voss nodded. Like Kawecki, he had spoken with the agent named Lucy by radio, but never met her. And that was before they left Arkansas some three months earlier. A lot can happen in ninety days. "If you're ready, let's go. We're supposed to meet her at the Hotel Constantine. My guess is that she's watching us from one of those buildings."

"Roger that," Kawecki said, as he fastened his binoculars into place. "All right, everybody, let's move out. And don't forget to eyeball the windows all around. A stink with an Auger could do lots of damage from up there. Over."

Voss heard a crunching sound under his boots as he followed Lang and Kawecki across a field of fresh snow. He knew the stinks could follow and wondered if they would. How many humans remained in New York anyway? Enough to make tracks a common sight? Or were signs of habitation so rare as to merit an immediate follow-up? The politician didn't know but figured he was about to find out.

Lang must have been thinking about it too, because he made it a point to walk on bare concrete in the few places where that was possible, and cut through stores when it made sense. Fifteen minutes later they slipped through the front door of a run-down hostelry called the Constantine. It was a residential hotel from the look of it, which made sense given all the factories and warehouses in the area. An imposing reception desk stood off to the left, backed by a key rack, and a framed list of "House Rules."

Broken glass crackled under Rigg's boots as he walked over to the reception desk and slapped the dome-shaped bell that sat next to a black telephone. It made a lonely ringing sound.

Voss eyed the lobby's worn chairs, the shoe-shine stand, and the magazine kiosk that was decorated with cigarette advertising. Taking a closer look, he saw that a two-year-old copy of *Time* magazine was still for sale. The cover photo consisted of an open-mouthed Steelhead. The caption read: "What do they want?"

The answer, as it turned out, was *everything*.

Voss's thoughts were interrupted when Chu said, "We've got company," and a woman walked in off the street. She was decked out in a fashionable fur hat, a pink ski jacket, and a bandolier of red shotgun shells. The rest of her outfit consisted of black stirrup pants and fur-trimmed boots. A Winchester pump gun was tucked under her right arm. She looked like a socialite on a skeet shoot. "Hi," she said cheerfully. "I'm Lucy. Welcome to the Big Apple. Which one of you is President Voss?"

Voss stepped forward. The woman in front of him appeared to be in her early thirties. Blond curls peeked out from under the cap. Her wide-set eyes were China blue and her skin was alabaster white.

Lucy was a beautiful woman, or had been back before something ripped her face open and left a jagged scar that started high on the right side of her face. The white line zigzagged down across a softly rounded cheek to the left corner of her mouth. The stitches looked like the work of an amateur. Voss could tell that she knew what he was thinking as her chin came up and her eyes narrowed. "I'm Tom Voss," he replied. "It's a pleasure to meet you. Thanks for agreeing to help us."

"You're the one who deserves thanks," Lucy replied sincerely as her eyes darted from face to face. "Odds are that the stinks know you're here by now, so it's best to keep moving."

Lucy led the team out onto Canal Street, and from there to Varick, where they took a right. Voss would have felt very exposed if it hadn't been for the snow. It was falling more thickly now, reducing visibility to little more than twenty feet, and erasing the team's tracks within a matter of minutes.

Warehouses crowded in all around as Varick merged with Broadway. A short time later the party turned left onto Chambers, where they passed a building that appeared to have been pulverized by a giant foot. Then it was time to stop and check their back trail. The lack of visibility cut both ways. If the Chimera couldn't see the humans, the reverse was true as well.

"Okay," Lucy said, as she used a boot to scrape some snow aside. "See that manhole cover? If one of you big, strong men would be kind enough to lift it up I would appreciate it. You'll have to remove your packs in order to drop through, however."

It took the better part of ten minutes to lift the cover out of the way, send two men down the steel ladder, and drop the packs through the hole. Then, once the rest of the party was safely belowground, it was Mason's job to ease the metal lid back into position. With that accomplished, it was time to gear up again.

Lucy was holding a flare. The light threw black shadows up onto curved walls. "We're in a storm drain," she informed them as the men shouldered their packs. "We use them to get around. The stinks know that, so they send hunter-killer teams down to look for us, but they pay a high price for doing so. Keep your eyes peeled and remember, pipes come in from every direction."

"And if we get into a fight, be careful where you aim," Kawecki added. "We have enough problems without shooting each other."

Like the rest of the team, Voss was armed with two primary weapons. Given the situation, he thought it best to exchange the M5A2 carbine for a cut-down Rossmore stored in the scabbard strapped to his pack. With the shotgun at the ready he followed Lucy, Lang, and Kawecki out of the collector manifold and into a large pipe. They had to walk bent over, which not only was uncomfortable but would make it damned hard to fight if attacked.

Lucy led them through a series of left- and right-hand turns. Voss tried to memorize the route but soon gave up. It was too damned complicated.

A short time later, the team arrived at a point where explosives had been used to open a side passageway. The tunnel was about ten feet long. Heavy beams had been used to shore up the passageway, but the work had obviously been carried out by amateurs, so Voss had no desire to linger. Lucy directed the team into a subway tunnel. "We're close," she promised. "Now stay together. I wouldn't want to lose anyone."

It was good advice, and Voss was careful to keep the interval between Kawecki and himself short as they followed a set of rusting tracks past a train and the empty platform beyond. Voss had been to New York on at least a dozen occasions back before the war. He wondered if he had stood at that very station, his mind focused on an upcoming meeting, blissfully unaware of what the future had in store.

Suddenly Voss's thoughts were jerked back to the present as Alvarez yelled a warning: "Drones!" Each of the beetle-shaped machines was equipped with a headlight, and the beams crisscrossed each other as a loud thrumming noise sounded and a swarm of at least twenty Drones swept in to attack the humans.

Alvarez put a burst of projectiles into the lead machine and it exploded. The resulting flash of light strobed the tunnel as the rest of the team opened fire. The noise generated by automatic weapons and shotguns blended with the percussive boom of exploding Drones to produce a hellish cacophony of sound.

Voss saw a bright light angling down at him, fired the Rossmore, and heard a metallic clang as the slugs struck.

Instead of exploding, the badly damaged Drone kept coming, and crashed into his chest!

The impact put Voss on his ass, and electricity crackled around the machine as it struggled to lift off. The Drone was about five feet off the ground and wobbling badly when Voss sat up. He fired the shotgun and felt a series of pinpricks as the machine exploded and small pieces of shrapnel hit him.

"Nice one, Mr. President," Lucy said, offering him a hand. "It looks like we have what we need. A leader who can shoot straight."

As Voss came to his feet, he saw that the battle was over. Drone carcasses littered the tracks. Some of them smoked and sputtered impotently as components shorted out.

"What have we got?" Kawecki demanded. "Any casualties?"

"Yeah," Rigg said solemnly. "Mason took one in the ass."

"It snuck up behind me," the big man said defensively. He had short hair, dark skin, and a moon-shaped face.

Kawecki chuckled. "I'll put you in for a medal. Okay, check your weapons, and let's get going. Target practice is over."

After a ten-minute walk, the team arrived at a spot where a construction project had been under way. Lucy led the group back behind a pile of lumber to a point where three sheets of plywood were leaning against the wall. Once the sheets were lifted out of the way, a hole was revealed. "You'll have to crawl on your hands and knees," she commented. "But it's okay to leave your packs on."

The woman led the way, and one by one the men followed her. Light flooded the tunnel, and when Voss stepped forward, he was completely unprepared for the sight that greeted him. Lucy saw the look on his face and nodded knowingly. "This station is located underneath the public area in front of City Hall. It was intended to be a showpiece when it opened in 1904. But passenger service was discontinued in 1945 and the station was sealed off later on. We use it as a gathering place, and one of our people is a damned good engineer. He tapped into the Chimeran power grid and restored the lights."

"It's beautiful," Voss said as he looked down the tunnel. The first decorative arch featured intricate tilework, the next boasted insets of colored glass, and brass chandeliers hung in between. The effect was stunning.

"Come on," Lucy said. "The rest of them are camped in the mezzanine."

As the team followed Lucy into the lobby-like mezzanine they saw that dozens of soldiers, ex-soldiers, and citizen freedom fighters had responded to the nationwide call. Some of them knew one or more members of the incoming team, so there were lots of raucous greetings, friendly insults, and man-hugs as old comrades were reunited.

Kawecki, Mason, Rigg, and the rest were soon lost in the social melee. Voss was standing by himself when Lucy reappeared with a bespectacled man at her side.

"President Voss? This is Doctor Fyodor Malikov. I understand that you two have been in frequent radio contact but have never met face-to-face. Doctor Malikov, this is President Thomas Voss."

"Tom is fine," Voss said, as he shook the other man's hand. His handshake was surprisingly strong for one who looked so frail. Judging from appearances, Malikov was in his late fifties or early sixties. He was mostly bald, with a halo of white hair and a full beard. His face was gaunt and his clothes were tattered.

Voss knew Malikov had been forced to flee Europe for the United States after the Chimera broke out of Russia. He'd been instrumental in creating the serum that the

Sentinels relied on and the new Hale vaccine as well. This vaccine could not only alleviate human suffering by making humans immune to the Chimeran virus, it could reduce the number of pod farms and the forms they produced.

"It's a pleasure to meet you in person," Malikov said. "How is the vaccine production going?"

"We aren't producing as many doses as we'd like," Voss replied, "but it's ramping up. And getting the vaccine out to the people takes a lot of effort, as you can imagine."

"I understand," Malikov said. His eyes were bright. "Meanwhile ve must either shut the tower down or destroy it."

"And how is that going to work?" Lucy wanted to know.

A long moment of silence passed as Malikov looked down, then up again. "I don't know," he confessed.

"You don't *know*?" Voss demanded incredulously. "We brought all of these people here to New York, and you don't know?"

"That's the reality of the situation," Malikov said defensively. "Vonce ve get inside, and fight our way up to the control room, I'll figure it out."

"And if you don't?"

Malikov met Voss's eyes. His gaze was unapologetic. "Then we're going to die for nothing."

The attack on the tower was scheduled for 0830 the following morning, but for Kawecki and the rest of the soldiers the evening was a rare opportunity to get together in groups of five or six and shoot the shit. And whenever soldiers gather, talk inevitably turns to old battles and old buddies. So as Kawecki and some of the surviving Sentinels sat on their packs and passed a bottle of Jim Beam around, the subject of Joseph Capelli was bound to come up.

"I say Capelli did the right thing," a soldier named Budry said as he took a sip and wiped his mouth. "Hale hadn't had an inhibitor treatment in a long time. The poor bastard was about to turn. Joe did him a favor."

"That's bullshit," Yorba replied bitterly. He had a head of unruly hair and a beard to match. "Hale was the best we had! And maybe Malikov could have saved him. Plus this is the U.S. Army, goddamn it! Or what's left of it. Since when is it okay to shoot your commanding officer? No, I'd say Capelli got off easy. They should have put the SOB in front of a firing squad."

"How 'bout you, Captain?" a Sentinel named Russ inquired, as the bottle came his way. "Was Capelli right or wrong?"

"The asshole was *wrong*," Kawecki said darkly. "I fought alongside Hale and he was a fine officer. And, if I run into Capelli, I'll blow his fucking brains out. Any further questions?"

"No," Russ said with a boyish grin. "I think that covers it."

"Good," Kawecki said as he stood. "This meeting is adjourned. Go get some sleep. We have a whole bunch of stinks to kill in the morning."

It was July 4th, and Voss had been up all night. Not because he had to be, or wanted to be, but because he couldn't sleep. Now the task that once seemed so achievable, and even glamorous, was beginning to look like a suicide mission. The tower was much larger than he had imagined it to be, and it was crawling with stinks. Worse yet, Malikov wasn't sure of what to do if they made it to the control room. So, having allowed his visions of glory to get the better of him, Voss was going to die.

But it was too late to change plans or back out. All Voss could do was shoulder his pack and follow a double column of soldiers up the Lexington Avenue Line towards the intersection of 42nd and Third. That was where the alien tower had grown to dwarf the Chrysler Building and touched the sky itself. A six-inch-thick Chimeran power conduit led the way.

A scouting party had been sent ahead and reported everything was quiet so far. But that couldn't last for long—and it didn't.

The battle began fifteen minutes later as they passed under 35th Street. The first sign of resistance came when three elongated Hunter Drones dropped out of a ventilation shaft and opened fire. The effort wasn't enough to stop Voss's team, so Voss assumed the machines were supposed to simply delay them.

If so the tactic wasn't very successful, because Kawecki had been expecting something of the sort and his men had two L210 LAARKs (Light Anti-Armor Rockets) prepped and ready to go. The Drones barely had time to open fire before they were destroyed in quick succession.

The rocket launchers were a bit of overkill, but Kawecki figured the LAARKs wouldn't be of much use inside the tower, and he wanted to hold casualties to a minimum going in. "That's what I'm talking about," one of the men said, as a still-smoking carcass clattered onto the tracks. "We're kicking ass and taking names."

Once the party's leaders arrived at the point where the tower's metal roots blocked the tunnel, they climbed up onto the platform and took up positions around the stairs as the rest of the troops came up to join them. Over Voss's objections, Alvarez, Mason, and Rigg had been assigned to guard Malikov and himself. So wherever they went the others followed.

"Okay," Kawecki said over the radio. "Let's go upstairs and waste some stinks. Over."

With a shout of approval, the single-file column of soldiers surged up the stairs, past an empty ticket booth and into the tower itself.

Voss *heard* the battle before he had a chance to join in it, as the human invaders made violent contact with a force of snarling Hybrids. Heavy fire lashed back and forth, and Voss heard screaming as people began to fall.

The politician had to negotiate his way around a half-dozen bodies as he and the rest of the soldiers pushed their way into a huge lobby. Voss tilted his head back to see a circular platform with thick supporting columns on both sides of it. A walkway spiraled up and away from the platform. It was connected side-to-side by a network of crisscrossing sky bridges.

As Steelheads appeared on the platform above and fired Augers down into the crowd below, Lucy jerked spastically and went down. A soldier fell as Kawecki said, "Kill those bastards! Everyone else onto the elevators. Move!"

Voss had seen the elevators too, three of them on each side of the lobby. He led Malikov, his bodyguards, and a dozen other soldiers over to one of the circular platforms. Mason slapped a control, curved doors slid into place, and the elevator began to rise.

Malikov studied a brightly lit panel on the wall. "This symbol is for the control room," the scientist said confidently, pointing at a star-shaped icon. "If we stay on the elevator it will take us there. Tell the others."

At that moment the platform jerked to a halt and the doors opened. "Hold that thought," Voss said. "It looks like the stinks shut the elevator system down."

That prediction soon came true, as *all* of the tubular lifts opened to spill their passengers out onto the circular platform Voss had seen from the lobby below. As the humans exited, they were immediately confronted by the stinks who were already on that level. More of them were charging down the spiral ramp from above as a swarm of Drones appeared.

A hellish battle ensued. Wraith miniguns harvested the Chimera like wheat in a field, V7 Splicers chopped the stinks into chunks of raw meat, and an L11-2 Dragon sent tongues of fire up the ramp. But it made no difference, as the now flaming 'brids, Steelheads, and Ravagers charged through the conflagration to grab humans and wrap them in fire. The screams they produced overlaid each other.

Every time the President tried to advance and join the force at the foot of the ramp his bodyguards cut him off. So Voss assigned himself the task of dealing with the seemingly endless waves of Drones. But no matter how many of the machines he destroyed, there were always more.

He fired the carbine until it ran dry, reloaded until all of his spare magazines were empty, and switched to the Rossmore. Malikov was firing too. Patrol Drones exploded left, right, and center as empty casings arced away and bounced off the floor.

But there was no cover to speak of, and the floor was slippery with human blood as men fell in twos and threes. Bodies lay everywhere, and the sound of gunfire started to dwindle as the Chimera began to run out of targets.

Voss was convinced he was going to die. He was resigned to that fate, when Mason stepped in to clip a rope to the D-ring at the center of his combat harness. Voss opened his mouth to object, but Kawecki was there to cut him off.

"Mason is going to lower you over the side, sir. We're sending Malikov down too. Once you hit the floor, unhook the rope so we can use it again."

Voss said, "Wait just a goddamn minute," but that was as far as he got when Mason plucked him off the floor and dumped him over the side. There was a sudden jerk as he fell four or five feet, followed by a twirling descent. That was when Voss spotted the seething mass of Leapers waiting below. They made a horrible gibbering sound as the President freed a grenade, pulled the pin, and let it fall. The bomb hit, bounced, and went off with a loud boom.

Voss knew that shrapnel from the explosion could hit him as well but figured that was the chance he'd have to take. He needed a landing zone and got one as the exploding grenade created a bloody 360-degree bull's-eye for him to put down in. Pieces of hot metal hit him, but he barely registered the pain while his boots hit and he hurried to free the rope. Then the line was gone, quickly snaking upwards, while Mason peered down at him. There was a muted thump when Malikov landed a few feet away. "Ve are supposed to run!" the scientist yelled, as his line was retracted.

"Screw that," Voss replied, while he blew a half-dozen charging Leapers to bits. "The rest of them need a safe place to land."

Malikov nodded and began to blast away. Kawecki landed a minute later, quickly followed by Mason and Rigg, all of whom had rappelled from above. Rigg's nickname was "Pretty Boy." But it was hard to tell if he deserved the title because of the bloody bandage wrapped around his head.

"How many more?" Voss inquired, shoving shells into the Rossmore.

"There aren't any more," Kawecki answered grimly. "Shuck that pack, Mr. President, and follow me. It's time for us to get the hell out of here."

Fire lashed down as the humans dropped their packs and zigzagged across the floor, firing while they ran, killing anything that moved. Then they were through the open door, following a well-plowed path east, as Hybrids poured out of the tower and gave chase. "The-East-River," Kawecki said as they pounded along. "We'll-look-for-a-boat."

They paused a few hundred feet farther on, turned to fire on the Chimera, and had the satisfaction of seeing a dozen of them go down before resuming their flight. The snow continued to fall as they followed a well-worn stink-path through the wreckage of FDR Drive and down to the East River. And that was where Voss saw a broad expanse of drifting ice! It was moving at a good three or four miles per hour. Visibility was poor, but they could still spot open channels, as the entire mass drifted towards New York Bay.

"Come on!" Voss shouted, skidding down a slab of concrete to the river below. "It's our only chance!" And with that, the President of the United States ran for his life.

CHAPTER TWO
HEAD CASE

The Deep Home Saloon and Pleasure Emporium occupied the lowest level of a parking garage in Burlington, Colorado. The top two levels had been bombed into rubble, a half-dozen vehicles trapped inside. What light there was came from lanterns hung at regular intervals. They conspired to produce a soft, smoky glow and shadows that danced the walls as people moved about.

One corner of the space had been walled off with sheets of plywood to create a kitchen, where everything was cooked over charcoal fires. The mouthwatering odor of barbecued meat wafted out into the larger room, and from there into the ruins above, which acted to trap it.

An improvised bar was set up along one wall. The rest of the furnishings consisted of mismatched tables and a wild assortment of chairs. They sat willy-nilly on top of the diagonal parking slots and the grease spots centered between the white lines.

The saloon's clientele came in all sorts of shapes and sizes, but they all had certain things in common. They were dressed for the outdoors, they were heavily armed, and they were doing business. Most of it consisted of straightforward "I'll give a John Deere 'Trapper' jackknife for your magnifying glass" type of barter. But darker bargains were being struck as well, at packed tables where burly men and hard-faced women eyed each other over drinks.

One man sat alone. His name was Joseph Capelli. He wore a knit cap pulled down over his ears, a black sweater, and military-style wool pants. A pistol rode in the shoulder holster under his left arm. His shotgun was within easy reach, too, as was the Marksman rifle he wore strapped to a pack frame.

Capelli was finishing a huge steak as a waitress delivered a second mug of home-brewed beer. She had blond hair, steely blue eyes, and was wearing a short skirt. The latter being a surefire tip-getter. "Will there be anything else, sir?"

"No. What do I owe you?" Capelli's voice was hard and inflectionless.

"A box of .22s, five twelve-gauge shotgun shells, or half a dozen rifle rounds," she said in a singsong voice. "The boss prefers 30-06 cartridges, but 30-30s are okay, and he's willing to consider .303s."

Capelli's sage-green Type N-3 military parka was hanging on the back of his chair. He slipped a hand into a pocket, felt for the bottle, and pulled it out. "How 'bout this? One hundred tablets of Bayer aspirin. Never opened."

The waitress accepted the bottle and examined it more closely. "How do I know they're real? The boss'll take it out of my pay if they aren't."

"They're real," he assured her. "And so is this." The lipstick appeared as if by magic. It was one of six tubes he had come across in a previously looted five-and-dime. A look of greed appeared on the woman's face as the bottle of aspirin went into the sack that hung at her side and the bribe disappeared into her bra. "Thanks, mister." Then she was gone.

Having paid for dinner, it was time for Capelli to enjoy his second mug of home-brewed beer. It was full-bodied, and reasonably smooth, but a little too sweet for his taste. Capelli's thoughts were interrupted as a little boy in a plaid coat dashed into the room and went over to speak with the man behind the bar. The bartender had slicked-back hair and two days of salt-and-pepper stubble. He listened, nodded, and rang a silver bell, which made a gentle, tinkling sound. "Quiet! Two Hunter Drones are sniffing around outside."

The Chimeran machines could detect heat. Capelli knew that. But sound? That wasn't entirely clear. It was a good idea to play it safe, though. So all of the customers were careful to minimize their movements, and keep their voices down, until the bartender rang the silver bell again.

That was when Capelli heard a rustling sound and turned to find that a big, bearlike man was standing next to his table. "Mr. Capelli? My name's Locke. Alvin Locke. Mind if I sit down?"

Capelli opened his mouth to reply, but the other man had already dumped his pack on the floor and taken a seat. "I'm looking for a runner," Locke announced. "And people tell me that you're one of the best."

"I'm still alive."

Locke chuckled. "And that's a mighty fine recommendation. Especially these days."

Locke opened his mouth as if to continue, but stopped when he heard a low and very menacing growl. He turned to discover a large dog looking up at him with teeth bared. The animal looked a lot like a German shepherd but had a Mohawk-like ridge of fur that ran the length of his spine. "Is that *your* dog?" Locke inquired nervously.

"Nope. Rowdy belongs to himself."

"Then why is he growling at me?"

"Because you're sitting in his seat."

Locke got up, circled around the table, and sat down.

After jumping up onto the vacated chair, the dog sat on his haunches and yawned. "What's so special about that particular chair?" Locke wanted to know.

"I'm right-handed," Capelli replied, tossing a chunk of steak up into the air. With an audible snap, Rowdy intercepted the piece of meat and gulped it down.

Locke grinned. "Makes sense. So, like I was saying, I need a runner."

Capelli nodded. The U.S. Mail was a thing of the past, so anyone who wanted to send a letter or package badly enough hired a runner. And that was the way he'd been making his living ever since the Army kicked him out. So people knew about him. That was how most clients came his way—through referrals. "How big is the package? And what's the destination?"

"I'm the package," Locke replied. "And the destination is Haven, Oklahoma."

Capelli opened one of the pockets on his pack, withdrew a well-worn Texaco road map, and opened it up. Then, after a minute or so, he put it away again. "Sorry, Mr. Locke, I can't help you. I specialize in short runs. No more than a couple hundred miles or so. Your destination is at least twice that. Plus we're talking about thirty-five or forty days of travel through territory I'm not familiar with. That adds more danger. So, I suggest you find someone else." As if to signal the end of the conversation, a piece of gristle soared into the air and disappeared with a *snap*.

"I see," Locke replied thoughtfully. "My sister and her family live in Haven and, since I have no family of my own, I plan to join them. It was a nice little town back before the Chimera shot it up. And it could be again, because what the stinks don't know is that people still live there. Not on the surface, mind you, but underground, where a network of tunnels tie their homes together.

"I had a good hiding place and enough supplies to last me for ten years up near Glenwood Springs," Locke continued. "But, after spending the last couple of years in hiding, I came to the conclusion that mere survival isn't enough. I want to be part of something, I want to help make life better, and if that means walking a few hundred miles, then so be it. But I'm a businessman, Mr. Capelli, or was back before the shit hit the fan, so I lack the skills to make the journey on my own. That's why I need a runner. I hope you'll reconsider. If you'll take me to Haven I'll give you ten of these right now—and ten more when we arrive."

Locke pushed a 1920 gold piece through a puddle of beer. It came to rest next to Capelli's mug. The runner pushed it back.

"Put that away. Half the people in this saloon would slit your throat for a tube of Ipana toothpaste."

Like so many other things, the American monetary system was a thing of the past. Most business transactions were handled via barter. But precious metals still had value to those willing to bet on some sort of future. Locke smiled as he made the coin disappear. "But not *you*, Mr. Capelli, or that's what I hear. They say you're an honest man."

Capelli took a sip of beer and pushed his plate to the right. Three squares of carefully cut meat were waiting for Rowdy and the dog hurried to lap them up. "You could join a community here in Colorado. New ones start up all the time."

"And they fail just as frequently," Locke replied. "Usually because of internal dissention, a communicable disease, or an attack of some sort."

"So what makes Haven different?"

Locke was quick to follow up on a possible opening. "They have elected leaders, some of whom were smart enough to see what was coming, and lay in supplies before the stinks took control of North America. The soil under the town is reasonably easy to dig through, they have a good source of water, and a doctor! A young one, thank God. The place isn't perfect, of course, nothing is, but there's a chance. And that, my friend, is better than nothing."

The little boy came scooting into the room and to the bar. He said something to the bartender, who then rang the bell and brought a double-barreled shotgun out from under the counter. "It looks like the stinks are on to us," the bartender announced grimly. "Follow the signs to the emergency exit and good luck! We'll set up somewhere else if we can."

With a great deal of shouting people sprang to their feet, swung packs up onto their backs, and grabbed their weapons. Then, like a herd of spooked cattle, they stampeded towards a door with the words "Emergency Exit" scrawled on it. Only one person could pass through the doorway at a time, so there was an immediate backup.

Rowdy jumped off the chair and barked. Capelli's movements were casual as he stood and slipped his arms into the parka. "No, boy. Not yet."

Locke was on his feet, his pack was on his back, and he held a .30-30 Winchester in the crook of his arm. He gestured towards the crowd. "Shouldn't we get in line?"

"Keep your eye on the bartender and his son," Capelli replied, as he hoisted the pack frame onto his back. "We'll follow them."

Locke looked and saw that rather than head for the emergency exit with the others, the bartender and the boy were headed towards the main entrance. And, judging from the pack on the bartender's back, he was carrying that evening's receipts. Locke swore softly. "Well, I'll be damned. They're using their customers as decoys!"

"Roger that," Capelli agreed matter-of-factly. "Come on. There must be a third way out of here."

The bartender and his son had already passed through the door and entered the stairwell by the time Capelli arrived. But where the locals turned right, they turned left. Then they climbed the stairs to the level above, and to what had been a dead space until a bomb fell on the building. The explosion had left a crevice wide enough for father and son to slip through. Rowdy led the way and Capelli was quick to follow. Muted gunfire could be heard by then, which meant that at least some of the saloon's customers were doing battle with the stinks, who had been topside waiting for them.

Capelli heard Locke swear and turned to discover that the other man was too big to fit through the narrow opening. "Give me the rifle, shed the pack, and slip through sideways. Hurry!"

As Locke handed the Winchester through the crevice, the dog growled a warning and Capelli heard the gabble of stink speech coming from the stairs above. Then Locke passed his pack through the opening, quickly followed by Locke himself, who then reclaimed his rifle.

Capelli had been hoping to avoid combat, but it was too late. He motioned for Locke to squeeze past him, leveled the Rossmore at the passageway, and waited for a Hybrid to appear. One of the slope-headed monsters arrived seconds later. It was backlit by a single lantern that dangled out in the hall. The Chimera snarled loudly, and was raising a Bullseye, when a full load of double-ought-buck blew half of its head away. Blood and gore painted the concrete wall behind it.

But as the first stink collapsed, another appeared to take its place. And so it went until the Rossmore's tubular magazine was empty and it was necessary to reload. That was a dangerous moment, and one in which Capelli would have been forced to pull his pistol had he been alone, but Locke was tugging at his pack.

So Capelli stepped into a gap, let the big man take his

place, and was pleased to see the calm manner in which Locke fired the Winchester. Brass casings arced through the air and tinkled off concrete as Locke worked the lever. The battle came to an end as two more Hybrids went down.

Capelli was satisfied with the weapons he already had, and couldn't carry more, but it was tempting to strip the Hybrids of ammo. Even if *he* couldn't use it, someone else could, and ammo was the equivalent of money. But there was no way to know how many Chimera were in the area, or when more of them would decide to come charging down the stairs, so he let the opportunity pass.

"Come on," Capelli said, as he pumped a round into the chamber of his newly reloaded shotgun. "Let's get the hell out of here. Rowdy—take the point."

The dog, standing stiff-legged next to Capelli, barked. Then, having turned within his own length, he was gone.

"That's quite a dog," Locke said admiringly.

"He'll do," Capelli replied. "Don't forget to reload."

Locke had forgotten. He smiled sheepishly as he slipped a couple of shells into the rifle's receiver and picked up his pack as if it were a suitcase.

Activating the light attached to his shotgun, Capelli followed the pale blob through a zigzagging passageway until he came upon a wooden ladder. It slanted up through a dark hole, and the angle was such that Rowdy could climb it. The dog was already halfway up the crudely built structure by the time Capelli arrived.

Wood creaked as Capelli stepped aboard, and it gave slightly as he made his way upwards. Cool night air greeted him as the light from the shotgun splashed the underside of a slab of concrete. From there he had to get down on his hands and knees and crawl through a short tunnel to the spot where the bartender, his son, and Rowdy had escaped into the darkness beyond. The light was a potential liability, so Capelli paused to turn it off, and took the opportunity to listen. The air was chilly, hinting at things to come.

Capelli heard something rattle behind him. It was Locke, and Capelli wished that the big man could move more quietly. He took note of the fact that the sound of gunfire could no longer be heard. It seemed that one side or the other had won. Capelli would have put his money on the stinks.

Shotgun at the ready, he eased his way out onto what had been a ramp and froze. A little bit of light shone from the street beyond. When Locke appeared, Capelli held a finger to his lips and began to slide along the sloping wall. He found a corner at the bottom, just inside the big doorway, a good place to hide while he looked outside.

It was a horrible scene.

A bonfire blazed in the middle of the street. But the Chimera *liked* cold air, so it wasn't for the heat. They were cooking with it. Half a dozen human bodies had been dragged into the circle of flickering firelight, where they were being systematically butchered and eaten. The axes made a thunking sound as they rose and fell. Was the blond waitress among the victims? Capelli hoped not. "Follow me. And be quiet," he whispered to Locke. "Or they'll have us for dinner too."

Locke looked ill. But he managed a nod and followed Capelli out onto the sidewalk. The ruins of the parking garage were at the very edge of the firelight's reach. Moving stealthily, the men were able to slip from shadow to shadow, steadily putting distance between the stinks and themselves.

The Chimera were ghastly silhouettes by then, gathered around the leaping flames, gnawing on human flesh. Capelli had seen a lot of horrible things during his days as a Sentinel but nothing worse than the scene in the middle of Rose Avenue.

It was a clear night, and the stars were out, leaving just enough light to navigate by as they sought to put the stinks behind them. Moving carefully, Capelli led Locke east about a quarter of a mile until the taller buildings began to thin out. Then he was faced with the usual conundrum. Should they find a place to hole up because it was dangerous to travel at night? Or should they keep going because it was dangerous to travel during the day?

That's a tough one, the voice in Capelli's head said unsympathetically. *If you make the wrong decision you could wind up like me—which is to say dead!*

Shut up, Hale.

That's shut up "sir" to you, the voice responded sternly. *Because I'm an officer. Or was, until you blew my brains out.*

You were changing, Capelli countered, for what might have been the thousandth time.

You could have taken your concerns to the Major, or to Dr. Malikov, the voice said accusingly, *but you didn't. Why was that, Capelli? Was it because you were afraid I would turn into something like Daedalus? Or was it because you're an insubordinate sonofabitch who can't take orders?*

Screw you.

Peals of laughter echoed inside Capelli's head. The laughter faded away as he heard the familiar click of claws and Rowdy materialized out of the gloom. He was panting and he produced a soft whining sound as he bumped Capelli's leg. Then, having announced his presence, he surged forward to take up a position roughly fifty feet ahead.

They went on like that for another ten minutes when the bulk of a barely seen building blotted out a section of stars. Capelli gave a low whistle to let Rowdy know that he was turning off the road, then activated the shotgun's light as a church loomed in front of him.

They climbed a few stairs, the blob of white light playing across the gaping door and probing the chapel beyond. It revealed signs of a battle: spent casings, the projectile-riddled pews, and what might have been dried bloodstains. Then, as Capelli made his way down the center aisle, he saw that some words had been painted to the right of the altar. *"Why, God, why?"*

It was a good question. One that Capelli couldn't answer.

Locke gave the only eulogy the people who had taken refuge in the church were likely to receive. "Poor bastards."

"Yeah," Capelli agreed as he spotlighted the choir loft above. "See that? We'll spend the rest of the night there. Then, immediately after daybreak, we'll follow U.S. Route 40 east."

Locke looked from the loft down to the man next to him. "So you'll take me to Haven?"

"Yes."

"But you said you wouldn't."

"That was then," Capelli answered. "This is now. Let's get some rest."

No matter where Capelli found himself, he was almost always able to get a reasonable amount of rest since Rowdy's finely tuned senses were on duty twenty-four hours a day. That night the dog, a half German shepherd, half Rhodesian ridgeback mix, gave no warnings, so both Capelli and Locke were able to log six hours of sleep. But it seemed like only a matter of minutes before a beam of bright sunlight slanted down through a dirty window and threw a carpet of gold across the choir loft's wooden floor.

That woke Capelli, who wiggled out of his sleeping bag and slipped the Magnum back into its shoulder holster. Both Locke and Rowdy were awake and watching him. "I'm going to climb up into the tower and take a look around," Capelli announced as he laced his boots. "Assuming the area is clear I'll be back down. Then we'll make breakfast and hit the road." If Locke resented taking orders from what amounted to an employee, he showed no signs of it as he began the process of extricating himself from his bedroll.

After retrieving a pair of binoculars from his pack Capelli went over to a narrow door, pulled it open, and began to climb the twisting-turning stairs. The stairs delivered him to a small platform just below a large pair of church bells. Four vertical windows allowed Capelli to scan the area without being seen. The air was cold, but the clear sky suggested that the day would warm up later.

After about ten minutes of peering out through the narrow slits, he saw that with the exception of a wispy column of smoke spiraling up into the sky from town, there were no signs of life, Chimeran or otherwise. Having eaten their fill and resterilized the town, it appeared that the stinks had left for parts unknown.

Satisfied that there weren't any imminent threats to worry about, Capelli returned to the choir loft. Locke was in the midst of preparing breakfast for the two of them, black coffee and thick oatmeal, with some precious raisins thrown in, all brewed over a can of Sterno. The meal was followed by half a Tootsie Roll each.

Haute cuisine it wasn't, but Capelli felt pleasantly full after the meal, and ready to begin the thirty-five-mile hike to the city of Goodland. He figured it would take about two days, unless the weather turned bad or some stinks got in the way.

After checking the surrounding landscape, the threesome left the church and made their way east onto Route 40. The two-lane blacktop led them through mostly flat farmland with overgrown wheat fields on both sides of the highway. Houses could be seen here and there, along with barns and silos, and trees that had been planted to shelter the buildings from the wind.

Once in awhile a feral Chimera could be seen in the distance, searching for something to eat, and they passed the rotting remains of a cow. But other than an occasional bark from Rowdy as he took off after a rabbit, and the eternal hum of the wind, the land was silent.

They saw cars of course, and trucks, and even a yellow school bus, but all were motionless. Some sat as if abandoned only moments before, out of gas perhaps, or broken down. Others lay every which way, having been attacked from the air, and shot full of holes. That had been at least a year earlier, of course. The drivers and passengers who could be seen through filthy windows looked like skeletonized half-mummies, still clad in scraps of rotting cloth, waiting for the elements to bury them.

And they saw graves, too, with improvised crosses standing like lonely sentinels beside the road. Each marked the end of a desperate journey, back when there had been places to go and the strength required to dig.

But amidst these signs of death there were unmistakable signs of life: Route 40 was a natural trail for people to follow. Capelli's practiced eye took note of a recent campfire, a signpost with a cryptic message written on it, and a couple of .22 casings too bright to have been lying on the road for very long. All signs that, in spite of Chimeran efforts to exterminate them, human beings still walked the surface of the planet.

They had been walking for three hours by the time Capelli called a halt just short of a bridge. The sun was high, and other than the white scar that a Chimeran shuttle had left on the blue sky, it was as if the threesome had the entire world to themselves. From the highway they had to skid down a steep bank into the shadowy area below. A stream ran under the bridge, and judging from the trash left by others, they weren't the first people to pause there. "You supplied breakfast," Capelli said, "so lunch is on me."

Capelli opened his pack and brought out a jar of applesauce he had found in an abandoned farmhouse—plus two cans of Vienna sausages purchased a couple of weeks earlier. "Looks good," Locke said. "Shall I heat the sausages?"

Capelli shook his head. "No, save the Sterno for later. Rule number one is never light a fire during the day."

Locke nodded. "If you'll give me your mess tin I'll divide everything up."

Locke and Capelli made small talk during lunch, but not much, since the two men didn't know each other that well. But Capelli learned that Locke had done a hitch as a hospital corpsman in the Navy after high school, inherited some money, and gone into business as a car dealer back before what he referred to as "the plague."

Then, after the Chimera overran Great Britain, Locke had been quicker than most to see how things were going. So he purchased a large quantity of supplies while they were still available, stashed them near his cabin in the mountains, and eventually moved there. At first, Locke had been satisfied to simply hide out, but after receiving a couple of runner-delivered letters from his sister, he eventually resolved to join her in Haven.

Capelli was intrigued by the possibility of a truly successful survival community. But when pressed, Locke had very few details to add. *Still,* Capelli thought to himself, *it's worth taking a look at. And the truth is that I don't have anything better to do.*

So Capelli finished the last of his applesauce, washed his plate in the stream, and removed a pair of binoculars from the top of his pack. "See the tree over there? The one on the east side of the stream? I'm going to climb it and take a look at our back trail."

Locke looked around. "Where's Rowdy?"

"Wherever he wants to be," Capelli replied.

The stream was shallow enough to wade through without overtopping his boots. So Capelli followed it as far as he could, knowing that he wouldn't leave any tracks. His caution wasn't the result of a specific threat, but because it was always best to be careful, even when there was no apparent danger.

Having left the streambed at a point approximately thirty feet from the cottonwood, he made straight for it. The dry calf-high grass swished past his boots and a raven made a throaty cawing sound as Capelli arrived at the base of the tree. With a flapping noise, the bird took to the air.

He passed his binoculars around so they hung down his back and shinnied up the textured trunk, up to the point where he found reliable footholds in a series of sturdy branches. A few minutes later Capelli was as high as he could safely go and scanning the countryside through the binoculars. *I taught you that*, the voice said. *I taught you to stop, look, and think.*

Yeah, Capelli agreed. *You were a fucking genius. Now shut the hell up.*

The voice could be quite insistent, but this time it did as it was told, and Capelli was free to examine the horizon without any distractions. And it was then, while scanning the highway, that he saw the tiny figures coming up the road. His heart began to beat faster. Were they Hybrids? Grims?

No; as Capelli rolled the image into perfect focus he saw that they were humans. And that was when he swore. Not because they were headed east on Route 40; lots of people did that. But because these individuals were jogging! And nobody runs while carrying a heavy pack unless they have a very good reason to do so.

Like catching up with people ahead of them.

Turning the glasses to the right, Capelli scanned the area beyond the bridge, before making his way out of the tree. Once on the ground it was a simple matter to hurry down to the streambed and follow the water back to the bridge. He found Locke reading a leather-bound book. He closed it as Capelli approached. "See anything?"

"Yeah, I sure as hell did. How many people did you show those gold coins to back in Burlington?"

Lock frowned. "Not many. Two, no *three* people, counting yourself. I exchanged one of them for some silver coins and I gave the other away."

"You did *what*?"

"I gave it to a woman with a sick child so that she could pay for a doctor," Locke answered defiantly. "Why do you ask?"

"Because five men are hot on our trail," Capelli answered darkly. "Maybe it was the money changer, or maybe it was the woman, but somebody fingered you. And now some very unpleasant people are coming to take your gold."

Locke looked doubtful. "What makes you so sure?"

"Because they're *running*, goddammit, and that's the only explanation that makes sense. Now, here's what we're going to do. I want you to head over to the rise on the other side of the stream and build a little fire."

Locke frowned. "You're going to use me as bait."

"That's right," Capelli replied, as he removed the Marksman from its scabbard.

"How do I know I can trust you?" Locke wanted to know. "You could let them kill me."

"You should have considered that before you went to sleep last night."

Locke grinned. "That's true! I'm alive, aren't I?"

"For the moment. Now take your pack and rifle, cross the stream, and build that fire."

"Okay," Locke said reluctantly. "But what if they shoot me from a thousand yards away?"

"Then you'll be dead. Now get going."

Rowdy had reappeared by then. He nosed the ground, then ran to catch up as Locke splashed through the stream and climbed the slope beyond. Rowdy was always up for an outing and followed along behind, pausing every now and then to lift a leg.

Capelli considered calling the dog back, thought better of it, and took a moment to stash both the pack and the Rossmore on top of the retaining wall that ran under the bridge. Then he returned to the stream and followed it north. That enabled him to move quickly and stay off the skyline as he made his way towards the spot he had chosen while up in the tree.

A sharp left-hand turn took him up a slope and into a field of unharvested wheat. His boots produced puffs of dust, and a squadron of grasshoppers fled ahead of him as he went facedown on the hard ground and elbowed his way up onto a rise. Even though the land *looked* flat there were slight undulations, and even a few feet of additional elevation would give him a slight advantage.

Once at the highest point, and with a screen of wheat stalks to conceal him, Capelli put his eye to the Marksman's scope. It was, as the name implied, a very accurate weapon. Though not appropriate for the task at hand, the semiautomatic rifle could launch a small semiautonomous Drone as well, which would fire on any life form it encountered.

The highway seemed to leap forward as Capelli found the strip of blacktop and followed it back to the five-person column. They looked bigger than they had before, the heat rising off the blacktop causing them to shimmer slightly, and the left-to-right breeze would be a factor as well. Not to mention the fact that the bastards were still running.

Still, Capelli was confident of his ability to make the shot as he led the first figure slightly and wondered which one of the would-be thieves was the group's leader. The one in front was a good bet. Unless the number-two man had enough power to force someone else into the point position. Capelli was running through the possibilities when he saw the lead figure wave the others forward.

Confident that he knew which person to shoot first, Capelli glanced over his left shoulder, and saw that a thin column of smoke was rising up into the sky. Locke was doing his part and the thieves were taking the bait.

Capelli turned back, nuzzled the rifle with his cheek, and felt a sudden emptiness at the pit of his stomach. Suddenly the column was close, a *lot* closer, which left very little margin for error. Capelli made a slight adjustment for windage, squeezed the trigger, and felt it break. The butt kicked his shoulder, and the report was nearly lost in the vast grasslands, as the group's leader appeared to stumble and fall.

It was tempting to stay on him, and make sure he didn't get up, but that would be dangerous. The column was breaking up, so he had to send a second projectile after the first, and do so quickly. The trigger gave, and another man threw up his arms in a gesture of final surrender, as the rest of the thieves sought cover in the wheat field beyond.

That was good, but not good enough, as the wheat rippled and the surviving thieves made a beeline for Locke. Capelli swore. He'd hoped that after two pursuers went down the rest would pause, giving him an opportunity to thin the group even more.

But these people were not only tough, they were determined, and that made them that much more dangerous. And as the road rose to meet the bridge deck, it was going to provide the thieves with more cover if he remained where he was.

So Capelli was forced to pull back, slide down the slope, and splash south. As he passed under the bridge and emerged on the other side, he noticed that Rowdy was nowhere to be seen. And, having heard the gunshots, Locke had gone to ground.

Capelli didn't have time to look for his client as he climbed up out of the streambed and looked towards the west. He could see them now, plowing their way through waist-high wheat, weapons at the ready. And they could see *him*. The man on the right fired a Bullseye tag, which missed by a foot. Then, as the thief triggered half a dozen poorly aimed projectiles, Capelli shot him in the chest. He appeared to throw the Chimeran weapon away as he fell over backwards.

The others were firing by then, so Capelli had no choice but to throw himself facedown, and roll sideways. The man on the far left fired a carbine, and geysers of dry dirt shot up all around the ex-Sentinel as he came to a stop. He was pinned at that point, or would have been except for Locke and his Winchester. The rifle made a *crack, crack, crack* sound as the businessman triggered three rounds. That was followed by a familiar growl and a cry of pain as Rowdy attacked one of the men from behind.

Capelli popped up at that point, and saw that another thief was down as the last one whirled, trying to bring his shotgun to bear on Rowdy. However, the dog's teeth were locked onto his butt. So as he turned, Rowdy spun with him.

Capelli's first shot was hurried. It nicked the man's shoulder, and produced a puff of aerosolized blood, but failed to bring him down. Capelli was worried lest the man shoot Rowdy, but he forced himself to concentrate, and fired again. The second projectile was dead-on. The would-be thief staggered, appeared to lose his balance, and collapsed.

It had been a brief but bloody battle, and as Capelli stood there in what should have been a peaceful wheat field, the scene had a surreal quality. "Damn," Locke said, as he arrived. "You're good."

That's true, the voice said mockingly. *You are good. At killing people.*

Capelli felt the usual post-combat tremors, as a surfeit of adrenaline coursed through his circulatory system, and he sought to hide them. "We need to check each body, strip it of anything that has value, and get the hell out of here."

It was clear that Locke didn't want to deal with the bodies, but he understood the need to do so, and followed along behind as Capelli went from corpse to corpse. And it turned out that the third one, the thief he'd shot immediately after emerging from under the bridge, was a woman. That didn't surprise Capelli, but his client was shocked. "That's her!"

"That's who?"

"The woman I gave the coin to. The one with the sick baby."

Capelli nodded expressionlessly. "That comes under rule six."

"Which is?"

"Mind your own business. Search her pockets! See if you can find the coin."

Locke knelt, and it took him less than a minute to find what he was looking for. He shook his head as he slipped the gold piece into a pocket and stood. "This world sucks."

"Tell me about it," Capelli said, and that was when Rowdy began to bark. Capelli turned towards the highway, raised the Marksman, and looked through the telescopic sight. "Shit."

Locke squinted into the afternoon sun but couldn't see anything. "What is it?"

"Stinks, at least a dozen of them, all coming on strong."

"After us?"

"No, not originally. I think they were following the people who were planning to rob us," Capelli said as he eyed the oncoming mass. There were Hybrids, a couple of Steelheads, and an eleven-foot-tall Ravager. "But now they're after us," he added. "Or will be in a couple of minutes."

"So what are we going to do?" Locke inquired nervously.

Capelli lowered the rifle and turned back towards the bridge. "We're going to grab our gear and run like hell."

CHAPTER THREE
GOOD AS GOLD

Saturday, September 26, 1953
The Lucky Buckle Mine near Idaho Springs, Colorado

Colorado State female inmate 26301 was in a lateral, working to shore up a section of Tunnel Five, when the rock under her boots trembled. Bits of rock rattled as they rained down on her helmet, a column of particulate matter shot up out of a ventilation shaft located ten feet behind her, and dust swirled through the beam projected from her headlamp.

The inmate's name was Susan Farley. Her heart skipped a beat as she waited for the next tremor and the sudden blackness, as tons of granite crushed the life out of her. Then the moment was past. The people around her began to cough and Mary Howe said what everyone else was thinking. "That felt like it was directly below us. It's my guess that Tunnel Four collapsed."

That was Susan's theory as well, and if it was true, then the inmates working immediately below were in big trouble. She turned to look at Red Cooper. The middle-aged guard was of medium height, with carrot-colored hair and a face like an Idaho spud. His double-barreled twelve-gauge shotgun was aimed upwards as if the weapon could defend him from the possibility of a rockfall. "How 'bout it, Boss Cooper?" Susan inquired. "Should we check on the people in T-4?"

Cooper glanced at her. His face looked pale in the

glare from her light. Tiny dots of perspiration populated his forehead. It was easy to see that the guard was frightened and trying to hide it. "Yeah, sure," he said hoarsely. "Take Howe and go down for a look-see. The rest of you can get back to work. This ain't no tea party."

As the guard who was closest to the cave-in, it was Cooper's responsibility to go down and check on the crew himself. But it was relatively safe where he was and it looked like Cooper had plans to stay.

Susan followed shiny narrow-gauge railroad tracks back to Shaft Three. The wooden platform was where the crew had left it an hour earlier. The elevator was large enough to handle a single ore car and powered by the generator on the first level. Immediately after the levers were pulled, the cage dropped three inches before coming to a momentary halt. That was followed by a loud clanking noise and the squeal of an unoiled pulley as the elevator began to descend. If the cable broke, or something went wrong with the machinery that controlled the lift, both women would plunge to their deaths. It wasn't where either one of them was supposed to be.

The inmates had been housed in a standard prison facility near Canon City before the Chimera swept into Colorado, the state government collapsed, and everything went to hell in a handcart. That was when Susan and her fellow inmates had been transferred to the Lucky Buckle Mine, where the sentence "twenty-five years at hard labor" took on new meaning. Because the existence that Susan and the other prisoners had been subjected to was more like slavery than a prison sentence. Especially since it was pretty clear that whatever gold the mine produced was going to Warden Brewster and his guards rather than the citizens of Colorado.

Susan saw a white line flash through the blob of light projected from her headlamp and pulled on the cable brake. It took a considerable amount of muscle to stop

the elevator, but Susan was a lot stronger than she had
been months earlier, and brought the box to a stop.

Howe was a short, stocky woman of thirty-three.
She'd been sent to prison for beating her husband sense-
less with his own whiskey bottle. Nobody messed with
her. She slid the safety gate out of the way, entered Tunnel Four, and sent the light from her headlamp skipping
ahead. Susan came up to join her, and the two women
followed the shiny tracks back into the darkness. They
hadn't traveled more than a hundred feet when they
found the cave-in.

As Susan's light played across the jumble of granite,
she could see the glitter of quartz crystals and the lengths
of shattered timber that stuck out of the pile like the
ends of broken bones. She knew some of them dated
back to the early 1930s, when the upper laterals had
been driven deep into the mountainside. So was that it?
Were some half-rotted supports responsible for the rockfall? Yes, that was the way it appeared, although there
was no way to be sure.

The rubble was head-high, but Susan could see what
looked like a gap at the top, so she crawled over chunks
of rock in order to get closer. "This is Susan Farley," she
announced. "Can anyone hear me?"

"Farley?" a distant voice answered. "This is Mundy.
Boss Atkins is dead. Johnson has a broken leg, and Liddy
is unconscious. Her pulse is weak—and I'm worried
about her. Can you dig us out?"

"I don't know," Susan replied uncertainly. "We're about
a hundred feet in. How far back are you?"

Susan heard the characteristic clatter of loose rock, and
suddenly the other woman's grimy face was there, peering
through a small hole. "Another fifteen feet or so."

"That's a lot of rock to clear," Susan observed doubt-
fully. "And we'll have to put up new support beams as
we go. That'll take two or three days at least."

"I don't think Liddy will survive that long."

"Okay, hang tough. There might be a faster way to get the crew out of there, but I'll have to get an okay from Boss Cooper. And you know that chickenshit bastard. He'll want to check with the warden. You've got air. What else do you need?"

"A first-aid kit and more water."

"Howe can work on that while I go up and talk to Cooper."

"Thanks, Farley, we won't forget."

Susan's mind raced as she returned to the elevator, stepped aboard, and closed the gate behind her. There was a sudden jerk, followed by the usual clanking sounds, as the pawls were engaged and the cage rose.

Her idea was to drop a rope down through the ventilation shaft that connected Tunnel Five with Tunnel Four. The vertical passageway was narrow. Very narrow. But most, if not all, of the women were smaller than the average man. So the logic was there. But would that be enough? It was difficult to predict how Warden Brewster would react, because his decisions were almost always based on what was good for *him*, and Tunnel Four hadn't been all that productive of late. So if forced to choose between spending hundreds of woman hours clearing a played-out lateral and removing gold-bearing rock from Tunnel Five, the heartless sonofabitch might go with the second option. Leaving the crew in Tunnel Four to die.

It wouldn't be the first time. Four months earlier, after the bottom of the shaft that served Tunnel Three caved in, Brewster had left the crew in the lateral above to starve rather than invest the time and energy necessary to repair the elevator. All of which was on Susan's mind as she left the lift and went looking for Boss Cooper.

After listening to her plan, he frowned. "I don't know," the guard said, rubbing the stubble on his chin.

"Your idea *might* work—but we'd better check with the warden."

"Yes, sir," Susan said evenly. *Well, you're predictable if nothing else,* she thought to herself.

It took nearly twenty minutes of precious time to reach the lowest level, or "main" as the prisoners referred to the large tunnel, and follow the tracks back to Shaft One. Most of the mine had a fairly reliable source of electricity thanks to the Cummins V12 diesel generator positioned near the main entrance. A long string of lights dispelled the gloom as they made their way down the corridor to Shaft One.

Then they had to summon the cage again and ride it up a level to the played-out lateral, where a pair of armed guards were waiting to receive them. Their job was to protect Brewster from the inmates, his own correctional officers should they decide to turn on him, *and* any Chimera who might find their way into the mine.

Cooper had to surrender his shotgun, and consent to a cursory pat-down, but that was nothing compared to what Susan was forced to endure. She was ordered to lock her hands behind her neck and spread her feet, so the guards could search for weapons. Not that squeezing her breasts and rubbing her crotch had anything to do with keeping Brewster safe.

Like the rest of the women in the Lucky Buckle Mine, Susan had been forced to endure the humiliating process many times before, and it never got easier. She kept her eyes forward, gritted her teeth, and tried to ignore Pete Pardo's rank body odor as he pawed her body and nuzzled a cheek. "Uh-oh," Pardo said, "this one is carrying concealed weapons. Two of 'em!"

It was an old joke, but Tom Olson never got tired of it, and laughed appreciatively. "You'd better let me check 'em out, Pete. Who knows? Maybe you're wrong."

And so it went until both men had groped Susan more

than once and Cooper chose to intervene. "Save some for later, fellas. We've got a collapse in Tunnel Four—and Atkins is dead."

He didn't mention the women, injured or otherwise, but Susan didn't expect him to. *"Dead?"* Pardo demanded incredulously. "He owed me half a box of .22s. The bastard."

"You'd better get going," Olson put in. Now that the guard knew about the cave-in, he was worried about how Brewster would react if the twosome were delayed.

Susan was ordered to enter the tunnel and Pardo gave her a pat on the fanny as she walked past. A line of dangling lightbulbs led her back to the natural cave where Brewster's quarters were located. Susan felt the usual sense of fear as she brushed between a pair of makeshift curtains and entered what she thought of as "the lair." A fitting analogy. Brewster was a beast, and he lived in a cave.

The relatively narrow entrance opened up into an irregularly shaped chamber that was about thirty feet long and twenty wide. The rocky floor was covered with overlapping mismatched rugs. The main furnishings consisted of a black potbellied stove, an imposing desk, and an enormous bed.

At the moment, a prisoner named Corly Posner was sitting on it with her back resting against the mahogany headboard. She was painting her toenails red, and when she looked up, the puffy black eye was plain to see. Though servicing Brewster had its privileges, not the least of which was escaping the sort of fate that had befallen the women in Tunnel Four, it had its risks as well. The warden's temper being one of them.

Susan's thoughts were interrupted as a Hudson's Bay blanket was thrown aside and Brewster entered the cavern. He was wearing a waist-length leather jacket, khaki pants, and a pair of hiking boots. After placing his Fareye rifle in a rack alongside some other weapons, Brewster removed his jacket and turned to face his visitors. He had dark eyes, a formidable nose, and had chosen to shave his head rather than wear a halo of hair. "Aren't you supposed to be up in Tunnel Five?" Brewster demanded, as he eyed Cooper.

Cooper's feet shifted nervously. "Tunnel Four collapsed, sir. Atkins was killed—and what's left of the crew is trapped."

Brewster circled the desk and sat in a thronelike chair. "Okay," he said calmly. "That explains your presence. Why bring *her* along?"

Cooper's eyes flicked towards Susan and back again. "Inmate Farley believes there's a way to rescue the crew in Tunnel Four in a matter of hours rather than days."

"So rather than steal the idea, and claim credit for it, you brought her along to take the blame if I think it's stupid."

Cooper seemed to wilt under Brewster's unblinking stare. "I thought she should have an opportunity to speak for herself," he said lamely.

The warden laughed contemptuously as his eyes shifted to Susan. She felt as if his gaze were stripping her clothes off. "So, Inmate Farley, let's hear this idea of yours."

Susan swallowed the lump in the back of her throat and tried to muster more saliva. Then, careful to keep her sentences short, she told Brewster how the ventilation shaft could be used in a rescue effort. He toyed with an ivory letter opener while she spoke—and nodded when she was through.

"Short and to the point. I like that," Brewster said, as he studied her. "Some women don't know when to keep their mouths closed."

Susan saw Corly flinch out of the corner of her eye. "It's hard to know for sure," Brewster continued conversationally, "but I have a suspicion that you might look pretty good without those overalls. Or anything at all, for that matter.

"So here's what I want you to do. Accompany Boss Cooper back to Tunnel Five, pull the crew out of Tunnel Four, and report to me. Oh, and one other thing."

By that time Susan was scared, and sorry she had put her idea forward. What had begun as an attempt to help some fellow inmates had turned into a nightmare. "Sir?"

Brewster jerked his head in Corly's direction. "Take that piece of shit with you."

More than two hours had elapsed since the cave-in by the time a tripod was set up over the ventilation shaft and Susan was lowered down through the narrow chimney that connected Tunnel Five with Tunnel Four. She used a claw hammer to bang away at the worst obstructions as the beam produced by her headlamp played across the glittering surface in front of her.

Then she arrived in a circle of light, where three anxious women were waiting to receive her. Mundy's face was smeared with dirt. "You're a sight for sore eyes, Farley. We owe you."

"You'd do the same," Susan replied, and wondered if it was true. "How's Liddy?"

The other woman shook her head. "She stopped breathing. We couldn't bring her back."

"I'm sorry," Susan said soberly.

"Yeah, we all are," Mundy replied. "We've got a splint on Johnson's leg. We'll send her up first."

They spent the next hour piling rocks over and around Liddy's body while a succession of women were winched through the shaft to the lateral above. Finally it was Susan's turn. Her body twirled gently as the rope pulled her upwards. Eager hands were waiting to pluck her out of the hole and unbuckle the harness. A boss named Riley had arrived to take charge. Cooper couldn't meet her eyes. "Let's go, Farley! It's time to get cleaned up. The warden is waiting for you."

"Yeah," Riley put in, as he grinned lasciviously. "Brewster wants to thank you in a very special way!"

Cooper didn't laugh, but a couple of the women did, which showed how hard some of them had become. Susan was following Cooper towards the elevator when a hand touched her arm. As Susan turned, her light came around to illuminate Corly's battered face. She blinked.

"Farley?"

Susan paused. "Yes?"

"Be careful. He's mean."

"Why did he hit you?"

Corly looked away. Tears cut tracks through the dirt on her face. "I told him that I'm pregnant."

"I'm sorry," Susan said softly. "But I have some good news for you."

Corly wiped her nose with the back of a wrist. "Really? What's that?"

"Brewster is going to die."

Corly might have spoken, might have asked how, but Susan was gone by then.

It took Susan about an hour to finish a lukewarm shower, fix her hair as best she could, and apply some color to her cheeks and lips with a borrowed lipstick. Then, certain in the knowledge that she wouldn't be back, she made her way through the sparsely furnished dormitory. The workday was over, so the other inmates were present, and all of them knew where she was going. Most of the women pitied her. A few no doubt thought she was a slut. Some even envied her, absurd though that clearly was.

But Susan's thoughts were elsewhere. She wasn't sure exactly when the decision to kill Brewster had been made. The last time she was groped? When she saw Corly's black eye? It hardly mattered. What *did* matter was to do the job quickly. *Always take your first opportunity. Odds are there won't be a second one.*

That was what she had learned at the Freedom First training facility near Custer, Montana, during the run-up to the assassination attempt on President Grace. The crime for which she had been arrested, tried, and sentenced to a federal penitentiary. Except that facility had been overrun by the stinks—causing the government to send her to Canon City, and then to the mine. So unlike the other inmates, even those convicted of murder, Susan was a *trained* killer. And that could make an important difference.

Taking Brewster out wouldn't be easy, however; she knew that, and what felt like a lead weight was riding in the pit of her stomach as Cooper waited for her to step off the elevator. Susan was received quite differently now that she had been selected to serve as Brewster's companion. There were no lewd comments, and no unnecessary physical contact, as Cooper rode the elevator down and Susan was subjected to a perfunctory search.

"Okay," Pardo said, gesturing towards the tunnel. "It's time to go to work."

"Yeah," Olson agreed. "We're counting on you to keep the warden real happy!"

The guards were still chuckling as Susan walked the length of the passageway. She pushed one of the shower curtains aside and entered the cavern beyond. Brewster was seated at his desk, oiling the Colt .45. He put the pistol down on a rag next to a handful of gleaming bullets. "Not bad," he said admiringly. "Not bad at all. And I hear the rescue was a success."

Susan came to a stop in front of the desk. Her eyes took everything in. That included Brewster, the Colt, and each object on the desk. She spotted a variety of weapons to choose from besides the pistol. An ivory letter opener.

A pair of scissors. Even the ruler had some potential. "Yes, sir," Susan replied woodenly.

" 'Sir' might be a bit too formal," Brewster said, as he stood. "I have a first name, you know. It's Hiram."

"Yes, sir. I mean Hiram."

"That's better," Brewster said, as he circled the desk. "I like your style. No attitude, no games, no silliness."

Susan turned to face him so that he couldn't get between her and the desk. She forced herself to maintain eye contact with Brewster as he ran a knuckle down the curve of her cheek. She shivered. "Are you afraid of me?"

"Yes," Susan answered honestly, as she turned a couple of degrees to the left.

"Good. If you do what I say, and behave yourself, life could be very comfortable."

Susan knew that Brewster was going to kiss her, and as their lips met, she forced herself to kiss him back. She even went so far as to open her mouth for him as she completed the half-turn and felt his hands begin to explore her body. The desk was directly behind her now and at least two feet away.

Brewster was kissing Susan's neck by then—and chuckled as he felt her fingers fumble with his belt buckle. "You are a hot little minx! No messing about! I like that."

And he was telling the truth, which became quite apparent as Susan pushed his pants down and cupped his genitals. "I want to do something special for you," she whispered huskily. "Are you ready?"

Brewster grinned. "I was born ready!"

"Really?" Susan inquired sweetly, as she closed a callused hand around his testicles. "Let's see if you're ready for *this*."

Brewster screamed, and his hands went to his groin as he fell over backwards. That was Susan's cue to turn and snatch the Colt off the desk. First she had to thumb the loading gate open. Then she had to insert the cartridges while rotating the cylinder. But it was child's play, really, since she had been taught to fire her father's .45 at age fourteen, and mastered the weapon shortly thereafter.

Meanwhile, Susan could hear Brewster swearing as he battled to regain his feet and hoist his pants up. Did she have time to load four of the six chambers? Or only three? It was a life-and-death decision. Because Brewster was a lot bigger and stronger than she was. And if he got his hands on her, the fight would be over very quickly indeed.

Susan chose to close the gate after inserting three rounds. She turned just in time. Brewster shouted something incoherent and charged. Susan squeezed the trigger and heard an impotent click as the hammer fell on an empty chamber. It was a single-action revolver. So before she could fire the weapon a second time she had to pull the hammer back again. Was there enough time? Or was she about to die?

Brewster was only inches away when the pistol went off. The lead slug punched a hole through his intestines and blew a bloody divot out of his back. He swayed drunkenly, looked down at his belly, and was still trying to inspect the damage when he keeled over backwards.

Susan brought the Colt up and was holding it with both hands as Pardo and Olson charged into the cavern. The men were heavily armed and with only two bullets left, each shot would have to count. Pardo took a slug in the chest, stumbled, and took a nosedive.

Olson fired, missed, and paid the price when a well-aimed bullet smashed through his forehead. His boots left the floor, and he seemed to float briefly, before landing with arms spread. Dust exploded up out of the carpet.

Susan stood there for a moment as gun smoke swirled around her head. Then, conscious of how vulnerable she was, she circled around behind the desk. Less than a minute later, the pistol was reloaded and ready in her hand as she crossed the room to where the green Hudson's Bay blanket hung.

After slipping through the doorway, she followed a short tunnel to a wooden ladder. A patch of gray sky was visible above. Brewster had been careful to provide himself with a back door and Susan planned to use it. But not until she returned to the cavern and collected at least some of what she would need in order to survive outside.

She had just reentered the cave, and was about to visit the weapons rack, when Brewster uttered a heart-rending groan. "I'll bet that smarts," Susan said unsympathetically. Then she shot him in the head. "Have a nice trip to hell."

CHAPTER FOUR
BAD COMPANY

Friday, September 25, 1953
The Badlands

The sky was blue, the highway was gray, and Capelli was running. With each stride, his sixty-pound pack parted company with his sweat-slicked back and hit him. He could just drop it, of course. But what then? How long would he last without food or backup ammo? Although that would be a moot point if the stinks caught up with him. At least a dozen of the creatures were closing in on them including a squad of Hybrids, a couple of Steelheads, and a hulking Ravager. None of which was of any concern to Rowdy, who was loping along at Capelli's side with his mouth open and his tongue flapping in the breeze.

Capelli glanced back over his shoulder, only to see that Locke had lost even more ground. He knew it was just a matter of time before the stinks caught up with the businessman.

Capelli felt the ground start to rise as he passed a black Ford, a yellow Buick, and a work-worn John Deere tractor. The machine was hooked to a trailer that had been looted of everything except a rotting couch. But the combination of the incline and the presence of some abandoned vehicles gave Capelli an idea. A desperate one to be sure, but anything was better than letting the stinks gnaw on his bones, so he began to scan the cars ahead.

Their batteries were dead, and had been for a long time, but maybe, just maybe, he could start one of the vehicles by compression. All he needed was a downhill slope, a key that had been left in the ignition, and tires that weren't flat. And some gas. Enough to get them five miles down the highway.

Laughter echoed in his head. *Sure,* the voice said mockingly. *That would be wonderful. By why stop there? How 'bout a VTOL, complete with a beautiful stewardess, and a well-stocked bar?*

Capelli wasn't about to be baited. The top of the rise was just ahead. The pack slapped him on the back as he ran, his lungs were on fire, and his feet felt as if they were made of lead. Then, just when it seemed as if the torture would never end, he was there. The burgundy Oldsmobile was riddled with holes, and bones spilled out onto the highway when he opened the door. They rattled as they hit the ground.

A skull grinned at Capelli from the passenger seat as he eyed the floor and saw two pedals. No clutch, so the 88 had an automatic transmission. And Capelli knew it was damned near impossible to push-start one of those, so he slammed the door and looked back.

Locke was struggling. What had been a clumsy running motion had deteriorated into an awkward shamble. And farther back, partially concealed by the shimmering heat, the Chimera could be seen. And if they were tired, there was no evidence of it.

Capelli swore, turned back towards the top of the rise, and forced himself to run. He passed a truck, but it was blackened by fire. The first vehicle on the reverse side of the slope was sitting atop three good tires, but the fourth was flat. It wasn't perfect, but it was worth investigating.

Capelli uttered a silent prayer as he approached the

1949 Nash Airflyte and opened the door. What he saw was sufficient to elicit a whoop of joy. The Nash had a stick shift! But his spirits fell when he realized that the ignition key was missing.

Then Capelli remembered that the trunk had been left open. A quick inspection revealed that a set of keys was dangling from the trunk lock. And while everything else was gone, the spare was right where it was supposed to be. As was a jack.

"What-you-got?" Locke inquired as he coasted to a stop and stood with chest heaving.

"A way to outrun the stinks," Capelli answered, dumping his pack onto the ground. "How are you at changing tires?"

"I was a car dealer, remember?" Locke replied, as he shrugged his pack off.

"Good. Put the spare on as quickly as you can. Then, when the car is ready to roll, give me a holler. We'll start it on compression."

Locke pulled the jack out of the trunk and turned to meet Capelli's gaze. "What if this baby is out of gas?"

"Then all of our troubles will be over," Capelli predicted grimly.

"What are you going to do?"

"I'm going to slow 'em down," Capelli answered. "Or try to. Don't forget to throw our packs into the car. Rowdy. Stay." Then he was gone.

Rather than go over the rise, and lose visual contact with Locke, Capelli knelt next to the burned-out truck's half-melted rear tires. As he brought the rifle to bear on the Chimera, he was shocked to see how much closer the aliens were. But that put them within range, which meant an opportunity to slow them down.

Capelli panned from left to right as a variety of heads bobbed up and down within the circle of his telescopic sight. But the one he wanted most towered above all the rest. Because if he could nail the largest and most powerful stink, it would not only reduce the overall threat but cause the lesser forms to advance more slowly.

But he had to bag the monster with a single head shot. Because if he didn't, the Ravager would activate a shield so powerful his rifle wouldn't be able to punch through it. And that would submarine his plan.

The stinks were at the bottom of the slope. It took all the nerve Capelli could muster to focus on the Ravager and capture the rhythm of the creature's movements. Up-down, up-down, up-*blam!*

Capelli felt the rifle kick his shoulder, saw the spray of blood, and had the satisfaction of seeing the Chimera fall. The rest of the stinks immediately went to ground in the wake of the Ravager's death. And that was just fine, since it meant they were stationary for the moment.

Capelli turned to look back over his shoulder and saw that Locke had removed the flat and was about to mount the spare. Rowdy was lifting a leg over one of the good tires. The whole thing was going to be close. *Very* close.

The truck shook as a blast from an Auger ripped through it and a hail of Bullseye projectiles pinged all around. Capelli knew the Chimera could "see" his heat signature, and was forced to back away, in hopes that the top of the rise would offer additional cover. That was dangerous, of course, because the moment he stopped firing, the stinks would advance.

Rather than allow the aliens to climb the slope unopposed, Capelli took the opportunity to switch from the Marksman's primary to secondary firing mode. He felt the recoil and heard the report as a semiautonomous Drone took off and cruised downslope.

It was only a matter of seconds before the airborne

turret "sensed" the presence of living targets and opened fire. There was quite a commotion as Hybrids fell, the Drone took fire from below, and Locke yelled, "Hey, Capelli! It's ready."

Capelli turned and ran as lethal Auger bolts flashed through dirt and thick concrete before stuttering off into the distance. The spare was on, the jack was lying where Locke had left it, and the big man had the driver's-side door open so he could push and steer at the same time. "Come on!" he shouted. "Let's get out of here."

Capelli slipped the sling over his head and let the Marksman hang across his back as he caught up with the Nash from behind. With both men pushing as hard as they could, the bathtub-shaped sedan began to roll. Slowly at first, due to its considerable weight, but faster as it gained momentum.

When Locke thought the speed was sufficient he jumped behind the wheel. The transmission was in neutral. So he put the clutch in and pulled the shifter down into first gear. The Nash jerked as he lifted his foot, but nothing happened. So Capelli continued to push.

Was the car out of gas? It was starting to look that way as the sedan gathered speed once again and Locke popped the clutch for the second time. This time there was a loud bang when the engine backfired, coughed, and finally caught.

Locke gunned it as Capelli ran to catch up, pulled the back door open, and dived inside. The rear window exploded and showered the men with safety glass as the surviving stinks topped the rise and opened fire.

But the engine had steadied by then, Locke had upshifted into second gear, and the sedan was gaining speed. Thirty seconds later they were out of range—and the stinks were dwindling in the rearview mirror. The race had been won. But for how long?

Capelli worked his way out of the sling, pulled himself

forward so he could look over the other man's shoulder, and eyed the gas gauge. It appeared that they had a little less than a quarter of a tank to work with. "Not bad, huh?" Locke remarked cheerfully, as the needle on the speedometer continued to climb. "I'm a Ford man myself! But I have to admit that this thing is roomy."

Rowdy was sitting in the front passenger seat with his head out the window and tongue flapping as Capelli allowed himself to fall back into the seat. The last few hours had been exhausting, and now as the shadows began to lengthen, he was tired. The engine hummed, the slipstream roared, and miles melted away. The situation wasn't perfect. Nothing ever was. But right then, in that moment, Capelli was happy.

East of Goodland, Kansas

Capelli and Locke were standing at a crossroads about half a mile off the highway when the first drops of rain fell. There was a gas station, a general store, and a forlorn-looking post office. None of the buildings appeared to be occupied. The sky was increasingly dark, the occasional bolt of lightning could be seen to the north, and the threesome had been looking for a place to hole up when they happened across the dead body. Rowdy, for reasons known only to him, was busy barking at it. Capelli told Rowdy to shut up, and he did.

Two days had passed since the Nash had run out of gas, thereby forcing them to abandon it. They had been walking ever since, and the trip had been wonderfully uneventful until now.

Locke stepped forward to inspect the corpse. It was roped to a telephone pole. He grabbed a handful of greasy hair and jerked the man's head up. Lightning strobed, a loud crack was heard, and Capelli saw that the man's face was badly swollen. It appeared as though he had been beaten to death. That was too bad, but dead is dead, and there was nothing they could do about it. "Come on. It isn't safe out here. We need some cover."

That was when the rain fell harder, hitting the man's face and reviving him. His eyes popped open.

"Well, I'll be damned," Locke remarked. "The sonof-abitch is alive."

"Cut him loose," Capelli instructed, as another bolt of lightning zigzagged across the sky. It was closer now and the bang came quickly. "Let's try the post office. Maybe we can take shelter there."

By sandwiching the man between them, and half-carrying, half-dragging him across the empty street, Capelli and Locke were able to help him into the post office. Like everything else in the state of Kansas, it had been looted.

Locke lowered the man onto the floor as Capelli activated the light on his shotgun. He knew from experience that the building could be home to just about anything. That included pods, Grims, and Leapers. So it was necessary to check the place out before taking up residence. As Capelli's light played across the floor he saw dozens of unopened envelopes, many of which were stamped with dirty boot prints. Rowdy's claws made clicking noises as he nosed along, pausing only to sniff an oak bench, before continuing his investigation.

Capelli figured the walls were pretty much as they had been before the area was overrun. A red, white, and blue Uncle Sam stared out at him from a recruiting poster. The old man's gaunt-looking face was stern and his right index finger was pointed at Capelli's chest. "Uncle Sam needs you!" the caption read.

Uncle Sam kicked your ass out of the Army, the voice put in. *And for good reason.*

Laughter that only Capelli could hear followed him

through a door and into the postmaster's office. There was a counter that faced out onto the main room, plus shutters that could be closed in order to seal the space off from the public area beyond. A potbellied stove occupied a corner and the south wall consisted of nothing but niches, many of which contained undelivered letters.

It was 2:36 according to the clock mounted on the back wall. The timepiece was flanked by Wanted posters on one side and copies of postal regulations on the other. All of them were held in place by red thumbtacks.

Then, turning back to face the door, Capelli saw that most of the north wall was taken up by a glass-covered American flag. It had been punctured more than once and, according to the plaque below, had been carried into the battle of Seicheprey in 1918 by local troops.

Not having detected any signs of Chimera, Capelli returned to the main room as thunder rolled outside. It was dark by then and rain pattered on the roof. The man was coming around, after receiving half a Hershey bar from Locke and some water to wash it down. He blinked owlishly as Capelli's light stabbed him in the eyes. "Come on," Capelli said. "We'll hole up in the inner office. If we pull the shutters, less light will show."

Locke helped the man to stand and gave him a shoulder to lean on as they followed Capelli and Rowdy into the office. The next half-hour was spent building a fire in the stove, clearing away some of the litter, and laying out their bedrolls. Once the baked beans were hot, and everyone had a mug full of black coffee, the man told his story. Long, lank hair served to frame a narrow face. One eye was swollen shut. The rest of his face was puffy, his upper lip was swollen, and judging from appearances it was difficult for him to chew.

His name was Pete Sowers, and it seemed that he was

part of a community living in the huge salt mine located under Hutchinson, Kansas. Originally most of the salt from the mine had been used to make pharmaceuticals, baked goods, and chemical products. In post-industrial America, those markets didn't exist anymore.

But, to hear Sowers tell it, survivors were increasingly in need of common table salt. Both to flavor their food and to preserve meat. So business was on the upswing. "I'm one of twelve salesmen," Sowers explained earnestly. "My job is to deliver salt to existing customers and identify new ones. I generally travel with two bodyguards. Calvin, Ted, and myself were headed for the rendezvous in Colby when at least two hundred Leapers jumped us in a dry wash about ten miles south of here. We fought like hell, but I'm the only one who made it out, along with one of the pack animals."

"I'm sorry to hear that," Capelli said sympathetically. "You mentioned a rendezvous in Colby. When is it supposed to take place?"

Sowers wiped his lips with a grimy sleeve. "In a couple of days. The stinks are a big threat—so the rendezvous won't last for more than five or six hours."

The door to the potbellied stove was open and firelight danced the walls. Rowdy was lying in front of the fire with his head on his paws. His eyes were open, and Capelli knew the dog was alert to the slightest sound.

Locke took a sip of coffee. "So how did you wind up *here*? Tied to a telephone pole?"

"I figured I'd go to the rendezvous, sell the remaining salt, and head home," Sowers replied. "But a group of bandits spotted me and gave chase. They caught up, beat the crap out of me, and I passed out. When I came to, they were gone. Maybe they left me for dead."

"So what now?" Capelli inquired.

"I'm a charity case," Sowers said, as he glanced from

face to face. "I know that. But if you'll let me accompany you to the rendezvous, there's a good chance that some of my folks will be there. If not, I'll borrow some ammo from one of our customers. Either way I'll pay you."

"We aren't looking to make a profit," Capelli responded. "But food is always welcome."

Locke eyed Capelli. "So we're going to Colby?"

Capelli was seated on an upside-down waste-paper basket. He shrugged. "Why not? It's on the way."

Sowers opened his mouth as if to ask, "On the way to where?" but closed it again. A terrible darkness had fallen over America and everything was different. People were generally reluctant to say where they were going and it wasn't polite to ask.

The fire crackled as it consumed pieces of what had been the postmaster's desk drawers, thunder muttered to the south, and Rowdy produced an elaborate yawn. The day was done.

Colby, Kansas

It took two days to reach Colby. The weather had improved by then, although there was a nip in the air, and some of the trees were starting to turn. And with each passing mile there were more and more signs that other people were headed for the rendezvous as well. As the two-lane road carried them east, Capelli spotted campfires, so recent that some of them were still smoking, piles of fresh horse dung, and a so-called message tree. It was located at the center of a town too small to have a name.

The stinks couldn't read. That was the theory, anyway, and insofar as Capelli knew it was true. But humans could, so many of the messages that were pinned to the big oak tree located at the center of town were cryptic. One said, "J.C., So far so good," and was signed "H.N." And another read, "Luke, dad's better, Love, T."

But some of the messages were open and direct, such as a pistol-shaped card that read, "Need a gunsmith? Ask for Hank Fowler."

There were hundreds of them. So many that the lower part of the tree trunk looked as if it had been painted white. Sowers read them all, or tried to, looking for any sign that other salt salesmen were in the area. Some of them made him very upset. Like the one that read, "My husband needs penicillin! Will do *anything* for it. Ask for Amanda Hartly."

By that time, Capelli had come to the conclusion that Sowers was a bit too naïve to be out roaming the badlands alone. The man had a tendency to see everything in simple black-and-white terms. And that reminded him of another person who had all of the answers: a lieutenant named Nathan Hale.

As they approached Colby, the men found themselves sharing the highway with a steady stream of other people. Some were mounted, some were on foot, and in spite of the danger represented by such a gathering, most of the travelers were in a good mood.

The same couldn't be said for their dogs, however, many of whom saw Rowdy as a threat. They growled whenever the big mix approached them. But if Rowdy was offended, there was no sign of it as he made the rounds of people and animals alike, his tail a-wagging.

As they entered Colby, Capelli saw a sign that read, "Colby, The Oasis on the Plains," and thought there was some truth to it. Except for a swath of destruction that cut across the town at an angle, the city was largely intact. That included the Romanesque courthouse, which, though partially burned, still had a stately appearance and served as the backdrop for the chaotic rendezvous spread out in front of it.

The gathering was part picnic, part yard sale, and part revival meeting. As Capelli looked around, he saw people sharing food around small fires, merchants selling everything from homemade candles to blocks of cheese, and preachers of every stripe. One of them claimed to be in touch with the Chimeran hive-mind and was wearing a Leaper skull on top of his head. And there were musicians, too. Along with jugglers, hollow-eyed beggars, medicine men, and a man who claimed to represent President Thomas Voss. He stood on a park bench and gave a speech about the attempt to destroy a tower in New York City, but only six people paused to listen.

In spite of the country fair–like atmosphere, there was an overlay of fear as well. It could be seen in the way that people continually scanned the sky for any sign of a Chimeran shuttle and never ventured more than a foot or two away from their possessions. And there were other dangers, too. Because all manner of thieves were roaming the crowd. They ranged from fast-talking con men to heavily armed thugs. Capelli was just about to warn Locke of that when Sowers uttered a shout of outrage. "There they are! The bastards that stole my salt!"

Then Sowers was off, winding his way between clumps of people, as he hurried to confront a group of five heavily armed men. They had a string of horses hitched to a picket line, and from what Capelli could see, they were selling bags of something off a wide-spread blanket. "Come on!" Locke said. "Sowers is unarmed. He's going to need some backup."

"Wrong," Capelli responded as he reached out to grab the other man's arm.

"Why not?"

"Rule six."

"Which is?"

"Mind your own business."

Locke jerked his arm free. "There's more to life than looking out for yourself, Capelli."

Yeah, the voice said, as Locke hurried away. *There's more to life than what's in it for Capelli.*

Capelli sighed, whistled for Rowdy, and followed his client over to the spot where Sowers was locked in a heated confrontation with a much larger man. He had thick black hair, a unibrow, and a crooked nose. And, judging from his expression, he was pissed.

"You stole my horses *and* my salt," Sowers said accusingly. "And I want them back."

Predictably enough, the man with the black hair drew a pistol and pointed it at Sowers's head. "You *want* to die, don't you? Well, you're about to get your wish."

"I wouldn't do that if I were you," Locke said coolly.

The man looked up, saw the Winchester that was leveled at him, and frowned. "Who the hell are *you*?"

"I'm the guy who's going to blow your head off unless you put that pistol away."

"Oh, really? What about *them*?" the man demanded, as his companions drew weapons and pointed them at Locke.

"It looks like they're going to die too," Capelli said, as he stepped forward. At that range the Rossmore could blow two or three men away with a single blast, and all of them knew it. Rowdy, who was standing at Capelli's side, growled menacingly.

The result was a Mexican standoff. People who were in the line of fire hurried to clear the area as time seemed to stretch. Then it snapped as Locke fired, the man with the black hair was thrown off his feet, and all hell broke loose. A bandit shot Sowers in the left leg; Capelli blew him away with the Rossmore, and was pleased to see the man standing next to him fall as well.

The Winchester made steady *bang, bang, bang* sounds

as Locke worked the lever and brass casings arced through the air. A second BOOM from the shotgun was like the period at the end of a sentence as a load of double-ought buck nearly cut the last bandit in two.

That was followed by a moment of silence while the crowd absorbed what had occurred. Then it was as if someone dropped a needle onto a record. A baby cried, Sowers groaned as he clutched his thigh, and hawkers went back to haranguing the crowd. Time was short; scores had been settled the only way they could be, and life went on.

Locke fished a first-aid kit out of his pack and went to work. Having cut Sowers's pant leg away, he checked to see if there was an exit wound. When he found one, he announced the good news. "The bullet went through— and it looks like it missed the bone. I'll pour some gin in there, slap pressure dressings on both of the holes, and wrap everything with gauze. That should hold you for awhile."

"Thanks for backing me up," Sowers said, as Locke opened a bottle of gin. "I know what I did was stupid. But I was pissed!"

"Yeah," Capelli said, as he eyed the crowd. "We noticed. Of course, Locke is just as stupid as you are. Although I do give him credit for shooting first."

Sowers swore as the gin trickled into the entry wound. Locke wiped some blood-tinged alcohol away and placed a gauze pad over the wound. "I didn't have a choice," the businessman said. "It was either that or allow something bad to happen."

Capelli thought about Hale. The gun, the look in the officer's golden eyes, and the explosion of gore. "Yeah, it's like that sometimes."

A sturdy-looking woman appeared. She was wearing a broad-brimmed hat, a buckskin jacket, and faded jeans.

A pair of scuffed cowboy boots completed the outfit. There was a frown on her homely face and her voice was gruff. "Sowers? Is that *you*? God damn it, son, you're supposed to sell salt, not lay around on your ass."

Sowers's face lit up and he grinned. "Capelli, Locke, I'd like you to meet Meg Bowers. Meg's a salesman, just like me, only pushier."

"I'm a sales*woman*," Bowers put in combatively, "and that ain't all. I'm pushier, meaner, *and* better-lookin' than Sowers is. But, worthless or not, the sonofabitch is ours! So we'll take him off your hands."

A trio of rugged-looking men had appeared by then. They were armed to the teeth and leading horses. Once Locke's rough-and-ready first-aid efforts were complete, they loaded Sowers onto a horse and placed his boots in the stirrups. "Two of those horses over there are mine," the salt vendor said, "plus the bags of salt But I reckon the other mounts are yours."

Capelli looked across the scattering of dead bodies to where the horses stood. There were seven of them. "We'll take three of them. Two to ride and one to sell. You keep the others."

Sowers shrugged. "It's a deal. Take the ones you want."

Capelli looked at the string of horses but stayed where he was.

Bowers laughed. "You don't know the first thing about horses, do you, son?"

Capelli shook his head.

"Hanson," Bowers said, "go over there and cut out some mounts for our friends! And I'll be watching you. So give them something decent."

One of the riders obeyed, and five minutes later Capelli and Locke had three horses, complete with saddles and related gear. Sowers waved as he followed

Bowers down the crowded street and was soon lost to sight.

Then it was time to carry out the gruesome task of stripping the dead bodies of valuables as members of the crowd looked on. The take included a small arsenal of weapons, a quantity of ammo, and some food. As soon as the process was complete, Capelli insisted that they move a block away before trying to figure out what to do with the extra horse and nine guns.

"Stay here," Locke said. "If I can sell cars, I can sell a horse! I'll be back." And with that, both he and the extra mount disappeared into the crowd.

Capelli wasn't so sure about his client's claim, but Bowers had been correct. He *didn't* know the first thing about horses. So maybe Locke could pull it off.

The ex-soldier *was* an expert where weapons were concerned, however, and having laid his wares out for potential customers to look at, was soon haggling away. He had attracted plenty of possible buyers. But Capelli had a limited amount of time to work with—and didn't want to haul the weapons around. So he set the prices low but refused to accept anything less than quality ammo.

Twice, Capelli had the funny feeling he had come to associate with danger. Back during his days as a Sentinel, a SRPA psychologist named Cassie Aklin had told him that such sensations were thought to originate in something called the "reptilian complex," meaning the part of the brain that higher mammals share with reptiles and is responsible for basic fight-or-flight responses.

Whatever it was, Capelli had come to trust such warnings. So on both occasions he interrupted what he was doing to take a quick look around. But there were dozens of people in the area, and when Capelli scanned their faces, none of them looked especially suspicious. So all he could do was continue to sell the weapons, stash his profits, and hope for the best. He was down to a beat-up Luger and a .303 Enfield when Locke returned with a stranger in tow.

The man was tall, with a ruddy complexion and a well-tended mustache. He was wearing a tweed cap, a shooting jacket, and knee-high riding boots. His armament consisted of a riding crop, a double-barreled pistol in a cross-draw holster, and a knife that could be seen sticking up out of a boot. There was a pleasant smile on his face.

"Capelli, this is Mr. Patrick Murphy! He's a packer and the new owner of what was our horse. Patrick, this is Joe Capelli."

"It's a pleasure to meet you, Joe," Murphy said genially. "You'll be glad to know that Al got a fair price for your animal."

"I'm pleased to hear it," Capelli replied, as he stood to shake hands.

"Patrick and his men are packers," Locke explained as Rowdy arrived to check the newcomer out. "And they're headed for Hoxie. That's our next stop, right? So I asked Patrick if we could tag along and he said yes!"

"That's right," Murphy agreed. "The word is that there are plenty of stinks over that way, and the more guns the better."

Capelli was anything but pleased. What Murphy said was true. But a large group of people could attract trouble too. And the arrangement Locke had in mind was a clear violation of rule eight, which was "Never trust anyone."

But Murphy seemed to be okay, and Locke was so pleased with the arrangement he had made that Capelli couldn't bring himself to say no. "That sounds good," he agreed. "When do you plan to leave?"

"In about fifteen minutes," Murphy replied, as he

looked up at the empty sky. "We want to put some distance between ourselves and Colby. A rendezvous is hard to resist—but they're damned risky. The stinks nailed one near Lincoln a few months back. I hear there were hundreds of casualties."

"I agree," Capelli said. "We'll be ready."

Murphy delivered a salute with the riding crop, gave Rowdy a pat on the head, and melted into the crowd. Capelli felt the strange tingling sensation at the back of his neck, took a long fruitless look around, and wound up selling the Luger for two .38s and a pocket knife. Later, when he went to open it, he discovered that the second blade had been broken off.

As the sunlight began to fade, and the shadows lengthened, Capelli figured they were a good five or six miles east of Colby. His knees hurt, his butt was sore, and the horse he was riding seemed to know that he was a novice rider. A fact made obvious by its tendency to make a side trip whenever a clump of especially succulent grass appeared.

The pack train included six wranglers, all of whom were amused by Capelli's lack of equestrian expertise, and never tired of poking fun at him. Besides the mounts the men were riding, the group had a spare purchased from Locke. The actual cargo, whatever it was, had been loaded onto ten mules, each of which could carry about eighty pounds. So Capelli figured the group was moving eight hundred pounds of *something*. Less supplies, of course. Not that it mattered to him so long as everything went smoothly.

It was clear that the wranglers not only knew what they were doing, but had been working together for quite awhile as they laagered for the night. The site consisted of a rise crowned by a sturdy rock wall and a burned-out farmhouse. There wasn't any shelter to speak of, but the waist-high wall would offer cover if the group was attacked, and the ruins were a plentiful source of firewood.

As the camp was set up, most of the animals were unloaded and given a chance to graze under the watchful eye of a mounted wrangler. All of which struck Capelli as very professional. And after darkness had fallen the well-screened fire, an excellent dinner, and the neatly aligned tents all combined to reinforce this impression. In fact, it was almost *too* well run in Capelli's estimation.

The whole thing was reminiscent of the Army. And, as he listened to the men chatter among themselves, he was struck by the frequent use of phrases like "Roger that," "He's on the far side of the perimeter," and "What's for chow?"

Of course there were lots of ex-soldiers around, and the fact that a group of them had banded together could be explained in all sorts of ways, but Capelli resolved to keep his eyes peeled nevertheless.

Locke had no such reservations, and clearly felt at ease with the wranglers, as a group of them sat around discussing the finer points of Ford flathead engines. A subject of very little interest to Capelli, who was sore after more than three hours spent in the saddle and looking forward to turning in early. And, more than that, to a full night's sleep, since Murphy insisted that his men would take all of the two-hour watches.

So the packers were gathered around the fire when Capelli got up and slipped away. Rowdy had been gone for an hour by then, hunting probably, because that was the way he got most of his food.

Capelli wasn't trying to walk quietly. Doing so was second nature. And that was the reason why the wrangler who was kneeling next to Locke's open pack failed to hear him. Capelli froze as the beam from a penlight played across his client's gear. The fire threw some light into the surrounding area, but because the runner was standing in the dense shadow cast by the farmhouse's freestanding chimney, he was impossible to see.

Capelli's first instinct was to draw his pistol, step forward, and challenge what appeared to be a thief. But what if the man wasn't acting alone? What if he had *orders* to search the packs? Given what he'd observed earlier in the day, such a thing seemed to be all too possible. The thought sent a chill down his spine.

Putting the flashlight down in order to use both hands, the wrangler bent forward to inspect the inside of the pack. For a brief moment part of the man's face was illuminated. Only then did Capelli recognize him as a packer named Cody, a wrangler who had been standing nearby as he sold weapons back in Colby. He wondered if there was some sort of connection.

No more than a minute had passed since Capelli had left the circle of firelight. He heard a low whistle, saw Cody kill the light and melt into the darkness. It didn't take a genius to realize that he'd been missed and a wrangler had been sent to warn Cody.

Capelli turned back towards the fire and pretended to zip up his pants as he reentered the firelight's soft glow. Murphy was seated on the ground and leaning on a saddle. His eyes seemed to glitter as he looked up. "It's a nice evening, don't you think?"

"Yes," Capelli said, agreeably, as he held his palms towards the warmth. "It is. The nights are getting colder, though."

Capelli and Locke announced their intention to turn in about twenty minutes later. As soon as they were alone, Capelli told Locke about what he'd seen and his decision to part company with the pack train as soon as possible. They couldn't do so that night, not with a sentry on duty at all times, but an opportunity would arise soon. Or so he hoped.

So they agreed that they would take turns sleeping with weapons at the ready just in case the wranglers attacked during the night. That was why Capelli was awake when dozens of Grims burst up out of the farmhouse's basement, killed the sentry, and attacked the men trapped in their sleeping bags.

CHAPTER FIVE
A SHOT IN THE ARM

The President of the United States was living in a cave. Not because he *wanted* to, but because it wasn't safe to live out in the open. So when the wind-up alarm clock began to ring, he was sleeping in what he jokingly referred to as the "Executive Residence." Meaning a side room off the cavern's main gallery, where what remained of the federal government convened daily. It was pitch black, so his first attempt to locate the obnoxious clock failed. But the second succeeded.

Most of the facility had electric power, thanks to the presence of an underground lake and the turbine generator placed in the tube through which the outflow had been forced to pass. So the lamp located next to his sleeping platform came on as he turned the switch and the limestone walls were flooded with a soft yellow glow.

That was the easy part. Then he had to steel himself for what came next. The temperature inside the caves was a constant 58 degrees Fahrenheit. That was bearable when fully dressed but felt cold as Voss rolled out of the sack.

But there was no way to escape the moment, not and get his work done, so Voss sat up and began to work his way out of the bag. Once his legs were free, he hurried to pull the robe on before making his way over to a corner where all he had to do was hold a bowl under a steady stream of water in order to collect enough for a quick sponge bath. Later, assuming he found enough time, he would shave and take a hot shower in the communal facility down on the main floor.

Voss donned an Army uniform that bore no insignia, and slipped his arms into the Magnum's shoulder holster harness, before stepping out onto the natural balcony just outside of his quarters. A downward-slanting trail led from his quarters to the main floor below. The pathway was one person wide and most of it had been excavated by hand.

The main gallery, which was at least one hundred feet high and three times as wide, was absolutely spectacular. It was illuminated twenty-four hours per day by lights that splashed the cathedral-like ceiling and painted the walls with gold.

Hundreds of spiky stalactites hung from the rocky surface above and some of them cascaded down the sides of the main room like frozen waterfalls. All of the formations had been created by the steady drip, drip, drip of mineralized solutions over thousands of years.

Pointy stalagmites, too, stuck up from the floor, as if reaching for the stalactites above. And sometimes they came together. Whenever that occurred, columns of variegated limestone were formed. They looked like carved ivory and added to the otherworldly, surreal beauty of the place.

But spectacular or not, Voss and his staff had been forced to destroy hundreds of stalagmites in order to clear the main floor. Having been taken apart and brought into the cavern piece by piece, a carefully reconstructed D-7 Caterpillar tractor was used to grade the surface. The machine had to be used sparingly, though, because the ventilation inside the gallery was poor, and it didn't take long for carbon monoxide to build up. Just one of the many problems associated with living in a cave.

When Voss stepped off the trail and onto the main floor, Cassie Aklin was there to greet him. She was about five-eight, had light brown hair, and intelligent eyes. She had a hot cup of coffee ready and he paused to accept it. As he did so, Voss knew he was surrendering himself to whatever Aklin had scheduled for the day. In fact there were times when Voss wondered who was in charge. Him? Or the woman with the PhD in psychology?

Aklin had been employed by SRPA. Then, when what remained of the government had been forced to flee Denver, she had agreed to act as his chief of staff and nothing more, in spite of his best efforts to engineer a closer relationship.

For her part Aklin claimed to be attracted to him, but insisted that it wouldn't be ethical to be both his lover and chief of staff. "Let me put it this way," she had said recently. "Which do you want more? My body? Or my mind?"

Voss wanted both, but he knew that even a marriage wouldn't be enough to erase the ethical dilemma. And he knew something else as well, or thought he did, and that was the fact that Aklin had been in love with the legendary Nathan Hale. Part of her was still mourning his death at the hands of another soldier. So, with the exception of whatever affection was implied by the morning coffee ritual, their relationship was dishearteningly professional.

Aklin smiled as he took a sip. "Good morning, Mr. President."

Voss wasn't sure that the "Mr. President" thing was appropriate given their circumstances. But Aklin insisted on it, because as she put it, "The title is an important part of what we're trying to restore."

Voss smiled. "Good morning, Cassie! What have you got lined up for me? Will I be meeting with foreign dignitaries? Or cleaning out the filter for the septic system?"

Aklin grinned. "Neither one, although you did a great job with the pump, and the maintenance crew was grateful. You're meeting with a member of the press this morning."

Voss raised his eyebrows. "Really? Who?"

"His name is George Truitt. He works for KGHI in Little Rock and he walked more than a hundred and fifty miles to talk to you."

Voss knew that a handful of radio stations were still on the air across the country. All of them were operated by brave men and women who couldn't broadcast for more than a few minutes a day for fear of being tracked down by the Chimera and killed.

But so long as the stations continued to exist, Aklin saw them as an important way to get the administration's primary messages out to the public and Voss knew them by heart: "The United States government still exists, we are going to inoculate the population against the Chimeran virus, and this country *will* rise again."

It was more than a message of hope, it was a promise, and one Voss intended to keep. "Good. Where is Mr. Truitt?"

"In conference room one."

It was an old joke, but Voss laughed anyway. The cavern's main floor was divided into three sections. The lab facility run by Dr. Malikov occupied one end of the huge room. The kitchen, a medical clinic, and two sets of communal showers were located on the opposite side of the oval space. Everything else was right smack dab in the middle. And that included "conference room one."

The rectangular space consisted of little more than a table, some chairs, and plywood partitions for an illusion of privacy. There was no conference room two. "So, if you don't mind," Aklin added, "we'll serve your breakfast in the conference room."

"I'm sure Mr. Truitt would appreciate one of Ruth's famous cinnamon rolls," Voss put in, as they followed a gravel path to "Main Street," where they took an immediate right. Half a minute later they were in the screened-off conference room where Truitt, Kawecki, and two of his soldiers were waiting. Truitt was about six feet tall and dressed for the outdoors. His head was covered with a black hood, the idea being to keep the exact location of the facility's entrances and exits a secret.

"Please remove Mr. Truitt's hood," Voss said.

Kawecki obeyed, and Truitt blinked repeatedly as his eyes adjusted to the light. He had dark skin and a receding hairline. Judging from the amount of white hair in his neatly trimmed mustache and goatee, Truitt was in his late fifties. He had a deep basso voice that thousands of people were familiar with. "Mr. President! This is both an honor and a pleasure."

"Thank you for coming so far to see me," Voss said as he stepped forward to shake hands. "I'm sorry about the hood."

"There's no need to be. I understand," Truitt assured him, as he looked up at the dramatic formations that circled the main gallery. "It isn't the White House—but it's very beautiful."

"Yes," Voss replied. "I agree. Please take a seat. I'm told that breakfast is on the way—and we can talk while we're waiting."

Once the two men were seated, Truitt produced a battery-powered recorder, which he placed on the table between them. Having plugged a mike into the machine, he turned it on. "Are you ready, Mr. President?"

Voss smiled. "As ready as I'll ever be."

"Good," Truitt replied. "The first question will follow my introduction."

Voss couldn't help but notice the way the timbre of Truitt's voice changed as his radio persona took over. "This is George Truitt. I am with Thomas Voss, the acting President of the United States, reporting to you from an undisclosed location in Arkansas. It's early in the morning, the President is sipping a cup of coffee, and appears to be in good health."

Truitt paused as he repositioned the microphone. "First, before we go any further, could you comment on how you came to be President? As I understand it, you were Assistant Secretary of Interior during the previous administration."

Voss was expecting the question and had an answer ready. "As Assistant Secretary of Interior I was subordinate to a person on the succession list. And, if someone on the official list steps forward, I will immediately surrender the reins of government to them. But," Voss continued, "no one has done so thus far. Probably because all of them are dead. So, as acting President, I'm trying to do everything in my power to protect our citizens and take our country back from the Chimera."

"And that brings us to the attack on the tower in New York," Truitt said, as a cup of coffee and a huge cinnamon roll arrived at his elbow. "Tell us about that."

Even though the attack had been a horrible failure, Voss knew it was the only thing he had to support his claim that he was trying to take the country back. So he was eager to explain the tower's function, and why it was so important that he and a group of volunteers had attempted to shut it down.

"Finally," Voss concluded somberly, "all we could do was run. We went east, towards the river, which was clogged with chunks of drifting ice. At least a dozen

Hybrids were on our tails, so we jumped onto a passing floe in hopes that they would give up. They didn't.

"That was the beginning of a horrible death dance. As we jumped from one chunk of ice to the next, they fired at us and we fired at them," Voss said darkly. "But we eventually whittled them down, and Captain Kawecki killed the last of them, as the floe carried us past Governor's Island and out toward the Statue of Liberty. It took some fancy footwork, but we were able to get off the ice, and scramble ashore in Jersey City. It was a long walk to Arkansas, but we made it."

Truitt had managed to eat a couple of bites of cinnamon roll and wash them down with coffee by then. "So what now, Mr. President? Are you planning further attacks?"

"I can't address the possibility of more attacks for security reasons," Voss answered. "But I do have a very exciting announcement to make . . . one that will improve the lives of our citizens and prepare the way for a counterattack."

Truitt brightened. "I'm all ears, Mr. President."

"Here's how things stand now . . . when a human is bitten by one of the forms that we generally refer to as a Spinner, he or she is immediately incapacitated by a viral infection that leaves the victim conscious, but unable to move. At that point the stink spins a cocoon around the individual, who remains conscious throughout. A fate that's truly worse than death.

"After an excruciating incubation process the person is transformed into a Grim or a Menial, depending on how long the changeling is allowed to mature. At some point the newly formed Chimera bursts out of its pod and begins to serve the hive-mind, or to roam the countryside killing everything in sight in the case of the Grims.

"Now," Voss said, as his eyes took on additional intensity. "Here's my announcement. Thanks to a staff of brilliant scientists, and a brave soldier named Nathan Hale, a new vaccine has been developed. Prior to his unfortunate death, Hale was part of a top-secret government program to inoculate our soldiers with the Chimeran virus. And now, using antibodies taken from his blood, we've been able to develop a vaccine for use by the *entire* population.

"That means that if a vaccinated human is bitten by a Spinner they *won't* be incapacitated. In fact they will be able to fight back, much as such a person would if attacked by a dog. So once the population is vaccinated, a major battle will have been won and the stage will be set for a coast-to-coast uprising."

Truitt was clearly impressed, but a frown came over his face. "That's wonderful news, Mr. President. My listeners will be thrilled to hear it. But shouldn't you keep the program secret?"

"There's risk in making the announcement," Voss admitted. "But people need to know that the vaccine exists, and what the benefits are, so that they will agree to be inoculated. With that in mind, I think the benefits of releasing the information outweigh the need for security."

"How effective is the vaccine?"

"It's 97.6 percent effective," Voss replied. "I took part in a field test in which people who had been inoculated allowed themselves to be bitten by a captured Spinner. And you'll notice I'm still here," Voss said levelly, as he pushed a sleeve up out of the way. "You can see the scar on my arm—and there were witnesses."

"You're a brave man," Truitt observed. "So you have the vaccine, and it's effective. But how are you going to develop sufficient quantities—and get it to a population that is in hiding?"

"Production was already under way when we attacked the tower in New York," Voss replied. "And since that time Dr. Malikov has been able to help improve our methodologies. So we have more than a hundred thousand doses on hand.

"But I admit that informing the public about the program and getting the vaccine out to citizens are major undertakings. At this point I suggest that we adjourn to the lab, where you can speak with Dr. Malikov regarding the production process—and Chief of Staff Aklin about distribution."

Truitt reached in to turn the recorder off. Then he looked Voss in the eye. "You may be the acting President in the legal sense, but insofar as I'm concerned you're the *real* thing, and I plan to tell my listeners that."

That was music to Voss's ears. "Thank you. Is there anything you need before we visit the lab?"

Truitt grinned. "Yes, there is. I want another cinnamon roll. And a vaccination would be nice, too."

To protect it from falling debris, and to keep potential contaminants out, the lab had a peaked roof, plywood walls, and no windows. Workstations were positioned around three sides of the facility, all of them equipped with microscopes and a variety of lab ware. Most of the facility's two dozen scientists and technicians were busy carrying out quality control tests, working on ways to increase output, or tending the so-called production line at the center of the room.

That was where minute quantities of the Chimeran virus were injected into carefully chosen chicken eggs. Once that part of the process was complete, the eggs were moved to incubators, where they would remain for three months. Then the refining process would finally begin.

And one of the technicians responsible for some of the more routine aspects of the production process was frightened. Her name was Monica Shaw and she was in a terrible situation. If she refused to betray her country, and was caught doing so, she would be imprisoned or worse. And if she failed to betray her country, a man named Judge Ramsey would kill her husband and her three-year-old daughter, both of whom were being held virtual prisoners inside his complex in Oklahoma. Which, to hear him tell it, was going to be the seat of government for the *new* United States of America. A dictatorship run by him.

But only if Ramsey could compete with and destroy the real government. Which was why he had taken Shaw's family prisoner and sent her to Arkansas with instructions to infiltrate the federal government. An assignment she'd been able to accomplish with relative ease. First as a volunteer, then as a lab worker, trained to help produce the Hale vaccine.

Such were Shaw's thoughts as Voss, Truitt, and Malikov neared her workstation.

"This is Monica Shaw," Malikov said, as the three men came to a halt. "Her job is to help grow cultures."

Truitt said "Hello" to her and Voss smiled. Then they were gone. It was a trivial interaction really, but her heart was beating like a trip hammer, and her palms were sweaty. And Shaw knew why. She felt guilty, *and* she owed Ramsey a report.

The drop consisted of a rusty Hopalong Cassidy lunch box, which was located outside the cavern about half a mile from the main entrance. And, since she was one of those scheduled for a so-called outing that afternoon, there would be an opportunity to leave a written report. Then, if she was lucky, a letter from her husband would appear a few days later. It would be at least two or three weeks out of date, of course, but would include precious details about their little girl, and an awkward attempt to tell her how much he missed her. Awkward because both of them knew that Ramsey and/or one of his minions would get to read it before she did. Still, the possibility of such a communication was enough to send Shaw back to work. She was alive, and so were her loved ones, but the price was very, very high.

CHAPTER SIX

A DAMNED SHAME

Tuesday, October 6, 1953
The Badlands

Capelli was inside his sleeping bag when the Grims came surging up out of their underground lair to attack the unsuspecting humans. The basement of the burned-out farmhouse was the perfect place for dozens of pods to mature. And because of the charred debris piled on top of the ground floor, the unsuspecting humans had no idea what was lurking below.

The lone sentry managed to get off a single shot before a charging Grim threw its skeletal arms around him and opened its mouth to expose two rows of needle-sharp teeth. The man tried to push the foul-smelling creature away, but it was too strong. So the wrangler started to scream. But the sound was cut off as the Chimera tore his throat out. The sentry's eyes rolled back in his head, his body went limp, and he collapsed.

The gunshot, and the gibbering sounds that the Grims made, offered some warning but not enough. Most of the humans were still in the process of exiting their bags and scrabbling for weapons when the Chimera fell on them.

But unlike the rest, Capelli was not only awake but on guard against a possible attack. Not from the Grims, but from the wranglers, at least one of whom had been acting suspiciously earlier in the evening.

So he was fully dressed and his sleeping bag was un-zipped as the stinks swept across the encampment and a scattering of shots were heard. He didn't have enough time to do more than sit up, however. Capelli had battled Grims in the past and knew how important it was to keep them at a distance. They liked to attack en masse. And once the Chimera made physical contact with their victims the battle was over. So Capelli fired the Ross-more, heard the sharper *blam, blam, blam* sound pro-duced by Locke's Winchester, and knew the other man was fighting as well.

As Capelli's buckshot tore into them, the Grims liter-ally flew apart. But the runner knew there was reason to worry because he was going to need time to reload. Even if it was only two or three shells. Fortunately, that oppor-tunity came as the last of what might have been a dozen Chimera disintegrated and Capelli was able to thumb two rounds into the Rossmore's magazine as a grotes-querie collapsed at the foot of his sleeping bag.

But *another* group of stinks was already charging to-wards him, and it was only a matter of seconds before the shotgun was empty. Capelli was reaching for the Mag-num when Rowdy flew past him and tore into the Chi-mera with such ferocity that the attack stalled.

As the growling dog tore gobbets of bloody flesh out of the Grims, Capelli was able to not only shove six shells into the Rossmore, but throw the sleeping bag off his legs and scramble to his feet. "Rowdy! Here, boy."

The dog broke contact and whirled away. That al-lowed Capelli to fire freely. Now, with only half a dozen stinks left to deal with, he was able to blow them away two at a time. Finally, after what seemed like an hour but was actually a matter of minutes, the last Grim went down. A profound silence settled over the encampment, broken only by the *click, click, click* sound the shotgun shells made as Capelli thumbed them into the tubular magazine. He was still in the process of absorbing what had occurred when Locke groaned.

As Capelli swiveled towards his client, he saw that a dead Grim was sprawled across Locke's body and immediately knew what had taken place. Once the big man had expended all of the rounds in the Winchester's tubular magazine, the stink had been able to close in on him. Then, seeing the knife hilt that was protruding from the left side of the Chimera's skull, Capelli knew that Locke had managed to kill the monstrosity.

But as Capelli rolled the corpse off the big man's body, he saw Locke's badly bloodied shoulder, and his heart sank. His client wouldn't turn into a Chimera, not without being infected by a Spinner, but Grim bites were known to be extremely toxic.

Capelli put the shotgun down and knelt next to Locke's pack. The first-aid kit was sitting on top of everything else.

"Find the bottle of gin," Locke instructed through gritted teeth. "Give me a swallow and pour the rest into the wound."

After removing the bottle, Capelli used the pack to prop the other man up, and set about giving him first aid. Locke swore a blue streak as the alcohol made contact with his raw flesh—and Capelli did the best he could to blot the puncture wounds dry.

As fresh blood continued to well up from below, Locke told Capelli how to create a pressure bandage and tape it in place. The truth was that Capelli had been forced to treat dozens of wounds over the last few years, many of which were worse than Locke's. But there was no point in saying so and he didn't.

Once Locke was stabilized, Capelli took the shotgun and set about the grisly process of inspecting the rest of the encampment with Rowdy at his side. The average Chimera smelled like rotting flesh even at the best of times.

So their body odor, plus the smell of spilled intestinal matter, combined to form a stench so powerful it made Capelli gag. Bodies lay everywhere, Grims mostly, but with badly mauled human corpses mixed in.

But Capelli wasn't interested in either one. Not at the moment, anyway. What he wanted was two or three horses. Capelli thought he had heard screaming noises during the worst of the fighting, so he figured that at least some of the mounts were dead. And as the light from the shotgun swept across the ground ahead, he saw that he was correct. Two of the horses were down and one was dead. The other whinnied pitifully and kicked its legs in a futile attempt to stand.

Capelli was disappointed to see that with the single exception of an animal tied to a tree, rather than the picket line, all the rest of the horses had broken free. He went over to make sure that the remaining mount was secure before putting the wounded animal out of its misery. The Magnum made a loud boom, the horse jerked reflexively, and Capelli was about to turn away when he heard a barely audible croak. "Capelli? Is that *you*?"

The pistol was back in its holster by then. The beam from the Rossmore swept across the huddled mess and returned to it. Gravel crunched under Capelli's boots as he made his way over to the spot where the man lay. It didn't take a degree in medicine to see that Murphy was dying.

Judging from the sprawl of bodies around him, the head packer had given a good account of himself before a couple of Chimera were able to break through and take him down. It wasn't clear what had taken place after that, except to say that a hole had been torn in the middle of the sleeping bag, and the area around it was dark with blood. Murphy blinked as the light flooded his pain-contorted face. The words arrived one at a time. "Don't-leave-me-like-this."

"I won't," Capelli promised. "But, before I send you on your way, there's something I want to know."

Murphy winced and bit his lower lip. "Anything."

"Were you and your men going to kill us?"

Murphy tried to smile. It came across as a grimace. "Yes, we were. Locke is carrying a large quantity of gold. Did you know that?"

Capelli nodded. "Yes, I did."

With another loud boom the Magnum went off. An even louder explosion followed as Capelli triggered the pistol's secondary fire function. Murphy ceased to exist.

The horse's hooves made a soft clopping sound as Capelli led the animal over to where Locke sat with his back resting against the pack.

"Who were you shooting at?"

"Just tidying up, that's all. This is going to be tough, Al, but we need to get out of here, and that means you've got to climb up onto this horse."

"I can do it," Locke said gamely. "But I'll need some help."

It took a full twenty minutes to saddle the horse, get Locke up onto the animal's back, and load his belongings into some saddlebags. Then Capelli led the heavily laden horse down the graveled drive. He planned to head east, in the direction they had been going originally, and find a place to hole up. They could hit the road again once Locke felt better.

But finding such a hideout wouldn't be easy. Locke was slumped forward in the saddle, morning wasn't that far away, and Capelli had no idea where to look for shelter.

The next few hours unwound slowly. The journey was interrupted on two different occasions when Locke fell out of the saddle and hit the ground. After the second incident, Capelli tried to rope his client in place. But the horse didn't like the way the rope passed under her belly,

and during the periods when Locke was lucid, he complained about the fact that his wrists were secured to the
saddle horn.

There was quite a bit of starlight, so Capelli could see
some of the features around him, and take occasional
side trips to inspect anything that might serve as a hideout. But none of the deserted houses, barns, or silos felt
right. And Capelli had learned to trust his instincts.

So the first blush of dawn was visible along the eastern
horizon by the time he spotted the concrete grain elevator
and left the highway to check it out. The ten-story-high
concrete cylinder held very little interest for him. The out-
buildings were worth a look, however. They included a
small stand-alone office structure and a storage shed,
both of which had been looted and would offer little or
no protection during a firefight.

But about fifty feet away, right next to a faded sign that
read "Storm Shelter," was a slab of angled concrete to
which a rusty steel door was attached. Metal squealed
as Capelli pulled the barrier open and pointed the Rossmore's light down into the black hole below. A short
flight of stairs led down to a room about eight feet wide
and twelve feet long, furnished with metal benches that
ran along both walls, a folding card table, and some
rickety chairs.

Had the elevator workers used the underground shelter as a lunchroom on hot days? Or gone there to take
illicit naps? Yes, judging from the half-naked pinup girls
on the walls, Capelli thought they had. A brunette with
the title "Miss October" seemed to watch him, her smile
forever frozen in place, as he checked the inside surface
of the door. He was pleased to find a steel bar that would
allow him to lock the shelter from within.

An Auger could send blasts of transient radiation right
through the barrier, of course, but the underground shel-

ter would be impervious to just about everything else, and was unlikely to draw attention from all but the most meticulous of searchers. Especially if he removed the sign.

All these factors played into the final decision. But the first rays of light from the steadily rising sun, and Locke's deteriorating condition, settled the matter. The shelter would have to do.

Capelli's first task was to prepare a bed on one of the long benches, and revive Locke long enough to get him down off the horse, and into the shelter. Then it was time to take all of the supplies down, whistle Rowdy in, and remove the horse's bridle, saddle, and blanket. He wasn't especially good at the task, but Capelli got the job done.

Then, painful though the decision was, he had to turn the animal loose. Partly because he lacked the knowledge required to care for the beast, but for another reason as well: the horse was like a neon sign pointing at a human presence. A simple slap on the hindquarters was enough to send the animal trotting away.

Capelli knew it was important not only to take cover but to tend Locke's wound. But water was critical too. And a line of very lush trees about two hundred yards away hinted at the presence of a river or stream.

Arming himself with the Marksman, and picking up a couple of galvanized buckets taken from the storage shed, Capelli made his way across a grassy field to a spot where a game trail led to the stream below. Sheets of water flew and droplets of moisture sparkled in the morning sun as Rowdy charged into the brook.

Capelli followed the dog into the stream. After quenching his thirst, he filled the buckets and carried them back to the shelter. Rowdy entered on his own, so all Capelli had to do was put the buckets down, and close the door behind him. It was safe to do so thanks to the presence of an air vent. The metal lock bar screeched as it slid into place.

Then it was time to light candles and turn his attention to Locke. The big man was only semiconscious, but he came to for a moment, as Capelli removed the bandage. "Capelli? Where are we?"

"We're in a storm shelter. All you need to do is get better. Here . . . Have some water."

Capelli held the cup to Locke's lips and the big man took a couple of sips. "Sorry," Locke croaked. "Sorry to be so much trouble."

Then he was gone again. Either asleep or unconscious. Not that it made much difference. The good news was that the bleeding had stopped. But Locke's forehead was hot, his breathing was shallow, and the margins around the puncture wounds were red.

Capelli found three packets of antibacterial sulfa powder in Locke's first-aid kit, sprinkled one of them over the holes, and replaced the old dressing with a new one.

Then it was time to pour some water into a pan for Rowdy, heat some beans over a can of Sterno, and eat. Just minutes after finishing his meal an overwhelming sense of fatigue came over Capelli. He extinguished all but one of the candles and slipped into his sleeping bag, giving himself permission to take a one-hour nap.

Capelli awoke more than five hours later with a painful headache, a foul taste in his mouth, and an urgent need to pee. All of which had been sufficient to wake him. Or had they? The candle had burned out, so it was pitch black as Rowdy growled, and what felt like an earthquake shook the shelter.

Capelli fumbled for the flashlight, found it, and sat up. "What is it boy? What do you hear?"

The answer came as something hit the ground nearby and Capelli felt the resulting vibration through the soles of his feet. There were a number of possible causes. And none of them were good. Was a Chimeran hunter-killer team outside? Complete with a big spider-like Stalker? Or was something even larger on the loose?

Of course Capelli knew there were flesh-and-blood possibilities as well. Like a Titan, or God forbid, a Leviathan. Although that seemed unlikely, because monsters like the one that had laid waste to most of downtown Chicago were rare. Not that the exact size of the menace made much difference, since all he could do was sit in his hidey-hole and hope for the best.

Then Capelli heard the whine of powerful servos through the vertical air vent and knew that one of his earlier guesses had been correct. Some sort of Chimeran mech was in the area. Looking for the two humans? Or just *looking*? And alone? Or in company with a force of Hybrids? There was no way to know as he waited for the Auger blasts to tunnel down through the concrete roof and kill him.

But Capelli's fears began to dissipate as the noise faded away. He waited for a couple of minutes and, not having heard or felt anything, concluded that they were safe for the moment.

Having taken care of his own physical needs, Capelli went to work on Locke's. The big man was in a bad way. He was semiconscious at best, his skin felt unnaturally hot in spite of the cold air, and Capelli knew his client was dehydrated. All of which were bad. But worst of all was the foul odor that invaded his nostrils when the bandage came off. Capelli's spirits plummeted.

Why so glum? the voice inquired cheerfully. *There's nothing like a bullet in the head to put a patient right! Go ahead! Take care of Locke the way you took care of me.*

Screw you, Hale.

In addition to everything else, Locke had soiled himself. So the next hour was spent cleaning the big man up, putting a new dressing on the suppurating wound, and trying to pour some water into him.

Finally, once Capelli had done everything he could, he allowed himself to take another nap. Rowdy wasn't too pleased with that decision, and he spent a good five minutes whining by the door, before curling up in front of it.

When Capelli awoke it was evening, and time to work on Locke again, before fixing a large dinner that he shared with Rowdy. It seemed as if Locke was dreaming, because he spoke occasionally, and even laughed out loud once.

After darkness fell, Capelli opened the door and stuck his head out. There was a scattering of clouds, but the moon was up, and threw a ghostly glow over the land. It was cold, *damned* cold, and Capelli figured it would freeze later.

Rowdy stood in the opening for a moment as his supersensitive nostrils sampled the night air and his ears stood at attention. Then he was gone, and Capelli knew better than to try and call him back. Rowdy was tired of being cooped up and eager to hunt.

Capelli wanted to stretch his legs too. But first there were chores to take care of. He took a broken shovel he'd found earlier and the Rossmore out to a spot a couple of hundred feet from the shelter and dug a hole. After dumping a load of garbage into the depression, Capelli covered it with a thick layer of dirt. Because if *he* could smell it, then Howlers could too, and the last thing Capelli needed was to have a couple of those monsters hanging around.

Once he was done, it was time to fetch more water from the river. So Capelli armed himself with the shotgun, two buckets, a grimy towel, a bar of Lava soap, and some clean clothes before making his way to the stream.

After placing everything on the bank within easy reach, Capelli removed his clothes, took the bar of soap, and waded out into the freezing water. It wasn't deep enough to swim in. But he could sit down, and that was a shock.

Working quickly, Capelli scrubbed his skin with the highly abrasive soap, rinsed it off, and hurried to wash his hair. Then he stood up quickly and made a grab for his towel. The moment he was dry enough to put them on, Capelli slipped into clean clothes and a warm jacket.

Once he'd filled both buckets with water, he returned to the shelter, where he took a look at Locke before returning outside. Not for any particular purpose, but to enjoy the night air, and escape the confines of the shelter.

As Capelli sat on the mound of earth over the shelter and looked upwards he saw three bright lights streak across the blue-black sky. He wondered if they were meteorites but knew they weren't. Not only did the Chimera own the Earth, they owned the sky, and as far as he could tell, they owned the future, too.

It took Locke the better part of three days to die.

When the end came, it came quietly; Locke simply stopped breathing. Capelli might have been able to resuscitate him, but knew it would be pointless if he couldn't solve the *real* problem, which was the raging infection that had taken over the big man's body.

Capelli would have needed more than a day to dig a proper grave. And he had no way of knowing who or what might catch up with him while he did it. Not to mention the fact that he would have had a hard time moving the corpse by himself.

So Capelli closed Locke's eyelids, arranged his body in a peaceful repose, and went looking for something to write with. He found half a can of black paint in the storage unit, plus a still-serviceable brush, and took them back to what was about to become a crypt.

Capelli wrote the epitaph in military-style block letters on the wall directly above the body. Miss October smiled as she watched from across the room. "HERE LIES ALVIN LOCKE. A GOOD MAN, FORCED TO LIVE IN BAD TIMES, WHO WAS ON HIS WAY TO DO GOOD THINGS WHEN THE CHIMERA KILLED HIM."

Afterwards he sorted through Locke's belongings and took what he could use. Food mostly, since Capelli had no use for .30-.30 cartridges, or clothes that were way too big for him. The money belt, however, was still heavy with gold coins, and his to keep if he wanted to do so.

But at some point over the last few days he had made the decision. Though he could not deliver his client to Haven, Oklahoma, he *could* deliver the money belt—and take a look at the community at the same time. Maybe it was just another group of pathetic survivors eking out a day-to-day existence while they waited to die. Or maybe Haven was something more. Locke had thought so, and Capelli was determined to find out.

So Capelli tidied up, left the rifle and the supplies he couldn't use in plain sight on the card table, and made his way up the stairs, where Rowdy was sitting with one leg up in the air, nibbling at his fleas.

Having lowered the door into place, Capelli turned towards the access road, and the highway beyond. He figured he was pretty close to Hays, Kansas. After that it would take a good six or seven days of walking to reach what had been Salina, Kansas, and was currently referred to as "Tank Town" by runners who had been down that way.

It was early morning, a good time to travel. As Rowdy led the way, and Capelli followed along behind, farms gradually gave way to light industry and a scattering of houses. But rather than enter Hays, and be forced to deal with whatever might be lurking there, Capelli elected to give the city a wide berth by swinging south. He crossed a set of railroad tracks, and pushed down into farm country, before heading east again.

That took him into the early evening, when the weather turned bad and he sought refuge in a barn. One end of the structure was filled with pods. They made raspy breathing sounds, and with no way to know when they might pop, Capelli couldn't stay there. He could set the barn on fire, however—which he did before going back out into the rain. Capelli knew the flames could attract some stinks, but it was a chance he was willing to take rather than leave the pods intact.

Half an hour of walking brought him to a road, a sizable junkyard, and the opportunity to hole up in the back of an old bread truck. And with Rowdy acting as his alarm system he felt reasonably safe. Rain rattled on the roof as he ate cold beans out of a can. Then, after finishing his meal, he brushed his teeth. The floor was hard but the sleeping bag was warm. Sleep came quickly.

The next day dawned bright and clear. Capelli made breakfast for himself, packed his belongings, and was on the road by eight. He followed it north to Route 40, where he took a right-hand turn, and continued east.

Following the highway was a dangerous thing to do. Both the Chimera and humans used it. But cross-country travel was often extremely slow due to the need to traverse occasionally difficult terrain, cross rivers, and cut through barbed-wire fences. So having chosen speed over safety, Capelli was on high alert as the ribbon of highway carried him through rolling grasslands.

And that was why he spotted both the body and the child from a half-mile away.

The sighting was enough to send Capelli off the road into a cluster of trees. A low whistle brought Rowdy in, and the dog lay panting at his side as Capelli freed his binoculars. The body that lay sprawled on the highway was clearly that of a woman. A pack was strapped to her back and a rifle lay on the pavement next to her. There were no obvious signs of injury—though that didn't rule out a bullet wound. But why shoot her, and leave the rifle? No, an illness of some kind seemed more likely. The little girl, who Capelli judged to be three or four years old, was squatting next to the body as if waiting for it to come back to life.

It was a pitiful sight. But Capelli had seen a lot of pitiful sights and wasn't about to move forward without a careful examination of the surrounding countryside.

However, having quartered the ground ahead, he came up empty. So with the Marksman at the ready, Capelli left the protection of the trees and returned to the highway. The sun was past its zenith by then, so his shadow pointed east, and an intermittent breeze ruffled the grass to either side of the road as Capelli approached the body.

The little girl looked scared, but also determined to remain right where she was. She had black hair worn in a bowl cut, a grimy face, and was dressed in raggedy clothes. "Is that your mother?" Capelli asked as he came to a stop.

The girl said, "Yes," Rowdy growled, and Capelli saw motion out of the corner of his eye. He turned in that direction as a man rose from his hiding place. He was wearing a hat made out of freshly cut grass and a burlap bag to which more green stuff was attached. The apparition had already raised his weapon, and Capelli was still bringing his rifle to bear when the scarecrow fired on him.

The oncoming bolt looked like a black dot at first. Capelli was formulating a plan to duck beneath it, when the ball-tipped missile hit him in the forehead. The force of the blow knocked him off his feet and dumped him onto his back. Capelli caught a glimpse of blue sky, and felt a brief moment of pain, before the voice had its say. *Hey, Capelli . . . What happened to rule six?* "Mind *your own business?*" Then a tidal wave of blackness rolled him under.

Capelli was somewhere a long way off when the bucket of water hit his face. The voice sounded as if it were coming to him through a tunnel. "Get up."

Capelli's eyelids felt like they were glued shut. He forced them open. The face hanging over him was blurry. He blinked and it came into focus. The man's forehead and cheeks were covered with tattoos. When he smiled, Capelli saw that his teeth had been filed down into points.

"Aha," the man said, "there you are. There's a bump on your forehead, but you'll survive. Now get up."

Capelli felt dirt under his right hand, turned, and attempted to stand. Metal rattled, something brought him up short, and he fell. The tattooed man laughed, and Capelli felt a humiliating mix of shame and fear. That was when Capelli realized that he was wearing a metal collar to which a chain was attached. And, with the exception of his clothing, his possessions were missing. Including Locke's money belt. All taken from him so effortlessly that it was embarrassing.

"They call me Inkskin," the man said. In addition to his face, almost every inch of the man's bare torso was covered with tattoos. "What's your name?"

"Capelli."

"Well, Capelli . . . It's time to get up off your ass." Inkskin had a Bullseye Mark III, which he used as a pointer.

Capelli swore, lurched to his feet, and swayed uncertainly. His head hurt, blood pounded in his ears, and the late afternoon sun felt hot. He was standing in what looked like a gravel pit. That impression was reinforced by the presence of a downward-slanting chute, an ancient road grader, and an old shack. All of which were a fit.

What looked odd was the open-sided circus wagon parked about thirty feet away. The brightly colored paint was faded, but he could read the name "Zenda Brothers Circus" painted across the side of it, and could see the creature within. But it wasn't a lion, tiger, or bear. It was a Steelhead!

"Meet El Diablo," Inkskin said, "but don't get too close. He's hungry."

As if to emphasize the point, the Chimera made a horrible screeching sound and rattled the bars. The Steelhead had a hairless skull, six golden eyes, and a powerful physique. It was dressed in scraps of Chimeran armor, and Capelli could smell the creature from thirty feet away.

"That's enough gawking," Inkskin said. "You can get acquainted with El Diablo later! Who knows? Maybe you'll get to dance with him!"

Apparently the guard thought that was funny, because he laughed as he gave the leash a vicious jerk, and led Capelli away. The runner searched his surroundings for Rowdy, but saw no sign of him, and wondered what that meant. Had the dog been able to escape? Or had he been shot? He had no way of knowing.

Inkskin led Capelli past the wagon into a messy campsite. Boxes, trunks, and bags were scattered all around a central fire pit. The "dead" woman was seated on a camp chair, combing the little girl's hair as Capelli walked past. Neither one of them so much as glanced his way.

A group of raggedy-looking men were seated in the shadow thrown by the shed. All wore neck collars and sat to either side of a heavy chain. Some of the prisoners were asleep, but the rest regarded Capelli with dull-eyed interest.

"Meet your new friends!" Inkskin said cheerfully, as he padlocked Capelli's leash to a heavy chain. A second guard was watching over the prisoners. He was wearing an orange wig, white face paint, and a red nose. An inverted mouth made it appear that the clown was permanently sad. "Get some rest," Inkskin advised, as Capelli took his place on the ground. "You're going to need it." The loose gravel made a crunching sound as he walked away.

"He's right about that," the man sitting opposite Capelli said. "My name is Escobar—but most people call me Bar."

Bar had short black hair, brown eyes, and high cheekbones. Like the rest of the prisoners, he was unshaven. Chains rattled as they shook hands.

"My name is Capelli. What's with the circus thing?"

Bar shrugged. "You're looking at what remains of a family-owned circus. Back before the stinks came it employed about fifty people. They had a dozen exotic animals in those days, plus twenty vehicles, and all sorts of equipment. Now they're down to the single wagon. Ain't that right, Bam-Bam?"

The clown nodded. "That's right, donkey."

Capelli looked around. "So how do they move the wagon? With horses?"

Bar shook his head. "Hell, no . . . Horses are expensive. We haul the wagon. That's why they call us donkeys."

"And you'd better do your share," a man sitting nearby said. He had black hair, penetrating eyes, and dark skin.

"Loomis don't like slackers," Bar observed. "But his bark is worse than his bite. The ugly-looking piece of work next to him is Askin. Then there's Valova, Omata,

Nix, Kilner, and Ganson . . ." And so it went until Bar
had named twenty-two men other than himself.

"So," the man named Omata said, "which scam did
they run on you? The woman who blackjacks you in the
middle of the night? The woman lying in the middle of
the road? Or the woman with the sick child?"

"The woman lying in the middle of the road."

Omata nodded soberly. "Alfonso is pretty good with
that crossbow, isn't he?"

"He's very good," Capelli conceded.

"And he's a crack shot with a rifle and pistol, too,"
Bar added. "The woman's name is Leena. She's Alfonso's wife, and the little girl is their daughter."

"Damn the little bitch to hell," Nix put in bitterly.

"He fell for the sick daughter routine," Bar explained.
"Leena blackjacked me in the middle of the night. But
the two of us had a very good time first. I'll bet she
didn't mention *that* to Alfonso!"

"And you'd better hope she doesn't," Bam-Bam put in
darkly. "He'd put a bullet in your head. Then we'd have
to find some other idiot to replace you."

"Which brings us to the Steelhead," Capelli said. "How
did they capture it?"

"Same way they got *you*," Bar replied. "Leena was
lying in the middle of the road, the stink comes strolling
down the highway, and *pow!* Alfonso bags the sonofabitch."

"Of course, that was before our time," Ganson said.
"All of the donkeys from back in those days are dead."

Capelli frowned. "Two dozen men? How come the
mortality rate is so high?"

Loomis glanced over at Bam-Bam and saw that the
guard had stepped away to take a leak. He was careful
to keep his voice down. "Malnutrition and disease. But
every time Ringmaster Jack can assemble an audience,
he selects one of the donkeys to fight El Diablo."

"And El Diablo always wins," Bar observed darkly. "That's how the stink gets most of its meat."

Capelli remembered Inkskin's comment. Something about dancing with El Diablo. Now it made sense. "Has anyone ever escaped?"

Bam-Bam had returned by then. "No," the guard said. "No one ain't never escaped. But feel free to try if you want to. I could use the target practice."

Bar smiled. His teeth were yellow. "Welcome to the circus."

Three long, hard nights had passed since Capelli had been captured by members of the Zenda Brothers Circus. Ringmaster Jack, who was generally referred to as "Master Jack," wanted to rack up at least fifteen miles per day. In order to maintain that pace it was necessary for the donkeys to work extremely hard.

Not only was the circus wagon heavy in and of itself, but Capelli figured that El Diablo, the corpulent Ringmaster, Leena, her daughter, and all the luggage tied to the wagon's roof represented at least a ton of additional weight. All of which made it difficult to drag the wagon up even a gentle slope.

But with Master Jack wielding a long, thin whip from his seat at the front of the wagon, plus Bam-Bam the clown and Inkskin pacing along to either side, the slaves had no choice but to throw themselves against the four-man crosspieces. So each night seemed like an eternity of strenuous effort, punctuated by the sting of Master Jack's whip and occasional blows from the guards. Cold rations were served at about one in the morning.

That was when Capelli thought about Rowdy. The big mix was dead. That was what Bam-Bam claimed, anyway. But Capelli wasn't so sure. Some kind of dog had been nosing around the camp the previous day and Inkskin had taken a shot at it. All Capelli could do was hope. And more than that, plan. Because even if no one had ever escaped from the Zenda Brothers Circus, that didn't mean it was impossible.

Meanwhile, as the donkeys slaved, Alfonso ranged well ahead of the wagon. He was mounted on a golden palomino and had taken to carrying Capelli's Marksman rifle in a fancy buckskin scabbard. The sharpshooter's job was to act as a scout *and* drum up business. A mostly hit-or-miss process that relied on word of mouth, posters tacked to message trees, and a certain amount of luck. Like arriving in a tiny town called Hamley, Kansas, just as a revival meeting was about to take place. Such an event could easily pull in a hundred people from the surrounding countryside, most of whom were starved for entertainment.

In order to take advantage of the opportunity, the donkeys had been forced to work through the night and well into the next afternoon. The plan was to stay in Hamley for two days, so long as the Chimera left the town alone. Something the exhausted slaves would have welcomed had it not been for the high price that one of them was going to pay. A stop meant that one of them would be forced to fight El Diablo—and everybody knew how that would turn out.

So the mood was somber as chains rattled, wood creaked, and the raggedly dressed donkeys pulled the wagon through the center of town. Master Jack was wearing a fancy black suit, Leena was practically naked, and a brightly attired Bam-Bam was working the crowd on the right side of the street. A stripped-down Inkskin had responsibility for those on the left. Both had pieces of hard candy for the wide-eyed children and were mouthing a spiel prepared by Alfonso.

"Come see us when the revival is over, folks," Bam-Bam said. "There will be juggling and fire eating! But that's not all. One of our brave warriors will fight El Diablo!" A pitch made all the more effective when the Steelhead rattled the bars on its cage and screeched loudly.

And so it went as the men pulled the wagon to the point where Alfonso was waiting for them. He was dressed as a cowboy, complete with a ten-gallon hat, a western-style red shirt, pearl-handled Colt revolvers, leather chaps, and high-heeled boots. His horse whinnied loudly and reared up onto its hind legs as Alfonso removed his hat and waved it at the crowd. That got cheers and applause as Capelli and the rest of the prisoners towed the wagon into the parking lot next to the feed store.

The revival tent was set up only a block away, and the locals were drifting in that direction, as Master Jack began to shout orders. First a couple of slaves had to dig a hole for the twelve-foot-long section of telephone pole that they had been forced to cut. The rest of the donkeys were split into two groups and sent out to bring back anything and everything that could be used as seats. Capelli wondered if the chore would offer a chance of escape. But all such hopes were dashed by the fact that he was chained to the other men in his work party and Inkskin was sent to accompany them.

Once the wooden benches, bales of hay, and the bleachers taken from the high school were set in place, the whole area was roped off. The idea was to herd the locals past Leena so she could collect an admission fee from each spectator. Food and ammo being the preferred medium of exchange.

Finally, when everything was ready, or as ready as it would ever be, the donkeys were chained to a telephone pole located at the edge of the roped-off area. All of the slaves were frightened, and for good reason, since there was no way to know which one of them would be forced to fight El Diablo.

They had theories, of course, such as the one that held that Bam-Bam didn't like Loomis. But from what Capelli had been able to pick up over the last few days, there had been very little rhyme or reason to many of the previous choices that Master Jack and his performers had made. So as the paying customers began to filter into the arena, he felt a horrible emptiness invade the pit of his stomach. The others must have felt the same way, because all of the slaves were unusually quiet as they sat at the edge of the roped-off ring.

Master Jack's booming voice could be heard far and wide as he strode into the arena, and welcomed the steadily growing crowd to what he claimed was "the biggest little show on Earth."

Then Bam-Bam appeared. First he juggled two red-and-white-striped clubs. That was followed by four and six. The crowd started to applaud as the clown put eight clubs in the air, began to catch them behind his back, and hurried to get them airborne again. Then he missed, or that was the way it appeared, and a club fell on his head. Something at least part of the crowd thought was hilariously funny.

He shook the blow off, and still juggling, the seemingly dizzy clown walked into the thick center post and knocked himself unconscious. It was supposed to be funny but garnered only halfhearted applause as Master Jack and a scantily clad Leena came in to drag Bam-Bam away.

That was when Inkskin took over. The light had started to fade. But thanks to the fact that he was wearing nothing more than a loincloth, the audience could see all of Inkskin's colorful tattoos. A likeness of an openmouthed Hybrid lurked in the spot between his prominent shoulder blades and appeared to glare at the audience. With a dramatic flare of light, Inkskin set afire a specially designed sword and waved the flaming weapon over his head.

But Capelli and the rest of the donkeys weren't paying any attention to Inkskin as Alfonso appeared in front of them. "So," the sharpshooter said, as he scanned the faces before him. "Who's it going to be? Hmmm! I know. Let's give the runt a shot."

Capelli followed Alfonso's pointing finger to a small man named Nix. He had sandy-colored hair, even features, and was known for his dead-on John Wayne impression. And as Capelli saw the look of hopelessness come over Nix's face, he felt a sense of relief, followed by shame. Because his good fortune was at the other man's expense.

Suddenly Bam-Bam was freeing Nix from the main chain and fastening what looked like a ten- or twelve-foot lead to the slave's rag padded collar. That was when Capelli realized that Inkskin's sword-swallowing routine was over—and Master Jack was about to announce the main act as Nix was led out into the make-shift arena.

"Laaadies and gentlemen . . . Children of all ages . . . Please welcome the brave warrior who, armed with nothing more than a knife, is about to face the fearsome El Diablo in a full-bore, no-holds-barred, battle to the death. If our warrior wins, he will be freed. And should El Diablo win, he will be fed!"

The whole thing was so barbaric, Capelli expected some of the townspeople to object, if not put a stop to the one-sided battle. And a year or two earlier they probably would have. But many of those who had survived the invasion were inured to violence, had been forced to kill many times themselves, and had come to regard strangers with suspicion. And Nix was a stranger. So rather than demand that the slave be released, they applauded instead. And Capelli was shocked to see a scattering of children in the crowd.

El Diablo screeched in pain as Bam-Bam and Inkskin used pole-mounted cattle prods to force the Hybrid out of its cage, down a ramp, and into the arena. The Chimera had been fitted with a neck collar similar to Capelli's.

The slaves came to their feet as Leena made her way out to where Nix stood, took one of his arms, and raised it above his head. The audience had grown to at least sixty people. Capelli was reminded of the stories he'd heard about Rome's Colosseum as the crowds cheered the man who was about to die.

Then the yelling stopped, and there was a mutual inhalation of breath, as Leena took hold of the chain that was coiled near the center post and began to drag it out to El Diablo. And as she came within reach of the beast's arms, the crowd waited for the Chimera to kill her. But it didn't. Why?

The answer could be seen standing in the shadow next to the circus wagon. Alfonso was aiming Capelli's Marksman at El Diablo. A safety precaution? Yes, Capelli thought so, as the chain was secured to the beast's collar. Then Leena turned her back on the Steelhead and walked away. The act of bravado earned a burst of applause.

By then both Nix and El Diablo were chained to the center post so neither one of them could run. Capelli didn't know Nix. Not really. But he felt sorry for him as the other slave was given a large, single-edged knife. Nix tested the edge with a thumb as he turned to face the Chimera.

But in spite of the sympathy he felt, Capelli was a survivor. So as El Diablo screeched and shambled towards Nix, he was determined to learn whatever he could from the impending slaughter.

Nix reacted the way most people would—he backed away from the Chimera. But that meant his chain was gradually wrapping itself around the thick center post. And as it became shorter, the distance between the combatants grew shorter as well. Capelli could see that eventually Nix would be forced to go one-on-one with El Diablo. At that point he would slash the Chimera a few times, and having survived dozens of such battles in the past, the Steelhead would charge the human. The end would come quickly.

Capelli wanted to shout a warning, to give Nix some advice, but knew the other slave wouldn't be able to hear him over the crowd noise. But then, just when it appeared that the deadly dance was about to come to its inevitable conclusion, Nix did something entirely unexpected.

Nix did not keep backing away. Instead, he put the blade between his teeth, and turned towards the vertical center post. Then, with the agility of a monkey, he swarmed up it. The weight of the chain slowed Nix down, but failed to stop him, as he pulled himself up onto the flat surface above. Then, having taken control of his chain, Nix passed it over his head three times. That gave him some additional slack and a momentary advantage. The crowd reacted with a cheer.

El Diablo roared its anger, but was plenty tall enough to snatch Nix off his roost, so the human's situation had only marginally improved. The Hybrid was shuffling forward, clearly intent on sweeping Nix off his perch, when the human launched himself into the air. Nix had extended the knife point down. He was a real threat if he could manage to drive the blade into the Steelhead's neck.

And the plan might have worked except that as Nix landed on the Chimera, the tip of his knife hit El Diablo's iron collar and skidded off. That was the only break the monster needed. It wrapped Nix in a stinking embrace and proceeded to crush the life out of him. Bones crackled like broken twigs, a horrible farting noise was heard, and the battle was over.

Capelli, who had been hopeful up until the last moment, uttered a groan of disappointment. It was echoed by the men around him. And it seemed as if the crowd felt the same way, because as the Hybrid began to feed, most of the people booed and got up to leave.

"Nix had balls," Bar said admiringly, as the spectators began to file out.

"Yeah," Capelli agreed. And sadly enough, that was the only memoriam Nix was likely to receive.

CHAPTER SEVEN
HOLE CARD

Thursday, October 15, 1953
Concordia, Kansas

Susan Farley awoke hundreds of feet up in the air. As the first rays of sunshine slanted down to splash Level 12 of Defense Column Five with golden light, Susan resolved to enjoy the cozy warmth of her sleeping bag a little bit longer.

And why not? The central elevator that served DC-5 back before the top fifty feet of the tower had been blown off was no longer operational. The only way to access her lofty perch was a series of flights of switch backing stairs. And, thanks to the booby trap she had left down on Level 10, no one could sneak up on her using the stairs. Not without setting off a Chimeran hedgehog grenade.

Drones were a danger of course, but having done nothing that would attract them, Susan had been free to enjoy her first good night's sleep in many days. A couple of weeks had passed since she'd killed Warden Brewster and his bodyguards. After arming herself with weapons stolen from Brewster's quarters, and exiting the mine via the emergency bolt hole the warden had provided for himself, Susan found herself partway up a mountainside.

From there she scrambled down a scree-covered hill to a trail that took her halfway around the mountain. After a short hike to a logging road, she'd come to a paved highway. She had to decide which way to go. And that was a tough decision. Because, with the possible exception of her adopted brother, Susan's entire family was dead. And, since Nathan had chosen to work for a corrupt government, he was as good as dead insofar as she was concerned.

So with no family to seek out, Susan resolved to hook up with Freedom First, the underground resistance group that opposed the Grace administration *and* the stinks. Their base in Montana had been destroyed. Susan had heard that much before she and her fellow prisoners were transferred to the mine. But the organization had other cells, one of which was in Concordia, Kansas.

It wasn't much to go on, but with no better destination in mind, Susan began what she knew would be a long walk. She had weapons, including a single-action Colt .45, an Army-issue Fareye rifle, and a lightweight Reaper carbine. All liberated from Brewster's private quarters. She kept the Reaper handy day and night because of its capacity to provide a heavy volume of fire. Something neither one of her other weapons was capable of.

Susan also had a good knife, plus the green Hudson's Bay blanket from Brewster's quarters that now served as a poncho. But what she lacked was a pack, camping gear, and boots to replace the ones on her feet. Both of which had holes.

So as Susan made her way down out of the mountains, she'd been on the lookout for an opportunity to buy what she needed. And thanks to the silver dollars taken from Brewster's desk, she had the means. There must have been a stash of gold somewhere as well. The Buckle was a gold mine, after all. But rather than take the time to look for it, and be forced to deal with the guards, Susan figured the silver would be enough to get started. If not, she could sell the Colt.

The opportunity came when Susan caught up with a group of survivalists, all headed for what they called a rendezvous. She followed them to a tiny ranching town called Falcon. It had been important once because of its location at the intersection of two railroads. But those days were over. So the town was of little interest to the Chimera, making Falcon the perfect spot for a rendezvous.

At least two hundred people were present when Susan arrived, and she was pleased to discover that there were all sorts of things for sale. That included handmade pack frames, women's clothing, and boots. Thanks to the pouch of silver dollars, Susan was able to purchase everything she needed without sacrificing the .45 or any of her precious ammo. And she was pleased to acquire two hundred rounds for the Reaper.

Having obtained the items she needed, Susan left the rendezvous before dark. Half the crowd was rip-roaring drunk by then and she wanted no part in what was to follow. As an unaccompanied female, she was something of a target, and had already been forced to deal with half a dozen come-ons.

That was why Susan left Falcon quickly. She kept her eyes peeled as she hurried up the road and made for the first firing position she saw. The water tank sat atop wooden stilts, which were at least twenty feet tall. A maintenance ladder led upwards and she hurried to climb it. Once on the walkway that circled the metal tank, Susan shucked her newly acquired pack, took the Fareye, and lay flat. Then, using the rifle's scope, she looked back towards the edge of town.

It wasn't long before a couple of people pulling a cart on bicycle wheels came her way. They were talking to each other, completely oblivious to the danger above as they passed the water tank and continued on their way. Then a trio of horsemen galloped by in the other direction. They were late, but clearly determined to take part in the rendezvous before it melted away.

A full five minutes passed after that with no sign of pursuit. So Susan was just about to pack up and leave when one of the men who had come on to her appeared. He was armed, but wasn't wearing a pack, which seemed to suggest an errand of some sort. Of course that didn't mean he was looking for her, since there were lots of other reasons why he might venture out.

But if the man *wasn't* looking for her, then why was a bloodhound straining at the leash in his hand, and leading the way? Susan remembered the big animal now. It had been with the man, sniffing around her ankles, as he invited her to have a drink with him. Something that seemed innocent at the time but took on added significance as the beast bayed and towed its master along.

As the twosome made a beeline for the water tower, Susan was well aware of the fact that many months had passed since she'd fired a rifle. But the skills learned as a little girl, and subsequently honed by the Freedom First instructors, were there waiting to be used.

With no crosswind to speak of, and the air relatively dry, all Susan had to do was squeeze the trigger. The Fareye produced a loud report. The bullet knocked the man's right leg out from under him, and he went down hard. The dog stopped, circled back, and stood next to its master.

Susan could have killed her pursuer, and probably should have, but was satisfied to shoulder her pack and hurry down the ladder. By keeping the tower's stiltlike support beams between her and the wounded man, she hoped to prevent any possibility of return fire.

The man was about three hundred feet away. He had a bushy beard, wild uncut hair, and was dressed in denim overalls. And he was tough. Having secured a makeshift pressure dressing with a blue bandanna, the man was back on his feet. Or foot, since he couldn't put much weight on the other one. "I'll find you!" he shouted. "And when I do, you'll wish you had never been born."

Susan stopped in her tracks, uttered a sigh, and turned back towards the man. Then, having moved to the left in order to get a clear shot, she raised the Fareye. The man could have fired at her then—but was using his rifle as a cane. So Susan shot him in the head and was already turning away as the body fell. *Some people are just plain stupid. That's what Dad said, and he was right.*

After securing supplies in Falcon, Susan headed north through Limon and Last Chance, Colorado, to U.S. 36. It paralleled U.S. 40 to the south, but was likely to be less traveled by both humans and the Chimera. That made it ideal insofar as Susan was concerned. Of course, "less traveled" didn't mean safe. Far from it.

A pair of Howlers had picked up Susan's trail just west of Atwood, Kansas. It had taken eight long hours, and all the skill she possessed, to establish an ambush, and to take the lion-sized beasts down.

Then, a few miles east of Norton, Susan had been forced to take shelter in a line shack for two days due to heavy rains. Although that had been good in a way: she had taken the opportunity to bathe in a nearby stream, wash both sets of clothes, and fine-tune her gear. That included converting Brewster's western-style holster into a shoulder rig.

Once the weather cleared, Susan returned to the road. She spotted the jagged top of the defense column seven days later. The tower grew steadily taller as the afternoon wore on. She was a quarter-mile away when the sun began to set.

Having scanned the area for a good ten minutes to

determine that the way was clear, Susan passed through a hole in what had been part of the perimeter fence, and crossed a fire-blackened defense moat.

From there it was a short trip up an embankment, through a gap between a couple of gun positions, and into the debris-strewn area that surrounded the column's sturdy base. Tons of material had fallen from above. The only sounds were generated by the eternal whine of the prairie wind, her own footsteps, and the rattle of metal treads as she climbed the stairs. She could not help but think about the others who had made the same journey and were almost certainly dead. If not as a result of the battle that had rendered the column impotent, then as a result of some other fight, as the Chimera systematically pounded North America into submission.

But after a good night's sleep, and with the sunshine angling in from above, Susan was in a good mood as she rolled out of the bag into the chilly air and went about her morning routines. All of the metal surfaces around her were covered with a layer of glittering frost. Water was limited to what she had in two Army canteens, but she was used to such inconveniences, and it wasn't long before she was dressed and cooking breakfast over a can of Sterno. She still had plenty of oatmeal, but was running low on everything else. That included tea, which she missed very much.

Once the meal was over and her gear was packed, Susan took the Fareye and made her way over to the east side of the deck. It had been too dark to scan the surrounding countryside the evening before, but now she could see for many miles.

Just before President Grace's death, and over the objections of those who spoke for Freedom First, the Grace administration had not only constructed defense columns like the one Susan was standing on, but so-called Protection Camps as well. They were small towns, really, in which hundreds of thousands of displaced citizens could be housed, and kept under control.

The city of Concordia had been host to such a camp, and as Susan swung the Fareye from left to right, she could see what remained of it. Hundreds of barrack-style buildings were all set up on a grid, complete with little parks that were positioned with checkerboard-like regularity. The open areas were overgrown now, but Susan could imagine children playing in them, as their parents looked on.

It was a reasonably peaceful scene at the moment, or would have been, were it not for the strange flower like structure that had blossomed at the southern end of the camp. Susan thought it was some sort of Chimeran spaceship at first. But, after studying the object for a while, she concluded that it was a prefab fortress. The sort of thing the aliens could drop wherever a small base was required.

The black metal dome sat about six feet off the ground. It featured a com mast and three petal-shaped ramps. She assumed there was a fourth on the south side of the structure. A hodgepodge of human vehicles were parked around the dome, which suggested that the stinks had learned to use them.

Susan was too far away to make out very many details. But she could seen tiny figures coming and going and knew that they were Hybrids. It was difficult to keep count, since it was hard to know how many Chimera were inside the structure at any given moment, but Susan estimated that fifteen to twenty of the aliens were in residence. And the longer she watched, the angrier she became. She was sick and tired of running and hiding from the creatures who had murdered her family.

Those emotions gave birth to an idea that was both audacious and more than a little absurd. What if Susan could wipe out all of the stinks associated with the base?

It wouldn't mean a damned thing where the big picture was concerned. The Chimera would still be in control of the United States. But it would be a victory of sorts. That got her to thinking, and a plan started to come together.

The Chimera had taken Concordia. And now it was time for the bastards to pay.

Having left the tower a little after noon and stashing her gear in a culvert, Susan was waiting at the west side of the Protection Camp when darkness fell. Now, being right next to one of the outlying buildings, it was easy to see why critics including Freedom First had been so opposed to what they called "citizen concentration camps." Meaning places where a substantial portion of the population could be forced to live according to rules laid down by an increasingly dictatorial government.

But Susan knew it was important to put such concerns aside as she entered the maze of buildings with the Fareye slung across her back and the Reaper in her hands. She didn't want to use the weapon, though. Not yet anyway. Because in order to execute her plan, she needed a stink magnet and a reliable source of light. Something other than the Chimeran base, which was lit up like a Christmas tree.

As Susan darted from building to building, she had to watch out for the debris that lay everywhere—and for either a Chimera or one of their Drones. Although judging from the way the firebase was illuminated, the aliens hadn't been attacked in a long time.

After counting the streets from the tower, Susan knew when she arrived at what she thought of as 15th Avenue. She circled a burned-out car and crossed the street. Having entered the long, narrow building on the other side, she used blips of light from a hand torch to navigate down a dusty hallway. It was lined by tiny apartments, glorified bedrooms really, all equipped with bunk beds and basic furnishings.

Susan had a pack of cigarettes. Not to smoke but to trade, one coffin nail at a time, to those who did. But in this situation she was about to turn a tube of tobacco and a pack of matches into a trigger. She placed a cigarette crosswise inside the packet of matches, being careful to keep the tip well away from the match heads.

According to Susan's Freedom First instructors, the average burn time for a Camel was four to five minutes. Plenty of time in which to reach her next destination. But first she gathered a pile of flammable materials together, lit the cigarette, and placed the triggering device next to a big wad of dry newspaper.

With that accomplished, she hurried out into the night and made for the nearest watchtower. The two-story structures were located at regular intervals throughout the camp. Their purpose being to protect the inhabitants and control them.

Susan let the Reaper hang crosswise over her chest so both her hands and feet were free to climb the ladder. A series of quick steps carried her up through a circular opening to the point where she could step off it onto a wooden deck. It was surrounded by four waist-high walls and topped with a conical roof. The structure wouldn't protect her from .22-caliber bullets, much less blasts from an Auger. But hopefully the element of surprise, and the cover of darkness, would offer sufficient protection.

Kneeling in front of a south-facing window with the Reaper within easy reach, Susan brought the Fareye around and slipped the sling up over her head. By that time she could see a red-orange glow through the windows of the building in which the fire had been set. And it wasn't long before flames escaped through open doorways and began to climb the outside walls.

Would the Chimera ignore the blaze? Or would they attempt to put it out? There was no way to know. But one thing was for sure: If the neighboring structures caught fire, and the conflagration began to spread, the fire would threaten their base. And that was a good thing.

So she watched with interest as a Chimeran transport roared up the street and came to a halt. Half a dozen Hybrids got out. But, rather than fight the fire, they began to scan the area with Augers in an effort to locate the person or persons responsible for the blaze. The whole thing was absurdly easy at first, thanks to the fact that the Hybrids were silhouetted against the flames. All Susan had to do was move the Fareye from target to target and pick them off one at a time. Five of them went down before the survivors realized what was happening and sought cover.

Rather than try to figure out where the Hybrids were hiding, Susan turned her attention to the heretofore brightly lit dome. It suddenly went dark as an engine started and reinforcements piled into a second transport.

Susan smiled grimly as the headlights came on and she inserted a fresh magazine into the rifle's well. It appeared that the hive-mind, or whatever it was that controlled the Hybrids, hadn't run into that situation before. By using the headlights as reference points, she was able to put three bullets into the area where the windshield should have been. The transport swerved left, then right, and smashed into a building. It didn't blow up, which was unfortunate, but Susan was happy nevertheless as she passed the sling over her head and felt the Fareye thump her back.

Having grabbed the Reaper, Susan was in the process of turning towards the opening at the center of the room when a Patrol Drone popped up through the aperture and a bright light speared her eyes. The robot exploded as a burst from the Reaper struck it. But other machines were visible outside the windows by then, and she felt a searing pain as a couple of projectiles grazed her ribs.

At that point the situation became desperate as Susan held the trigger down while turning a full circle. Drones exploded one after another, bits of shrapnel stung her face, and the Reaper clicked empty.

Susan ejected the empty magazine and replaced it with another as she made for the ladder. She clamped the side rails between her boots and slid to the ground. Her boots thumped as they hit the ground. Auger bolts flashed around her and lesser projectiles kicked up geysers of dirt. It was time to run.

As Susan zigzagged through the firelit maze of buildings, the whole notion of taking on a couple dozen Hybrids by herself seemed stupid now. She would be lucky to survive. A breeze came up as a Bullseye tag blipped past her head. Sparks flew high into the air, where they circled for a moment, before being carried to other buildings. In no time at all, cedar-shingled roofs caught fire and the blaze began to spread.

The surviving Hybrids stopped firing within a matter of seconds, and Susan could imagine them running towards the suddenly vulnerable dome. At that point it would have been smart to keep going, retrieve her pack, and clear the area as quickly as possible. But one of her father's favorite sayings was "Never leave a job half finished."

So Susan switched to offense. The open wound hurt, but she forced herself to ignore the pain as she jogged south. At least ten buildings were on fire by then, and there was plenty of light to see by as she neared the dome. The lights were back on and half a dozen 'brids were standing in front of the structure as if to guard it.

Susan brought the Fareye around, braced the rifle against a signpost, and triggered a series of quick shots. All but one of them flew true. Then the weapon was empty as the sole surviving stink spotted the weapon's final muzzle flash and turned in her direction. It charged straight at her, firing as it came. Projectiles buzzed past her.

She didn't have enough time to reload the Fareye, and the Reaper was hanging by its sling, so Susan pulled the Colt. Then, walking *towards* the oncoming stink, she raised the pistol, pulled the spur-shaped hammer back, and began to fire. "That's for Dad! And that's for Mom, and these are for our ranch hands."

The heavy slugs hit the Hybrid, threw it back, and dumped the creature on its back. The Chimera was dead, but Susan had one bullet left, and was determined to use it. "And this one," she said as she pointed the revolver downwards, "is for *me*."

With a loud bang, the .45-caliber slug smashed the Hybrid's grotesque face, flames shot a hundred feet up into the sky, and the past continued to burn.

CHAPTER EIGHT
ONE-ON-ONE

One step at a time. That was the way Capelli made it through each long and exhausting night. Fortunately the terrain was relatively flat. But even a slight incline required the slaves to throw their combined weight against the wooden crosspieces as Master Jack's whip nipped at their backs and they pushed the wagon upwards.

Nine days had passed since the stop in Hamley and Nix's ill-fated battle with El Diablo. And now, according to Bam-Bam, the circus was on its way to a place called Tank Town. A community which, to hear him tell about it, was like a miniature city. Except Capelli had no intention of going to Tank Town or anyplace with Master Jack and his so-called performers. Because he planned to escape.

It was on the fifth day out from Hamley that Capelli found the broken hacksaw blade. He and the other donkeys were crouched inside a large equipment shed at the time, waiting for night to fall, when he caught a glimpse of the object, partially covered with soil. The implement was half the length it should have been, and dull as well, which probably accounted for why it had been thrown away.

Shortly thereafter, Capelli went to work on link thirty-two of the chain that ran from the wagon's tongue to his metal collar. But his task wasn't easy. The teeth were worn down and there was rule eight to consider: "Don't trust anyone." Not even his fellow donkeys—who might try to take the tool for themselves, or sell him out to one of the guards.

So sawing through the link had been a long, arduous process often carried out with cold fingers when the others were sleeping. And with nowhere else to hide the object, Capelli had been forced to stick the ribbon of steel down into his right boot, where it rubbed his skin raw.

But finally the cut had been completed and camouflaged with a paste made from oil-soaked dirt mixed with spit. Now, all Capelli needed was the right opportunity to pull himself loose and run like hell. And when he and his fellow slaves toiled up a 3-percent grade, he saw his chance.

Alfonso was the only member of the troupe who had a horse, and he was scouting somewhere up ahead. There was no moon. But with a clear sky and some starlight, Capelli could see the mixture of grass and unharvested wheat that flourished along both sides of the road. It was tall enough to hide in, and given the need to protect the wagon, it seemed unlikely that Inkskin and Bam-Bam would pursue him for very long.

So as the slaves reached the top of the rise, Capelli felt for link thirty-two, found it, and broke free. Then, cognizant of the fact that it was important to move quickly, he ran. Inkskin saw the motion and hurried to block the slave's escape route.

Capelli had about two feet of chain to work with, and the metal flail struck the guard across the bridge of his nose. He fell, the Bullseye clattered as it hit the ground, and Capelli kept running.

Master Jack was bellowing orders by that time, and projectiles blipped past Capelli's head, as Bam-Bam opened fire on him. Capelli was in the wheat by then. But after hours of hard work, his legs felt as if they were made of lead. He drove himself forward anyway, knowing that every yard of progress took him closer to freedom. The firing had stopped by then, because a dead donkey was nothing more than Hybrid fodder.

But then, just as Capelli was about to drop to his hands and knees in an attempt to disappear from sight, he heard the sound of thundering hooves. Voices shouted, a loop of rope fell over his shoulders, and a horse rushed past him. Suddenly, Capelli was jerked off his feet and towed towards the highway. The ground was reasonably smooth, but there were small rocks, and they pummeled his back until he came to a sudden stop in the drainage ditch.

Inkskin was there to lift Capelli up, drag him onto the pavement, and beat him back down. The lower part of the guard's face was black with blood and he was furious. From his vantage point on the ground, Capelli realized that there were three horses in all as the man who had roped him swung a leg over his mount's back and stepped down. "Thanks," Bam-Bam said, as the rope was removed from Capelli's shoulders. "The bastard damned near got away."

Master Jack had arrived on the scene by then and took advantage of the opportunity to kick Capelli in the ribs. The blow hurt like hell. Capelli curled up into the fetal position. Then, turning to the rider, the ringmaster spoke. "Are you from Tank Town by any chance?" he inquired conversationally. "We were told to expect a contact roughly five miles out."

"You heard right," the man replied, his breath fogging the air. "My name's Grady. I'm what the boss calls a 'coordinator.'"

"So Tank Town is still in operation?"

"We've been in business for fifty-three days without being attacked by the Chimera. And that ain't no accident," Grady added, as he coiled his rope. "In order to enter Tank Town you'll have to do it at night, you'll have to follow one of our guides, and you'll have to obey the house rules once you're inside."

"Okay," Master Jack replied. "That sounds reasonable. What's this I hear about an entry fee?"

"You'll have to pay a fee to get in," Grady confirmed. "Plus the boss takes ten percent off the top of anything you make."

There wasn't much light, so Capelli couldn't see the expression on the ringmaster's face, but he could tell that the fat man was annoyed from the tone of his voice. "*Ten percent?* That's kind of steep, isn't it?"

Grady put a foot in a stirrup and swung up onto his horse. "That's a matter of opinion, I guess. But a large audience is real hard to find these days."

Master Jack was in no position to push back and knew it. "Point taken. We'll follow your guide in."

Inkskin jerked Capelli to his feet, shoved him towards the rest of the donkeys, and added a kick for emphasis. "Welcome back, Capelli. You're going to be sorry. *Real* sorry."

Capelli stumbled, caught himself, and knew that he was.

Both Boss Orley's guide and Ringmaster Jack wanted to make it into Tank Town before sunrise. And for good reason. So long as the stinks controlled the sky, everyone on the ground was vulnerable. Especially during daylight hours.

All of the slaves were ordered to push harder. But when Master Jack's whip cracked, it was Capelli who felt the pain most often. Because everyone was angry with him. Including most of the other donkeys. They blamed him for the extra work, even if that didn't make sense.

So it was back to one-step-at-a-time as the hours ticked away, the sun began to peek over the eastern horizon, and the guide led the slaves off the highway. Her name was Tupo, and Alfonso rode at her side as she led the slaves into a shallow river. After a hard right turn, the donkeys were forced to drag the heavy wagon upstream. A strategy clearly intended to prevent traffic from creating the sort of trail that might be noticed from above. "Put your shoulders into it!" Bam Bam demanded, as the wagon lurched over loose rocks, and El Diablo screeched.

It was difficult to find a solid footing on the river bottom, but Capelli did the best he could, as the tip of the whip found his left ear and left it numb. Fortunately, the trip from the highway to the point where a massive pipe opened onto the streambed was mercifully short. A left turn took them into the metal tube. A wood floor had been installed to accommodate vehicles, and occasional lights hinted at the presence of a generator.

Finally, after passing various points where raw sewage was pouring out of smaller pipes into the main tube, they came to the place where some sort of a pump had been demolished to make way for a wooden ramp. Pieces of machinery and chunks of broken concrete had been piled to either side, leaving the way clear for the slaves to muscle the wagon up the slope, through a ragged hole, and into the empty reservoir beyond. Judging from the presence of pens filled with pigs, cattle, and horses, it was being used as a communal barn. The odor that pervaded the place was only slightly less nauseating than the one in the big pipe.

Tupo led Alfonso and the rest of them over to a spot

where the wagon finally came to a halt, and Master Jack paid the entry fee with what Capelli felt sure was one of Locke's gold coins.

It was blessedly warm inside Tank Town. After being ordered to strip, the slaves were hosed off like animals. They were then allowed to dress in the same filthy clothes and led to a pen where they were watered and fed. Once his stomach was full, Capelli lay down on a fresh scattering of straw and went to sleep. It was like falling into a bottomless well, and he felt grateful as the blackness swallowed him up.

The sun was just about to set, and Susan Farley was gnawing on a raw carrot as she sat on a ledge with her back against a rock. From her vantage point on the hillside, she could look down into the gully a couple of hundred feet below. The family, as she thought of the group, had chosen to camp under a railroad bridge next to a gurgling stream. An attempt had been made to screen the fire with pieces of canvas draped over a framework constructed with sticks, but she could see hints of the orange-red glow nevertheless, and took an odd sort of comfort from it.

Susan had been following along behind the group of five men, three women, and two children for the better part of three days, with occasional breaks to forage for food. There were lots of overgrown vegetable gardens in Kansas. Not to mention wild carrots and so-called prairie potatoes, although she was tired of being a vegetarian.

There was game, of course—plenty of it, given how few people there were. But Susan had been reluctant to shoot anything for fear of giving herself away to the Chimera, or alerting the "family" to her presence, which might cause them to break contact.

That was silly, of course. Especially since the original plan had been to follow along behind and let them flush out any stinks that might be lying in wait. And the strategy worked, because a horde of about thirty Leapers attacked the group early the next afternoon, only to be decimated by the heavily armed humans.

But gradually, as Susan watched the family through the Fareye's scope, an unintended bond began to form. The members of the group appeared to be relatively happy, judging from the way they interacted with each other. It gave Susan a vicarious sense of companionship. Something she was surprised to discover that she both needed and felt guilty about. *They're going somewhere*, Susan thought to herself. *And I need supplies. So I'll follow them. Then, once we arrive, I'll break it off.*

So Susan ate a raw potato, made herself a cup of slightly bitter dandelion tea, and slipped into her sleeping bag half an hour later as a way to combat the cold. The family was still up, and the evening breeze brought occasional bursts of laughter her way. It felt good to know that some form of happiness was still possible—and the thought led to a pleasant dream.

When Susan awoke the next morning the sun was up, although barely visible through a thick overcast, as a light drizzle fell. It was a miserable beginning to the day. But Susan had no choice but to get up, boil some vegetables for breakfast, and break camp.

And it was then, as she was fastening the straps on her pack, that she spotted the Hybrids—a file of them, all crossing the railroad trestle, and silhouetted against the pewter-gray sky. Her heart skipped a beat. Would they look down? And see the family below? Or continue on their way?

While mostly hidden from the family her position was

visible from the bridge, so Susan took cover behind a large rock, before bringing the Fareye up. She was watching the stinks when one of them pointed downwards. Then it fired down between the railroad ties. The others did likewise, and the family answered from below.

But the humans were going to be slaughtered. That much was obvious given how exposed they were and the fact that the stinks held the high ground. So she reacted accordingly. The Fareye barked and a Chimera fell. The body flipped end-for-end before splashing into the stream and being swept away.

Meanwhile, as both the aliens and the group below them continued to exchange fire, Susan shot another Hybrid. A halo of blood appeared around its head before the creature collapsed onto the bridge, where it lay with an arm dangling over the side. Then, as suddenly as it had begun, the battle was over as the last stink staggered and went down.

Susan watched from above as the family broke camp. One of the men had a white bandage wrapped around his left bicep. But none of the group had been killed, and Susan was grateful.

Once the family was ready to go, the woman Susan thought of as Nancy stepped out into the open. She held something over her head as she turned a full circle. Then, as if performing a pantomime, she bent over to place whatever it was on a flat rock next to the stream.

After watching the group leave, Susan shouldered her pack, and made her way down the slope to the brook below. Once she splashed across she came to the rock, saw what the woman had left for her, and felt a sense of warmth. Because while the family didn't know her name, or anything about her, they knew someone had been watching over them. And the Hershey bar was their way of saying "thanks."

Susan toyed with the idea of making herself known to the family during the next couple of days, but it didn't feel right somehow, so she was still tagging along behind them when the oil refinery appeared on the far horizon. That's what she assumed it was, anyway, although she was no expert.

Was that where the family was headed? It looked that way. The complex was occupied, because the group was still a half-mile away from the assemblage of stacks, towers, and tanks when a group of three men popped up out of nowhere to intercept them.

She watched their interaction through the Fareye's scope, taking comfort from what appeared to be a friendly conversation. She continued to observe as the family was hustled off the highway. The people she had come to think of as her friends vanished shortly thereafter, only to reappear hours later as darkness settled over the land. All of which was a clear indication that the people associated with the refinery were very cautious indeed. An attitude that she approved of.

Susan was close by then, *much* closer, and followed along behind as the family was led into the deep ditch that was designed to contain an oil spill, and from there into an open pipe. At that point she thought it best to make herself known, and was about to do so, when she caught a whiff of human sweat and felt something hard nudge the base of her skull. "That's a .22 Ruger," a male voice said. "Drop the rifle and put your hands on top of your head."

Susan did as she was told. A group of people dressed in black clothing and armed with Augers closed in around her. Here was the security team *behind* the security team. And, judging from the efficient way in which they questioned and then released her, they were used to intercepting people who wanted to enter Tank Town. It was, they informed her, open to anyone who could pay the entry fee. But the price was so steep she almost said no before finally caving in.

Because the truth was that she needed supplies, and needed them badly. She'd consumed all of her food and had used up most of the Fareye ammo. That left Susan with no choice but to part with the Colt, the shoulder rig, and the remainder of her .45 ammo. A few minutes later she had the pleasure of entering a world where there were electric lights, sleeping cubes that could be rented by the day, separate showers for both sexes, self-service laundry facilities, a medical clinic, three restaurants, a gambling casino, and the so-called bowl, where all kinds of entertainment was available. All for a price of course, which was bad news for Susan, who was very nearly broke.

Having found her way into a dimly lit female dormitory, Susan was forced to part with twenty-five Reaper projectiles to buy a much-needed shower, wash her clothes, and rent a locker. Still, it was a thrill to crawl in between clean sheets for the first time in months and drift off to sleep without fear of being attacked.

She awoke feeling refreshed and went in search of a big breakfast. The circular restaurant was crowded with people of every possible description. The common denominators being hard eyes, the fact that none of her fellow diners were over the age of sixty, and that they were all armed. She paid five projectiles for a rib-eye steak, three fried eggs, and several mugs of tea. And the meal was well worth the price.

From there she set off for the casino, where if things went well, Susan hoped to recoup at least some of her losses. The entire complex had been emptied of oil and gasoline at some point. Probably during the desperate days just prior to the big collapse. But the odors lingered. And as Susan followed hand-printed signs through a maze of pipes, she noticed that the smell was stronger in some places than in others.

The casino occupied a medium-sized tank. It was a simple affair that consisted of twelve tables, two of which were set up for blackjack. The concepts of day and night didn't mean much inside Tank Town and the facility was about half full. What light there was emanated from cone-shaped fixtures that dangled over the tables. A thick cloud of cigarette, cigar, and pipe smoke eddied around them. A bar had been set up on one side of the tank and a booth labeled "Cashier" was located directly opposite it.

After speaking with the woman inside the cage, Susan learned that she could borrow up to a hundred house tokens in various denominations by using the Reaper as collateral. "And if I lose?" she wanted to know.

"Then we keep the Reaper," the woman with frizzy red hair replied. "It's up to you."

Susan didn't want to risk the Reaper, but the only other way to make a significant amount of money in a relatively short period of time was to sell her body, and she wasn't that desperate. Not yet.

So she took the money and gave the Reaper over, wishing she still had the Colt. Because if the stinks attacked while she was playing cards she would be shit out of luck. A scary thought indeed, even though she could steal a weapon if she had to.

After scanning the tables, Susan spotted one that had two empty slots and wandered over. A man who introduced himself as Tom was running the table. He was wearing a ball cap and a pair of glasses that had been mended with black electrical tape and was in need of a shave. When she asked if she could play, he looked her up and down and produced a phony-looking smile. "Sure, honey! You sit yourself down and we'll deal you in. Are you familiar with seven-card stud?"

"I used to play it with my family," Susan said truthfully. "Dad said I was pretty good." What Susan failed to mention was the fact that she had spent months playing poker in the Lucky Buckle Mine with a dealer from Las Vegas as her tutor.

"I'm glad to hear it," Tom said condescendingly. "Because we wouldn't want to take advantage of a pretty little thing like yourself."

The other men nodded agreeably, and Susan thought she could see dollar signs in their eyes, as she stacked the tokens in front of her. It didn't take a genius to see that her fellow players thought they had an easy mark. But Susan had a good memory for cards and had an ability to read faces. That was the edge she needed. Or so she hoped.

During the first hour of play, she discovered that Tom was an erratic player who allowed surges of emotion to influence his betting and wasn't doing as well as the house should have.

The man seated directly across from Susan was very different. His name was Carl. He was smarter than Tom, a lot more patient, and willing to take risks when it made sense to do so. He had a large bald spot surrounded by a fringe of hair that hung down to his shoulders, and he was chewing on a kitchen match.

The third player was named George. His narrow-set eyes had a tendency to blink rapidly when he was going to bluff. A tactic he used far too often. And he had a hollow cough. The kind that kept people from sitting too close.

So those were the personalities Susan had to interact with as rounds were won and lost, the towers of tokens in front of her continued to grow, and those belonging to the others dwindled. George lost the most, and was eventually forced to cash out, followed by Tom an hour later. That shut the game down and left Carl and Susan as winners.

Susan had 326 tokens by then, which allowed her to pay back the advance, *and* reclaim the Reaper. Then, being more than two hundred ahead, it was time to enjoy a good lunch.

Two hours later she returned to the casino determined to make some more money, buy the supplies she needed, and get the hell out of Tank Town as quickly as possible. Because even though the facility was well run, it was too big to last forever, and she wanted to be a long way off when the stinks brought the party to a close.

Rather than play poker again, Susan decided to switch things up and, being a good card counter, blackjack was the obvious way to go. The objective of the game was to beat the dealer, and there were two ways to accomplish that. She could achieve a total higher than the dealer's without exceeding twenty-one, or stay below that magic number while the dealer went over it.

The homemade blackjack table stood waist high and consisted of a half-circle of plywood covered with a gray blanket, with mismatched bar stools for five players. The dealer, who was renting the table just as Tom had rented his earlier that day, stood on the other side of the flat surface. There was no shoe, which meant the table was set up for hand-held blackjack. Susan knew that in hand-held games, cards are dealt facedown and the players peek at them in order to see what they have.

Piles of differently denominated house tokens were arrayed in front of the dealer. He had slicked-back hair and a neatly trimmed mustache, and he handled the single deck of cards with the confidence of a professional.

But Susan had seen him sitting at the bar before lunch. And as she took her place on one of the wooden stools, she thought she noticed a slight slur to his speech. Was the dealer inebriated? If so, that could make a difference. She resolved to keep a careful eye on him.

One man was already seated to her right, and it wasn't long before three more bellied up to the table. The first few hands went smoothly enough. Susan won three times out of five and felt good about it. Meanwhile, one of the men won *four* times.

His name was Cecil, and he looked ordinary enough, except for one thing. In a time and place when it was very difficult to stay clean, much less pursue the finer points of good grooming, Cecil's long, slim fingers were manicured. In addition to that his fingernails were longer than Susan's, filed to points, and appeared to be quite sharp.

Was that a coincidence? Or was Cecil using his fingernails to mark cards? If so, that would enable him to know the value of at least some of the cards that were facedown in front of the dealer. But card marking was a well-known method of cheating at blackjack, so it seemed logical to suppose that the dealer would be watching for it.

But as Susan watched the dealer, and saw the slightly glassy look in his eyes, she was reminded of her earlier observation. If he wasn't drunk, he was impaired, and it appeared that Cecil was taking full advantage of that fact.

So what to do? Make a public accusation, which could lead to an ugly confrontation? Or watch the cards and try to figure out which ones had been scratched? That would be dishonest, of course. But Susan figured that anyone stupid enough to deal blackjack while drunk was going to get cleaned out anyway.

So she followed the cards, came to the conclusion that all of the aces were marked, and made her bets accordingly. Not with absolute consistency, which would have been enough to tip off the drunk, but often enough to rake in more money than she would have otherwise.

Cecil had heavy brows, a beak-shaped nose, and thin lips. They were turned down disapprovingly, and Susan could tell that he was on to her. But he couldn't complain without revealing his own perfidy, so the card shark was forced to settle for less, and share his ill-gotten gains.

But not for long. Once Susan had what she judged to be enough, she excused herself rather than wait around to see Cecil clean the dealer out. Or get shot. Whichever came first. The 112 tokens won while playing blackjack brought her total winnings up to 338 tokens, minus the cost of lunch.

It was time to go shopping.

Capelli was going to fight El Diablo because Master Jack wanted to punish him for trying to escape. But there was a second reason as well—and that was to keep the rest of the donkeys living in fear. So they were allowed to watch from one of the animal pens that fronted the stands as Bam-Bam and Inkskin used their stick mounted cattle prods to drive El Diablo out into the circular arena. The Hybrid screeched loudly, which was sufficient to claim the audience's attention as Capelli was forced into the ring by blows from Alfonso's whip. The runner was naked except for a loincloth, because as Bam-Bam put it, "The audience wants to see some blood."

Capelli heard the roar of applause and wondered who the onlookers were rooting for. Him? Or El Diablo? They were seated all around the circular arena, but their faces were a blur, as Ringmaster Jack came out to address the crowd.

"Laaadies and gentlemen! Children of all ages! Tonight you are about to witness a battle between a human, armed only with a knife, and the Chimeran Steelhead we call El Diablo. If the human wins, he will be freed. And if El Diablo wins, he will eat well tonight! Now, settle back, and enjoy the show."

As Jack left the ring, Inkskin was there to give Capelli the single-edged knife. The blade was about six inches long. "Maybe you should slit your throat with it," the tattooed man suggested, as he backed away. "The whole thing would be less painful that way."

Capelli tested the blade with his thumb, was pleased to discover that it was quite sharp, and turned his back to the eight-foot-high wall that surrounded the bowl. He estimated that the arena was about seventy-five feet across. The dirt under his bare feet had clearly been brought in from outside and there were some sizable rocks mixed in with it. A cluster of lights dangled from above and Capelli had to keep his chin down to avoid the glare. He was frightened, but alert, with blood pounding in his ears.

El Diablo was shuffling sideways. The Chimera had a good six inches on Capelli. In addition to six gold-colored eyes, and a reptilian jaw that could open extremely wide, the Steelhead had an animal-like muscularity. Its reactions were quick, it had the benefit of experience, and it was hungry. All of which were advantages.

Could the stink draw on knowledge possessed by the Chimeran hive-mind? Or call on it for help? Maybe, but Capelli didn't think so, because if the hive-mind knew about El Diablo's situation, why hadn't a force of Hybrids been sent to destroy the circus weeks or months before?

No, Capelli figured El Diablo was on its own for some reason, just as he was. So what to do? He could throw the knife, of course. But the ex-soldier knew that the best throwing knives were double-edged, which his wasn't. And accurate knife throwing requires lots of practice and a good eye. If the thrower isn't the correct distance from the target, the weapon can easily hit hilt-first.

No, Capelli reasoned, as some in the crowd booed the lack of action, throwing was out of the question. That suggested stabbing or cutting. Except that according to Bar and the rest of the donkeys, none of the previous attempts to slice and dice El Diablo had been successful. Which was why the big Hybrid was not only alive but seemingly fearless.

The beast extended both arms and charged.

Fortunately, Capelli had a plan. And that was to forgo the sort of offensive strategies used by previous combatants in favor of what he'd been taught by a burly hand-to-hand combat instructor named Sergeant Major Brierson. *Forget anything you think you know about knife fighting,* the noncom had advised. *Because most, if not all of it, is bullshit. I'm going to turn you into street surgeons, which is to say people who make cuts with a very specific purpose in mind, and that's to disable your opponent.*

So as El Diablo surged forward, Capelli chose his primary targets—which were the muscles on the top surface of the Steelhead's sinewy forearms. Specifically the extensors that enabled the stink to uncurl and extend its bony fingers. The challenge being to stay out of the sort of death hug that ended Nix's life.

Time seemed to slow, and Capelli was only vaguely aware of the crowd's roar, as he ran straight at the Hybrid. Then, at the very last second, he made a grab for the stink's right arm, got hold of the creature's wrist, and brought the blade down. It sliced through skin, muscle, and tendons before grating on bone.

As El Diablo screamed in pain, and brought its left arm inwards, Capelli dropped to the dirt and rolled away. Having missed the opportunity to grab its opponent, the

Steelhead paused to examine the bloody injury. After three attempts to straighten its fingers it uttered a grunt, turned towards Capelli, and hissed.

The crowd was in a complete uproar by that time and Susan, who had a front-row seat, was staring at the man in the ring. Especially the large tattoo on his back. It included the capital letters "SRPA" and the likeness of a Hybrid skull wearing an Army helmet. The last time she had seen such a tattoo was on her brother's half-naked body as members of Freedom First attempted to beat information out of him. Was this man from Nathan's top-secret unit? Yes, she thought he was.

Her presence at the event had been the result of boredom plus idle curiosity. And having seen the absurd matchup, she had been about to leave rather than witness the slaughter. But now there was a personal connection, even if it was to a man who had been a member of SRPA, an organization that supported the Grace administration.

Bets were being placed all around—most of which were on the Chimera. Susan felt for the pouch of tokens, bet all of them on the man with the SRPA tattoo, and wondered if she was going to regret it.

Legs, Brierson said, as he spoke to Capelli from the past. *Cut them correctly and your opponent won't be able to move. And remember, while Hybrids are somewhat different from humans, they were human at one time. That means they have a similar musculature.*

So as Capelli and El Diablo circled each other, the runner was eyeing the area just above the Chimera's knees knowing that if he could sever the stink's *vastus medialis*, *vastus lateralis*, or *rectus femoris*, it would immobilize the Steelhead.

But how? El Diablo's right hand was little more than

a club now, but there was nothing wrong with its left, or its teeth for that matter. Still, he had to try. So it was Capelli's turn to charge. A fistful of soil was concealed in his left hand and the knife was gripped in his right, as he dashed forward. Then, the moment Capelli was close enough, he threw the dirt into the Chimera's face.

Perhaps the tactic would have been effective against another human. But the Steelhead had *six* eyes, and even if four of them were blinded, it could still see. So rather than make the cut as planned, Capelli felt an explosion of pain as the Chimera's good hand found his throat and a bony fist came around to hammer his skull.

Everything went black for a second, the strength went out of Capelli's knees, and he began to fall. But the darkness lifted after a moment or two, and as it did, Capelli brought the knife up and in. That saved him. Because as three inches of steel entered El Diablo's abdomen, it let go.

However, the talons on the Chimera's left hand had left deep puncture wounds in Capelli's neck and slashed his chest as they fell away. Blood gushed, Capelli back-pedaled, and the crowd went wild.

People were on their feet, and the betting became even more frenzied as the odds shifted again. Because now that the human was wounded, and bleeding profusely, the smart money expected the contest to end quickly.

But Capelli was a Sentinel. Or had been one. And he still had the capacity to recover from nonlethal injuries more quickly than other people could. So even as the odds turned against him, Capelli's wounds had begun to close. That didn't mean he was safe, however, as El Diablo began to follow him around the ring.

What happened next was more accident than plan as Capelli backed over a stone that was mixed in with the dirt and tripped. El Diablo uttered a roar of triumph as the human fell over backwards.

Capelli's first impulse was to roll out of the way as the Hybrid came towards him. But another possibility occurred to him, and he went limp instead. Certain of victory, the Steelhead bent over, and was in the process of reaching for Capelli's already bloodied throat when the human came back to life.

The blade cut deep, found the sartorius muscle in the Hybrid's right leg, and sliced all the way through it. Suddenly, without lateral rotation, flexion, and abduction, El Diablo was crippled.

As the Chimera screamed, and made a grab for what hurt, Capelli brought his knees up to his chin and kicked. His feet hit the stink in the stomach and pushed it over. Dirt flew, and a cloud of dust rose as the Hybrid landed on its back.

Bam-Bam, Inkskin, and Alfonso were rushing into the arena by that time in a belated effort to save their Chimeran meal ticket. But those who had money on Capelli weren't having any of that. There was a sudden stutter of gunfire as someone fired a burst from a .45 M3 submachine gun. Geysers of soil flew into the air and drew a line between the circus performers and the Chimera.

So the men were forced to retreat as Capelli scrambled to his feet and El Diablo made futile efforts to stand. That was when the pro-Capelli part of the crowd began to chant. *"Kill it! Kill it! Kill it!"*

And Capelli was happy to oblige. As he circled the beast, it made a pathetic effort to match his movements but couldn't keep up. That allowed the human to step in and slash El Diablo's throat. Blood sprayed the dirt, the Chimera's head wobbled, and the beast collapsed.

Absolute pandemonium broke out as the winners celebrated and the losers were forced to pay up. Capelli knew there was something he should do, but he couldn't summon the energy to do it, as the circus performers swept in to confiscate the knife and carry him towards the exit. "No!" Capelli protested. "I'm free. You promised."

Bam-Bam's brightly painted face loomed above as Capelli was borne away. "We lied," the clown replied. "You killed El Diablo—and you are going to pay."

CHAPTER NINE
NOWHERE TO HIDE

Tuesday, October 27, 1953
Freedom Base, Blanchard Springs Caverns,
Ozark National Forest, Arkansas

It was eternally black inside the caverns, or would have been, were it not for the generator and electric lights. But the side gallery in which Monica Shaw and the other women slept was kept dark so they could get some rest whenever the opportunity presented itself. Except that Shaw couldn't sleep, because she was in pain.

Not physical pain, since there was nothing wrong with her body, but emotional pain that stemmed from the horrible decision she'd been forced to make. Within the next hour, acting on information obtained from her over the last few months, Judge Ramsey's regulators were going to attack the base. Their goal was to destroy the nascent government and steal the five thousand doses of Hale vaccine that were ready for distribution. Except that under the dictatorship that Ramsey planned to establish, the only people receiving the vaccine would be his supporters.

None of this was of interest to Shaw. All she wanted to do was protect her husband and three-year-old daughter, both of whom were under Ramsey's control.

But what was right? And what was wrong? Or did such concepts have meaning anymore? Survival of the fittest. That was the new morality. Or so Shaw continually told herself. Except now, faced with the imminent slaughter of the President and his staff, Shaw realized that she'd been wrong. If there was any hope for humanity, it lay in battling not only the Chimera, but people like Ramsey. Even if that meant sacrificing her husband and daughter.

Tears were streaming down Shaw's face as she threw the blanket off and swung her boots over onto the floor. She was fully dressed in anticipation of the coming attack. Carefully, so as not to wake the others, Shaw made her way over to the cot occupied by Cassie Aklin. Then, having touched the other woman's shoulder, she said, "Cassie! It's Monica."

Aklin had been dreaming. Nathan Hale was sitting on the other side of her kitchen table in Denver. His strange golden eyes were locked with hers and he was smiling. "There isn't any point in worrying about tomorrow, Cassie! We have tonight. Let's enjoy it."

Then Hale disappeared as someone else said her name. "Cassie, it's Monica. I need to talk to you."

Aklin resented the loss of her time with Nathan and felt a rising sense of irritation. "Monica? Can this wait? I need some sleep."

"No," Shaw whispered flatly. "I did something terrible, Cassie! Something I'm ashamed of. I told them when President Voss would be in the cave—and when the latest batch of Hale vaccine would be ready. They're going to kill the President *and* steal the shipment."

Aklin sat up straight, threw off her covers, and made a grab for the clothes on the chair next to the cot. "They? Who are *they*?"

"They call themselves regulators, although they're more like outlaws. They work for a man named Ramsey. He's holding my husband and daughter prisoner up in Oklahoma. He said he'd kill them unless I cooperated. So I went along. But I couldn't go through with it."

Aklin swore as she tied her boots. "How much time do we have?"

"Forty-five minutes, give or take."

Aklin came to her feet, slipped a chest protector over her head, and grabbed the Bullseye that was leaning against a wall. If looks could kill, then the one she aimed at Shaw would have been fatal. "You made a difficult decision—but you made it late. I hope you aren't expecting a medal or something. We're going to see President Voss. You lead the way. And Monica!"

Shaw wiped some of her tears away with her wrist. "Yes?"

"If you try to run, I'll shoot you."

Thomas Voss was not only awake, but hard at work when the emergency klaxon began to bleat, and Shaw entered the cubicle people jokingly referred to as "the Square Office." Aklin was right behind the technician, her face grim.

"We have a confirmed condition five, Mr. President. I don't have enough time to explain—but this isn't a drill. Please follow me."

Voss wanted to say, "No," and demand an explanation. But he knew that if Aklin said the facility was about to come under attack, then it was. So he swore, made a grab for the jacket that was hanging on a nail, and followed the women out of the cube.

Voss could tell that Shaw had been crying and that Aklin was angry with her. Was it tied in with the condition-five evacuation somehow? Yes, he figured it was, and wondered what Shaw had done to make his chief of staff so upset.

As the trio left the office and crossed the floor of the cavern to the escape route, soldiers ran towards the main entrance, and they heard muted gunfire.

"We have reason to believe we're up against about a hundred hostiles," Aklin said. "All human."

Shaw's head was down, and Voss was about to demand more information, when Kawecki and a squad of heavily armed soldiers appeared. They wore armor, plus packs kept ready for such a situation, and immediately took the lead. "They'll make sure our escape route is secure," Kawecki said as the men jogged past.

Malikov and four heavily burdened scientists arrived a couple of seconds later. Voss knew they were carrying everything required to start making Hale vaccine. Unfortunately, there was no way to save the lab equipment or the five thousand doses that were scheduled to go out the following day. That would take mules and a pack train.

"Ve are ready," Malikov said stoically. Voss knew Malikov had survived at least a hundred close calls over the last few years. And, judging from the Rossmore in his hands, the cadaverous-looking scientist was ready to fight again.

"Thank you, Doctor," Voss said. "Your people will bring up the rear. It's imperative that we protect them *and* the cultures they're carrying."

"Ve understand," the scientist responded.

But then a series of explosions sounded. The time for conversation was over.

Kawecki led the way and Shaw was next in line, closely followed by Aklin, Voss, Malikov, and his scientists. The sounds of fighting began to fade as the group followed the path through a narrow opening and into the passageway beyond.

Having passed through the gap, Kawecki ordered the rest of the group to continue on while he paused to start the timer on a pre-positioned demolition charge. Voss heard the explosion a minute later as the officer caught up and managed to squeeze past.

From there the trail led gradually upward. What illumination there was originated from the lights attached to weapons and a few hand torches. Voss caught occasional glimpses of wet limestone walls, stalactites hanging from above, and crystal-clear pools of water that shivered as they passed.

Finally, after climbing a couple of hundred feet, the path delivered the group into a small cave where emergency supplies were waiting for them. Voss selected a pack with his name on it, and was in the process of putting his arms through the straps, when a dull thud was heard.

"They blew the doors," Kawecki said darkly. "They're inside now."

Voss looked at Shaw as she began to sob. "They work for a man named Ramsey," Aklin said. "He's holding Shaw's husband and daughter hostage. That's why she volunteered to work for us. You can view her as a traitor or a patriot. Both descriptions are accurate."

Voss selected a Rossmore from a rack of weapons and checked to make sure that the shotgun was loaded. "Watch her, Cassie! Don't let her do anything stupid. I want to know more about this Ramsey person. A lot more.

"Marvin, order the men in the main cavern to break contact, and pull out. Let's save as many people as we can. Tell them to report to Freedom Base Two."

Kawecki nodded grimly. "And once they're clear?"

"Blow the cavern."

Kawecki raised a radio to his lips and gave a series of orders. Then, walking single file, the government of the United States of America was forced to abandon Freedom Base One. Another battle had been lost.

It took more than two days for the group to make its way out of the national forest onto Route 7, which they followed south towards the city of Russellville, and the Ouachita Mountains beyond. Voss and his senior team had been well aware of the need for a backup location, and a site that was located northwest of Hot Springs had been selected over two other possibilities.

Route 7 was very scenic, thanks to the hilly terrain and a wealth of evergreens and oaks. The fall foliage was pretty to look at. And that would have been nice had Voss and his party been on a vacation. But the journey was extremely stressful, because everyone knew the Chimera could be hiding in the trees or waiting around the next bend in the road.

It was better than the alternative to following Route 7, however, which was to leave the highway, and travel cross-country. A process that would take too long, and would force the party to cross treacherous rivers and climb steep slopes. So all the group could do was stay alert, hug the side of the road, and hope for the best.

They saw lots of rusting cars, trucks, and buses along the way. But in spite of the signs of past carnage, the group had only one close call during the first part of the trip. A Chimeran shuttle came speeding down the highway only fifty feet above the pavement. The angular machine looked like a collection of flying knife blades. With a high-pitched scream, it flashed past the roadside picnic area where Voss and his party had paused to eat.

They were hidden by a screen of trees from the shuttle as it followed the road south. But had the machine arrived even ten minutes earlier, the group would have been caught flat-footed out on the highway. The timing was a piece of good luck—and a reminder that the stinks were still very much in charge.

On the third day the group arrived on the outskirts of Russellville, where they faced an important decision. Should they stay on Route 7? And cut through the devastated city? Or circle around it in hopes of avoiding whatever might be lurking in the ruins?

Kawecki favored the second option. And having made the long, dangerous trek to New York and back, Voss knew the soldier was correct. Cities, or the remains of them, were typically infected with Leapers, Grims, and worse. Or, if the stinks weren't in residence, then some very nasty humans probably were.

But Voss was very conscious of the time that a detour would consume and the need to restart vaccine production as quickly as possible. So as commander-in-chief he made the decision to camp the night, depart just before dawn, and put the city of Russellville behind them as quickly as possible.

They spent the night in what had been a power plant. A careful search of the building turned up a room with more than a dozen pods in it. Or what *had* been pods, since the Grims or Menials had already been "born," and had left their cocoons to rot. The stench was horrible, but fortunately the power plant was large enough that the group could camp some distance away.

They had a long and mostly sleepless night, illuminated by the full moon and the faint glow off to the east that signaled the presence of a Chimeran base. At first the city was quiet, but it wasn't long before a mournful howl was heard, and answered from miles away. Voss was on the roof at the time and felt a chill run down his spine.

"What the hell was *that*?" the soldier standing next to him wanted to know. He'd seen a variety of Chimera, but the long, drawn-out cry was new to him.

"That was a Howler," Voss answered grimly. "Or, to be more accurate, *two* Howlers. If you haven't run into one of them, they're big, about the size of a lion, and fast. But that isn't the worst of it. Once they pick up your scent they'll follow it anywhere."

The soldier, a kid named Hostler, was armed with a Bellock grenade launcher. It was pointed up at the night sky. His teeth were white in the moonlight. "Maybe so, sir! But if them Howlers come after us I have the answer right here."

Voss recognized the bravado for what it was, and was about to say something cautionary, when he was distracted by the distant *pop, pop, pop* of gunfire. Chimera hunting humans? Humans defending themselves? Or humans fighting humans? Anything was possible.

A necklace of five Patrol Drones sped by the building about an hour later, seemingly intent on an errand of some sort, as their lights slid down the street. But to Voss's relief the humans remained undiscovered.

After what seemed like an eternity the first hint of dawn appeared in the east and, having already broken camp an hour earlier, the presidential party filed out onto the street. They were too heavily burdened to run, but Kawecki insisted on a fast walk.

Malikov, Aklin, Shaw, and the rest of them had no complaints, however. They knew how important it was to put the city behind them as quickly as possible. Route 7 was thick with wrecks. That forced the party to thread their way through the maze, constantly on the lookout for a variety of potential threats.

Perhaps it was the early hour, or maybe it was dumb luck, but for whatever reason, Voss and the rest of the group were able to successively make their way through the downtown area and onto the stretch of road called South Arkansas Avenue.

Then it was time to cross the Arkansas River to the town of Dardanelle. The bridge had been hit from above and there wasn't much left of it. But although it would have been impossible to drive a car across the bridge, a couple of remaining beams offered a precarious path over the river. At one point Voss paused to look down, saw that at least half a dozen Furies were patrolling the water below, and knew that a fall would mean certain death.

The others recognized the danger as well and were careful to maintain their balance as they completed the crossing and followed Route 7 through Dardanelle's empty streets. Having reached the town undetected, Voss felt a tremendous sense of relief. The decision to cut through Russellville had paid off.

So as the group left the south end of Dardanelle for the relatively open countryside beyond, the President was in good spirits. But that changed when the party came across a convoy of shot-up Army trucks, a burned-out half-track, and a cluster of improvised crosses. And the farther they went, the worse the carnage became.

As the group topped a hill, a vast field of bones appeared. Thousands upon thousands of bones, some lying on the surface, the rest partially protruding from the dirt as if trying to bury themselves.

Were they human? Yes, they were, Voss concluded, as he and his companions made their way down into the dip beyond. And Chimeran? Yes, judging from the six-eyed skull that stared at him from a few yards away, and the enormous Titan-sized thigh bone sticking up out of the soil.

And there were machines, too. Or what had been machines. Their metal skeletons stood here and there like pieces of abstract sculpture, each carcass marking a moment in what must have been a desperate battle. As Voss followed Kawecki around the remains of a Jeep, he could see a downed VTOL that half blocked the highway. It was riddled with holes and one engine was missing. In the cockpit was a picture of a pretty blonde just below the cockpit, marked with the name "Vera."

Off to the left, a burned-out tank could be seen with its cannon pointed impotently at the sky. And a couple of hundred yards down the road they came across the shattered remnants of a Chimeran Stalker. One of its four legs had been blown off and it lay slumped to one side.

Had that been the totality of the evidence, Voss might have been able to convince himself that the battle had been a draw. But the truth lay up ahead. That was where the burned-out remains of a Protection Camp could be seen. And there, lying like the remains of a huge tree, were three sections of what had been a heavily armed defense column.

It looked as if the tower had been sheared off about fifty feet above the ground, then fallen across a section of the camp it was supposed to protect, and shattered into three pieces. It was possible that the stinks had a ground weapon capable of such a thing, but Voss was inclined to believe that the column had been attacked from orbit. Aklin was standing next to him. Her face was pale and a tear was trickling down her left cheek. "They fought! They fought hard."

"Yes," Voss replied soberly. "Now it's our turn. Come on. I want to clear the battlefield before sundown."

But it wasn't to be. There was no straight path through the maze, and the battlefield occupied at least five square miles of wreck-strewn land. As the sun dropped into the west, the group had to either make camp or travel during the hours of darkness. Something that both Voss and Kawecki opposed.

It wasn't sufficient to simply make camp, however. Not in the open. The prudent thing to do was to find a spot that could be fortified in a short period of time, using the minimum amount of effort. Kawecki considered a number of different possibilities before eventually settling on a rise crowned by the remains of a small house. It appeared as if the structure had been hit by an artillery shell and burned. Subsequent to that a tank or a Stalker had flattened what remained of the dwelling, scattering scorched lumber all around.

The added elevation, and the presence of a well and a nearly intact stone foundation, made for a good start. But to make the camp even more secure, Kawecki ordered his men to create a 360-degree free-fire zone by clearing away any piece of debris large enough for a stink to hide behind.

Then the soldiers were given orders to prepare firing positions at regular intervals around the perimeter. Finally, once the work was done, they posted sentries and then gathered around small fires. Any blaze could attract the wrong sort of attention, but Kawecki thought that the practical as well as psychological benefits were worth the risk, and Voss agreed.

So it wasn't long before people were getting water from the squeaky hand pump, heating rations over one of three fires, and preparing for bed. It was dark by then, and the stars were out, as Voss made the rounds with a mug of coffee clutched in his hand. The idea was to keep people's spirits up, give them a chance to gripe if they wanted to, and get to know them better.

That was what he had in mind as he sat down next to Monica Shaw and asked how she was doing. It was something he had been meaning to do for days. Everybody knew what she had done, so the technician had been something of a pariah, and she looked surprised when Voss spoke to her.

"Okay, I guess," she said dispiritedly.

"Good," Voss said, as he took a sip of the lukewarm brew. "So tell me about this Judge Ramsey person. How did you come to know him? And how did you wind up the way you did?"

Shaw shrugged. "My husband and I were refugees. Looking for a place to live. We left our home in Kansas City, and were headed for Tulsa, when a bunch of men who called themselves regulators captured us. Then, along with some other folks, we were taken to a railroad tunnel near Haven, Oklahoma. That's where Ramsey's factory is—and where he lives."

"Factory?"

Shaw nodded. "The judge manufactures ammunition, which as he likes to put it, 'is like making money.' We were invited to work in the factory in return for food, medical care, and a twelve-by-sixteen-foot room next to the track."

Voss finished his coffee with a single swallow. "Did you accept?"

Shaw stared into the fire next to them. "There wasn't any choice. You either agree or the regulators take you five miles away and leave you without anything other than the clothes on your back. And we have a daughter. Her name is Amy and she's three."

Voss nodded. "That isn't much of a choice. So, how did you wind up in Arkansas working for us?"

"The judge called me into his office one day," Shaw said dully. "He told me that somebody was trying to start a fake government down in Arkansas—and that I was to go there and become part of it."

"And you agreed?"

Shaw looked up from the flames. Her eyes were huge and her chin trembled. "The judge said Roger—that's my husband—and Amy were to stay behind. I knew what that meant. So I agreed."

"He said it was a 'fake' government?"

"Yes," Shaw replied. "Not that it matters, since he wants to run everything himself."

Voss was silent for a moment. "I can't say I approve of the choice you made, but I certainly understand it. And I'm glad you changed your mind."

He was about to ask Shaw about the shipment of Hale vaccine, and what Ramsey planned to do with it, when he heard a long, drawn-out howl. He heard another, and then another, until a chorus of spine-chilling cries came from all points of the compass. Voss rose, went over to where his gear was laid out, and put his mug down. Then, with both the Rossmore and a bandolier of shotgun shells in hand, he went to see Kawecki. The soldier was on his feet, holding a Bullseye Mark III pointed up at the sky. Orders had been given and soldiers were rushing to man their various positions.

"So, what do you think?"

"I think we're in a heap of trouble, Mr. President. There must be fifteen or twenty Howlers out there."

"Yeah! Why so many, I wonder?"

Kawecki was silent for a moment. "I figure it's the bones, sir. Maybe the Howlers are hungry. If so there's plenty of marrow in those bones."

The comment was punctuated by a prolonged howl. The noise was not only closer, but soon echoed by other Howlers, who were clearly closing in on the encampment.

"I wish we had more shotguns," Voss said, as he pumped a shell into the Rossmore's chamber.

Kawecki, who was well aware of the manner in which Howlers could absorb bullets and other projectiles, nodded. "I suggest that we make the rounds, Mr. President. You go left and I'll go right. Please remind those with shotguns to hold their fire until the beasts are in close. We have a Splicer, a Bellock, and a Wraith. We'll use those to keep the Howlers at a distance."

The men split up, and had just started to circle the defensive wall, when a five-hundred-pound Howler came rushing out of the surrounding darkness. Hostler opened up on it with the Bellock, but he missed, and by the time the explosive round went off, the stink was already in the air. It landed on Shaw, bore her to the ground, and ripped her throat out.

Then Voss was there, firing into the monster with the Rossmore, and killing it with three loads of double-ought buck. But more Howlers were galloping towards the compound by then. Some tumbled end-for-end as tracers from the Wraith minigun found them, or a Splicer blade ripped through their muscular bodies.

Yet others seemed unaffected by a hail of Bullseye projectiles, rounds from M4A2 carbines, and lighter backup weapons. Then as a flare soared into the air, and went off with a gentle pop, the humans got their first look at the army of Howlers bounding towards them, and one of the scientists began to scream. Malikov ordered the man to shut up and was there to blast a stink as it soared in over the wall. It landed on a fire, produced an explosion of sparks, and lay in a smoking heap.

Unable to keep the monsters at a distance, the humans found themselves trapped in a horrible melee. Three stinks were inside the defensive wall by then. Two soldiers and a technician went down. Voss swore as his Rossmore clicked empty. There wasn't enough time to reload as one of the beasts turned towards him and charged.

The Magnum came out of the shoulder holster smoothly enough, but Voss wasn't sure if he could bring the heavy revolver to bear in time, as the Howler launched itself into the air. So he fired a second too soon and knew the bullet had gone wide. Then he pulled the trigger again, saw the hit, and barely had time to activate the secondary fire function as a quarter-ton of Chimera slammed into him.

Voss was falling backwards as the large-caliber bullet exploded deep inside the Howler's chest, and blew chunks of bloody meat in every direction. But the crushing impact of the Chimera's body drove Voss to the ground and forced all the air out of his lungs. And that's where he was, gasping for breath, when Kawecki and one of his men arrived to roll the corpse off him.

"It's over," Kawecki said, as he pulled the President to his feet. "I think so, anyway."

Voss was bent over with his hands on his knees. He felt like he was going to puke. "How many?"

"Four dead, counting Shaw. Two or three wounded."

"Shit."

"Yeah."

"And Cassie?"

Aklin appeared out of the gloom. "I'm fine, but you look like hell. Come on! Let's see if we can get some of that blood off you."

Kawecki watched the President walk away. "We could do worse," he said to himself. "Much worse."

The private standing next to him frowned. "Sir?"

Kawecki looked at him. "What the hell are you doing here? Get Perkins and drag the stinks out of here. What do you think this is? A frigging picnic?"

The private nodded. "Yes, sir! I mean, no, sir." *Officers. Who could understand them?* There was no answer, nor did he expect one, because some things simply are.

CHAPTER TEN
BE CAREFUL WHAT YOU ASK FOR

Tuesday, November 3, 1953
South of Tank Town

Capelli had been crucified. The cross consisted of a post from which the U.S. Route 81 sign had been removed—and a length of two-by-four scrounged from a nearby barn.

It was a little past noon. That's what Capelli figured anyway, as the sun inched across the cloudless sky, and his shadow swung towards the east. His arms were tied to the crosspiece and about five feet of clothesline had been wrapped around both the upright and his legs.

Capelli had been there for hours by that time and he was cold. *Very* cold. Eventually, assuming that this day passed as the last two had, Bam-Bam and Inkskin would arrive with some hot soup.

Unless a group of Hybrids happened along, that is. Then, if there were more stinks than the circus performers could handle, the Chimera would be allowed to kill him. But if there were only two or three Chimera, Alfonso would pop up and stun one of the 'brids with a bolt from his crossbow. Meanwhile, Bam-Bam and Inkskin would cut the rest of the stinks down.

Once they had captured a replacement for El Diablo the circus would be back in business. And, according to Inkskin, Capelli was already slated to fight the new Hybrid. Without a knife.

Capelli attempted to generate some body heat by flexing his muscles. The result was a little bit of warmth. It was a small victory, but it made him feel better nevertheless. The afternoon wore on.

It was mid-afternoon by the time Alfonso, Bam-Bam, and Inkskin emerged from their various hiding spots and wandered out onto the two-lane highway. There hadn't been any traffic, Chimeran or otherwise, which meant the effort to capture a stink would resume the following morning. Unless Ringmaster Jack decided to pull up stakes and go looking for another site, that is.

All three of the circus performers were carrying canteens and blankets in addition to their weapons, and Capelli figured that at least a couple of them had been napping. The clown's makeup was badly smudged, which made him look even more sinister than usual. "What a waste of time," Bam-Bam complained, as he loosened a knot. "You couldn't draw flies, much less a Chimera."

There was no point in answering, and Capelli didn't as loops of rope fell away. His arms were next, and as Capelli lowered them, Inkskin was there to reattach his collar. Except that as the tattooed man opened the device, and was about to clamp it in place, a high-velocity bullet blew the top of his head off. The report was like an afterthought.

Capelli felt something warm wash across his face as all of the strength went out of Inkskin's body and he collapsed. There was a momentary clatter as both the collar and the guard's weapon hit the pavement.

And then Capelli's training kicked in. He was already in motion, sprinting for the side of the road, when a slug snatched Bam-Bam off his feet. With a thump, he landed facedown on the white line.

By then Capelli was in the ditch and trying to figure out what was happening. Two bullets—two kills. A pro, then. Or a talented amateur. But why? And more importantly, *who*? Not the stinks, because they would have shot him. Or, failing that, would be surging out onto the highway.

Capelli heard the distinctive sound of a Marksman firing a three-round burst. *His* Marksman. Which meant Alfonso was firing back. *The rotten sonofabitch.* And there was Master Jack to consider, not to mention Leena, who could use a weapon when called upon to do so. What were *they* up to?

Capelli raised his head for a second, spotted the Bullseye Bam-Bam had been carrying, and wondered if he could make it. The weapon was a good fifteen feet away—and there was the return trip to consider. Say ten seconds out, five on the scene, and ten back. Twenty-five in all. Plenty of time for the mysterious marksman or Alfonso to shoot him. Except they were focused on each other. A notion that gained credence as another shot rang out. Capelli got up, scrambled onto the highway, and made a beeline for the weapon.

Susan felt a sudden stab of fear, and rolled away, as a bullet nicked the top surface of her right shoulder. It didn't hurt. So chances were that the projectile hadn't broken the skin. But the return fire was completely unexpected. Yes, there was a third man stationed next to the road, but he was armed with a crossbow. *And* a rifle, as it turned out. Something she had missed.

That was bad. But what made matters worse was the fact that the bastard was a very good shot. As good as *she* was? Yes, Susan thought that was possible. She elbowed her way down off a slight rise, and snaked towards the pile of rocks where her pack was hidden. A farmer had painstakingly removed the stones from his field and she was grateful.

No sooner was she behind the pile of rocks when a

bullet spanged off the rock in front of her. Had the shot been an honest-to-God attempt to nail her? Or was the projectile supposed to freeze her place? Giving the third man an opportunity to reposition himself?

Suddenly Susan regretted the impulse that caused her to follow both the circus and the man with the SRPA tattoo on his back. He was free though, and that was a good thing, or would be so long as she managed to survive.

Susan was kneeling behind the pile of stones with two inches of the Fareye's long, slender barrel poking out through a gap. A really good sniper could put a bullet through the hole. Hell, she had met one Freedom First operative who could have shot her through the telescopic sight, but he was dead. Not from a sniper but a massive heart attack.

As Susan watched a light breeze play across the grass, she noticed a spot where the feathery stems were leaning in the wrong direction. She made a tiny allowance for the breeze and squeezed. The rifle butt nudged her shoulder, and as the bullet sped through the air, it broke the sound barrier.

The wagon and the humans who had to pull it were hidden inside a barn that was located two hundred yards off the highway. And that's where Ringmaster Jack, Leena, and her daughter were. Having heard the gunshots, they knew something was amiss. Otherwise Alfonso, Bam-Bam, and Inkskin would have returned by then.

So Jack was faced with a dilemma. Should he venture out in order to provide his employees with some fire support, or remain in the barn and guard the donkeys? They were lined up against the south wall staring at him. He frowned. "What the hell are *you* looking at? Keep your eyes on the floor."

"They aren't looking at you. They're looking at *me*."

The voice came from behind him. And as Jack turned, he saw a man silhouetted in the side door and felt a gentle nudge. A tag! The Ringmaster knew what that meant and shouted, "No!"

But the projectiles were already on the way. They sparkled like jewels, swarmed the Ringmaster like angry bees, and tore into him. His corpulent body shuddered as if afflicted by some terrible disease, wavered uncertainly, and slumped to the ground.

"Capelli!" the man called Bar shouted. "The hayloft!"

Capelli brought the Bullseye up and took a step sideways as Leena fired her pistol. The bullet kicked up dirt just beyond where he'd been standing.

It was relatively dark up in the loft, so Capelli couldn't see his assailant, but he had a pretty good idea of who it was. The same rotten bitch who'd suckered him into the trap weeks before. As he pulled the trigger and held it back, a dozen beams of sunlight appeared as projectiles punched holes in the wooden floor and the roof beyond. Leena uttered a cry, took two uncertain steps, and toppled forward.

Her body hit the dirt with a thump and threw a cloud of dust into the air. It was still settling as Capelli hurried up the ladder and onto the platform above. That was where he found the little girl. She was dead, having been hit by at least two projectiles, and Capelli swore softly. That hadn't been his intention. Far from it. But there was nothing he could do. She, like so many before her, had been in the wrong place at the wrong time.

His captors had been sleeping in the loft, which meant their belongings were spread about, an opportunity too good to pass up. Capelli took a moment to select a good pack and spent the next ten minutes filling it with carefully chosen items. He also appropriated Leena's Colt

Commander and took an adjustable shoulder holster from her sleeping bag.

Then, as Capelli went through Master Jack's belongings, he came across what he recognized as Locke's money belt. It felt lighter than before but still held a small fortune. So he buckled it around his waist before returning to the ground.

The prisoners yelled at him, rattling their chains, and trying to break free from the tractor to which they were tethered. Capelli raised a hand as he stood before them. "Listen up."

The noise stopped and they stared at him. "I've got good news for you. As soon as I finish collecting the things I need, you'll be freed. And since there's a limit to how much I can carry, there will be plenty of stuff left for you. How you divide it, and what you do next, is up to you. So please take it easy and I'll turn you loose shortly."

The prisoners *didn't* take it easy. Some of them shouted demands and others pleaded with him as Capelli took what he wanted from the wagon. Once Capelli was fully equipped, he retrieved the key from Master Jack's vest pocket. It was slippery with blood.

Capelli shouldered his pack and checked to make sure that the Bullseye was full up before going over to turn the donkeys loose. They grew very quiet, their eyes following his every move, as the big padlock fell free and landed in the dirt.

Capelli was backing away by then—with the assault rifle raised. "I'll leave it to you to find the key to those collars. Bam-Bam and Inkskin are on the highway. That's where I would start if I were you."

Because the prisoners were hooked to the master chain, and Capelli was armed, they couldn't prevent him from leaving. Bar said, "Thanks," but the rest were yelling insults as Capelli paused to confiscate Jack's Bullseye before backing out through the door.

Once outside, Capelli paused to check his surroundings. Where was the mysterious sniper? And more important yet, where was Alfonso? Especially given all of the gunfire. That seemed to suggest that Alfonso was wounded or dead.

But Alfonso was a cagey bastard, and a crack shot, so he couldn't take anything for granted. Capelli crossed the open area between the barn and the highway in a series of short dashes and flopped onto his belly after each sprint. But even as the prisoners exited the barn and shuffled his way, no one shot at him.

The scene on the highway was just as Capelli had left it, with two bodies sprawled on the concrete. As he eyed the field to the east, he felt a strange crawling sensation, and wondered if he was under surveillance. Was the sniper there? Watching him? Yes, that was a distinct possibility.

Capelli turned and saw that the donkeys were only a hundred feet away and closing fast. That was when he realized that he would have to collect Inkskin's Bullseye or run the risk that one of the prisoners would use it against him. Having scooped the weapon up, he lugged all three assault weapons through the ditch and into the field beyond. Then, as soon as he thought it was safe to do so, he removed the magazines from two of the Bullseyes and left the weapons behind.

Capelli had seen the bullet take the top off Bam-Bam's head, so he had a pretty good idea of where the shooter must have been hiding. He began to walk in that general direction, but he hadn't traveled more than twenty feet when he ran into Alfonso's body.

The circus performer was lying facedown, and judging from the messy exit wound, had been shot in the forehead. Capelli's Marksman rifle lay in front of the body. After slinging the Bullseye over his shoulder, he bent to pick it up. Once he'd straightened, he saw that a woman was standing thirty feet away.

She was tall. Maybe five-eight or so. A gentle breeze ruffled her light brown hair. She had green eyes, a high forehead, and a spray of freckles across her nose. "You have blood on your face."

Capelli reached up, felt the crusty stuff, and remembered the way the top of Bam-Bam's head had flown off. "Yeah, I guess I do."

"That's a nice weapon."

"Yes," Capelli replied. "It was mine before it was his."

"Now it's yours once again."

"Thanks to you."

The woman smiled bleakly. "You're welcome. You took care of the rest?"

"Yes."

"And the prisoners?"

"They're free by now. Why did you do it?"

The woman shrugged. "I saw the fight in Tank Town. My brother had a tattoo identical to yours. There were a whole lot of things we disagreed on. But he was a brave man. So I freed you for him."

"Your brother was a member of SRPA? What was his name? Maybe I knew him."

"Hale," the woman answered. "My brother's name was Nathan Hale. My name is Susan Farley. Mom and dad adopted Nathan after his parents died."

Sardonic laughter flooded Capelli's mind. *Surprise!* the voice said. *My sister saved your life. How weird is that? Are you going to tell her?*

"I knew him," Capelli admitted. "More than that, I reported to him. And you're correct. He was a very brave man."

That's all? the voice wanted to know. *Come on, Capelli. Tell her what you did. Maybe she'll shoot you. Lord knows you deserve it.*

The light had started to fade. "Which way are you

headed?" Capelli inquired. The words sounded awkward. Like those of a schoolboy hoping to escort a girl home.

Susan smiled. "Was that an invitation?"

"Yes," Capelli answered honestly. "It was. But I won't try anything. I promise."

"I'll shoot you if you do," Susan replied. "But I'd like to hear about my brother. If you don't mind talking about him, that is."

The last thing Capelli wanted to do was talk about Hale. But he didn't want to part company with Susan Farley, either. "No, I don't mind. Are you ready to go?"

"I will be as soon as I get my pack," Susan answered.

Rather than return to the highway, and a possible confrontation with the newly freed prisoners, the twosome stuck to the fields. Half an hour later they entered a rocky depression where an overhang offered protection from above and a ring of fire-blackened stones marked the site of a previous fire. "So, what do you think?" Susan inquired.

Capelli raised a hand. Had there been a noise? The sound of a twig snapping? The answer came in the form of a joyous bark, followed by a blur, as a large dog bowled Capelli over. "Don't shoot!" he yelled, as Rowdy licked his face. "He's friendly! Most of the time, anyway."

"I've seen him before," Susan said, as Capelli struggled to his feet. "He was roaming the area when I caught up with the circus. What kind of dog is he anyway?"

"I'm not entirely sure," Capelli said, as he gave Rowdy a pat. "But there's some Rhodesian ridgeback in him. Or so I've been told. It's good to see him. I thought he was dead."

It was nearly dark by then, so Susan produced a flashlight. The beam played over the campsite. "So as I was saying! Does this look okay to you?"

"It's fine," Capelli said. "Let's perform a quick check to make sure there aren't any pods in the area."

Susan agreed, and thirty minutes later they had a fire going, and were cooking a communal meal. The warmth felt good. "So," Capelli said, in hopes of delaying the Hale conversation for as long as possible. "How did you wind up in the audience watching a Steelhead beat the crap out of me?"

"The Steelhead wound up dead, as I recall it," Susan observed dryly.

Capelli served the food, and as they began to eat, Susan told him about the attack on her parents' home, the dangerous trip through stink-held territory, and how she had been recruited by Freedom First. An association that led to a failed assassination attempt, prison time, and forced labor in the Lucky Buckle Mine. "So I broke out," she concluded, "traveled east, and wound up in Tank Town."

Capelli sensed there was more to the story. A lot more. But he figured she would share the details when and if she felt like it. "You're lucky to be alive," he observed. "Although skill clearly had a lot to do with it."

The firelight illuminated Susan's face from below. She shrugged. "Country girls know how to survive. Enough about my adventures. Tell me about the Sentinels—and my brother."

Yeah, the voice said. *Tell Susan about me.*

Capelli stared into the flames. "You know he's dead."

"Yes," Susan said soberly. "That's what I figured. But I never received anything official."

"That's because the Sentinels were top secret," Capelli explained, "and all of us were listed as KIA. Then the government collapsed and millions of people were buried in unmarked graves. Or not buried at all."

Susan blew steam off her mug of tea. "How did Nathan die?"

Capelli tried to meet her eyes but couldn't. "Your brother was infected while fighting in England. The virus should have taken over his body, should have turned him into a Chimera, but for some reason it didn't. Not right away.

"Then a scientist named Malikov injected experimental subjects with the Chimeran virus as part of Project Abraham. Later on he developed an inhibitor treatment to keep the virus under control. All of the Sentinel troopers received it, including your brother, but there were signs that he was beginning to change in spite of the injections. And, as the fighting grew even more intense, he refused treatment in order to battle the stinks."

Capelli's words were followed by a moment of silence as tears began to roll down Susan's cheeks. "What are you saying? That my brother turned into a Chimera?"

Capelli forced his eyes to make contact with hers. "No. He was *beginning* to change. I thought so, anyway. And if he had, the entire team would have been in danger. So I shot him."

There was an audible gasp as Susan took a deep breath. "You-you shot my brother?"

"Yes," Capelli said woodenly. "I thought it was my duty to do so. Some people agreed with me. But most of them didn't. So I was thrown out of the Sentinels—and I've been wandering around the badlands ever since."

Susan's eyes narrowed as she wiped the tears away with the back of her left hand. Suddenly Capelli found himself looking down the barrel of a .22 pistol. Her voice was matter-of-fact. "I should shoot you."

Capelli nodded. "That would make sense. Sometimes I think I should shoot myself."

Ten long seconds dragged by. Suddenly the pistol disappeared under her jacket. Capelli's eyebrows rose. "You aren't going to shoot me?"

"Not tonight."

"And tomorrow?"

"Possibly. It's too early to say."

"Okay, then! Would you like some more tea?"

"Yes, please."

The fire crackled, their shadows loomed against the cliff, and Rowdy yawned. He was content.

When Capelli awoke it was to a cold, gray morning. A front had moved into the area overnight, and judging from the look of the pewter-gray sky, it was going to rain. But that was okay with Capelli, because after weeks of imprisonment he was free! And thanks to Rowdy's presence he'd been able to sleep well.

So Capelli was in a good mood until he rolled out of the sack to discover that Susan had left. It wasn't surprising. Not after what he'd done to her brother. But, unlikely though such a scenario was, he'd been hoping that she would manage to forgive him.

Oddly enough, the voice tried to console him. *Look at it this way, Capelli! She could have shot you. The fact that she didn't is forgiveness of a sort.*

He spent the next half-hour brushing his teeth, taking a chilly sponge bath, and starting a fire. The water was boiling, and Capelli was about to pour some oatmeal into it, when Rowdy bounded into camp, his tail a-wagging.

"Is that hot water for me?"

Capelli's head came up. Susan was standing about ten feet away. "I took a look around," she announced. "The area is clear. For the moment at least."

So saying, Susan shrugged her pack off, put it down, and opened the flap. Two minutes later she was crouched on the other side of the fire, drinking tea.

Had she really been out looking around? Or was that a cover story? What about the possibility that Susan left, changed her mind, and doubled back? There was no way to know—and Capelli wasn't about to ask. "It looks like you have a new friend," he said with a nod towards Rowdy.

The dog was lying next to Susan, looking up at her with worshipful eyes. "He's a sweetheart," she said. "He reminds me of the dog I had back home. So where are we headed?"

Capelli felt a rising sense of hope. There had been no discussions, no negotiations, just the casual use of the word "we." Did that mean what he thought it did? That Susan had chosen to remain with him for a while? The possibility of that made him unexpectedly happy. But the situation was delicate, he could sense that, so he chose his words with care.

"I was on my way to Haven, Oklahoma, when the circus people captured me." Having told her that much, Capelli went on to share the rest of the story, including the deal with Locke, and the way the big man died. "So I can't take him to Haven," Capelli concluded. "But I can deliver *this*. He wanted his sister to have it. And, thanks to you, I was able to take it back."

Capelli removed the money belt from his open pack, went around the fire, and gave it to her. When Susan peeked into the pocket and saw the coins, she gave the gold back. She was impressed by Capelli's determination to deliver what he could easily have kept for himself—as well as his willingness to trust her. Maybe the decision to turn back hadn't been so stupid after all. Even if she should hate him. But Nathan was stubborn. Very stubborn. And, if he refused treatment, then Capelli might have been correct. Either way, he'd been honest about it—and that was worth a lot.

"And there's something else," Capelli said, as he

returned the belt to his pack. "Locke believed that Haven is special. A place where he could settle down. I'd like to find out if he was correct."

Their eyes met across the fire. Susan sipped her tea. "So would I."

Days passed. Then a week, as they circled the city of Wichita, and continued south. There had been sightings, and a run-in with some Grims, but the strategy had been successful. Now, after a long day of walking, the twosome had arrived at an airfield outside the small town of Wellington. It consisted of a three-story control tower, a single runway, and three hangars. Two were empty and a dusty Piper J-3 Cub occupied the third.

"So what do you think?" Susan inquired. "Should we camp here?"

"It looks deserted," Capelli answered. "But I saw some Leaper scat on the way in, and we'd be very exposed. What if they swarmed us?"

"How 'bout the tower?"

Capelli eyed the structure. The glassed-in control room would provide them with a good view of the surrounding area and make it easier to stay warm. But once inside the structure it would be impossible to leave if they were surrounded. Of course, perfect camping spots were nonexistent. "Let's find some water, top off the canteens, and go for it. We'll use Sterno for cooking."

The airport had its own water tower and the faucet outside the tiny terminal building was still functional. It wasn't long before the pair were up in the tower making themselves at home. They even brought Rowdy inside, closing the door behind him.

Capelli and Susan were used to each other by that time and went about their various chores with very little discussion. Because of the tower's height, and the flat country all around, they knew that even the least bit of light would be visible through the windows. So as the sun went down, the couple went to considerable lengths to minimize the use of flashlights as they cooked a simple dinner and got ready for bed. And it was then, just as they were about to turn in, that the Chimera began to arrive.

The invasion began with a roar as two fighters dropped out of the sky, skimmed the airfield, and soared upwards again. Capelli's first thought was that they had been spotted, and he was reaching for the Marksman, when Susan touched his arm. "Look!"

By kneeling in front of the window, with only the top of his head and eyes exposed, Capelli could look out over the airport with very little chance of being seen. And the sight that met his eyes was both amazing and frightening.

There were Drones. Dozens of them. All sweeping in from the north. The overlapping beams they projected lit the way for at least a hundred Hybrids. And he could see Stalkers bringing up the rear. Capelli was quite familiar with the big spider-like machines, which he knew to be the equivalent of human tanks. "This isn't about us," he concluded. "There are far too many of them. The stinks are on the move for some other reason."

And the prediction proved to be true as both the Drones and Hybrids passed the tower by. Then they divided themselves into smaller groups and spread out. "They're securing the airport," Susan observed. "With us inside."

Capelli was impressed by Susan's calm, no-nonsense manner. "Yeah! Look at the Stalkers. They're settling in for the night."

And it was true. As each machine came to a halt, Hybrids could be seen exiting the mechs. Most of them were heading towards the far side of the airstrip, but a few were wandering around. "It's just a matter of time before a stink comes up here," Susan observed.

"True," Capelli agreed. "And since there's no place other than the washroom to hide in, we'll have to kill it and do so quickly. So quickly that it doesn't have a chance to send a mental image to the Chimeran hive-mind. Then, if we're lucky, the rest of them won't notice."

Susan looked skeptical. "Really?"

"Hybrids are like ants," Capelli replied. "At this moment thousands of them are dying worldwide for a variety of reasons. Kill one and the rest won't notice unless they see it occur—or the hive-mind has reason to think that something unusual has taken place. That's when the you-know-what hits the fan."

Both of them ducked as a Patrol Drone paused outside and a beam of light played across the back wall. Then it was gone, and Capelli heaved a sigh of relief. "That was close."

Susan took a peek. "Uh-oh! Two stinks left the nearest Stalker and they're coming this way."

"Damn," Capelli said disgustedly. "We could handle one of them with a knife. Now we'll have to use a gun."

"True," Susan replied calmly, as she removed the Ruger from its shoulder holster. "But that doesn't mean we have to make noise. Here's a little something I purchased back in Tank Town."

Capelli watched as she removed a fat tube from one of her pockets and began to screw it onto the .22's barrel. "A silencer? Perfect. Let's hide in the washroom. Remember, it has to be quick."

The restroom was so small that Capelli had to stand on the toilet, and Rowdy was forced into a corner as Susan took up a position next to the door. The dog growled but stopped when Capelli ordered him to.

Susan stood with her pistol at the ready. She could

hear brief bursts of stink speech as the 'brids came up
the stairs. Then it was possible to smell the Chimera as
they entered the control room. The odor was reminiscent of rotting meat.

All of their gear had been pushed back into a corner.
But it wouldn't take the Chimera long to find it. So as
the Hybrids paused to look out through the windows,
Susan pushed the door open and stepped into the control room. She held the pistol with both hands.

The semiauto produced a soft *phut, phut, phut* sound
as Susan fired. The stink on the left fell like a rock as two
.22 slugs punched their way through the back of its skull.
The second 'brid started to turn. Susan pulled the trigger,
saw the Chimera's head jerk as a bullet hit it in the jaw,
and corrected her aim. The next bullet hit the Hybrid in
the left ear and penetrated its brain. The ugly-looking
monster was already dead and falling when Susan reflexively triggered another shot. It shattered the front
window and sent shards of glass tinkling onto the concrete below.

Rowdy growled and rushed out to investigate the dead
bodies. Capelli was right behind him.

"I broke a window," Susan said tightly. "Glass hit the
concrete below."

Capelli eyed the scene outside. There were no signs of
alarm. "This would be a great time to get the hell out
of here."

"It would," Susan agreed. "But *how*?"

"See the Stalker down below? The one these two arrived in? We'll drive it out of here."

Susan's eyebrows rose. "You are one crazy bastard."

Capelli grinned. "You got that right. Get your stuff—
and one more thing . . ."

"Yes?"

"I like the way you kill stinks."

Susan smiled. "I'll bet you say that to all the girls."

Capelli shook his head. "No, just you."

Ten minutes later they were packed and ready to go. Susan descended the spiral staircase first, her silenced pistol at the ready. Capelli was right behind her with Rowdy on an improvised leash. Then they were out the door and into the cool night air.

Capelli paused for a moment and scanned the immediate area. There were no stinks to be seen. So he led Rowdy and Susan around the corner and out towards the Stalker. The belly hatch was open and a narrow ladder extended downwards. "Shuck your pack and climb in," Capelli instructed. "I'll shove Rowdy up the ladder. There's a gun turret up above the cockpit. He can ride there. Be sure to tie him in. Then, once you're ready, I'll push the gear up."

Susan shrugged her pack off, climbed up into the machine, and gagged as the cockpit's fetid odor caught in the back of her throat. But there was no time to think about that as Capelli shoved the big dog up through the hatch. With a firm grip on Rowdy's leash, Susan guided him up a couple of steps into the gun turret. He made a whining noise but stopped as she scratched behind his ears. Once the animal was secured she hurried back down.

Capelli passed the packs up to her, and while she looked for a place to stow them, he entered the cockpit. "You'd better get that harness on," he suggested, dropping into the pilot's chair. "This thing is going to throw you around."

"So you've done this before?"

"Twice. Once in a captured unit that was used for training purposes—and once in the field when there was no other choice."

Capelli lifted a cover out of the way and thumbed a switch. Susan heard a loud whine, more than two dozen indicator lights came on, and the hull began to vibrate. He flipped a switch and she felt a violent jerk. "Sorry about that," Capelli said, as he took hold of the aircraft-style control stick. "I'm a bit rusty. Here we go."

The machine lurched from side to side and generated whine-thud sounds as four articulated legs carried it across the airstrip towards the access road on the far side of the airport. Susan was looking up at the rearview monitor. "None of them are following us."

"Good," Capelli replied. "That's what I was hoping for."

Ten minutes later they were approaching Route 81 when Capelli saw lights on the highway and realized that he was looking at a southbound convoy. Susan looked from the screen to Capelli. "What are we going to do?"

"We'll join them," Capelli said. "And hope for the best."

"Which is?"

"We get forty or fifty miles down the road and bail out."

"And if we can't?"

"Then it's been nice knowing you," Capelli said, as he glanced her way. "Are you sorry you came?"

"No."

Capelli reached over to hold her hand. "Neither am I."

CHAPTER ELEVEN
WHAT'S YOURS IS MINE

Friday, October 30, 1953
The Badlands

Having successfully attacked the federal base and split his forces into three groups for the 290-mile trip home, Judge George Ramsey and twenty-two of his regulators were making their way through a narrow river gorge when the Leapers attacked. The Chimera were roughly the size of dogs, but because of their long, pointy tails they bore a vague resemblance to scorpions.

One or two Leapers would have been no match for such a large party of humans. But hundreds of the creatures were pouring out of caves in the rocky slopes on both sides of the shallow river. More than that, they had the advantage of height, and many were able to leap onto their victims from above. Once they gripped the outrider's head with their forelegs, the monstrosities opened their jaws wide to expose needle-sharp fangs. That was the last thing some of the humans saw as they were dragged off their horses to die in the river.

The whole thing happened so quickly, and the stinks attacked with such ferocity, that Ramsey and his entire party would have been killed had it not been for drills held at regular intervals during the journey. Ramsey was mounted on a huge Clydesdale named Thunder. As the attack began, he jerked the horse's head around and made a grab for one of two sawed-off shotguns holstered to either side of his saddle. "Form a circle!" he shouted. "Protect the pack animals!"

Ramsey's voice was barely audible over the staccato roar of gunfire and the screams of panicked horses as their riders fired at the Chimera. Some of the stinks were blown apart, but there were plenty more, and they kept coming. Ramsey fired both barrels in quick succession. Each blast of double-ought buck struck one of the airborne monsters and produced an explosion of blood as Thunder trampled a squealing Leaper beneath his massive hooves.

Then it was time to holster the first weapon and draw the second. The first shot went wide as Thunder took an unexpected step to the right. But the second struck an already wounded Leaper full-on and blew half of its skull away.

Then Thunder was part of the defensive circle. Ramsey pulled the Clydesdale around and kneed the big animal into line. The pack mules, each of which was loaded with a portion of the loot taken from the federal facility, were milling around at the center of the formation. Some of the braying animals were tangled up by then and began to nip at each other. But none of the regulators had time to sort the mess out.

The river ran red with blood as Ramsey and the surviving members of his party fired hundreds of rounds. Projectiles chewed up both the Chimera and the surrounding landscape as each man blasted whatever was directly in front of him. Three of the horrors took a rider named Carter down. All four of them perished as a hail of projectiles chopped the surface of the river into a bloody froth.

The battle came to an end about a minute later as the last of the Leapers launched a suicidal charge and fell in successive waves. "God damn it to hell," Ramsey said as the firing finally stopped. "It seems like there's more of

the bastards every day. Hunter? There you are! Let's find
out how many casualties we have. And why didn't our
scouts warn us?"

"I don't know," the hard-faced outrider replied. "But
I got a feeling they were cut down without getting a shot
off. We'll find 'em upriver."

"That makes sense," Ramsey agreed darkly. "They
might hit us again. So let's keep our eyes peeled."

It took the better part of fifteen minutes to count heads,
treat the wounded, and get the pack train straightened
out. Unfortunately, one of the pack mules had been killed
and part of its cargo destroyed. Ramsey still had more
than four thousand doses of Hale vaccine left, however.
That was enough not only to supply all of his workers
but to protect lots of other people, too. All of whom
would be required to swear fealty to him.

But that was in the future. At the moment, Ramsey
had other matters to attend to.

"Tully is in a bad way," Hunter told him. "Doc took
a look but says he ain't gonna make it. Tully asked for
you."

Ramsey was reluctant to dismount. Because at 290
pounds that was a chore. But if Tully was dying, then it
was Ramsey's duty to speak with him.

Hunter accepted Thunder's reins as Ramsey swung a
meaty thigh up and over the Clydesdale's enormous hindquarters and managed to lower himself to the ground
without assistance. That was a personal victory of sorts.

One of the regulators was waiting to escort Ramsey
downstream to the spot where Tully was laid out on
a horse blanket with his saddle for a backrest. It was
soaked with blood, as was the pressure bandage wrapped
around his chest. Tully was a tough man and knew the
score. The outrider managed a smile as Ramsey knelt
next to him.

"Thanks for coming, Judge. It looks like this is the

end of the trail for me. Please make sure that my woman gets my pay and gear."

"I will," Ramsey promised. "Plus I'll tell Mr. Perkins to scrub whatever you and the missus owe to the company store."

"That's right kind of you," Tully managed. He coughed, and blood trickled down his chin. Doc Laferty was there to wipe it away. "There's one more thing," Tully added. "A favor, if you're willing."

"Which is?"

"You can't wait for me," Tully replied. "I know that. But don't leave me alive."

"I won't," Ramsey promised, as he struggled to his feet. "Where do you want it?"

"In the head."

Ramsey favored a British .455 Webley Break-Top revolver as his personal sidearm. He removed the weapon from the shoulder holster under his left arm and took careful aim. The report echoed back and forth between the canyon walls, sent a bird flapping into the air, and marked mile 231 of the long journey home.

Two days after the battle with the Leapers, Ramsey and his men cut through what had once been a ranch and arrived at the edge of a huge crater. It was at least a mile across and roughly 600 feet deep. The riders made their way up over the lip that surrounded the depression and then followed a circular path down to the wreck below.

No attempt had been made to hide the path—a decision that would have been fatal elsewhere. But Ramsey knew the crater and the wreckage that lay at the bottom of it to be unique. Nobody was quite sure what type of Chimeran spaceship was interred there, or how the American military had been able to bring the huge vessel down, only that it had.

And even though there were more than 300 humans living in the wreck, it had never been attacked. Was that simply a matter of good luck? Or did the ship register on the Chimeran sensors as an active installation? If so, that reflected the hive-mind's limitations. It could see everything its minions saw but had to process all of the incoming data itself. Some things got lost, were misinterpreted, or were assigned the wrong priority. And with no one to question the hive-mind's conclusions, such errors went uncorrected.

The party was welcomed by a pair of well-armed guards and allowed to enter the hull via a hole that had been cut through the side of the ship. The power plant was still online, although no one knew how long it would remain that way. So the air was warm and the lights were on.

The uppermost levels of the vessel were reserved for livestock, so the horses and mules were left there, as the mayor of Shipdown came up to greet Ramsey. Piers Olmey was a tall man who had a long face and insisted on wearing a frock coat.

The two of them had a long-standing relationship that dated back to the days when Ramsey had been a district judge and Olmey had been a prosecutor. They shared a stern, no-nonsense approach to law enforcement.

Having installed Olmey as mayor of Shipdown, Ramsey knew he would be able to count on the community's citizenry when it came to the challenges that lay ahead, and there would be plenty of them.

Because, if humans were to take their planet back, they were going to need a strong authoritarian government rather than a dithering democracy. And that was one of the reasons he had undertaken the long, grueling trip to the Arkansas National Forest: to kill the government that was taking root there before it could grow any larger.

Ramsey was ushered onto the only elevator that still worked and taken to the spacious quarters Olmey had assigned to himself. They were decorated with a variety of furnishings packed in from a Sears store located twenty-five miles away. Ramsey thought the juxtaposition of 1950s Americana and Chimeran tech was a bit off-putting, but that didn't stop him from tucking into a huge dinner comprising of steak, potatoes, and freshly baked pie.

The meal presented an excellent opportunity for Ramsey to tell his host about the Hale vaccine and the role it was going to play in making the American Empire a reality. Ramsey had a luxuriant mustache that drooped to either side of his mouth. He made use of a napkin to dab at it as he spoke. "Not only will the vaccine provide our people with additional protection, we'll be able to offer immunity to other communities, and bring them into the fold as well. Then, once we have enough people to form an effective army, we'll take this part of the country back."

Olmey nodded sagely. "The sooner the better. That's what I say."

Once the meal was over, it was time for the obligatory tour of the weapons factory that Olmey ran on Ramsey's behalf. The facility was located two levels down from the mayor's quarters. That made it necessary for the men and their bodyguards to board the central elevator and ride it down to L-6, where an obsequious foreman was waiting to escort the VIPs through a narrow passageway into the open space beyond.

Workstations had been set up all around the circular deck. As Olmey led Ramsey from station to station he provided a running commentary. "As you know, the Marksman was developed by humans based on Chimeran tech. We're taking that process further by developing a model that allows the user to tag his or her target. That required us to sacrifice the secondary mode of operation, of course, but the Drones are difficult to manufacture under these conditions, so we believe it's a positive tradeoff."

Olmey paused next to a bench where a gray-haired woman was bent over another weapon. She continued to work, but her hands had begun to tremble. "You may recognize this as an Army-issue XR-13 Bellock," Olmey said, apparently unaware of the way his presence was affecting the woman in front of him. "But as you can see, the original rotary magazine has been rechambered to fire twelve-gauge shotgun shells. Unlike the Rossmore, which has a capacity of eight rounds, what we're calling the XR-14 can accommodate *sixteen* shells, and that makes it ideal for close-in combat with Grims and Howlers. As for human opponents, well, you can imagine."

Ramsey nodded. "Excellent . . . Well done. Let me know when I can buy some."

What both men knew, but never discussed in front of others, was the underlying strategy that governed who made what. While Olmey's people manufactured weapons, Ramsey's were producing ammo for them, and neither group had access to a large supply of both. It was an arrangement calculated to keep malcontents from rising up and taking over either community. Plus both men employed informants, whose job was to provide early warning of any plot to remove them from power. The price of power was eternal vigilance.

After the tour was over, Ramsey was shown into the guest suite adjacent to Olmey's heavily guarded quarters, where he looked forward to a good night's sleep followed by an early-morning departure. He'd been absent from Tunnel-Through for far too long, and there was a great deal of work waiting to be done.

Once in bed, and comfortable for the first time in weeks, Ramsey fell asleep quickly. There were dreams. Lots of dreams. And all of them were good.

Tunnel-Through, Oklahoma

Except for the pools of light thrown down from the fixtures mounted high above, it was dark and gloomy inside the railway tunnel. Because of the mostly flat terrain, it was one of only two such structures in the state. And thanks to Judge Ramsey's foresight, the tunnel had been stocked with supplies and sealed off during the days leading up to the government's collapse. That included a train with a locomotive, a flatcar-mounted diesel generator, a string of tank cars loaded with fuel, and three passenger cars, the last of which housed Ramsey's office and private sleeping compartment.

Now, as the sound of the locomotive's horn echoed through the tunnel, Roger Shaw was filled with joy as he lifted his daughter Amy up and carried her out of the family's cubicle onto the west walkway. "Here we go, sweetie," he said. "We're going to see Mommy!"

Amy had a head full of curly brown hair and a slightly upturned nose, just like her mother's. "See Mommy, see Mommy!" the child chanted excitedly.

Father and daughter joined the steady stream of people who were headed south onto the track-spanning wooden platform located to the rear of the train. Ramsey and the final group of regulators had returned from Arkansas, and all sorts of rumors were circulating as Shaw followed the crowd to the assembly area. "The Chimera are going to leave the planet," one woman said.

"No," a man insisted. "I heard that they turned the entire city of Tulsa into a gigantic pod farm."

"That's bullshit," another worker proclaimed sourly. "Ramsey wants to run his mouth. And we have to listen. It ain't no more complicated than that."

Shaw secretly agreed, but was afraid to say anything, knowing that some of Ramsey's most vocal critics were informers. Men and women who would prime the conversational pump, get someone to agree with them, and turn the sucker in for a favor of some sort. And he couldn't afford to wind up on Ramsey's shit list, not so long as the bastard had Monica under his control, and there was Amy to look out for.

So all Shaw cared about was the fact that Ramsey had returned. Because if the judge was back, then Monica should be back, and he couldn't wait to see her. But as Shaw joined the crowd behind Ramsey's passenger car, and maneuvered his way up front, there was no sign of his wife on the riser where Hunter and the others were gathered.

So Shaw felt a bit uneasy as Ramsey emerged from the passenger car and stepped onto the platform. His toadies led the tepid applause. The judge was resplendent in a gray cowboy hat, snowy white shirt, and string tie. A black suit and a pair of gleaming boots completed the outfit. "Thank you!" Ramsey said, as if in response to genuine applause. "It feels good to be back in Tunnel-Through after a successful campaign. It's my pleasure to announce that our brave regulators were able to dig the pretenders out of the hole they were living in—and destroy the fake democracy they planned to impose on the American people."

The toadies clapped. So everyone including Shaw did likewise, and Ramsey beamed happily. "But that's not all," he continued. "Not only were the usurpers trying to seize control of our country, they had developed a vaccine to protect themselves against the Chimeran virus, and we brought more than four thousand doses home!"

This line didn't generate any applause, largely because Ramsey's toadies didn't understand what their leader was talking about. "Think about it, my friends," Ramsey continued. "Once vaccinated, a Spinner bite won't mean anything more to you than an accidental cut would. Clean the wound, cover it with a bandage, and you'll be ready to go. And, because you are members of this community, every one of you will receive a vaccination during the next five days."

Ramsey's announcement was greeted with a moment of silence, followed by genuine applause, as the citizens of Tunnel-Through realized how fortunate they were. Not Shaw, though, because Monica was still nowhere to be seen, and there was a growing abyss where the bottom of his stomach should have been.

The workers and their families were dismissed a couple of minutes later, but Shaw carried Amy up onto the riser, where he was able to intercept a man named Martin Lewis. "Excuse me, Mr. Lewis," Shaw said formally. "But I was given to understand that my wife Monica would return with Judge Ramsey. Is she here? And if so, could we see her, please?"

Lewis had been a rancher before the Chimera took over, and his face was still brown despite many months of living in the tunnel. A network of wrinkles radiated away from his beady eyes. They rearranged themselves as he frowned. "Shaw, isn't it?"

"Yes, sir."

"Wait here . . . I'll see what I can do." Lewis disappeared into Ramsey's passenger car, and five long minutes elapsed before he returned. Shaw tried to read the toady's weather-beaten face but couldn't. "Follow me," Lewis said. "The judge would like to speak with you."

Those were ominous words, because such a summons was rarely a good thing. "Where's Mommy?" Amy wanted to know, and Shaw kissed her forehead.

"I don't know, honey," Shaw said, as he followed Lewis into the richly appointed railroad car. "I hope we're going to find out."

Two men, both armed with pistols, stood to either side of the doorway that led into Ramsey's office. The judge was seated behind a large desk. It was covered by a green blotter and stacks of paper, each held in place by brass apothecary weights. Ramsey had removed his jacket by then, which meant the Webley was visible, as was his enormous paunch. Ramsey nodded as Shaw entered, but he neglected to get up, or offer his visitor a seat.

"I'm sorry to say that I have some bad news for you," Ramsey said, as he selected a cigar from the box at his elbow. "As you know, your wife agreed to carry out a very important task on my behalf. And things went well at first. But then, according to what a couple of witnesses told us just before we shot them, she warned the so-called President that we were about to attack. Her misguided act made no difference to the outcome. But our casualties were unnecessarily high as a result of your wife's treachery."

Ramsey paused to clip the end off the cigar, strike a kitchen match on the underside of his desk, and turn the enormous tube of tobacco over the flame. Then, once the cigar was drawing to his satisfaction, he resumed speaking. "A small group of people escaped the complex," Ramsey intoned, "and your wife may have been among them. But, given the overall situation, and the speed with which they had to depart, I believe it's safe to say that all of the worthless scum are dead by now. Do you have any questions?"

Shaw felt a terrible sense of sorrow. Somehow, deep inside, he knew the story was true. Monica was dead. But he felt a strange sense of pride as well. Because even though her decision to give warning ran counter to her best interests, not to mention her family's, the act had taken courage. A great deal of it. "No, Judge," he said stoically. "I don't have any questions."

"Good," Ramsey said, as he released a puff of smoke. "Because I have very little time to waste on either traitors or their families. I told your wife that if she betrayed me I would banish you and your daughter to the badlands. And that's exactly what I'm going to do. Lewis! Take them away."

Shaw felt as though he was part of a living nightmare as he and Amy were escorted through a maze of side tunnels—and from there to a hatch that opened onto a ravine. Then, without so much as a word, the steel door closed behind them. Shaw put his daughter down on the ground and looked around.

Next to the hatch was an exhaust port, through which Shaw could hear the distant rumble of a generator. There were no other sounds. The Chimera owned North America, sunset was no more than two hours away, and all they had was the clasp knife in his pocket and the clothes on their backs.

"Daddy, I'm hungry," Amy proclaimed. "And I'm cold, too."

Shaw wanted to cry and swear at the same time. But he couldn't. Not with Amy holding his hand. "Come on, honey," he said gently. "We need a place to hide."

CHAPTER TWELVE
WELCOME HOME

Thursday, November 12, 1953
Blackwell, Oklahoma

The darkness made it difficult for Capelli to see beyond the Stalker directly in front of them. But when it passed through a curve, he could just make out that the brightly lit convoy consisted of about fifty vehicles. Some were Stalkers like the machine he and Susan had stolen. But the rest was a hodgepodge of human cars, trucks, and two Greyhound buses. Sleet was falling and could be seen slanting through the beams that probed the road ahead.

Being an ex-soldier, Capelli was surprised by the fact that no attempt had been made to conceal the convoy. And as a citizen he was depressed by the fact that there was no need for the stinks to turn off their lights, because that meant there wasn't any organized opposition for the Chimera to worry about.

As for the convoy's purpose, that was a mystery, and would probably remain so. All that Capelli and Susan could do was to wait the situation out and look for an opportunity to exit the column. In the meantime they had the satisfaction of knowing that they were lurching along at twenty-five miles per hour. That didn't sound like much, but they were lucky to cover fifteen miles a day on foot. About two hours had passed by the time they saw a sign that read, "Blackwell, two miles."

Susan had a much-creased and somewhat grimy road map spread out in her lap. The glow from the instrument panel was sufficient to read by. "We don't want to go any farther than Blackwell," she said. "Not if we can help it. Haven is located about twenty miles to the east."

"Roger that," Capelli replied. "But if we leave the highway all by ourselves there's no telling how the stinks will react. They might let us go or they might come after us. We could fight them, of course—but we'd be badly outnumbered."

That fear turned out to be groundless, because as the outskirts of the city came into view the lead vehicles slowed and turned off the highway. Headlights washed across deserted buildings, and a pair of eyes glowed as a feral cat stared at them from an overgrown garden. Then a dozen Patrol Drones swooped in out of the night sky to escort the convoy into what a large sign proclaimed to be the Blackwell Zinc Smelter.

But in spite of the name, Capelli got the impression of a military base as the convoy snaked between brightly lit buildings and entered a parking lot that was already 25 percent full. A thin layer of sleet covered the vehicles. "This is where it gets interesting," Susan said tightly.

"Yeah, I'm going to park out along the edge of the lot somewhere and hope the stinks don't care. Then, once we're ready, we'll make a run for it."

"That makes sense," Susan agreed. "And Joe . . ."

Susan had never called him by his first name before and Capelli took note of it. "Yes?"

"It isn't for me to judge what you did. What's done is done. Do you understand what I mean?"

Their eyes met, and Capelli swallowed the lump in his throat. "Yes, I do. Thank you."

The lead vehicles were parking in orderly rows by then. So Capelli guided the Stalker out and around them in an effort to place the machine under a burned-out light.

"Watch the Drones," he instructed. "If somebody takes exception to what we're doing, they will react first."

But as Capelli brought the Stalker to a halt, the Drones formed what looked like a necklace and sailed away. "Perfect," Susan said. "Now let's get the hell out of here."

"My sentiments exactly," Capelli agreed as the engine spooled down.

It took the better part of ten minutes to unload both the dog and the packs. Capelli felt a rising sense of tension, because now that he was on the ground he could see that two Hybrids were on the tarmac about fifty yards away. And if the stinks came by for a visit, the poop was going to hit the fan. Rowdy growled but didn't bark as Capelli kept a firm grip on his leash.

Fortunately the Hybrids ambled off towards the west, which allowed the humans to turn in the other direction. And, because there was no perimeter to speak of, it was relatively easy to exit the base.

Thirty minutes later they cleared the eastern boundary of the city and followed a foot trail that paralleled the two-lane highway. Capelli figured the well-trod path was a recent development. Something both the Chimera and humans had created since the government's collapse.

Haven was twenty miles away, so Capelli calculated that a day and a half of travel would be required to reach the town. Having gone without sleep, and with only a few hours until dawn, Capelli and Susan were in need of some shut-eye.

So when they came across one of the local phone company's bunker-like switching stations, they gave the facility a quick once-over and made themselves at home. A heavy desk was sufficient to block the metal door, and they knew Rowdy would warn them if anyone came poking around.

The plan was to grab a quick meal and take a two-hour nap. But when Capelli awoke, light was streaming in through the building's slitlike windows and it was well past noon. He shivered as he put a pot of water over a Sterno can to boil, woke Susan, and went to brush his teeth in the tiny washroom. The face in the mirror was in need of a shave.

The threesome was on the move an hour later. It was a chilly day, and while they saw occasional signs of human activity, there were no Chimera to be seen. But the ever-present danger was there, and Capelli was careful to keep his head on a swivel as they crossed fields, cut through fences, and splashed across streams.

As they walked, they talked. About the past mostly, since they were still in the process of getting acquainted, but the future as well. And as Capelli listened to Susan he heard echoes of his own desires in her words. Like him, she wanted to settle down somewhere, be part of something good, and lead a normal life. Or what passed for a normal life in post-apocalyptic America. Children were never mentioned, but they were implied, and Capelli was surprised to discover that the possibility had some appeal.

But mostly he enjoyed being with her. Susan wasn't beautiful, not in the movie-star sense, but she was pretty and he liked to look at her. More than that he liked to hear the sound of her voice, and especially her laughter, which he sought ways to provoke. And judging from the small things she did for him, Capelli got the impression that she felt something, too.

So if it hadn't been for the ever-present threat of attack, the day would have been quite pleasant. Rowdy scouted ahead and they followed a path through a grove of nearly naked oaks. Their fallen leaves lay like a beautiful carpet on the ground and rustled underfoot.

Then, at about four in the afternoon, they spotted vultures circling in the distance. Big birds that were already fat from feasting on death and were circling their next meal. Against the lead-gray sky they looked like black crosses. "Something died," Susan commented. "Or is about to die."

"Yeah," Capelli agreed. "I guess we should take a look."

With a low whistle he brought Rowdy in. Then, with the dog trotting alongside them, Capelli and Susan made their way up a gentle slope towards the top of a hill. Instead of breaking the skyline, they dropped onto their bellies short of the summit and crawled the rest of the way.

After securing Rowdy to a sapling, Capelli elbowed his way to the crest of the hill where Susan was eyeing the area through the Fareye's telescopic sight. Capelli brought the Marksman around for the same purpose. The first thing he saw was an overgrown field. Beyond that was some rusty farm equipment, a sad-looking farmhouse, and a barn.

The birds were circling over the area in front of the house. That's where what looked like a little girl was crouched next to a dead body. Capelli was reminded of Leena lying out in the middle of the highway with her daughter nearby.

"See the little girl?" Susan inquired. "She needs help."

"It's a trap," Capelli said firmly. "Just like the one the circus people used to capture me. And there's rules six and eight to consider."

Susan turned to look at him. "Which are?"

"Mind your own business—and don't trust anyone."

Capelli saw the quizzical expression on her face. "What?" he asked defensively. "You disagree?"

"You would be dead if I believed in rule six."

Capelli thought about that. "Has anyone ever mentioned how obnoxious you are?"

Susan chuckled. "My brother mentioned it almost every day as we were growing up."

Capelli heard laughter echo inside his head. He hadn't told Susan about the voice and didn't plan to. *She's smarter than you are*, Hale said, *so get used to it*.

Capelli sighed. "Okay. I'll go down. At least I'll have someone to cover me."

"Count on it," Susan replied. "And be sure to circle around behind the barn. If there are people lying in wait you'll see them."

It was good advice. So good it was what Capelli would have done anyway. He was about to say as much when he saw the look in her eye. He'd been talking to the ex–farm girl for the last few hours. This was the *other* Susan. The one who had been trained to kill people and was very good at it. He bit the words off. "Roger that. I'll leave the Marksman and the pack here."

"Good idea. And take Rowdy."

Capelli nodded, put the rifle aside, and shrugged his way out of the pack. After he backed down the slope, he released the dog and headed north. The Bullseye was at the ready, and it felt good to be free of the pack.

The dirt road cut through the saddle between two hills and offered a natural crossing point. Capelli slipped through, eyed the area ahead, and made for the barn. The vultures continued to circle overhead. But except for them, and the rabbit that led Rowdy north, the farm was empty of life. Or so it seemed, anyway.

But Capelli wasn't satisfied until he checked the barn's interior, approached the house, and entered through the back door. The house had been looted, but there were no signs it was occupied. So where had the man and the little girl come from? That question was still on his mind as Capelli exited through the front door. What looked like a recent campfire was visible in front of the house. The body was still there, as was the little girl, who was wearing a coat that was much too large for her. She looked frightened.

"Don't be scared," Capelli said gruffly. "I won't hurt you. Is this your father?"

"Daddy's sick," the grubby-faced moppet explained. "He won't wake up."

Capelli knelt on the east side of the body so that if it came to sudden life he wouldn't block Susan's shot. Then he felt for a pulse. It was thready, and the man's breathing was shallow.

Capelli was no doctor, but he was an ex-soldier, and familiar with the symptoms of hypothermia. He looked up at the girl. "What's your name, honey?"

"Amy."

"Tell me something, Amy! Are you cold?"

The little girl shook her head. "Daddy gave me his jacket."

Susan arrived at that point. She was carrying both packs and the Marksman. "Who's your new friend?"

"This is Amy," Capelli answered. "And the man is her father. I think he's suffering from hypothermia. As far as I can tell, Amy and her dad don't have any gear. And she's wearing his jacket. Let's get him into my sleeping bag, start a fire, and pour some tea down his gullet."

It took twenty minutes to warm the man to the point where he could speak. He was wrapped in Capelli's sleeping bag with his back against Susan's pack as he told the story.

"My name is Shaw. Roger Shaw. Amy and I were thrown out of a community called Tunnel-Through. They left us with nothing more than my pocket knife and the clothes on our backs," he said.

"We spent the first night huddled in a hollow between some big boulders. I managed to start a fire the Boy Scout way, with a bow, a stick, and a fireboard. I knew the light could attract trouble, but we needed the heat, and it worked out okay.

"When the sun came up, we set out to find a place where we could do some scavenging and wound up here. The house was pretty well picked over. There weren't any clothes. But I found a can of peaches in the back of a cupboard, and was still searching the place, when two men arrived out front. They looked rough, and were well armed, so I figured we should hide.

"I knew they'd search the house and I was right," he continued. "As they came in the front door, we went out the back, and made straight for that truck."

The man was pointing towards the jumble of rusting farm machinery northwest of the house. There an old flatbed truck was sitting on blocks. Capelli nodded. "Then what?"

"Then we got in, closed the door, and got down on the floor." Shaw shrugged. "It was a good hiding spot. The men never came close. But rather than leave the way I hoped they would, the men set up camp. And as night fell it got colder. A lot colder. I gave Amy the peaches and juice a little bit at a time. That got her through.

"Eventually morning rolled around, and the sun came up, but I couldn't stop shivering. I began to feel dizzy, and was about to pass out, when the men finally left. I got out of the truck, stumbled over to where the camp-fire had been, and realized that I was going to need some firewood. So I was about to go find some when the lights went out. When I woke up you were here. Thank you, by the way—I'm very grateful."

Capelli stood and made a beeline for the truck. Rowdy went with him.

Shaw frowned. "Where's he going?"

Susan was sitting cross-legged, trying to comb the tangles out of Amy's dirty hair. "I'm not sure. But, if I had to guess, I'd say he's going over to check on rule six. Or is it rule seven? No, that's 'pee when you can.'"

Shaw, who was completely mystified, watched Capelli return.

"So," Susan said, "what did you conclude?"

Capelli held an empty peach can up for her to see. "I found this in the cab."

"So they can come with us?"

"Yeah," Capelli said evenly. "They can."

Haven, Oklahoma

The walk from the farmhouse to the outskirts of Haven was eerily quiet. It was open country, with occasional groves of trees, and lots of flat farmland. All of which appeared to be deserted. But Capelli knew that appearances can be deceiving as they entered the town. It looked as if a Chimeran hunter-killer team had taken a stroll through Haven and leveled most of it. "I saw a flash of light from the direction of that tower," Susan said. "Somebody's watching us."

Capelli looked, saw a three-story structure poking up out of the ruins, and nodded approvingly. "As they should."

"What do you think they'll do?"

"I don't know. If it was me, I'd let people stroll through. But if they began to poke around, or set up camp, I'd scare them off."

That made sense to Susan as the group made its way down what a sign proclaimed to be Grand Street. It wasn't so grand anymore. The Chimera had left a broad swath of destruction through the town and no effort had been made to repair the damage, which made sense.

One thing was strange, however. Or so it seemed to Susan, who had a sharp eye for details. There wasn't very much lumber lying around. Of course, it takes plenty of wood to shore up tunnels and keep them in good repair. So if the locals were living underground, then most of the available materials had been put to use somewhere under her feet. Is this the place? she wondered. The kind of community she was looking for? Maybe. It was too early to tell.

Grand Street delivered the group into the center of town, where they found themselves facing what was once a park. The tower they had seen earlier was off to the left. Shattered storefronts, piles of rubble, and wrecked vehicles surrounded the square, the exceptions being a library, which looked to be intact; a whitewashed church; and a partially damaged bank.

Shaw had caught up with them by then. Amy was perched on his shoulders. "Are you sure people live here?"

"I'm not sure of anything," Capelli responded. "But yeah! I think people are watching us. Let's see if I can flush them out."

Capelli took a dozen steps forward to ensure that he could be seen from the tower and all of the other structures around the square. The sky was blue and the afternoon air was still. He took a deep breath and shouted as loudly as he could, "I'm a runner—and I'm here to see Terri Locke! If Terri Locke is here, I would like to speak with her on behalf of her brother Alvin."

No response. Not even an echo. Or so it seemed until Rowdy began to bark and an elderly man appeared. He was wearing a knit hat and a blue overcoat, and he walked with the aid of a cane. Capelli took hold of

Rowdy's collar as the man drew near. "Hello! My name is Capelli. Joe Capelli. And you are?"

"Expendable," the man answered with a grin. "That's why they send me out to talk with people."

Capelli laughed. "Well, you have nothing to fear from us. I'm a runner and I have a package for Terri Locke."

The man nodded noncommittally as he turned to Susan and smiled. "Welcome to Haven, my dear. My name is Frank Potter."

Susan took the opportunity to introduce both herself and the Shaws. Amy was hiding behind her father but came out when Potter offered her a piece of peppermint candy.

Capelli watched with interest. Potter might describe himself as "expendable," but his blue eyes were extremely bright, and they never lingered anywhere for very long. Capelli had the feeling that in a matter of three or four minutes the entire party had been evaluated, inventoried, and categorized. Whatever happened next would depend on Potter's judgment.

And that was clearly the case. After a few minutes of seemingly idle chatter Potter turned to Capelli. "Let's go over to my office and discuss the matter further. Please leave your pack and weapons here."

So Capelli shrugged the pack off and gave the pistol, Marksman, and Bullseye to Susan for safekeeping. Then, with Potter at his side, he walked east towards the bank.

"My grandfather founded it," the old man explained, "and it has been in the family ever since. It has seen better days, though. Watch your head as you pass through the front door."

Capelli had to duck under a sagging support beam in order to follow Potter into a generously proportioned lobby. From there the old man led him past a row of teller's cages to a damaged door. Broken glass and other bits of debris crunched under Capelli's boots as they entered an office that was open to sky. Weather had taken quite a toll, but the banker's huge desk was still there, and a pleasant-looking middle-aged woman was perched on one corner of it. She had brown hair and a full face, and was dressed for a winter day. "I'm Terri Locke," she said as she stood, and offered a gloved hand.

"It's a pleasure to meet you," Capelli said sincerely, as they shook. "My name is Joe Capelli. Alvin hired me to escort him from Burlington, Colorado, to Haven. He said this is a wonderful place to live and it was his intention to settle here."

Tears had begun to well up and trickle down Terri's cheeks. She wiped them away. "He's dead isn't he?"

Capelli nodded soberly. "We were ambushed by a large number of Grims near Colby, Kansas. Al was badly wounded and died a few days later."

Terri accepted a handkerchief from Potter and blew her nose. "And you came all the way to Oklahoma to tell me that?"

"No," Capelli answered as he unbuckled the money belt. I came to Haven to give you *this*. I knew Al would want you to have it."

Terri accepted the belt, peeked into one of the pockets, and looked up at Capelli. "Gold?" There was a look of consternation on her face.

"Yes, ma'am. There was more originally. However, I was captured by a group of people who took some of the coins and spent them. But, thanks to the woman who is waiting out in the square, I was able to recover the belt and bring it here."

"That's an amazing story," Terri said. "And you are an amazing man. Most people would have kept the coins for themselves. I'd like to give you a reward."

Capelli shook his head. "No thank you, ma'am. But there is something you could do for me. If you're willing, that is."

Terri's eyebrows rose. "Really? What's that?"

Capelli jerked a thumb over his shoulder. "Susan and I are looking for a place to settle down. And Roger and Amy need a place to live too. Is there any chance we could stay here?"

There was a long moment of silence. Potter was the one who broke it. He was seated in the same chair his father had occupied years before. "I vote yes."

Terri smiled. "I'm the mayor, and Frank sits on the city council, so you have two votes. But you'll need more in order to stay. And folks will want to get acquainted with you and your friends before they take you in. That means a trial period. One in which you will have some but not all the privileges of citizenship. Would you and the others agree to that?"

"I would," Capelli answered. "And I think Susan and Roger will as well."

"Good," Terri said genially. "Welcome to Haven."

Three weeks passed. The townspeople assumed that Capelli and Susan were a couple. And, since neither of them denied it, they were assigned to what was referred to as a "starter" just off the main north-south tunnel. The so-called starter was really no more than an opportunity to excavate their own underground home. It wasn't stated in so many words, but both of them knew that if they were invited to stay in Haven it would have a lot to do with how hard they worked on the starter, and for the benefit of the community.

So Capelli volunteered to help with the community center that was being dug under the town square, and joined the forty-six-person defense force, which was led by a no-nonsense ex-marine named Tig Kosmo. The ex-noncom was suspicious of Capelli at first, but was soon won over by the newcomer's willingness to follow orders, and understanding of everything military. None of which prevented Kosmo from referring to Capelli as a "doggie," which was his name for anyone who had served in the Army.

Susan was invited to participate in the food-gathering parties that ventured out to gather such edibles as were available at that time of year. A task that Terri Locke and many of the community's women took part in.

So there was a bit of a stir when Susan asked if she could be a hunter instead. Because as the lead hunter, a cantankerous man named Levi Smith, put it, "Outside of my momma, I ain't never seen a woman who could hit the broad side of a barn with a shotgun, and our job is to hunt meat, not excuses."

But at Terri's insistence, Susan was given an opportunity to prove her skill. And when Susan dropped a deer at 650 yards, Smith not only put her on the three-person team, he kicked a man off to make room for her.

So that, plus Susan's country-girl skills at everything from sewing to candle-making, won her fans among men and women alike. Meanwhile, it was her expertise at digging tunnels and shoring them up that enabled the twosome to take their "starter" and enlarge it into a relatively spacious twelve-by-sixteen-foot room complete with an eight-foot ceiling, built-in shelving, and a salvaged sink. The starter didn't have any running water, not yet anyway, but it was furnished with items scrounged from abandoned houses.

Meanwhile, Capelli thought that his relationship with Susan was going well. They agreed on the important things, were a good team, and had been sleeping together since arriving in Haven. And maybe that was enough. But by then Capelli knew that certain symbols were important to her.

Still, knowing that and doing something about it were two different things until the day when Kosmo led Capelli and a squad of volunteer fighters into a town about five miles from Haven. The objective was to find and destroy Spinners, their pods, and any stinks that might be in the area. And it was a good thing, too, because after entering the town the team flushed a Spinner out of the local grade school, and killed it.

Of course, the presence of a Spinner suggested the possibility of pods, so it was necessary to sweep the entire town, and it was while searching the inside of what had been a jewelry store that Capelli found the item he needed.

The store had clearly been looted more than once. But someone, a thief most likely, had dropped a piece of jewelry on the floor. And none of the people who had passed through during the subsequent months had been fortunate enough to spot it. Not until Capelli came along, a rare ray of sunshine penetrated the nearby window, and the unmistakable glint of silver caught his eye. Capelli bent over, picked the ring up off the floor, and smiled.

The wedding took place a week later. The location was the whitewashed church on the main square. It was a mostly happy occasion. Although it was cold, and people were on edge because two Ravagers and fifteen Hybrids had passed through town earlier in the day.

It wasn't the first time such a thing had occurred, and the tunnels were sufficiently deep that the people moving back and forth in them couldn't be spotted with an Auger. But such visitations were worrisome nevertheless. So Capelli and Susan suggested that the ceremony be held underground.

But the mayor wasn't having any of that. "We aren't worms," she proclaimed. "Weddings should be held in a church." Therefore it was agreed that while the nuptials would take place in the church, the ceremony would be kept brief in order to minimize the potential danger, and in recognition of how cold it was. A decision that Capelli and Susan understood and endorsed.

And so it was that as people gathered in the church, Tig Kosmo threw a security screen around the town, and a warmly dressed Reverend Rawlings began what promised to be a very short ceremony. In spite of the cold air, Capelli was dressed in a shabby tuxedo and Susan was resplendent in the white wedding dress that one of the women had loaned to her.

That's where Capelli's attention was, or should have been, but something was wrong. Not with the wedding, but with Rowdy, who was standing stiff-legged a few feet from the altar staring back at the front door. And there was no mistaking the growl that rumbled deep in his throat. So Capelli looked in that direction, saw the air shimmer, and made a grab for the Colt Commander that was holstered under his left arm.

The onlookers produced a gasp of surprise as he jerked the pistol out into the open. It was pointed at Susan until he turned and fired three times in quick succession. The nine-millimeter slugs brought the charging Chameleon down. The monstrous creature became visible as it died, so the townspeople could see the Chimeran field generator strapped to its back, and the long curved claws for which such beasts were known.

But even as the well-wishers tried to absorb this, Capelli fired again and a *second* stink fell not two feet from the first. It was second nature for Capelli to eject the partially used magazine, and insert a new one in its place, as members of the embarrassed security force entered the church, their heads swiveling back and forth.

There was a moment of silence. Terri was first to speak. Her breath fogged the air. "It was a trick," she said thoughtfully. "The stinks left two Chameleons behind to kill anybody who came out of hiding after they were gone. Thank God for Rowdy." The dog, who was oblivious to that sort of praise, continued to lick himself.

Capelli returned the Colt to its holster. "Sorry about that, Reverend! Where were we?"

The minister's face was ashen, and the hands that cradled the Bible began to tremble. "Do you, Susan Farley, take this man to be your husband?"

Susan smiled serenely. "I do."

"Give her the ring," Rawlings instructed. "I now pronounce you man and wife. You may kiss the bride." And with that, the minister hurried away. It was December 25, 1953, and the best Christmas Capelli could remember.

You don't deserve her, the voice inside Capelli's head observed. *But welcome to the family.*

It had been raining for two days when Tom Hunter and a force of twenty regulators closed in on the town of Haven. They wore cowboy hats of various hues and long oilskin dusters, split so as to hang down along both flanks of their well-groomed horses. All of them carried arms and ammo made at Shipdown and Tunnel-Through. A policy calculated to simplify training, logistics, and repair.

And making the regulators even more dangerous was the fact that one of them was armed with a pulse cannon, two men were equipped with Chimeran field generators, and four carried Ravager-style energy shields. They could not only take on a Chimeran hunter-killer team if forced to do so, but had the capacity to subdue most of the communities within a fifty-mile radius of Tunnel-Through.

But that wasn't Hunter's mission. He had been sent into the countryside to persuade the communities to join what Ramsey called the New American Empire. Because, as the judge liked to put it, "The smart ones will take one look at our regulators, realize that we could wipe them out if we chose to, and join up. We'll deal with the stupid ones later."

The plan made sense, and as the regulators thundered into Haven, they had already brought two isolated groups of survivors into the fold. And Hunter saw no reason why the community of Haven would be any different. Though hidden from the Chimera, the town was well known to the locals.

Horses snorted and their hooves clattered as the riders brought their mounts to an intentionally showy halt. With the exception of a few men who had been ordered to keep their weapons ready, the rest of the regulators sat with their hands on their pommels. Details that Hunter knew the citizens of Haven would take note of.

The town was deserted, or so it seemed as a steady drizzle fell, and water dripped from the brim of Hunter's hat. But he knew eyes were on him as he lifted the bullhorn that hung from his saddle and spoke into it. "Citizens of Haven! I know you're out there—and I know you can hear me. My name is Tom Hunter. I was sent by Tunnel-Through's founder, Judge George Ramsey, to deliver a very special invitation."

A good ten minutes of silence followed. But Hunter understood. The regulators had taken the community by surprise, and there was a need to confer before a response was forthcoming. But eventually the front door of what had clearly been a bank opened and four people emerged.

The delegation included an old man and a middle-aged woman, both of whom were sharing a large umbrella. Two bodyguards brought up the rear. One was bare-headed in spite of the rain and armed with a V7 Splicer. The other wore a knit cap pulled down over his ears and was carrying what Hunter recognized as an

HVAP Wraith minigun. And judging from the way he held it, the man with the cap knew what he was doing.

Both weapons had clearly been chosen because of the horrific damage they could inflict on the tightly massed regulators. Suddenly, Hunter wondered if the show of force had been a good idea. But it was too late to redeploy his men, so all he could do was put a good face on things. "Good morning," Hunter said, raising a hand to touch the brim of his hat. "Like I said earlier, my name is Tom Hunter."

"I'm Terri Locke," the woman replied, as she looked up at the man who loomed over her. "The man on my right is Mr. Potter. I'm the mayor and he's a member of the city council."

"Pleased to meet you," Hunter said. "I don't like having guns aimed at me. Please tell your bodyguards to point those weapons somewhere else."

"And we don't like uninvited guests," Terri replied grimly. "Order your men to pull out—and I'll tell my men to lower their weapons."

Hunter wasn't used to push-back and didn't like it. But his orders were clear: Bring people into the empire peacefully if possible. He forced a smile. "Have it your way. Who knows? Maybe we'll be on the same side soon. Judge Ramsey is trying to unite all of the local communities under a single government. He calls it the New American Empire."

"Why?" Terri inquired suspiciously. "So he can run everything?"

"No," Hunter replied patiently. "So we can fight the stinks more effectively and take our country back."

"That's what the federal government is for."

"Really?" Hunter said sarcastically. "What has the federal government done for you lately? More than that, where the hell *are* they?

"Whereas we're right here. And we can offer you and your citizens more protection than you can provide for yourselves, health care from a *real* doctor, and vaccinations against the Chimeran virus."

Hunter saw the look on Terri's face and nodded. "You heard correctly. I've been vaccinated and so have my men. So if a Spinner bites one of us we won't turn. Nor will our families. And that's a powerful incentive to join up. What do you say?"

"That's a wonderful development if true," Terri replied. "But a decision to place Haven under Judge Ramsey's leadership and control is no small thing. Especially in light of the fact that one of our residents used to live in Tunnel-Through—and he paints a rather bleak picture of life there. In any case, I will have to discuss this matter with my constituents."

"Who have you got?" Hunter demanded confrontationally. "Mathers? Shaw? Both of them are liars. But if you want more information, then send someone to talk the situation over with the judge. But don't take too long. Other communities are joining up—and you wouldn't want to be left out."

With that, Hunter jerked his mount's head around and sent the beast galloping out of town. The rest of the regulators followed suit. Half a dozen piles of steaming manure marked where they had been gathered.

Once the last rider had disappeared from sight, Kosmo turned to Capelli. "Well, doggie! That was fun, wasn't it? By the way, it's a good thing we didn't have to open up on the bastards, because the HVAP doesn't work."

Capelli looked down at the Wraith and back up again. "You're joking."

"Nope," Kosmo said matter-of-factly. "Wraith parts are real hard to come by."

"Why didn't you tell me?"

"I figured it might have a negative impact on your morale."

"You're a rotten sonofabitch . . . You know that?"

Kosmo grinned agreeably. "That's what they tell me. Let's go. I'm getting wet."

CHAPTER THIRTEEN
STARS AND STRIPES

Construction of the Blakely Dam in the Ouachita National Forest had begun in 1948 and ended when the Chimera invaded North America and it became necessary to divert raw materials like steel and concrete into the war effort. But a significant amount of work had already been accomplished. The wedge shaped dam was 231 feet high and more than a thousand feet wide. Two turbines had been installed but never brought online. Still, since it had a small auxiliary generator, the facility had enough power to meet its own needs. Something the humans who lived deep inside the dam were careful to conceal. The thickness of the steel-reinforced concrete all around him made President Thomas Voss feel that he and his staff were reasonably safe from detection as he clattered down a flight of metal stairs and arrived on the level below.

Pools of light led him between desks towards the glassed-in area that had originally been designed to function as the dam's control room, but was now generally referred to as "the think tank." Meaning the enclosure in which most of the presidential decisions were made.

A great deal had been accomplished since the harrowing journey south from Freedom Base One. Not only had the government reestablished itself deep within the dam, the vaccine production program had been restored and improved. Pack trains loaded with vaccine, and accompanied by federal marshals, were making their way out to communities throughout the southeast. That meant Voss was not only building political support but a healthy virus-resistant population from which an army could be recruited.

Of course, Voss still had the never-ending threat of the Chimera to contend with, as well as human predators like Judge Ramsey, the man responsible for the destruction of Freedom Base One and the deaths of thirty-six federal employees. Voss was determined to punish that outrage both as a way to prevent future attacks and as an example to others.

Which was why Cassie Aklin, Marvin Kawecki, and a civilian scout named Calvin Rawlings had been summoned to the think tank for an early-morning conference. A pot of coffee was sitting on a warmer and a buffet-style breakfast consisting of Spam, pancakes, and fresh berries was available. Voss rarely took time off to eat, so such meals were common.

There were greetings all around as the President loaded a plate with food and Aklin poured him a cup of coffee. After taking his place at the long, narrow table, Voss opened the meeting.

"Okay, you know the score. Monica Shaw was forced to work for this Ramsey character—and that's how his people knew when and where to attack.

"And, based on what Shaw told me before she was killed, Ramsey is a lot more than a bandit. It's his intention to destroy the federal government so that he can replace it with one of his own. So now that we're up and running again it's time for some payback. We know roughly where Ramsey is, so I'm sending Kawecki up to resolve the situation. Rawlings, you know the area between here and there; I'm counting on you to get our people through."

Rawlings had shoulder-length hair, a high forehead, and a hooked nose. He nodded solemnly.

Kawecki frowned and put his fork down. "No offense, Mr. President, but you must be joking. We estimate that Ramsey has hundreds of armed regulators. How am I supposed to take them on with a dozen men?"

Voss finished chewing and swallowed. "You're a captain in the United States Army! That means you can accomplish the impossible."

Kawecki produced a snort of derision. "Thanks. We'll be lucky if we get there—never mind the rest of it."

Voss grinned. "Don't be such a pessimist. Let's plan for success rather than failure. And that brings us to the following problem: If—no *when*—you kill Ramsey, it will result in a power vacuum. So, unless we want to run the risk that someone even worse will be sucked in to replace him, it will be necessary to establish an entity that's loyal to the *real* government. Which is to say us."

"Oh, great," Kawecki responded sarcastically. "Is there anything else, Mr. President? Should I make all the Chimera disappear while I'm at it?"

Voss blew steam off the surface of his coffee. "Yes," he replied evenly. "That would be nice."

Kawecki, Rawlings, and a force of twelve men left that night. They were on foot. But with the aid of sturdy mules, they weren't required to carry anything other than their weapons, ammo, and some emergency gear. That allowed them to move quickly.

Of course the animals had their drawbacks, too. The mules were hard to conceal, had to be fed, and could be obstinate at times. But Kawecki figured the tradeoff would be worth it if he could keep his men fresh, carry a larger payload, and reach his destination quickly.

They traveled at night, with Rawlings scouting a mile or so ahead. Doing so was colder, but safer, and safety had priority. The civilian had a radio, which he used to guide the soldiers around obstacles. The route was a zig-zag affair that followed secondary roads in a generally northwesterly direction. They passed through dozens of devastated hamlets, circled two Chimeran bases, and were forced to cope with Leapers, Grims, and a pack of feral dogs along the way. The dogs had been brazen enough to attack one of the mules in broad daylight before being wiped out. But it wasn't until day four, when they were almost halfway to their destination, that the team ran into what Rawlings described as "a major freak show."

It was about two in the morning when Kawecki ordered the men to hobble the mules and set them free to graze in an overgrown field while he and Sergeant Pasco went forward to meet Rawlings. As they closed in on the rendezvous, a glow appeared up ahead. The dark bulk of a hill prevented them from seeing the source of the light as the scout materialized out of the gloom. "Follow me," the civilian said. "You won't believe this."

As Kawecki and Pasco followed Rawlings up a winding dirt road the glow grew brighter. Then, having arrived near the top of the hill, they dropped flat and crawled the last few yards. And what Kawecki saw at that point was unlike anything he'd ever seen before.

Stretched out in front of him was what looked like a football-field-sized sheet of glass. Except having been exposed to a lot of Chimeran tech, he suspected that the object was made of something akin to plastic.

Even so, the roof clearly weighed hundreds of tons and was held up off the ground by six iridescent pillars. Based on previous experience, Kawecki knew the supports were beams of coherent energy similar to those the stinks used for a wide variety of purposes. Some of the light was coming from the columns. Pole-mounted spots were responsible for the rest. Taken together, they illuminated the conical structures visible under the see-through lid.

They were pods. *Thousands* of pods. All planted in neat rows like a crop of vegetables and protected from the weather by the roof that floated above them. Could the plastic be darkened during the day? To shield the cocoons from the sun in the summer? Kawecki thought such a thing was possible.

"Look!" Pasco said from a position near the officer's right elbow. "Titans!"

Kawecki saw that the noncom was correct. Two of the giants were patrolling the perimeter of the pod farm with cannons at the ready. That was interesting, but the real question was *why*? Did the hive-mind need more stinks to do its bidding? And if so, what did it plan to do with them? There was no way to know.

"Now that you've seen the freak show, let's get out of here," Rawlings said from his position off to the left. "I think it would be a good idea to swing west before heading north again."

Kawecki shook his head. "Nope. There's no way we can leave this place operational. Besides . . . those are people down there. Or they were. Every single one of us has been forced to bypass pods at one time or another. But not thousands of them. No, we're going to put those folks out of their misery, and keep the total number of stinks down at the same time. The only question is *how*?"

Rawlings looked at Kawecki askance. "You must be joking. I didn't sign up for anything like this."

"I'm not joking," Kawecki replied calmly, "and you'll do whatever I say. Isn't that right, Sergeant Pasco?"

Pasco grinned wickedly. He had brown skin and his

teeth were very white. "That's right, sir. Mr. Rawlings will do whatever you say."

"I thought so," Kawecki said evenly. "Come on! Let's get out of here. We have some planning to do."

Sparks, Oklahoma

Nearly twenty-four hours had passed by the time the attack on the pod farm began. The mules were hidden in a barn located about a mile and a half away, along with two soldiers to protect both the animals and the group's supplies. Kawecki had divided the rest of his men into three teams, each having its own objective.

The Alpha and Bravo teams consisted of two-man LAARK teams. The first person's job was to fire rockets at the black boxes located at the base of each energy beam. The other soldier was carrying reloads for the LAARK, plus an M5A2 carbine, which could be used to provide security.

Meanwhile, Charlie team, led by Sergeant Pasco, was going to attack the Titans. Kawecki knew the enormous stinks could absorb a lot of projectiles. So by targeting one of the monsters with the group's single Wraith, plus a half-dozen lighter weapons, he hoped to neutralize the giants early on. Success would depend on surprise, timing, and teamwork.

After a short pep talk, all of the soldiers were sent out to take up the positions assigned to them. That put Alpha and Bravo teams along the south side of the rectangular farm, with everyone else up on the hill. They continued to dig in as Kawecki scanned the scene below.

"Damn it."

Rawlings, who was still opposed to the attack, turned to look at the officer. "Why? What's wrong?"

"Hybrids," Kawecki answered, as he released the binoculars in order to blow on his cold fingers. "Maybe half a dozen of them. They're walking around in among the cocoons."

"Maybe we should break it off," Rawlings suggested hopefully.

"Or maybe we should kill them," Kawecki said clinically. "Our snipers can handle it. But the result will be less fire on the Titans. Find Cole and Okada. Tell them to kill the 'brids before they target the Titans."

Rawlings nodded and slithered away.

The first call came in over the team freq twenty seconds later. "Alpha Team. In position. Over."

That was followed by a burst of static and a second transmission. "Bravo Team. In position. Over."

Kawecki clicked his transmit switch twice by way of a reply. Then it was Pasco's turn to speak in his ear. The noncom was at the other end of the firing line, which extended along the crest of the hill. "Charlie Team. We're ready. Over."

Kawecki eyed the Titans. They were at the east end of the farm and about to turn back. The best time to attack them would be when they were close, so that the massed fire would have maximum effect. Kawecki pressed the button. "Charlie Team will fire on my command. At that point, teams Alpha and Bravo may fire at will."

The Titans turned. They had smooth skulls and six eyes, and wore cooling units on their backs. They carried their cannons at something approximating port arms, and Kawecki wasn't looking forward to the barrage of high-explosive projectiles that would be coming his way in the near future. His stomach muscles tightened at the thought.

There was nothing to do but wait as the seconds crawled by and the Titans loomed larger. Finally, just as the beasts were about to turn and head the other way, Kawecki gave the order. "Fire!"

The Wraith was resting on an improvised bipod. That allowed the gunner to not only lie flat but to fire his weapon with greater accuracy. So as the minigun roared, and a stream of high-velocity bullets slammed into the Titan's chest, it staggered and was forced to take two steps back.

Meanwhile, lesser weapons were firing on the beast to the right. It uttered a scream of rage and fired its cannon. The shell hit halfway up the slope and threw a fountain of soil into the air.

Kawecki swore, fired two grenades in quick succession, and saw both explode as they hit. Blood flew, but the grenades had very little effect, as the Titan put its head down and began to charge up the hill.

Kawecki knew that, as the commanding officer, it was his job to keep an eye on the big picture and give the correct orders. But that was impossible as the monster fired again, Rawlings ceased to exist, and his remains fell like a warm rain. "Grenades!" Kawecki shouted. "Throw everything you have at the sonofabitch!"

And the soldiers obeyed. Not that it made a whole lot of difference as the Titan's head and shoulders drew even with the top of the hill. That was when Kawecki stood, threw an air-fuel grenade at the Chimera's enormous head, and uttered a whoop of joy as it made contact with the upper part of the giant's chest and stuck there.

The Titan released its cannon in order to paw at the device, but it was too late. The grenade generated a soft whump as it went off and the Chimera's head, hands, and upper torso were enveloped in yellow-orange flames.

Even though the beast was blind and disoriented, it staggered uphill with blazing hands extended. That was when some of the outgoing projectiles punched their way through the Chimera's torso and slammed into the cooling unit strapped to its back. The result was a series of overlapping explosions that blew the Titan apart and hurled chunks of raw meat high into the air. They thumped down all around him as Kawecki shifted his attention to the larger battle.

The other Titan had been able to reach the top of the slope off to the left in spite of a steady stream of slugs from the Wraith. The Chimera was holding a soldier with one hand while ripping the human's extremities off with the other. Rather than run the risk of hitting their buddy, Charlie Team's fire had fallen off. "Fire, damn you!" Pasco roared. "Davis is dead."

So Charlie Team fired as Kawecki shifted his attention to the pod farm. Two of the supporting energy beams had been extinguished by then and there was a flash of light as a third exploded.

The Hybrids were down, thanks to some good shooting by the snipers. But no sooner had Kawecki noted that fact than a wave of zombie-like Menials flooded into the farm from the east. Once they spotted the Alpha and Bravo teams, the stinks split into two columns and ran straight at the humans. "Down below!" Kawecki shouted. "Supporting fire!"

The second Titan exploded at that point, but Kawecki didn't have time to look, as he and half of Charlie Team shifted their fire to the pod farm. The Menials looked like ants when viewed from the top of the hill, and like ants they kept on coming. But the hail of projectiles slaughtered so many of the Chimera that the newcomers had to climb over piles of their own dead in order to throw themselves at the humans.

Fortunately, the continued fire from both the hill and the rocket teams themselves was enough to stop the gruesome onslaught as Kawecki shouted into the radio, "Alpha and Bravo teams! Shift your fire to the supports! Take them out and pull back."

As luck would have it, the remaining energy beams

were evenly spaced. So even though the roof had begun to teeter uncertainly, it remained horizontal to the ground. Then, as the last of the power supply boxes exploded, the gigantic sheet of transparent material collapsed onto the cocoons below.

Now Kawecki could see down through the roof as the fleshy pods exploded. As each cocoon popped, it produced a wet farting sound that merged with all the rest to generate a muted roar. Bloody goo spurted sideways and was simultaneously pressed downwards to form what looked like an enormous laboratory slide.

Kawecki heard gagging sounds as one of the soldiers threw up and a horrible stench rose to envelop the hill. "I'm sorry," Kawecki said to no one in particular. "I'm sorry it had to end this way. But it's over now."

Pasco had been close enough to hear. *The day when every stink has been killed*, he thought to himself. *That's the day when it will be over.*

CHAPTER FOURTEEN

CAN YOU DIG IT?

Monday, December 28, 1953
Haven, Oklahoma

Capelli could see a dusting of stars through the arched openings on all four sides of the clock tower. He remembered the sense of awe he had felt staring up at the constellations from the roof of the apartment house where he had grown up. But now as Capelli looked up at glittering pinpoints of light, it was the darkness between them that captured his attention. Because if the Chimera were from another planet, what else was out there?

Capelli's ruminations were interrupted as the ladder rattled and a man climbed up through a hole in the floor and onto the platform. He was dressed in multiple layers of clothes. "Hey, Capelli! How's it going?"

Mike Unver had been a high school science teacher back before the Chimerans invaded, and Capelli liked him. Unver was in his late fifties. His graying hair was combed straight back, and a pair of large glasses lent him an owlish appearance. The scope-mounted .30-06 he was carrying had originally been used for deer hunting but had an even more serious purpose now. "It's going fine," Capelli answered. "I haven't seen anything other than a few stray dogs."

"Good," Unver replied. "I could use some peace and quiet after the city council meeting."

"It's still in session?"

"Oh, yeah! And will be for some time. Are you going?"

"I'd love to skip it," Capelli confessed. "But 'people who don't participate can't complain.' That's what Susan says. So there will be trouble if I don't show up."

Unver grinned. "Are you sorry you tied the knot?"

Capelli shook his head. "Hell no."

"That's the spirit. So go down and do your duty. As least it's warm. And Capelli . . ."

"Yeah?"

"Take some body armor with you. You're going to need it."

Capelli laughed, slung the Marksman over his shoulder, and backed onto the top rung of the ladder. It carried him down to the ground floor. A trapdoor provided access to a flight of wooden stairs and the main east–west tunnel below. From there it was a short walk to a door that opened into the recently completed meeting room.

As Capelli stuck his head inside, he saw that just about all of Haven's adult citizens had managed to cram themselves into the standing-room-only session. And that was unusual, because most of the council's meetings were sparsely attended. But, since the question of whether to place Haven under Judge Ramsey's control was up for discussion, everybody wanted to have a say. And no wonder, given how important the decision was.

Capelli saw Susan on the far side of the room, and began to work his way over to her as Potter stood at the front of the chamber, speaking in opposition to the proposal.

"It would be one thing if Ramsey was a member of the executive or even the legislative branch of state government," the ex-banker said. "Or if he was a duly appointed official of the federal government. But he's neither one of those. Simply put, Ramsey is an ex-member of the judiciary. A man who has taken advantage of the current situation to set himself up as a warlord, violating many of the laws he swore to uphold.

"And," Potter continued, as his eyes darted from face to face, "if you don't believe me, ask Roger Shaw. He and his wife lived under Ramsey's rule and were treated as little more than slaves. Ramsey forced his wife to become a spy, and after she warned federal officials that Ramsey's regulators were about to attack, Roger and his daughter were thrown out of Tunnel-Through with nothing more than the clothes on their backs."

Potter paused at that point as if to add emphasis to his final words. "Is that the sort of community you want to be part of?" he inquired rhetorically. "I think not. That's why I and a majority of the city council oppose placing Haven under Ramsey's authority. Thank you."

The speech got a round of enthusiastic applause from those who didn't want to give up Haven's autonomy, and that included Susan. She gave Capelli a peck on the cheek as he took his coat off. They stood with their backs to the earthen wall. Capelli slid the sling off his shoulder and allowed the rifle to rest on the floor. Most of the people around him were armed, and had to be, since an attack could theoretically come at any moment. And the next speaker, an ex-businessman named Mel Tilson, took advantage of that fact.

Tilson had thick black hair, a dark five-o'clock shadow, and the manner of the shoe salesman he had once been. "Take a look around you," Tilson demanded. "Is this the way you want to spend the rest of your lives? Living like gophers?"

Tilson had at least a couple dozen supporters and they shouted, "No!" in response to the questions.

"That's what I thought," the shopkeeper said, as if the entire room agreed with him. "If you want to live aboveground, and sleep better at night, the answer is to join forces with other people. Because there's strength in numbers.

"Now maybe you don't like the way Judge Ramsey's invitation was delivered. And I agree that it could have been more tactful. But that doesn't change the way things are. By joining up with the folks in Tunnel-Through we would have the regulators to protect us, living conditions would gradually improve, and we would receive access to the new vaccine. And that's a big deal, my friends! A very big deal. And even Roger Shaw, who Mr. Potter mentioned earlier, admits that such a vaccine exists. So let's take advantage of the heaven-sent opportunity to improve life for both ourselves and our children. Thank you."

Tilson's supporters were a lot louder than Potter's. But once the votes were tallied, the so-called Ramsey proposal was rejected by a vote of ninety-one to forty-seven.

"You'll be sorry," Tilson told some of his more vocal opponents as they filed out. "Ramsey won't let it rest. The regulators will be back. Then we'll have to fight them *and* the stinks."

"Tilson has a point," Capelli said, as Susan and he followed the north–south tunnel home. "The regulators will be back."

"Yes, they will," Susan agreed as she pushed the salvaged door open. "That's why we have to prepare for war."

Capelli turned his flashlight off as Susan lit a succession of candles. They produced a soft glow that made the primitive space look homey. "*War?* That's a bit extreme, isn't it?"

"No," Susan replied steadfastly. "It's logical. Once Ramsey has assimilated all of the communities that are willing to come over peacefully, he'll use the additional strength to come after holdouts like Haven."

Capelli placed the Marksman in the weapons rack and

turned to open his arms. Susan stepped in to place her cheek against the flat plane of his chest. "We were looking for a place to live," she said simply. "And we found one. Now we have to protect it."

Capelli kissed the top of her head. "Don't tell me! Let me guess. You have a plan."

"*We* have a plan," she corrected him, as she leaned back to look up into his face. "I've been talking to Mayor Locke, Mr. Potter, and some of the other pro-independence types. All of them agree. We need to form an alliance that's strong enough to fight Ramsey. And that means more weapons. Because the people of Tunnel-Through are busy manufacturing their own."

"That sounds logical," Capelli agreed. "But where are we going to find them?"

"I don't know," Susan answered. "But I told them that you would find a way."

Capelli kissed her smile. "You did, did you?"

"Am I in trouble?"

"Yes," Capelli said, as he led her towards the bed. "You certainly are."

Tunnel-Through, Oklahoma

It was a gray day, and an ice-cold wind was blowing out of the west. Mel Tilson was scared as he paused to check his back trail. And for good reason. He was traveling alone in a time and place when even large parties of humans were vulnerable.

But desperate times call for desperate measures. As Tilson scanned the dull monochromatic countryside, he knew that the anti-alliance crowd was wrong. Haven wasn't strong enough to survive on its own. The only hope was to form a close relationship with Tunnel-Through and Judge Ramsey. So rather than being in bed sick, the way his wife told people he was, Tilson hoped to meet with Ramsey. The problem being that something was wrong.

Tilson wasn't a trained warrior like Kosmo, or the new man Capelli, but he'd been raised on a ranch and knew a thing or two about the outdoors. One of which was that when the birds stop chirping, and the countryside becomes eerily quiet, chances are that a predator is on the loose. And since the birds had been singing in spite of his presence, *and* the gunshot he'd heard fifteen minutes earlier, it seemed likely that someone or something new had entered the area.

So with his Bullseye at the ready, Tilson backed into a thicket of trees, and sank to the ground. Then, in spite of an almost irresistible urge to run, he forced himself to remain motionless. Seconds later his instincts were proven correct as a soft thrumming sound was heard and three Hunter Drones drifted into the clearing.

Had they been following him? Or was their presence at that particular time and place a coincidence? Not that it mattered as the machines paused and Tilson held his breath. Then, with the surety of a compass needle swinging north, the machines swiveled in his direction and began to advance.

The Drones were armed with heavy machine guns that fired superheated kinetic projectiles. As they opened fire, Tilson heard the ominous roar and dived forward. The saplings around him seemed to vaporize into a cloud of wood, bark, and leaves. He felt the debris rain down on him as he covered his head with his arms and began to pray.

Then, for the first time in his life, God responded. There was the chatter of automatic weapons, followed by three partially muffled explosions, and a ground-shaking thump as something heavy landed within a few feet of him. Tilson looked to the right and saw the smoking ruins of a Hunter Drone.

"Come on," a male voice said, as strong hands pulled Tilson to his feet. "There's no way to know if the stinks will send reinforcements or write the Drones off to normal wear and tear. So let's get the hell out of here."

Tilson had been up in the clock tower on the day when the regulators rode into Haven. So he recognized the man in the cowboy hat and duster as the person who had spoken on Ramsey's behalf. "Is your name Hunter?"

"Yes, it is. Do I know you?"

"I was in Haven on the day you offered the community a chance to hook up with Tunnel-Through," Tilson answered, as a regulator returned the Bullseye.

Hunter had a firm grip on Tilson's elbow by that time and was steering him towards a horse. "So they sent you to say yes?"

"No," Tilson admitted. "The trip was my idea. I would like to meet with Judge Ramsey."

"Can you ride?" Hunter inquired noncommittally.

"Yes."

"Okay, once I'm aboard, swing up behind me."

Tilson did as he was told and quickly discovered that there were five men in all. One of them was leading a mule with a dead deer tied across it, which accounted for the rifle shot he'd heard earlier.

The hunting party trotted through broken country with the assurance of men who knew exactly where they were headed, which turned out to be a ravine that led straight towards a softly rounded hill.

A few inches of water was flowing along the bottom of the draw. It splashed and ice crackled as the horses passed between a pair of bushy saplings and a pair of guards before entering a huge drainage pipe. Or that's what Tilson thought it was until a series of widely spaced electric lights appeared, and the passageway opened onto a railway tunnel complete with a stationary train.

There were walkways to both sides, and people turned to look as the horses appeared, but none of them seemed to be surprised as Hunter pulled up next to the last passenger car. Tilson jumped to the ground, where Hunter joined him a few moments later.

"The judge is a busy man," Hunter said. "So you might have to wait. But I'll check to see if he can meet with you."

Hunter disappeared into the railroad car, and Tilson was left to stare at his surroundings, as Tunnel-Through's well-fed citizens came and went. The town had more people than Haven. A lot more. And Tilson was impressed by the purposeful feel of the place. Not to mention the steady rumble of a generator, the electric lights, and how warm it felt. Much warmer than Haven's tunnels.

Such were Tilson's thoughts as Hunter appeared on the platform above and waved him aboard. "You're in luck. The judge has fifteen minutes between meetings. Please leave your weapon with one of the guards."

After surrendering the Bullseye, and passing between a pair of grim-looking regulators, Tilson was shown into a richly furnished office. A man in a black suit came to his feet and extended a pudgy hand. "Welcome to Tunnel-Through. I'm Judge Ramsey."

"My name is Tilson. Mel Tilson. It's an honor to meet you, sir."

"Please," Ramsey said. "Have a seat. Mr. Hunter tells me that you're a citizen of Haven."

Tilson couldn't help but feel pleased by the way in which he'd been received. And, contrary to the stories Roger Shaw liked to tell, Ramsey was a pleasant man. "Yes, sir. My wife and I had a shoe store there back before the stinks took over. We were part of the original group that dug tunnels between basements to create a safe place to live."

"Except it isn't safe, is it?" Ramsey inquired shrewdly as he lit a cigar. "Because safety flows from strength, and there aren't enough of you to go it alone."

"That's what I told them," Tilson agreed, "after Mr. Hunter came by. But they have heard negative stories about Tunnel-Through. So the proposal to become part of your new government was voted down."

"I'm sorry to hear that," Ramsey responded, as a halo of cigar smoke formed around his head. "So what brought you here?"

Tilson shrugged uncertainly. "I wanted to talk to you and see Tunnel-Through with my own eyes."

Ramsey nodded. "That makes sense. I'd do the same. Tell me, Mr. Tilson . . . Are your fellow citizens aware of your trip?"

Tilson shook his head.

"That's just as well," Ramsey said judiciously. "There's no point in getting people all riled up. Now here's what I would suggest! How 'bout you and I stay in touch? Mr. Hunter could help you establish a message drop at the edge of town."

There were some obvious dangers associated with the proposal, and Tilson discovered that his mouth was dry. "What would you want to know?"

"Just everyday stuff," Ramsey said reassuringly. "What folks are talking about, community projects, that sort of thing. I feel certain that the rest of the citizens will come around eventually. And when they do, I'll need someone I can trust to provide the community with leadership. Do you follow me, Mr. Tilson?"

Tilson nodded eagerly. "Yes, Judge, I do."

"Excellent! We're of a mind then. Mr. Hunter will work with you to make all of the necessary arrangements. But, before you go, I have a gift for you."

Ramsey pressed a button and a man entered the office a few seconds later. He was small of stature, wore his hair parted in the middle of his head, and looked at Tilson through a pair of round lenses that were perched on the end of his nose. "This is Doctor Haffey. And if you would be so kind as to roll up a sleeve, he's going to vaccinate you against the Chimeran virus. More than that, he's going to send you home with a dose for each member of your immediate family. Just one of the benefits that will accrue to the citizens of the New American Empire."

"Thank you," Tilson said gratefully, as he rolled a sleeve up. "Thank you very much."

"You're welcome," Ramsey replied indulgently. "And one more thing . . ."

"Yes?"

"If you take care of me, I'll take care of you."

Tilson winced as the needle went in. "You can count on it."

Ramsey nodded. "I will."

Haven, Oklahoma

Snow slanted down as Capelli and Rowdy slipped into a dark shadow. They paused there, and when he was certain that he hadn't been followed, Capelli aimed a penlight at the clock tower. The signal was answered by two blips of light.

It was clear, so the twosome dashed across the open plaza and slipped into the bank. In less than half a minute they had pawed a pile of debris out of the way. The steel trapdoor was locked, just as it was supposed to be. Capelli made use of his rifle butt to rap on it three times. Then, having placed his mouth over a twisted piece of pipe, he gave the password. Metal squealed as two lock bars were withdrawn and a rectangle of buttery light appeared.

Rowdy was used to the trapdoor by then, so Capelli heard someone swear as eighty pounds of wet dog landed in her arms. But no one got hurt. Rowdy was on the floor shaking himself dry as Capelli arrived at the bottom of the ladder. "That dog smells worse than a Chimera," Katy Morris complained, wrinkling her nose.

"Tell me about it," Capelli replied, shrugging his pack off. "I had to sleep with him for three days."

"Which raises the subject of *your* odor," Susan said primly, as she entered the room and came over to kiss him on the cheek. "I heard you were back."

Capelli feigned surprise. "*Me?* I'm fresh as a daisy."

"Come on," Susan said, taking hold of Rowdy's collar. "It's time for a bath."

The couple left the ladder room for a corridor that led past the bank vault, which now served as the town's arsenal. And when Capelli walked past the open door he could see the racks of weapons that lined both walls, as well as the narrow workbench that ran down the center of the rectangular space. That was where Kosmo was busy putting an Auger back together. He waved as the Capellis passed by.

The image of more than fifty gleaming weapons should have been comforting. Especially given that there were at least that many racked in homes or kept close at hand throughout the community. But Capelli was painfully aware of the fact that the arsenal was barely adequate to meet Haven's growing needs, never mind those of the alliance the council hoped to create.

Susan eyed him as they followed a succession of lanterns down a side tunnel towards the public baths. "No luck, huh?"

Capelli shook his head. "I'm afraid not. Most of Kaw City is still standing, but it looked as though there had been a major battle at the police station, and you can guess how that turned out. So I came up empty. Whatever weapons the boys in blue originally had are gone."

She nodded understandingly. "Don't feel badly. It was a long shot. Everyone knew that. Besides, I've got what might be a lead."

"Good," Capelli said, as they entered what had been the basement of the local five-and-dime. "We're due for a break."

With the help of a convergence of pipes and a functional boiler, the space had been converted into showers plus six bathtub-equipped enclosures. "You haven't been around to use your allotment of hot water, and I saved mine," Susan said as she tied Rowdy to a vertical pipe.

Capelli brightened. "You mean . . . ?"

"Yes, I do. Followed by dinner in our start."

Capelli looked around the steamy room. A man was singing on the other side of a plywood partition and a child was putting up a fuss somewhere close by. "That sounds good. But what about the neighbors?"

"Try not to make as much noise as you usually do," Susan said sweetly. Then, having taken Capelli by the hand, she towed him into one of the enclosures, and closed the door behind them. Clean towels were waiting.

During the next half-hour Capelli discovered that the hot water felt good, as did his wife's soap-slippery skin. It was good to be home.

Later that night, after an absolutely delicious dinner of Vienna sausages and baked beans, the two of them sat side-by-side on their big four-poster bed. A literal steal from a house on the edge of town.

"Look at this," Susan said as she handed Capelli a package wrapped in a piece of oilskin. "Tell me what you think."

Once he'd unwrapped the notebook, the first thing Capelli noticed was the nicely executed drawing of a VTOL on the front cover and the name *Suzy Q* directly below it. "Lt. Tom Larson" was inscribed across the bottom in military-style block letters.

Capelli had seen dozens of similar notebooks over the last few years. Some of them functioned as diaries, others as sketchbooks, but most were quite utilitarian. That seemed to be the case with this one. Among other things, it contained a hand-drawn chart that showed how much fuel the *Suzy Q* could be expected to consume while carrying various payloads. It included a crew roster too, notes from briefings, and an unfinished letter to a girl named Betsy.

But the most interesting page, to Capelli's eye anyway, was the very last one. It was decorated with what might have been a splotch of dried blood, the words "Ordnance 6,000 lbs," and a string of numbers. Because of Capelli's military background, he recognized them as coordinates. He looked up and found that Susan's eyes were waiting to make contact with his. "Where did you get this?"

"It was lying under a partial skeleton," she replied. "We found it on a hunting trip two days ago. His bones were scattered about. Dogs, probably. But I found these near the book and the remnants of a uniform."

When Susan opened her hand, Capelli saw a dog tag with the name Larson on it and a pair of badly tarnished wings. "So the notebook was his, and judging from the last entry, his VTOL was loaded with weapons when it went down."

Susan nodded. Her eyes were shining.

"And the coordinates?"

"I looked them up."

Capelli smiled. "I'm not surprised."

"So, are you going to ask?"

"Yeah, I am. Where did the *Suzy Q* go down?"

"About twenty-five miles east of here," Susan replied. "That's the good news."

"And the bad news?"

"That's inside the Osage reservation. And they don't like uninvited visitors. That's what Mr. Potter says, anyway."

"Then we'll have to arrange for an invitation," Capelli responded. "Because this could be what we're looking for."

"So, I did good?"

"You did real good."

"Does that mean I get a reward?"

Capelli saw the look in her eye. *"Again?"*

"What? You aren't man enough?"

"Come here," Capelli said and Susan obeyed. The dog tag and the wings made a rattling sound as they hit the wooden floor.

Osage Reservation, Oklahoma

The meeting took place on a large sandbar near the eastern bank of the Arkansas River. The sun was out, and a thick layer of crusty snow sparkled, as a cold wind blew in from the west. Both of the groups were mounted— but they were very different. Susan, Tilson, and the rest of the delegation from Haven knew how to ride; Capelli was the only exception. They had good horses brought in from a variety of locations but they weren't familiar with the animals, and it showed.

The Osage had better mounts and sat atop them with the easy confidence of men who rode every day. They were twelve warriors in all, varying in age from about sixteen to sixty, and were armed with everything from powerful longbows to Chimeran Augers. All of them were dressed warmly, and some wore elaborate necklaces made out of stink fangs. Except for some red plaid here and there, they looked much as their ancestors had a hundred years earlier.

The Osage leader was notable not only for his skillfully made buckskin clothing, but a powerful physique and a shock of prematurely white hair. He sat with one leg crossed over his horse's neck. His boots were handmade and came almost to the knee. "Stick Walker sent a message. You wish to cross our land."

Capelli knew that the Osage called the banker "Stick Walker" because of his cane. Back before the stinks came, Potter had been willing to loan the tribe money when other people wouldn't, and the native Americans hadn't forgotten. "Yes," he said. "That's true. Thank you for agreeing to meet with us. My name is Joseph Capelli."

"I have three names," the other man replied. "I am called Pahusca, my council name is Papuisea, and my war name is Cahagatongo. But," the Osage added with a friendly grin, "my friends call me Bo."

Capelli smiled. "And my friends call me Joe."

"Good. So, Joe, what's on your mind?"

"Two things. First, the town of Haven would like to enter into an alliance with your people—and second, we would like your assistance in locating what might be a large shipment of arms."

A horse snickered and the river gurgled as Bo eyed Capelli from a dozen feet away. "An alliance against whom? And for what purpose?"

Susan took over the negotiations at that point, spending the next ten minutes describing Judge Ramsey's plans and laying out the reasons why the Osage should oppose him.

Eventually Bo nodded. "You make a convincing case. I will raise the matter with our council. In the meantime

there is the arms shipment to consider. Let's suppose that
it exists and that we manage to find it. What then?"

The possible split had been the subject of a good deal
of discussion prior to leaving Haven. Some, like Mcl Tilson, felt it should be 90–10, 80–20, or 70–30, all in Haven's favor. But Potter, Locke, and a majority of council
members agreed that anything other than 50–50 was
unrealistic. Not to mention the fact that an even split
would not only help bring about an alliance with the
Osage but serve to strengthen the native American community as well. So Susan made the offer.

Bo raised an eyebrow. "Now that we know the shipment is on our land, perhaps we should keep all of it."

"You can try," Susan admitted, as her horse took a
step sideways and she pulled up on the reins. "But you
haven't happened across it yet. And what if the stinks or
Ramsey's regulators find it first?"

Bo was silent for a moment. Then he uncrossed his leg
and nodded. "You have a deal. Let's ride."

It took a day of hard riding to reach the area where
the *Suzy Q* had gone down. Capelli had qualms about
traveling in broad daylight, and was in considerable
pain after hours on horseback, but there was no stop-
ping Bo and his war party. They all maintained that the
Chimera were afraid to enter the reservation because of
the large number of casualties they had suffered during
past incursions.

While respectful of the Osage nation's fighting prowess,
and inclined to believe many of their boasts, Capelli was
more than a little cynical regarding the theory that the
stinks were afraid to enter the area. The Chimera didn't
have emotions so far as he knew. But the hive-mind had
a limited number of forms available to do its bidding. So
perhaps the sparsely populated reservation had been
spared so the aliens could focus their energies elsewhere.

In any case there was no denying the fact that Bo and his warriors were very skilled at using whatever cover was available, hiding their tracks in streams, and avoiding open areas where the stinks could spot them from above. Which was one of the reasons why the party was able to reach the half-frozen floodplain called Broken Waters without incident.

The name stemmed from the way Hominy Creek split into a half-dozen competing channels before coming back together a few miles farther on. The water level was low at the moment, but Capelli could see where the creek had been pushed out of its bed by seasonal floods, and had stripped most of the surrounding soil away. Beyond that a white-capped bluff could be seen, with a line of bare-branched trees at the bottom, just back of the high-water mark.

Judging from Lieutenant Larson's coordinates and Susan's much-folded map, the *Suzy Q* was nearby. But *where*? The light had begun to fade, so there wasn't enough time to look around.

"We'll make camp," Bo announced authoritatively. "Then, when the sun comes up, the hunt will begin."

It was a good plan and, truth be told, the only one that was likely to work since stumbling around in the dark would almost certainly be fruitless. As those who weren't on guard duty sat around the communal campfire and tried to stay warm, Susan took advantage of the opportunity to lobby Bo regarding the possibility of an alliance.

And while Tilson peppered the mostly taciturn Osage warriors with questions about where they lived, and how large the tribe was, Capelli took the opportunity to clean his weapons.

Then it was time for Capelli and Susan to take a short walk before slipping into their sleeping bags. A flat rock sat next to one of the channels. Capelli swept a layer of snow off it before allowing Susan to sit down. With an arm around her shoulders, Susan snuggled in.

"Joseph?"

Capelli took note. Whenever Susan switched from "Joe" to "Joseph," it generally meant that something serious was at hand. "Yes?" he answered cautiously.

"There's something I need to tell you. Something important."

"Okay, what is it?"

Susan looked up at him. "I—that is to say, we—are going to have a baby."

Capelli was stunned. There had been so much going on, so much to do, that the possibility of a child hadn't occurred to him.

"Well?" Susan demanded. "Aren't you going to say something?"

"That's wonderful news," Capelli said warmly, and was pleased to discover that he meant it.

Then something else occurred to him. "Wait a minute! You knew you were pregnant and you came on this trip anyway? You've been riding a horse!" he said accusingly. "What about the baby?"

"I knew you'd go all Capelli on me," she said affectionately. "That's why I didn't tell you. Besides, these are early days. There isn't anything to worry about yet."

"So I'm going to be a father," Capelli said, as the realization continued to sink in.

"Yes," Susan replied, softly. "And a good one."

Capelli felt his wife's lips melt under his, and for that brief moment in time, they knew what true happiness was.

CHAPTER FIFTEEN
KNOCK, KNOCK, WHO'S THERE?

Monday, January 4, 1954
Osage Reservation, Oklahoma

The night passed without incident. Once the sun was up, breakfast was over, and nearly all traces of the encampment had been erased, it was time to go looking for the VTOL. By using a grid search, the humans were able to locate the downed aircraft in less than an hour.

The ice-encrusted fuselage was a hundred yards east of the floodplain, where it was hidden in a narrow ravine that the forces of wind, water, and time had cut into the bluff over the centuries. Judging from the dozens of holes in the fuselage, the *Suzy Q* had been badly shot up as Larson tried to bring the transport in. Capelli figured it had been dark. He could imagine the stomach-wrenching moment when both of the ship's stubby wings were torn off. But damaging though the blow was, it had slowed the VTOL down, and preserved the hull. It was wedged between two rock walls about fifty feet off the ground.

Capelli was ecstatic. And it wasn't long before he and a half-dozen other people had scrambled up to the point where they could enter the *Suzy Q* through an open hatch. Capelli had a flashlight, and as the beam played across the crates that were still strapped to the deck, he saw that the VTOL was loaded with everything from carbines to individually boxed MP-47 Pulse cannons that were sitting on top of the load. It was an extremely rich find, and he was still in the process of inventorying the newly acquired arsenal when something unexpected happened.

The interior lights came on. It took him a moment to process the development. Then he shouted, "Turn the power off!" As the lights went off, he followed the downward-sloping deck to the cockpit, where Tilson was seated next to a raggedy skeleton busily flipping switches.

"You fool!" Capelli said, as he jerked the businessman out of the pilot's seat. "The moment you drew power from the battery the plane's nav system came on, and the odds are pretty good that a light appeared on a stink control panel somewhere. If so, they know where we are and you can bet a shitload of the bastards will arrive soon."

"I'm sorry," Tilson said lamely. "I didn't know."

"Get Bo," Capelli ordered tersely. "And tell him to hurry."

The Chimeran drop ship came in from the west. It was all angles. Artificial lightning stabbed the ground as on-board sensors detected heat sources and weapons fired on them. Deer, wild horses, and rabbits died. Pressor beams crushed the water flat as the ominous-looking vessel drifted across the creek. Loose snow billowed into the air, icy pebbles sleeted sideways, and a wave of heat rolled over the land. And it was then, as the ship hovered, and a cloud of steam rose, that Capelli fired the Pulse cannon. He was hidden behind a cluster of snow-capped boulders that fronted the open area west of the crash site.

The bolt of concentrated energy hit the Chimeran vessel a fraction of a second before Bo fired the second cannon. The combination of two nearly simultaneous blasts caused the drop ship's bow to tilt alarmingly. It hit the ground at a steep angle and plowed a deep furrow into the rocky soil. A grinding crash was heard as the hull lost forward momentum and pancaked in. That was when Capelli swore. The plan had been to destroy the ship, not just damage it. He fired again and saw a flash of light as the bolt hit the hull. But it took a moment for the cannon to recharge, and that was long enough for half a dozen Hybrids to open a hatch and come charging out.

The humans had one thing going for them, however, and that was the element of surprise. As the stinks trotted forward, three Osage warriors rose from their various hiding places to release carefully aimed arrows.

Capelli saw a feathered shaft penetrate a Hybrid's neck as another arrow took a stink in the thigh. It stumbled and fell. At that point the humans opened up with a wide variety of conventional weapons. The battle might have ended then and there except for the Ravagers who lumbered out of the ship's hold with more Hybrids right behind them. And because of the powerful energy shields that the eleven-foot-tall monsters carried, they could protect both themselves and the 'brids to the rear.

The humans had two hand-held radios and Capelli spoke into his. "Sixkiller! Get around behind them if you can. We'll divide their fire."

The stinks were only yards away by then, and all Capelli could do was trade the Pulse cannon for a Rossmore in hopes of taking as many of the Chimera with him as he could. But Capelli had a guardian angel—and her name was Susan. She was positioned on a rocky ledge above the *Suzy Q,* firing over the shimmery energy shields. So as a Ravager arrived in front of Capelli he saw the stink's head jerk spastically. That was followed by an explosion of blood as the bullet blew a hole through the back of the Chimera's skull.

When the Ravager went down, it left the Hybrids sheltering behind exposed. Capelli was only a dozen feet away. The shotgun had a devastating effect. Projectiles pinged all around him as he fired again and again. A blood mist fogged the air and turned the snow pink as a succession of stinks fell. Some had the misfortune to be hit by both a hail of buckshot *and* a succession of skillfully aimed bullets from Susan.

As this took place, the warrior Sixkiller and three Osage braves thundered onto the scene. They controlled their mounts with their knees. That left their hands free to fire a variety of weapons. When the second Ravager and its escorts turned to confront the new threat, the humans were free to attack. There was a risk, however, which was why Capelli shouted at them, "Aimed fire only! We have friendlies out there."

Now, having been caught in crossfire, the aliens were going down one after another. The battle was far from one-sided, however, as a Hybrid jumped an Osage who had paused to reload. The stink left the ground with powerful arms spread wide, wrapped them around the warrior, and was in the process of ripping the human's throat out when they hit the ground together.

There was blood all over the 'brid's face as it bounded to its feet and ran straight at Sixkiller. The warrior released his bow to grab the cut-down Winchester Model 37 shotgun slung across his back. He pulled the weapon free, brought it to bear just in time, and jerked the trigger. The charge blew half of the stink's face away. Sixkiller's Pinto jerked his head wildly as the coppery smell of blood flooded the horse's nostrils. *What was that, anyway?* the warrior asked himself. *Number nine or ten?* Maybe a name change was in order. Tenkiller had a ring to it.

The voice came from the radio lying on the ground next to Capelli's right foot. It belonged to Bo. He was a hundred feet away, half concealed in a dry channel. "The ship! It's taking off."

As Capelli turned his attention back to the shuttle, he saw that the Osage was correct. He put the Rossmore down and brought the Pulse cannon up onto his right shoulder. The drop ship was a couple of feet off the ground by that time. Steam rose all around it. Once it was high enough, say fifty feet or so, the vessel would be able to fire down on the humans with impunity. So as Capelli pulled the trigger he was conscious of how high the stakes were.

The side hatch was in the process of closing as the bolt of energy passed through the opening and struck somewhere inside. After a flash of light came the partially muffled sound of an explosion. A gout of plasma shot out through the hatch. The ship shook wildly and blew up.

Capelli was flat on his stomach by that time. The shock wave rolled over him, sent small stones skittering east, and flattened a clutch of young trees. Capelli lay there for a moment, stunned by the violence of what had taken place, and gratified to be alive. Then he did a push-up and was in a kneeling position when Bo arrived to pull him up all the way.

"That'll teach the bastards," the Osage said grimly. "We sent at least two dozen of them to hell."

As Capelli looked at the still-smoldering wreckage of the ship and the bodies that lay helter-skelter all around, he saw that Bo was correct. But it wasn't over yet. There were millions more.

"Come on," he said soberly. "Let's get to work."

Tunnel-Through, Oklahoma

Captain Marvin Kawecki had been lying on the same spot for more than ten hours. He was cold and needed to pee. But he couldn't stand up. Not until complete darkness had fallen. Because if he did, one of Judge Ramsey's carefully hidden sentries would spot the movement and kill him. The well-camouflaged hide had been constructed the night before. Now, as Kawecki lay there, he continued to study the area through his binoculars.

Other than the hump-shaped hill through which the railroad tunnel had been bored, the surrounding area was mostly flat and open. A railroad siding was located to the east of his position, complete with an elevated water tank, and a low-lying brick building. And the sentry Kawecki feared most was located high on the walkway that circled the metal tank.

But there were other sentries, too, hidden in clumps of bare-branched trees, in carefully screened weapons pits, and behind the rocks on the hillside in front of him. All of which had been carefully mapped into the notebook that lay to his right. He figured that at least some of the outposts were serviced by underground passageways that led back to the main tunnel. And that was something of an enigma. However, he knew it was there thanks to a pair of rusty tracks that disappeared into a rockslide.

There was no way to know how thick the blockage was, whether it had been caused by a Chimeran attack or was the result of a human effort to create a place to hide. Although Kawecki would have been willing to put some serious money on the second possibility. Ramsey might be a ruthless bastard, but it appeared as if he was equipped with a good deal of foresight, and had been smart enough to make preparations back when such a thing was still possible.

All of which was interesting but less critical than the

need to pee. Slowly, careful not to disturb any of the leaf-less branches around his hiding spot, Kawecki rolled over to face what he thought was the downhill side of his position. Except that the ground was very nearly flat. So he wasn't absolutely sure that he had it right. And, when the moment came, it was clear that he didn't. Rather than trickle away as Kawecki had hoped, the urine pooled right next to him. The liquid was absorbed, but the odor remained. And like it or not, he had to roll back onto the damp ground. It took what seemed like a long time for the sun to go down.

Finally, once it was dark, Kawecki had the opportunity to emerge from his hide. Then, having turned south, he elbowed his way forward, where he hit a number of obstacles. He had to crawl around them, pausing every now and then to listen for signs of pursuit before continuing on his way.

Eventually, Kawecki decided it was safe to stand and make occasional use of his flashlight. That was how he found his way back into the ravine that led him south.

"Who goes there?" a voice whispered out of the darkness.

"Bob Hope," Kawecki answered, as a dimly seen sentry materialized out of the gloom.

"Welcome back, sir. I'll get Sergeant Pasco."

Fifteen minutes later, Kawecki was busy wolfing down some hot rations as Pasco and those who weren't standing guard listened to his report. "We don't have enough men to force our way inside, much less root Ramsey out," Kawecki observed. "These people have good security, they're well disciplined, and they're dug in."

"So what are we going to do?" Pasco wanted to know. "Head back to base?"

Kawecki took a swig of hot coffee. "Hell, no. The President gave us a mission and we're going to accomplish it."

"Okay," Pasco replied. "How are we going to do that?"

"I figure Ramsey has neighbors," Kawecki replied thoughtfully. "And, given the way he operates, at least some of them have got to be pissed. So they have a reason to help us. And there's another thing, too . . ."

The fire lit Pasco's face from below. "Which is?"

"We represent the U.S. government, god damn it! So we're in charge."

Pasco nodded. "Sir, yes sir." But his voice was flat, his face was blank, and it was clear he didn't believe it. Kawecki wasn't surprised, because truth be told, he didn't believe it either.

The team traveled north. It wasn't long before the difficulty with Kawecki's plan became painfully apparent. If there were communities other than Tunnel-Through in the vicinity, they were well concealed and, being strangers to the area, the soldiers didn't know where they were or how to approach them.

So rather than simply blunder around, and possibly wind up in an unnecessary fight, Kawecki decided it would be best to gather intel from the kind of people who knew the area and might be willing to talk. Namely itinerant merchants of the sort they had run into during the trip up from Freedom Base Two.

Of course that took some planning, because the traveling gunsmiths, preachers, and medicine men were a wary lot who went to great lengths to avoid being seen. Still, almost everyone succumbed to the temptation to use established roads at least part of the time. And Kawecki knew many of them liked to travel during the early morning or evening, when there was enough light to see by but less chance of running into trouble. With that in mind, he set up an ambush of sorts next to a long straightaway and resolved to wait until the right sort of individual came along.

A patrol made up of six slouching Hybrids walked past early on. Their lean frames were barely visible through a driving snow. Kawecki let them go rather than run the risk of attracting more. But the better part of a day passed before three humans, all mounted on horses, and leading a string of mules, appeared. A lookout located half a mile to the south had alerted him, so Kawecki shed his gear, with the exception of the Magnum revolver. That went down the back of his pants. He was standing on the badly faded white line with hands clasped behind his neck when the first rider clopped out of the quickly gathering darkness and stopped.

The woman was middle-aged and dressed in a Stetson, a duster, and a pair of cowboy boots. The businesslike M5A2 carbine that was resting sideways across her saddle quickly came to bear. "Who the hell are you?" she demanded suspiciously. It wasn't snowing anymore, but her words were accompanied by jets of lung warmed air.

Meanwhile, her companions were spread out to divide incoming fire and sat with weapons at the ready.

"Captain Marvin Kawecki, United States Army," came the reply.

"There *is* one?" the woman inquired incredulously.

"Yes, ma'am. And a President. He sent us here. And I need your help."

"*Us?*"

One by one, the soldiers rose from their various hiding places in the scrub next to the road. The woman's eyebrows rose incrementally. "Okay, Captain! My name is Meg Bowers. That's Sam Henry to my left—and Parcel Brown on the right. What sort of help are you looking for?"

Kawecki told her and she nodded. "You came to the right people, Captain. We're salt merchants, and we sell to everyone except the stinks."

"Including Judge Ramsey?"

"Yup, but that doesn't mean we like the bastard. It's getting dark. Let's camp. I'll tell you what I can—and you tell me about this government of yours. If it's for real, then there are plenty of people who are ready and willing to help."

The combined groups made camp near an abandoned farmhouse, and by the time most of them went to bed, Kawecki knew all about the community of Haven, and Bowers had a verbal contract to distribute Hale vaccine on behalf of the U.S. government. It was, as she jokingly put it, "a marriage made in hell."

The Osage Reservation

Now that the Haven group had found the *Suzy Q*, and won the battle with the Chimera, the race was on to unload the VTOL and clear the area before more stinks arrived. So a frantic effort ensued as mules were moved into position and crate after crate was lowered to the ground using ropes.

Then came the ticklish task of loading the often recalcitrant animals properly as even more boxes were sent down from above. After persuading Susan to function as a lookout, Capelli worked shoulder-to-shoulder with the others to get the pack train ready. It was difficult to keep his eyes off the sky, knowing it wasn't a question of whether stink reinforcements would arrive but *when*.

So Capelli felt a tremendous sense of relief when the final box was roped into place and Bo led the group away from the bluff and into the creek. It was impossible for the heavily laden mules to travel at anything more than a walk. And the relatively slow pace set Capelli's teeth on edge as the pack train followed the creek bed north before turning into a half-frozen stream. It led them in under the branches of trees that grew along both banks.

They offered a little bit of cover as a pair of sonic booms rolled across the land. Capelli couldn't see the Chimeran aircraft, but figured they were fighters, sent to scope out the situation before the shuttles arrived.

Bo led the pack train up out of the streambed into a covered sluiceway. The sound of hooves echoed back and forth between concrete walls as the group continued up a gentle incline to a point where the dry sluiceway ended and a metal roof hid them from above. Capelli saw the words "Osage Cement" on the huge processors all around and realized they were in what had been a tribally owned manufacturing facility. That was when Bo came to speak with him. "I suggest that we hole up here, split the load, and go our separate ways once it's dark."

Capelli was about to respond when Tilson took it upon himself to speak for the entire group. He had a noticeable tendency to show up whenever decisions were being made. "That will be fine."

A slow grin appeared on Bo's face as he made eye contact with Capelli. "I'm glad to hear it. But first we'd better check the plant for pods and post guards. I'll work with Joe here to take care of that."

Tilson nodded importantly and said, "Good. I'll wait here."

Haven, Oklahoma

It was nearly dawn by the time Capelli, Susan, and the rest of the team arrived in the town square, where the entire town turned out to greet them. And with lots of people to help, the effort to unload the shipment of arms and get it underground went quickly.

Once that task was over, Capelli and Susan were happy to let others take care of the mounts as they descended into the tunnel complex and began to make their way home. That was when Mr. Potter intercepted them.

"There you are!" he said cheerfully. "Welcome back, and please allow me to thank you on behalf of the council. I know you're tired, but we have some very special visitors, and it would be nice if you could say hi."

Capelli would have declined, but Susan responded by saying, "Sure, we'd be happy to." That left him with no choice but to go along.

Potter led the way. As Capelli followed the banker and his wife into the meeting room, he was shocked to see uniforms. *Army* uniforms, all worn by men he had never seen before, with one very notable exception. And that was Captain Marvin Kawecki.

Kawecki saw the old man enter, followed by a pretty woman, and a male who looked familiar somehow. Then came the moment of realization and the resulting flood of anger. Kawecki pulled his Magnum and aimed it at the man's head. "Joseph Capelli! You shot Hale. Now it's your turn to die."

The voice in Capelli's head had been largely silent ever since his marriage to Susan. Suddenly it was back. *What goes around comes around, Capelli.*

With a loud click, Kawecki thumbed the hammer back. Capelli knew there wasn't enough time to bring a weapon to bear. So he stood up straight and braced himself for the impact. It took all the willpower he had to stare into what looked like a railroad tunnel. The hammer fell.

CHAPTER SIXTEEN
FRIEND, OR FOE?

Mr. Potter's cane was already falling as Kawecki pulled the trigger. The wooden shaft hit the officer's forearm with a thunderous boom and the Magnum went off.

Capelli felt the bullet nip the top of his right shoulder while the revolver clattered to the floor. He was surprised to be alive as the soldiers raised their weapons. But Susan's Fareye was aimed at Kawecki by that time. "Hold your fire," she said grimly, "or the captain dies."

"That will be enough of that," Potter said firmly, stepping into the space between the potential combatants. "All of you will lower your weapons and do so now."

A long silence fell, during which Kawecki and Capelli glowered at each other. It ended when Kawecki said, "You heard the man. Lower your weapons."

The soldiers obeyed, but with obvious reluctance.

"That goes for you, too," Potter said, as he directed a look to Susan.

Susan brought the rifle's barrel up and back so that it was pointed at the ceiling and rested on the front surface of her right shoulder. A position from which the weapon could be brought to bear very quickly.

"Good," Potter said, as his eyes shifted from Capelli to Kawecki. "It appears that you two know each other."

"You could say that," Kawecki replied. "Capelli was

a soldier once. And a reasonably good one. Back before he chose to kill our commanding officer."

"Who had started to turn," Susan stated flatly.

Kawecki looked at her and frowned. "Excuse me! But who the hell are *you*?"

"My name is Susan Farley. I'm Nathan Hale's sister *and* Joseph Capelli's wife."

A look of astonishment appeared on Kawecki's face. He opened his mouth but nothing came out.

"Which brings us to you," Capelli put in. "Is that uniform for real?"

"The simple answer is yes," Potter replied sternly. "The President of the United States sent Captain Kawecki and his men here. And we are citizens. So regardless of what took place in the past, you will find a way to get along with these soldiers or leave Haven. Is that clear?"

Capelli nodded. "Yes."

"Good. That's enough for tonight. Everyone is tired. We'll come back together tomorrow."

Susan took Capelli's arm. "Come on," she said gently. "We're tired, and you're bleeding."

Capelli looked at his wife. He knew that when she said, "We're tired," she was referring to both herself and the baby. Somehow the past, present, and future had all come together in a single moment of time.

As the Capellis left, Kawecki bent over, retrieved his revolver, and returned the weapon to its holster. It was, he reflected, a very small world.

A strategy session was convened the following day. The entire city council was present, as were Kawecki, his soldiers, and leading members of the community. That included Mel Tilson, his strongest allies, and the Capellis.

Mayor Locke chaired the meeting. The first hour was spent listening to an off-the-cuff presentation by Kawecki, who brought the group up to date regarding the attack on Freedom Base One, the subsequent trek to Freedom Base Two, and the status of the Hale vaccine.

Capelli looked at Susan when Hale's name was mentioned. She was clearly determined to keep it together, but he saw a tear trickle down her cheek, and was reminded of the way she had been willing to kill for him the night before. Love, he decided, is a very complicated thing.

"So," Kawecki said, as his talk wound down. "My men and I were sent here to do something about Judge Ramsey. The problem is that we lack the manpower required to get the job done by ourselves. So I figured that communities like this one might be willing to lend a hand. Because if you don't fight the bastard off, he'll take over. Either by bribing people with stolen Hale vaccine or by force of arms."

That led to a short presentation by Terri, who reminded those present of the fact that the community had already voted to reject Ramsey's proposal. "And," she said, "thanks to the Capellis, Mr. Tilson, and all the other members of the party that risked their lives to reach the *Suzy Q*, we are much better armed than we used to be.

"Not only that," she continued, "we have what may be a very important ally in the Osage nation. They are going to consider a formal relationship—and we hope to hear from them during the next couple of days. In the meantime, I think I speak for the entire city council when I say that we not only have an obligation to cooperate with Captain Kawecki, but it's in our self-interest to do so.

"I'm going to assemble a delegation that will visit

other communities in the area in an effort to build an alliance strong enough to conquer Tunnel-Through."

Though not entirely unexpected by some members of the audience, the notion that Haven should switch from defense to offense was new to others, and a moment of silence followed. Mel Tilson was taking copious notes. Things were moving quickly—and Judge Ramsey would want to know.

Pop-Up, Oklahoma

The delegation sent out to visit the surrounding communities consisted of Mayor Locke, Capelli, Kawecki, and six heavily armed security people: three from the community of Haven and three from Kawecki's contingent of soldiers. They intended to show that at least one group of survivors continued to trust the government in spite of the mistakes that had been made by the preceding Grace administration.

The first community on the list was called Pop-Up. A name inspired by the fact that, like the citizens of Haven, the locals lived underground. But they did not live in a town or the remains of one. Instead each individual, family, or group of families occupied its own underground habitat. Some were very small, some were said to be pretty elaborate, but all had one thing in common: they were located at least half a mile apart. It made for isolated living conditions, but it meant that even if the stinks located one of the homes, the rest could possibly survive.

The area in question was near what had been the town of Kildare. A community so small the Chimeran juggernaut hadn't even paused on its way through. The complete insignificance of the place was its best defense. Nor did the residents share any common infrastructure other than a loosely knit co-op–style government that was mainly focused on providing some rudimentary health care and education.

But despite the fact that they were spread out, the people of Pop-Up were known for their volunteer militia, which could field as many as thirty soldiers. And that was a fighting force well worth trying to recruit.

The area was mostly flat and generally open, with groves of skeletal trees, streams that had to be crossed, and scattered homes. All of which were eerily quiet except for the soft whisper of the wind, a flapping blind, or the occasional caw of a crow. Capelli yearned for the sound of a car or the laughter of children in a schoolyard. The sort of background noise he had once taken for granted. But that, like so many other things, had been stolen from humanity.

Their scout was a man named Tom Riley. He had been a mailman back before the stinks came. So he knew the area well, and when Riley raised a hand, the column came to a halt inside a grove of trees. The only sign of a human presence was a fifty-foot-wide circle of wooden stakes. Each was topped with a Hybrid skull, and all of them were staring at a central fire pit. "This is the clearing where the local families meet," Riley explained. "They have lookouts, so they know we're here. All we have to do is wait. Somebody will come before darkness falls."

"Okay," Terri acknowledged. "What should we do as far as security is concerned?"

There had been very little interaction between Capelli and Kawecki up till that point. But because they had joint responsibility for security they couldn't ignore each other forever. And while Capelli would have preferred to set up the defensive perimeter by himself, he understood the dangers of a split command. Not to mention the fact that Kawecki's soldiers wouldn't take orders from a civilian. Especially one with his background. So he took the initiative. "I suggest that the rest of us place ourselves under Captain Kawecki's orders where military matters are concerned."

Capelli saw a look of surprise appear on Kawecki's face, followed by what might have been wary respect.

"I think that's an excellent idea," Terri responded. "Captain? How would you like to position your troops?" The last was delivered with a smile.

Kawecki responded by putting four lookouts in place and cautioning them not to shoot any of the locals. That allowed the rest of the group to build a fire, heat some food, and rest for a while.

Time passed, the light faded, and just as Capelli was beginning to wonder if the locals knew they had visitors, four men and a woman appeared. They were dressed in odd combinations of wool clothing, buckskin, and furs. And they seemed to materialize out of the gloom. That made sense, because anyone who hadn't mastered all of the various aspects of field craft wasn't likely to survive for very long.

Once in the glade, and crouched around the fire, Capelli realized something else about the citizens of Pop-Up: They smelled worse than the stinks did. Not too surprising given the lack of running water in their underground burrows. But it was off-putting nevertheless.

If Locke was aware of the odor, she gave no sign of it, as she thanked the locals for coming, and gave them five thousand rounds of ammunition in a variety of calibers. The gift was intended to convey goodwill and attest to Haven's strength. Once the formalities were out of the way, it didn't take long to discover that the community had been contacted by a man from Tunnel-Through, who claimed to represent Judge Ramsey and wanted Pop-Up to become part of something called the American Empire.

Pop-Up's spokesman had long, stringy hair, leathery skin, and eyes that looked like chips of turquoise. The fire lit one side of his face and left the other in darkness. "He called it an 'invitation,'" the man named Moxley added, "but it sounded like an order. So Harvey shot him."

"*What?*" Terri exclaimed. "Just like that?"

Moxley looked surprised. "Sure, why not? Who the hell was he to tell us what to do?"

Kawecki tried to conceal a smile. "Then what happened?"

"There were six of them altogether," Moxley replied, as vapor drifted away from his mouth. "Only one of them escaped."

"So Ramsey knows what happened," Capelli observed.

"I reckon he does," Moxley agreed noncommittally.

"And once Ramsey has enough people, they'll be back," Kawecki predicted.

"Maybe," Moxley allowed.

"And maybe not," Terri put in. "We're trying to create an alliance for the purpose of attacking Tunnel-Through and destroying it."

"Sounds good," a fierce-looking woman said. She was wearing a ratty fur coat and a necklace made out of what might have been Hybrid finger bones. "Let's kill the bastards."

"You know what?" Kawecki said, as he pulled a fifth of carefully hoarded whiskey out of his jacket pocket. "I think we should drink to that."

Brickyard, Oklahoma

Having successfully enrolled the citizens of Pop-Up in the alliance, the delegation traveled west towards the sprawling brick factory that had once been a major source of employment for the area. Because according to Tom Riley, some of the Acme Brick Company's managers and employees had moved into the factory and were eking out a living there. If so, they were well within Judge Ramsey's reach and therefore potential allies.

But long before the Brickyard's chimneys and buildings came into sight, the group saw an ominous column of black smoke rising to point at the sky. "I don't like the look of that," Kawecki said grimly, and Capelli had to agree. Suddenly he was glad that Susan had agreed to remain in Haven.

Once the factory's chimneys and buildings became visible, Kawecki signaled the group to stop while he and Capelli elbowed their way onto a rise where they could examine the facility through their binoculars. Huge piles of finished bricks obscured the source of the smoke.

But Capelli knew that whatever had caused the fire couldn't be good. Because if humans had been living in the factory they would try to avoid bringing attention to themselves.

"It's my guess that they were clobbered," Kawecki said darkly, lowering his glasses. "I reckon somebody should go forward and take a look."

Capelli turned to meet Kawecki's gaze. "Me?"

"If you're willing."

"So the stinks will do the dirty work for you?"

"No," Kawecki answered levelly. "Because you're the person Hale would have chosen for the job. The man he could count on."

It was a peace offering of sorts, and Capelli surprised himself by accepting it. The truth was that he cared what the Kaweckis of the world thought of him. Even if that was stupid. "Give me your radio."

Kawecki did so, and once the device was secured, Capelli made his way forward. A rusty fence barred his way. But after following the barrier north he came to a ragged hole, bright metal, and what he knew to be Stalker tracks in the patchy snow.

He paused to listen for a moment and then entered the inner compound. Huge stacks of red bricks formed a maze that had to be negotiated before Capelli could see the source of the smoke. The brick buildings were intact. But lesser structures were made of wood and one of them was on fire. Capelli could hear the crackle of flames and smell the tangy smoke. He could also see scorch marks, cratered concrete, and a scattering of bodies.

Capelli advanced with his rifle at the ready. The first corpse he came across was that of a Hybrid. Its body had been riddled with bullets. But there was no snow on the body, no signs of bloating, or damage from scavengers. A relatively recent kill, then. Probably no more than twelve hours old. That was one of the many things that made stinks different from humans: They never bothered to bury their dead. Even when they won.

And there were humans, too: a mélange of men, women, and children. All clustered around four fully loaded carts. Some of the bodies had been partially eaten. Not by crows or vultures, but by the Chimera. Other bodies were untouched. It was sickening. Capelli had seen such sights before but never got used to them.

He had the radio out, and was about to press the transmit button, when one of the bodies groaned. Capelli went over to kneel next to the woman. She'd been hit in the abdomen and the front of her shirt was wet with blood.

"Carl? Is that you?"

"No," Capelli said gently. "My name is Joe."

The woman blinked repeatedly as his body blocked her view of the gray sky. "Is Carl dead?"

Capelli looked around. The smoke eddied, but everything else was still. "Yes."

"Good. He isn't in pain then."

"No."

"I'm thirsty. Very thirsty. Could I have a drink?"

The water wouldn't be good for her. Capelli knew that. And he knew it wouldn't matter as he freed the canteen, unscrewed the cap, and cradled the back of her head. She got some of the liquid down; the rest ran off her cheeks onto the ground. She coughed. "We were going to move . . . Going to be safe."

"I'm sorry," Capelli replied lamely. "Where were you headed?"

But there was no answer. Just a blank stare. The woman was dead.

Capelli closed her eyes and lowered her head to the ground. After thinking about it for a moment, he drew his knife. The cloth parted easily as the razor-sharp blade sliced through it. His suspicions confirmed, he went over to examine another body.

Capelli put the radio to his lips. There was no point in using military radio procedure. "This is Capelli."

"I read you," Kawecki replied. "What have you got?"

"A lot of dead people. They made the stinks pay, though. There's at least a dozen 'brids lying around."

"Anything else?"

"Yeah. I think the residents were planning to move to Tunnel-Through."

"How so?"

"They were packed to leave, and they had been vaccinated," Capelli answered. "And recently, too. All of the human bodies have Band-Aids on their upper arms. And you can see the needle marks."

After a moment of silence, Kawecki replied. "So Ramsey is making progress."

"That's the way it looks."

"What now?"

The smoke swirled and rolled away as Capelli eyed

the battlefield around him. "We bury Ramsey's citizens. Or cremate them."

"We're on the way. Over."

Capelli thumbed the transmit button twice by way of an acknowledgment. *Over?* Would it ever be over? The fire crackled and black smoke rolled away.

Haven, Oklahoma

After cremating Brickyard's citizens, and leaving the factory, the delegation paid visits to three more communities. Two of them agreed to join the alliance. Members of the third fired on the visitors and they had no way of knowing why. Fortunately no one was hurt.

Now, three days after the group's return, the citizens of Haven were preparing for war. And Capelli was worried. It didn't take a four-star general to know that an attack on a fortified position like the railroad tunnel was an iffy proposition at best. Especially without air power, armor, or artillery to break the place open.

In addition, Terri had to work around the clock to keep personality conflicts and politics from tearing the alliance apart. Fortunately, she had been able to convince the various players that Captain Kawecki should be in overall command because of his status as an emissary from the President, the depth of his military experience, and his neutrality where local politics were concerned.

In an effort to provide Kawecki with a reliable command structure, all of his men had been assigned to act as advisors, with at least one of them being incorporated into each unit. The hope was that the soldiers, plus the heavy weapons and hand-held radios recovered from the *Suzy Q*, would be enough to overcome the advantages Ramsey's forces had.

Capelli wasn't so sure. He had argued for at least a week of joint training prior to the attack. But while acknowledging the dangers involved, Kawecki, Terri, and senior members of the alliance pointed out the importance of surprise and the fact that exercises like the ones Capelli had in mind couldn't be carried out without being noticed by the stinks. The latter represented another potential problem. What if they dropped out of the sky right in the middle of the upcoming battle?

The whole plan was fraught with danger. But, as Susan said when Capelli expressed his concerns to her, "This is our home now, Joseph. We will live with these people or die with them." It was a statement that left no room for doubt or backup plans. And the way she said it reminded Capelli of someone else. A man named Nathan Hale.

The community of Haven held a communal meal the evening before the scheduled attack. It was a somber affair, and rightfully so in Capelli's opinion. Because even if the alliance was able to win an overwhelming victory, lots of people on both sides were going to die. That's what he was thinking as Susan left the buffet line and took the seat beside him. Capelli eyed the huge mound of food on her plate. "Eating for two, are we?"

"Yup! We have to keep our strength up."

Capelli chuckled. "You're getting fat."

"That's the plan."

"Yeah, I guess it is."

"Joseph?"

Capelli looked at her. "Yes?"

"The Tilsons, the Wexlers, and the Haneys are missing. They left most of their belongings behind. As if they plan to come back and reclaim them soon."

Capelli felt his heart sink. A montage of images flickered through his mind. He saw Tilson pumping the Osage warriors for information, Tilson flipping switches in the

Suzy Q's cockpit, and Tilson taking notes. Lots of notes.

"The bastards."

"Yeah."

"So Ramsey knows."

Susan held her tea with both hands. "I think we should assume that."

"Maybe Terri and the rest of them will cancel."

Susan shook her head. "Not from what I heard in the kitchen. They feel the alliance *has* to attack at this point. If it doesn't, Ramsey will. Besides, all of the necessary arrangements are in place. Who knows if we would be able to bring everybody back together again."

That made sense in a horrible sort of way. But Capelli discovered that his appetite had vanished. He put his fork down. "You're staying home tomorrow."

Susan frowned. "First, I don't take orders from any man, and that includes you! Second, I'm the best shot in Haven, and that could make a difference. So little Joe and I will be there."

The "Little Joe" thing had become a running joke between them, but Capelli didn't smile. He moved to push his chair back but stopped when Susan put a hand on his.

"Don't be angry, Joseph. I know you're trying to take care of me. Of *us*. And I promise to stay way back. Okay?"

Capelli looked at her, saw what was in her eyes, and felt the resentment melt away. "Okay."

Capelli heard peals of sardonic laughter inside his head but didn't care. Perhaps Hale didn't realize it—but he was dead.

Tunnel-Through, Oklahoma

Dawn was still half an hour away as the alliance closed in on the habitat called Tunnel-Through. Because his mostly civilian army had never been able to train

together, Kawecki figured it would be a mistake to try
and launch the sort of massed attack that could fail due
to inexperience or miscommunication. Plus the enemy
knew the alliance was coming and was well entrenched.

So rather than rely on brute force, Kawecki chose to
give each group a job it was uniquely suited to do. Once
he gave the command, Kosmo and most of the fighters
from Haven were going to attack the north entrance to
the tunnel.

Then, as the defenders swarmed to that location, Shaw
was going to lead Capelli and a small group of carefully
chosen men to the side entrance through which he and
his daughter had been ejected. The job was to blow the
door, enter the underground complex, and hunt Ramsey
down. Because if they could capture or kill Tunnel-
Through's leader, the battle would end quickly. Meanwhile if the regulators came out to play, Bo and a group
of mounted warriors would engage them, thereby giving
Kosmo and his people an opportunity to withdraw with
minimal casualties.

Smaller teams, made up of people from Pop-Up, Junk
Yard, and a community called Marsh, had been given
maps. That included copies of the one Kawecki had drawn
while spying on Tunnel-Through. They were to target
specific sentries and weapons pits, take them out, and
penetrate the complex via whatever doors and tunnels
they happened across.

That was the plan. But Kawecki knew it would be dis-
rupted once the fighting began. At that point he would
have to rely on hand-held radios to redeploy his troops.
Were all of them in the proper position? Kawecki put
out a call and listened as the answers came back. Some
of the transmissions were consistent with military con-
ventions, but most weren't.

"The Two Team is in position. Over."

"We're here."

"Ready when you are," and so forth, until the correct number of people had answered.

"Okay," Kawecki said, "light the place up."

More than a dozen flare guns went off, a series of pops were heard, and a number of miniature suns were born. They jerked as tiny parachutes were deployed, swayed gently when a breeze hit them, and began to descend. The bright lights threw harsh shadows across the half-frozen land as one of Kosmo's men fired a Pulse cannon and scored a direct hit on the rockslide that blocked the entrance. The battle for Tunnel-Through had begun.

Ramsey was sitting astride Thunder about half a mile to the west as the flares went off and the bolt of energy from the Pulse cannon struck. "You were correct," the judge observed, peering through a pair of binoculars.

Tilson's horse was standing to Ramsey's right. The businessman felt a sense of satisfaction. There had been a good deal of risk associated with spying for Ramsey, and subsequently sneaking out of Haven, but the gamble was about to pay off. Because even though he hadn't been privy to every detail of Kawecki's plan, he was familiar with the general outlines of it. And that meant Ramsey was, too. So shortly, within a day or so, he would be sent back not just to live in Haven but to govern it. "Yes, sir," he said out loud. "It looks like the idiots are sticking to their plan."

"As we will stick to ours," Ramsey replied confidently. "While the main group attempts to suck us in, we'll circle around behind them and take out their command structure. Then, once the beast has been decapitated, it will die. Are you ready, Mr. Tilson?"

Tilson felt a terrible emptiness at the pit of his stomach but managed to keep his voice steady. "Yes, sir."

"Good. Let's ride."

*   *   *

Capelli and his team were already in the ravine when the flares went off and the battle commenced. He whispered, "Go," and followed the dark blotch that was Shaw up a steep bank. Rocks clattered as they fell; a guard detached himself from the surrounding murk, and staggered drunkenly as Tenkiller put an arrow in his throat.

The first man was still vertical and choking on his own blood when a second one fired. The quick succession of flashes revealed his position. He uttered a choking cry as another shaft sped through the air and buried itself in his chest. His body landed with a thump.

The first guard was on the ground by that time and Shaw had to step over the body in order to reach the door. "This is it," he said sotto voce. "You can hear the generator through the exhaust port."

And Capelli *could* hear the steady rumble and smell diesel fumes as well. "All right! Good job. Move aside so I can place the charge."

The block of C-4 explosive was ready and all he had to do was slap it onto the metal door and back away. Judging from the incessant chatter of automatic weapons, and the occasional boom of grenades, the feint was well under way. So the sooner he and his team got inside, the better.

There was a flash of light and then a loud bang as the C-4 went off and the door buckled inwards. Capelli kicked it open and entered with his Bullseye leveled. Not having encountered any opposition, he took a moment to thumb the radio's transmit button. "Capelli here. We're inside. Over."

"Roger that," Kawecki replied. "Good work. Now go after . . . Just a sec. Hold on."

Capelli heard Kawecki swear. That was followed by a sudden flurry of gunshots, some desperate shouting, and the thunder of what might have been hooves. Then there was silence. That wasn't good. Capelli forced himself to stay focused on the job ahead and waved the team forward. "Follow me!"

And they tried. But the group hadn't traveled more than a dozen steps before lights appeared down the tunnel and Auger bolts flashed towards them. Capelli fired back, but he could tell that his team was outgunned as two of his men fell. "Grab the wounded and fall back!" Capelli yelled, firing from the hip.

But there weren't any wounded. Just dead men as Capelli, Shaw, and two others backed out through the shattered door.

"Stand by," one of the fighters said, readying his V7 Splicer. "I have a surprise for those bastards."

The man fired and a spinning saw blade sped down the tunnel, sliced through the first defender's head, and tore into the man directly behind him. Then the whirling blade glanced off a wall and cut a third person down before finally losing its momentum and clattering to the floor.

That offered an opening, and Capelli was about to follow up on it, when a voice he recognized as Sergeant Pasco's came over the radio. "All units will pull back. Repeat, pull back. Prepare to implement Plan B. Over."

Capelli swore. Plan B was to regroup, withdraw in an orderly fashion, and try to prevent a follow-up by Ramsey. Something had gone terribly wrong.

In keeping with her promise, Susan was well back from the assault on the north end of the tunnel, lying prone on top of a rise. It was cold, but she was wearing four layers of clothing and a piece of canvas kept her up out of the damp.

Kawecki's command post was a hundred feet in front

of her, behind a jumble of boulders. The sun was starting to rise. The clouds had blown away and a golden glow suffused the area. That allowed her to search for targets.

And despite the fact that the defenders hadn't rushed out to defend the tunnel the way Kawecki wanted them to, she'd been able to pick off three of the defenders by watching for muzzle flashes, and aiming a hair above them. Her instructors would have been proud.

But with no one to watch her back, Susan knew it was important to take a break occasionally and check what Capelli liked to call her "six." Meaning the area behind her. And that was how she noticed movement off to the west, realized that Kosmo and his team had been flanked, and shouted a warning.

However, Kawecki was on his radio talking to someone. And precious seconds passed before he understood the true extent of the danger, began to shout orders, and turned to confront the oncoming horsemen. Kawecki fired his carbine as he ran forward to drag a regulator off his horse.

That was when a blast from a shotgun blew half of his face away. Within a matter of seconds the rest of the command party fell too—their bodies jerking spastically as a hail of projectiles tore into them.

War cries were heard when a group of mounted Osage warriors barreled in from the east. Regulators were snatched out of their saddles and a confusing melee ensued as Susan fired at the man on the huge Clydesdale.

But the shot missed, another man fell instead, and Ramsey's cavalry were forced to withdraw to the west. Heavily armed defenders were pouring out of Tunnel-Through's carefully concealed entrances, dozens of the alliance's best fighters lay sprawled on the ground, and Kawecki was dead.

As Susan began to elbow her way back off the rise, she thought about her husband and wondered if he was out there somewhere wounded or dead. She wanted to go and search for him but knew that was impossible. So, like the rest of them, all she could do was run.

CHAPTER SEVENTEEN
CUT AND RUN

Tuesday, January 12, 1954
Near Haven, Oklahoma

Capelli was running. And so were dozens of others, pounding towards the steel bridge, as a mob of angry regulators thundered after them. Bullseye tags stuttered past. One of them hit a woman in the back and drew half a dozen projectiles to her body. She staggered, threw up her arms, and landed facedown. One of their pursuers opened up with a grease gun and a hail of .45-caliber bullets dug divots out of the bridge deck as Capelli waved the survivors forward, shouting, "Stop at the end of the bridge! We'll hold the bastards there."

Some of the people who were fortunate enough to make it across the bridge continued to run. But most remained. "Take cover!" Capelli shouted. "Wait until they're halfway across and let 'em have it."

Capelli, Shaw, and a half-dozen others took up positions behind the rusting tow truck that was angled across the approach to the bridge. The rest of the fighters crouched to either side of the span, where steel girders and concrete supports would offer some protection. The regulators were on the span by then. They had seen their attackers turn and run, so they were confident of victory.

Ramsey had given his orders, and his followers were eager to obey: "Follow the scum home and annihilate them."

But the bridge was two lanes wide, which meant only four horsemen could ride abreast. And that made them vulnerable. "Fire!" Capelli ordered from his position behind the tow truck, and what happened next wasn't pretty. As members of the alliance opened up, the leading horses stumbled. Some tumbled head over heels; others reared up and threw their riders off as hundreds of projectiles ripped into the mass of tightly packed flesh. Horse screams overlaid human screams as a pink blood mist filled the air and the regulators located towards the rear of the column tried to stop.

But it was too late. As their mounts ran into the barrier of dead and dying flesh, the latecomers were caught up in the meat grinder as well. Some managed to dismount and take cover behind the pile of bodies. But it wasn't enough to save them as Auger fire stuttered through the mound and cut them down. The whole battle lasted less than five minutes. "Cease fire!" Capelli shouted. "Save your ammo. You'll need it later."

A heavy silence settled over the scene. The defenders seemed dazed by the way in which their fortunes had been reversed as a man went forward to put wounded horses out of their misery. By the time the gunshots were over, friends had sought friends, relatives had sought relatives, and small groups were beginning to depart.

Capelli tried to hold them by explaining the need to not only defend the bridge, but prepare for a second assault on Tunnel-Through.

"You must be joking," a man from Junk Yard said. "I lost my brother-in-law and a friend today. Sure, we stopped 'em here, but that won't put an end to it. Ramsey has more men. Lots of 'em. And they'll be gunning for us. We can knuckle under or run. And there's no place to run to. So stay if you want to—but there ain't no point to it."

Maybe Mayor Locke or Mr. Potter would have been

able to stop the exodus. But Capelli was no orator, and it wasn't long before he was left with three men from Haven and two Osage warriors. That wasn't enough to hold the bridge—not in the face of a concerted attack. And there was the town to consider. There were other bridges. And for all Capelli knew, Ramsey's forces had already crossed one of them. If so, Haven would need every gun it could muster.

After thanking the Osage for participating in the attack, Capelli released them. Then, with his fellow townsmen at his heels, he began to jog. Susan was very much on his mind at that point. Had she escaped the carnage? Fear for his wife's safety was like a lead weight that rode the pit of his stomach.

It took three hours of running and walking to reach Haven. And when they did, it was to find that the town was on high alert. Kosmo had lookouts posted all around the community, heavy weapons had been deployed to strategic locations, and a fast reaction team was ready to respond at a moment's notice.

All of which was good, but inadequate, considering the extent of the losses the town had suffered, and the likelihood of reprisals. But before Capelli could worry about that, something more pressing required his attention. So when he saw Terri inspecting a newly created barrier he went over to speak with her. The mayor's eyes were red with fatigue, her skin looked gray, and Capelli could tell that she was battling to maintain a positive attitude. "Have you seen Susan?"

Terri forced a smile. "Joseph! I'm glad you're safe. Susan arrived an hour ago along with Bo and some of his braves. They crossed the river up towards the east fork, where the water is pretty shallow this time of year. The first thing she wanted to know was whether I'd seen you."

Capelli didn't wait to hear more. He went in search of

Susan and found her in the underground meeting room, which had been converted into a makeshift hospital ward. There was no mistaking the look of joy on her face or the warmth of her embrace.

"Joseph!" she said into his shoulder. "Thank God. I've been so worried."

"Me too," Capelli said earnestly, as he led his wife over to a corner. "I have to leave soon, and I will feel a lot better knowing that you're safe."

Susan frowned. "Leave? Why? Where are you going?"

"Blackwell," Capelli answered grimly.

"Blackwell? The town where we parked the Stalker? It's crawling with stinks."

"Exactly," Capelli replied. "There are enough Chimera stationed there to destroy Tunnel-Through six times over. All I have to do is show them where the tunnel is."

Susan was silent for a moment. Then she nodded. "That's brilliant. And I think we can make it work. We'll go there, get the stinks to follow us, and lead them to Ramsey. And, if we do it fast enough, the Chimera will destroy Tunnel-Through before the reprisals begin."

"That's the idea," Capelli agreed. "Except for one thing. You aren't coming."

Susan opened her mouth to speak, but Capelli raised a hand. "I know . . . You don't take orders from any man. But there's an exception to every rule. And I'm asking you to make one now. For me, for little Joe, and for us. *Please.*"

Susan's eyes narrowed, then softened a bit. "Okay . . . But only if you agree to take someone else with you."

"I will," Capelli promised. "Plus Rowdy. He's been cooped up for days."

"When do you plan to leave?"

"Just before sunrise."

"Come with me," Susan said as she took hold of his hand. "We need to tell the mayor, find a volunteer, and collect the gear you'll need."

"And I could use a bath," Capelli added.

"With or without me?"

"I could drown without a lifeguard."

Susan laughed, and Capelli was reminded of all the little things that made life worth living.

Capelli, Rowdy, and Mike Unver left Haven at 0432. Mayor Locke, Mr. Potter, and other members of the council were present to see them off. "Thank you," Terri said earnestly. "Thank you very much." She looked like she was going to cry but managed not to.

Susan did cry, but didn't say anything other than, "Shoot straight."

Capelli and Unver were mounted on sturdy horses with a heavily loaded mule in tow. Having racked up only six hours of sleep, Capelli was tired, but painfully aware of how important the mission was and determined to accomplish it. The sky was clear, the stars glittered like diamonds, and there was enough light to see by.

They followed the same path Capelli wanted the stinks to use, only in reverse. The plan was to leave weapons, ammo, and a little bit of food at key locations along the route. That would allow him to travel light, which would be very important, with what could be hundreds of Chimera on his trail. And thanks to Unver's technical skills, Capelli was equipped to plant some very nasty surprises along the way as well.

With fresh mounts, and Rowdy out front, they made good time at first. But they had to hide when a shuttle appeared off to the west, and each one of the stops took time. Especially since they now had to cache the items left behind. So when the sun neared the western horizon, Capelli and Unver were still a good five miles short of Blackwell.

But that was to be expected. Capelli knew what was coming, and so he was in need of some hot food. Not to mention sleep. So they watered the animals, made camp in among some trees, and cooked a simple dinner.

"So," Unver began once the canned stew had been served. "What time are we going to get up in the morning?"

"I'm getting up about 0500," Capelli replied levelly. "But you'll be at least ten miles east of here by then—because you're leaving right after dinner."

Unver frowned. "Like hell I am."

"Oh, you are," Capelli replied confidently, as he swallowed a swig of water. "Because if you go with me, both of us are going to die. And I'm not ready to cash it in yet."

"Who says?" Unver demanded defiantly.

"*I* say. Look, Mike, no offense, but you're too damned old for this. And if you come along you'll slow me down. Then the stinks will kill you and me, and Ramsey will be free to take Haven. Is that what you want?"

"No," Unver replied reluctantly. "But I promised Susan that I'd stay with you no matter what. She said she'd shoot me if I came back without you."

Capelli chuckled. "That sounds like her all right. Don't worry about it. Her bark is worse than her bite. Listen, Mike . . . It took balls to volunteer for this mission. And you put me right where I need to be. But this is as far as you're going. So eat up, take those hay burners, and get the hell out of here."

Unver left forty-five minutes later. And as soon as the schoolteacher was out of sight Capelli broke camp, followed Rowdy west, and found a second place to sleep. That way Unver wouldn't be able to reveal Capelli's location if he was captured.

Capelli thought he was alone as he slipped into his sleeping bag, but that wasn't the case. *You don't trust anyone, do you?* the voice inquired.

I trust Susan. And Rowdy.

How about me? Do you trust me?

You don't exist.

Maybe I do and maybe I don't, the voice said evasively. *But I have a piece of advice for you.*

Which is?

When the stinks come after you, run like hell.

Peals of laughter were still echoing through Capelli's mind when he finally went to sleep.

Capelli awoke earlier than intended. The sun wasn't up yet, but he could see the stars through foliage above him, and figured it would be a sunny day. But cold. *Very* cold. Which would burn more energy.

Knowing it would be his last meal for a while, and that he was going to need lots of energy, Capelli forced himself to eat a large breakfast even though his stomach felt queasy. A sensation he had felt many times during the hours prior to combat.

Rowdy, who was feasting on a can of hoarded dog food, showed no such reservations. Of course he had no idea what lay in store for him, and ignorance is bliss.

Once the meal was over, Capelli wrapped his sleeping bag and cookware in a shelter half and hid them up in a tree despite the fact he was unlikely to return. Because he couldn't afford the extra weight—and it went against his grain to abandon good gear.

Then it was time to fill his canteens from a nearby stream before heading due west. The LAARK was heavy, as were the backup rounds, but critical to his plan. The idea was to send the stinks a message they couldn't ignore. Then, once they were hooked, it would be time to employ the Marksman. A Magnum completed his armament.

Security around the Blackwell base had been lax when Capelli and Susan passed through. But was that still the case? Capelli hoped so but knew better than to take something like that for granted. So as the sun started to rise, he entered the east side of town. The houses in front of him were silhouetted against a soft glow that came from up ahead.

He worked his way between abandoned structures and along darkened streets until what looked like a single headlight appeared in the distance. He grabbed Rowdy's collar and pulled the dog behind a garage as a Patrol Drone hummed past. Then, once the machine was gone, it was time to continue west.

As Capelli zigzagged through the streets, the light he'd seen earlier grew even brighter and the Chimeran base appeared ahead. The newly constructed fence glowed as if lit from within, and Capelli figured it was charged with electricity. Hybrids could be seen patrolling the perimeter as well. All of which was interesting but didn't matter, because Capelli had no intention of entering the base. The LAARK would take care of that for him.

Capelli told Rowdy to stay, placed the Marksman on the ground next to his right knee, and ducked out from under the rocket launcher's sling. He freed the weapon and then checked to make sure it was loaded, and that an extra two-round magazine was ready for use.

Now he had to choose a target. Something taller than the intervening fence. And as Capelli stared into the sight, he found he had a number of choices. Two buildings were tall enough to qualify as targets, in addition to the smelter's smokestack. It bore the company's name, and given the angle he would be firing from, looked like the best bet. So Capelli brought the LAARK to bear, aimed as close to the bottom of the structure as he could, and took a deep breath. After the first rocket left the launcher there would be no turning back.

Capelli thought about Susan, his right index finger tightened, and the LAARK jerked as a rocket sped through the frigid air. It hit dead center on the stack. A wink of red-orange light, then a resonant boom. The explosion blew a hole in the brick chimney but left it otherwise intact.

So Capelli fired a second missile. He heard the impact but was too busy loading a new magazine to view the results. Then the rocket launcher was up on his shoulder, ready to fire again. The ragged hole in the smokestack was bigger than before and an undulating siren could be heard. Capelli ignored the temptation to look around and focused all of his attention on the target. The third rocket hit home, but the fourth flashed through empty space, because the one-hundred-foot-tall stack was falling by then.

Capelli lowered the weapon in time to see the tapered cylinder land on the smelter's parking lot, where it crushed two Stalkers before breaking into three sections and sending a thick cloud of coal dust up into the air.

Rowdy barked excitedly as Capelli put the LAARK down and grabbed hold of the Marksman. The plan was to leave the launcher where the stinks could find it—and to eliminate as much weight as possible. "Come on, boy," Capelli said as he stood. "It's like the man said . . . Let's run like hell."

It would take the Chimera at least ten minutes to figure out the angle of attack, send some 'brids to check out the area from which the rockets had been fired, and find the LAARK. And Capelli planned to make the most of the lead time.

Rowdy took the lead as they followed a zigzag course between derelict houses and onto a street that led towards the rising sun. The fiery disk was big, bright orange, and a potential ally.

With that in mind he pounded his way toward the

church he had identified more than an hour earlier. It, like every other building in Blackwell, had been broken into during the many months since the fall. The structure's arched windows stared sightlessly at the street, the front door hung askew, and the interior was badly trashed.

But Capelli had no time for sightseeing. His left boot came down on a hymnal as he opened a door and followed a flight of twisting, turning stairs upwards. The steeple was home to a bell, with louvered shutters on all four sides.

Capelli used the rifle butt to shatter four horizontal strips of wood on the west wall and shoved the weapon's barrel out through the resulting hole. Then, he ordered Rowdy to stay, and put his eye to the telescopic sight. What he saw was what he had expected to see.

Having determined that the attack had come from the east, the Chimeran hive-mind sent two dozen Hybrids in that direction. Capelli's position was well concealed, and with the rising sun behind him, he eyed the oncoming mob. From his vantage point above and in front of the aliens he could see each one of them, including the stinks towards the rear.

So rather than alert the entire group by firing on the first row, Capelli took careful aim at the very last alien. The creature's head rose and fell rhythmically as it ran. Capelli waited for the 'brid to sink fractionally, applied pressure to the trigger, and felt the wooden stock kick his shoulder. A fraction of a second later, the Chimera's head came up and blossomed into a bloody cloud. Those at the front of the formation heard the gunshot, but assumed the projectile had missed, as they began to spread out.

But Capelli was ready for that and continued to harvest alien lives until the survivors realized what was happening and sought cover. That was his cue to exit the steeple as the half-blinded 'brids began to pepper the structure with Bullseye and Auger fire. It sounded like a hailstorm had hit the church as hundreds of projectiles struck the front of the building and pencil-thin rays of light stabbed the gloomy interior. Splinters flew all around them, and the church shook like a thing possessed as Capelli and Rowdy bolted out through the back door.

Now he had to run—confident in the knowledge that the Chimera were well and truly hooked. But could Capelli stay ahead of them? That was the question. And the answer was maybe. *If* he could sustain the right pace, stay hydrated, and maintain situational awareness.

And it wasn't too difficult at first. The air was cold, Capelli was fresh, and as he left Blackwell for the flat countryside to the east there was nothing significant to slow him down. So in half an hour Capelli covered about four miles. He had established a good rhythm, and was jogging down the white line, when two rows of projectiles blew divots out of the road to either side of him. A Chimeran fighter roared over his head seconds later and arced away.

Capelli swore, turned to the right, and jumped over a drainage ditch. Within a matter of seconds he was in knee-high wheatgrass. It had been taller back towards the end of summer, but a succession of snowfalls had beaten it down. Still, it was the only cover available, so Capelli went facedown in the field as the fighter came in for a second run. Projectiles struck, columns of half-frozen soil soared into the air, and dirt rained back down. But Capelli and Rowdy were a good ten feet outside the main impact area. So only a small quantity of dirt landed on them. The incoming projectiles had been close, however. Too close, as Capelli jumped to his feet.

The fighter was dangerous, no doubt about that, but

it was fast, so fast it couldn't slow down enough to effectively engage such a small ground target. While the aircraft was banking away, and preparing to make another gun run, Capelli had time to advance. Even if he couldn't get very far. Of course, that strategy wouldn't work for very long. Sooner or later the fighter pilot would get lucky. And even if the Chimera didn't, it seemed safe to assume that more stinks were closing in from the west.

So as Capelli jogged forward he kept an eye peeled for the grove of scraggly trees, the outhouse next to it, and the old travel trailer. The very sight of them was like an injection of energy. He ran forward as the fighter circled to the north, jerked the trailer's metal door open, and grinned. The L11-2 Dragon was right where he had left it. Along with a canteen full of water, a couple of candy bars, and a first-aid kit.

The Marksman went over Capelli's shoulder; he stuffed one of the candy bars into his mouth, and took hold of the flamethrower with both hands. Then, he backed away from the Airstream and turned and ran. A burst of explosive projectiles plowed through the trailer with a roar and shattered a tree beyond.

Capelli was pursuing a zigzag course by then, firing the Dragon as he ran. The wheatgrass was damp and slow to catch fire, but once aflame the stubble produced plenty of black smoke. It blew from west to east and provided Capelli with some much-needed concealment.

After ten minutes of continual use the Dragon ran out of fuel. So Capelli threw it away and continued east, knowing that every step carried him closer to his goal. He was starting to tire a bit, but knew it was important not only to keep running, but to reach the next dump. A place where he could make a momentary stand if he chose to.

As a veil of smoke blew over Capelli's head, and the

fighter strafed a spot half a mile to the south, he followed a game trail down into a gully. Rowdy came to a
stop and began to bark madly as hundreds of Leapers
surged up and out of the depression. Had they been sent
to intercept him? There was no way to be sure, but Capelli didn't think so. He figured it was a piece of bad
luck. As was the fact that he was armed with a Marksman rather than a Rossmore. The latter being far more
effective where massed targets were concerned.

But all he could do was rely on what he had. So Capelli was forced to back up towards the wall of fire he
had created as he sent one of the rifle's semiautonomous
Drones out over the gully. The device immediately went
to work killing the stinks, but even more boiled up out
of well-hidden caves.

Fortunately, Rowdy was there to keep the scorpion-
like horrors from surging in around the human. The dog
was like a whirling dervish as he darted in and out with
his jaws snapping. Leaper claws flashed, and potentially
lethal tails whipped back and forth, as Rowdy scored
kill after kill.

Thanks to the deadly turrets, plus well-aimed projectiles from the Marksman, and Rowdy's fighting prowess, the twosome managed to stay on their feet as the fire
closed in from behind. And that was when Capelli ran
out of ammo. It left him with no choice but to reach for
one of the four grenades he was carrying.

Rowdy snarled as he tore into a Leaper and the air-fuel
grenade arced into the mass of oncoming bodies. With a
loud whump the device went off; flames consumed the
remaining Leapers, and they began to scream.

"Rowdy!" Capelli shouted. But only a shrill whistle
could pull the dog away from the stink he was savaging.
The animal's muzzle and head were covered in gore. Capelli and Rowdy ran forward, jumping bodies whenever
necessary, making for the gully and the high ground be-

yond. Then something hit the field fifty feet in front of them and exploded.

Capelli paused to look back and saw that a Titan and two Ravagers had managed to pass through a gap in the wall of fire. A gang of Hybrids was following along behind. Another cannon shell was on its way, and it would have scored a direct hit on both man and dog, if they hadn't been scrambling up the bank.

With a Titan and two Ravagers on his tail, it was critical for Capelli to reach the supply dump and do so quickly. A big farmhouse appeared on the left as he topped the slope and paused to hurl his remaining grenades at the oncoming Chimera. They exploded in quick succession. The last was an air-fuel grenade that wrapped a Hybrid in a cocoon of yellow-orange flames.

Without waiting to see the results of his efforts, Capelli raced across an open area towards the southeast corner of the wraparound porch, where the stash was hidden. Pieces of lumber flew as he tossed them aside to reveal a piece of canvas and the items hidden beneath it.

The dump included two canteens of water, an M5A2 Carbine, and most important of all, a Wraith minigun. Not the faulty weapon from Haven's original arsenal, but a brand-new unit taken off the *Suzy Q* and transported to the site by mule. It was a weapon Capelli carried frequently during his days with the Sentinels.

The Wraith might work on the Titan, the Hale voice observed dispassionately, *but what about the Ravagers? Their shields will protect both them* and *the Hybrids.*

Capelli knew the voice was correct but could only handle one thing at a time as he shoved M5A2 magazines into empty ammo pouches, replaced his mostly empty canteens with fresh ones, and took the minigun into his arms.

The Titan was climbing up out of the gully by then. Only his head and shoulders were visible, but it wouldn't be long before the giant towered above Capelli, unless he could cut the stink down to size before then. Wraiths were notoriously difficult to fire, both because of their incredible weight and the fact that the rotary barrels could put out 1,200 rounds per minute. That produced a lot of recoil and caused the weapon to rise up off its target unless controlled.

But Capelli was not only strong, he was something of an artist with a minigun. He fired a tight grouping of bullets and the monster staggered. The Chimera was tough, however, and still managed to fire its cannon.

Capelli felt the heat the projectile produced as it flew past him and hit a tool shed, reducing the structure to kindling. *Stay on it*, the voice ordered sternly. *You've got to kill that thing before the Ravagers arrive.*

Capelli wanted to tell the voice to shut up but knew doing so would be pointless. So he kept the trigger down, walked the minigun projectiles back and forth across the Titan's chest, and swore when the weapon clicked empty. He dropped the Wraith and was reaching for the carbine as he backed away. The Titan swayed uncertainly, seemed to steady itself, and exploded.

That was good, but not good enough, as the Ravagers topped the rise and opened fire from behind their translucent shields. Hybrids were following along behind them. Rowdy barked and Capelli fired on them, but it was a waste of bullets. The big shields were impervious to rifle fire.

Capelli was left with one option. He'd been hesitant to use it up until then, and for a very good reason. Unver claimed the system would work, but what if it didn't? Projectiles whipped past Capelli like angry bees as he ducked down behind the concrete platform on which the old-fashioned pump sat. The remote was about the size of a pack of cigarettes, and Capelli could still hear Unver's words. "Wait until the bastards are right on top of the charge," the older man had instructed. "Then push the button. That's all there is to it."

But Capelli couldn't see where the Ravagers were. Not without sticking his head up high enough to get it blown off. So all he could do was push the button and hope for the best.

The block of C-4 went off with a loud boom that shook the ground, threw a column of debris up into the air, and shattered windows on the south side of the farmhouse. Capelli rose up from behind the platform at that point and was thrilled to see that one Ravager and at least three Hybrids had been killed. It was difficult to determine the number, with so many body parts lying around.

Unfortunately, the second Ravager was very much alive. Rowdy dashed out into the open as it continued to advance. Capelli shouted, "No!" as projectiles pinged all around him, but the dog wasn't listening. The Ravager swiveled a few degrees in order to fire on the animal.

Capelli saw his opening. He allowed the carbine to fall so he could grab his revolver. The moment the handgun was up and in position he fired. Due to the angle, the large-caliber slug hit the stink in the left shoulder. It rocked the beast back on its heels but wasn't enough to bring it down.

So Capelli triggered the secondary fire mode, causing the deeply embedded bullet to explode. That blew the Chimera's arm off, so both the limb and the shield fell together. The second bullet hit the Ravager in the skull and knocked it off its feet. The Chimeran body was still falling as Capelli took a hit in the side, dropped down behind the platform, and knew the whole effort had been for nothing. He was bleeding, his carbine was out of reach, and he had just four rounds left in the pistol. Once the Hybrids flanked him, the battle would be over.

Capelli had accepted that reality, and was thinking about Susan, when he heard a deep-throated *blam, blam, blam,* as someone fired a burst from what sounded like a Browning Automatic Rifle (BAR). That was followed by sustained fire and the sound of Mike Unver's voice. "Take that, you scabrous bastards! May all of you rot in hell."

At that point Capelli stood, weapon in hand, to discover that all of the remaining Hybrids were down. Bodies were sprawled every which way just short of his position. Unver had a big grin on his face as he exited the farmhouse.

"I thought I sent you home," Capelli said levelly.

"You did," the older man answered. "And I was half-way there when I realized that you are totally full of shit. So I came back."

Capelli grinned. "Thanks, Mike."

Unver nodded. "You're welcome, Joe. You were hit. How bad is it?"

Capelli returned the pistol to its holster so he could undo his combat vest and pull his shirt aside. The wound hurt, and his side was sticky with blood, but the hole had already begun to close. "Damn," Unver said in wonderment. "You heal fast."

"Yeah," Capelli said, as he refastened his clothing. "There's nothing like government health care."

Rowdy was miraculously unhurt. He paused to lift a leg over a dead Ravager, and both men laughed.

"Come on," Capelli said. "If the hive-mind was angry before, it's really pissed now. Let's get out of here."

The next half-hour or so passed without incident as the barely felt sun rose higher in the sky and the three-some continued to travel east. The momentary calm was a good thing, unless it meant that the stinks had given up. But they had nothing to fear; a Chimeran shuttle rumbled over their heads but then disappeared over the next rise. "They're trying to cut us off," Capelli said, as they paused to rest. "How much do you want to bet that stinks are closing in from the west as well?"

"I'd put money on it," Unver agreed. "If I had any . . . What do we do now?"

"We're still a good five or six miles out from Tunnel-Through," Capelli replied. "So we need to get closer. Let's move forward and see if we can slip between the stinks. If that doesn't work, maybe we can circle around them."

"It sounds like a plan," Unver said. His voice was steady, but Capelli could see the fear in his eyes. Fear *and* determination.

Capelli nodded. "Let's go."

Tunnel-Through, Oklahoma

Seven men were crammed into Judge Ramsey's office. A couple of them were seated, but most had been forced to stand. A large hand-drawn map had been fastened to the wall behind Ramsey's cluttered desk. All of the local settlements were identified by name as well as the estimated population.

Ramsey, who was just about to call the meeting to order, was a happy man. And he had every reason to be, because while the attack on Tunnel-Through had resulted in casualties, his forces had been victorious. And, based on information obtained from the prisoners they had taken, Ramsey felt sure that the so-called alliance had been crushed. A theory borne out by the fact that the attackers were all running for home—if their various burrows could be called homes.

But more than that, the failed assault on Tunnel-Through had boosted morale. Suddenly, having been threatened from the outside, the citizens of Tunnel-Through were united in a way that they hadn't been before. And that meant his position was secure.

Still, Ramsey knew that the history books were filled with examples of rulers who had underestimated their opponents, and had been severely punished for it. So he would not allow his enemies to plot against him—he intended to root them out. Starting with the town of Haven, which, according to Mel Tilson, was where the resistance effort had begun.

They were about to begin their meeting when the door opened and a trail-weary regulator was shown in. The man's hair was plastered to his head and he was in need of a shave. He held a Stetson hat in both hands and rotated it jerkily as Hunter introduced him.

"This is Rick Toby, Judge . . . He's been on picket duty west of here." Then, turning to Toby, Hunter said, "Tell Judge Ramsey what you saw. And don't leave nothin' out."

Ramsey listened with a growing sense of alarm as Toby described how he had seen a man and a dog fleeing from a large group of Chimera. Then, according to the regulator, the man had started a fire to slow the stinks down, and even managed to kill a few.

Toby wasn't sure what had occurred afterward, because after seeing such a large force of Chimera making a beeline for Tunnel-Through, he thought it was his duty to rush back and deliver a warning.

"And you were correct," Ramsey said approvingly. "Thank you."

As Toby was shown out of the office, Ramsey was left with more questions than answers. Who was the man with the dog? Why were the Chimera chasing them? For the same reason they would chase any human? Or had the man done something to aggravate them? And what if the fugitive managed to survive a bit longer? Would the stinks stumble across Tunnel-Through? Suddenly, Ramsey had something more than revenge to worry about. And that was survival. *His* survival. Which, according to Ramsey's perspective, was the most important thing in the world.

Near Tunnel-Through, Oklahoma

Being very much aware of how visible the dog would be if he broke the skyline, Capelli kept a firm grip on Rowdy's collar, as he and his companion neared the top of the rise. "Stay," Capelli said emphatically, and he pushed Rowdy down. The mix made a whining noise in the back of his throat but obeyed nevertheless.

With Rowdy taken care of, Capelli elbowed his way to the top of the slope where Unver was waiting.

"You aren't going to like this," the schoolteacher said, as he held a pair of binoculars to his eyes.

And Capelli saw that the other man was correct. The drop ship had landed, the cargo-bay door was open, and a dozen Hybrids were on the ground. Then something unexpected appeared.

The Attack Drone was identical to those Capelli had seen in the past, except for one thing: This unit was carrying a rider! As were the two machines that followed it out of the cargo compartment and into the bright sunlight.

Such a thing wasn't unheard of. In fact, Capelli knew that a Sentinel named Hawthorn had successfully ridden a Drone. But such occurrences were very rare. And the stink–machine combination was potentially quite dangerous.

"They're coming this way," Unver warned, and it was true. The Chimera had formed a skirmish line that consisted of alternating Hybrids and piloted Drones.

Capelli had a sudden thought and rolled over in order to look west. He was pleased to see that there weren't any stinks coming from that direction. Not yet, anyway.

"Okay," Capelli said as he turned back. "Here's what I want you to do. Once the stinks are in range, kill a couple of them. But don't waste any bullets on the Drones. Their shields will protect the pilots. Then I want you to stand up, let the bastards see you, and run west. There's an old combine a couple of hundred yards to the west. Take cover behind that."

"Yeah?" Unver said suspiciously. "And what are *you* going to do?"

"I'm going to lie here, let the stinks pass by me, and shoot them in the back."

Unver grinned. "I like it. But you'd better find some cover. Start looking. I'll handle the rest."

And the teacher was as good as his word. While Capelli worked his way sideways, careful to keep Rowdy in close, Unver opened fire with the BAR. The M1918A2 was firing armor-piercing .30-06 rounds, which produced an ominous roar as Capelli settled in below some bushes and pulled the dog in next to him. The firing stopped as Unver got up, paused to make sure the stinks had seen him, and turned west as projectiles kicked up dirt along the crest of the hill. Then he was gone and hidden from their sight.

Capelli was lying on his back. By raising his head slightly he could look left and right. That was how he saw four Hybrids top the crest of the hill and head downslope. The Drones arrived a second later, and as luck would have it, one of them passed directly over Capelli's position. He could hear the thrumming sound, see the scratches on the bottom of the machine, and smell the stink of ozone as a wave of heat washed over him. Rowdy barked madly, but the Drone was loud enough to obscure the sound.

Then Capelli was up, carbine to his shoulder, firing from only yards away. The pilot's back was exposed and the Hybrid jerked convulsively before it fell to the ground. And with no one to hold the throttle open, the Drone drifted to a halt.

What happened next was the result of an impulse rather than a carefully conceived plan as Capelli dashed down the slope. Thanks to the height advantage the hillside gave him, he was able to enter the Drone and occupy the just-vacated seat. The vehicle bobbed and sank slightly as Capelli's hands sought the controls. It took him only seconds to figure out that the joystick on the left was used to steer the Drone—and that the grip on the right controlled the machine's speed.

Then Capelli was off. And not a second too soon, as a 'brid fired a burst of rockets at him. They passed through the space he had occupied moments before and slammed into the hillside. The battle could have ended there and then had the other Drones been able to gang up on him. But Unver was in position by that time. And every time a 'brid pilot turned its back on the schoolteacher it risked being shot.

That limited what the Chimera could do and gave Capelli a much-needed advantage as he guided his vehicle in behind one of the stinks and fired the Drone's automatic weapon. A steady stream of projectiles tore into the enemy pilot and its mechanical mount. The Drone exploded. Pieces of flaming debris flew in every direction. There was a clanging sound as a piece of metal struck the front of Capelli's machine and bounced off. Capelli put the vehicle into a tight turn and went after the third Drone.

But it, along with all of the remaining Hybrids, had already fallen victim to Unver's lethal BAR. The pilot was slumped forward against the controls as its machine drifted two feet off the ground. "We did it!" the ex-schoolteacher shouted exultantly, as he dashed upslope. "We killed every goddamned one of them."

It was the last thing Unver ever said, as a row of ten Stalkers appeared to the west. All of them opened fire at once and missiles rained down out of the sky. Capelli was spared as columns of soil soared into the air—but Unver vanished as if he had never existed.

Capelli swore bitterly as he turned the machine towards the east and opened the throttle all the way. There was only one thing he could do, and that was to keep going. For Unver, for Susan, and ultimately for himself.

Well, I'll be damned, the voice remarked. *You listed someone else first.*

CHAPTER EIGHTEEN
FINAL JUDGMENT

Thursday, January 14, 1954
Tunnel-Through, Oklahoma

Susan Capelli was sitting upright in the trunk of a 1953 Cadillac, peering out through the four-inch gap between the lid and the car's rounded body. She was wrapped in a blanket, leaning against her pack. The vehicle was sitting on four flat tires in a small parking lot. To her left, about three hundred feet away, stood a water tower. She could see the lookout stationed up on the walkway. The pimply-faced youth wasn't a day over eighteen. Too bad he was going to die.

The hill, and the tunnel concealed within it, lay beyond. After circling around and approaching from the south, Susan had been able to infiltrate the area the night before. The car, and the cover it gave her, were a godsend. Two regulators had passed within fifteen feet of the vehicle earlier that day without giving it a second glance.

Now, as the pale yellow sun began to sink towards the western horizon, she saw little activity in the area. The exception being the lookouts posted on the flanks of the hill itself. She couldn't see the north side, but knew where the sentries located in front of her were, and planned to kill them as soon as Joseph arrived. *If* Joseph arrived—which, as the hours crawled by, seemed less and less likely.

But he's a Sentinel, she told herself. *Possibly the last Sentinel. And Sentinels are hard to kill.* The thought provided her with a momentary sense of comfort. But that feeling soon fell prey to the unresolved doubts which had gone before. The result was a persistent uneasiness that, combined with the nausea she'd been experiencing, made Susan feel ill. *Please, God,* she prayed. *Please keep him safe. And deliver him to me.*

Moments later, as if to mock her, three Chimeran fighters roared over the hill. Susan's initial reaction was to view the aircraft as a bad omen. Then she realized that the fighters might portend good news. What if her husband's efforts had been successful? What if he was closing in on Tunnel-Through from the west? That would explain the presence of enemy aircraft.

Susan felt a sudden surge of adrenaline, checked her weapon for the umpteenth time, and wished more members of the alliance were present. But they were needed at home, where she was supposed to be. Capelli would be furious with her for coming. Susan knew that. But she wasn't about to let the regulators or the stinks kill her man.

It was difficult to sit there for hours on end, and her butt was starting to hurt. So she was about to shift her weight when the Cadillac shook slightly and a series of muffled explosions were heard. The Chimera were coming! And that meant Capelli was alive.

That was all the information Susan needed. After hours of careful observation she knew exactly where Tunnel-Through's lookouts were—and she knew Judge Ramsey would be counting on them to provide him with a constant flow of intelligence. So if she could blind the bastard, and cut him off from the outside world, it would be a big help to the stinks. And ironically enough, that was what she wanted to do.

So with the efficiency of a woman determined to protect what was, and what could be, she shot the teenager in the head. As his body fell away from the tower and plummeted towards the ground she was already swinging the Fareye towards the hill beyond. The second target was located behind a bush she had marked earlier. Having heard the shot, the regulator was on his feet, binoculars to his eyes, looking for her.

She had to raise the barrel slightly due to the distance involved—and there was a westerly breeze to consider. With the crosshairs centered on a point slightly above and to the left of the lookout's head, she applied pressure to the trigger. The man went down as if poleaxed. The battle for Tunnel-Through had begun.

Capelli could have flown faster, and would have had it not been for Rowdy, who was loping along below the Attack Drone as they headed east. Capelli felt an unexpected sense of elation as a dozen regulators charged out of a copse of trees to intercept him. Because rather than turn and run, as he had been forced to do recently, Capelli could tackle the horsemen head-on.

Projectiles sparkled as they hit the Drone's shield. Capelli responded with a burst of rockets, whooping with joy. The missiles exploded and sent chunks of bloody flesh flying in all directions. A burst of machine-gun fire was sufficient to put most of the survivors down. Then he had to pull up and circle around as the Stalkers continued to close in from the west. "They're over here!" Capelli shouted into the wind. "Come and get the bastards." Rowdy heard his voice, even if the stinks didn't, and continued to lope along below.

Then a shadow flickered over the Drone, a stick of bombs slammed into the hill, and black smoke billowed up to stain the sky. The first fighter was closely followed by a second and a third, as the Chimeran pilots began to prepare the objective for the ground assault to come.

Did the fly-stinks realize that the Attack Drone had been hijacked? He had no way of knowing. Not that it mattered a great deal, since Capelli's machine was too small and maneuverable for the fighters to engage effectively.

But the Stalkers *were* a threat, and a very significant one, as they fired a broadside that exploded all around him. The resulting shock wave threw the Drone into the side of the hill. Capelli fell, and everything went black.

For the first time in months Judge Ramsey felt scared. But he knew it was important not to show it. So as Hunter stood in front of the big desk, and waited for permission to deliver his report, Ramsey made a show out of lighting a cigar. "Okay," he said finally, once the tube of tobacco was drawing properly. "What's the situation?"

"I'm not entirely sure," Hunter replied honestly. "Someone or some*thing* began to kill the lookouts on the south side of the hill about half an hour ago. And when I sent men up to replace them, they got killed too."

Ramsey frowned. "What is the bastard using? Projectiles or bullets?"

"My guess is bullets. Although it's hard to tell with head shots."

"It's probably a human, then," Ramsey concluded. "Although that's kind of strange given the circumstances. So what have the lookouts on the north side got to say?"

The train shook, and some of the items on Ramsey's desk rattled, as more bombs exploded above. "We had reports of a piloted Attack Drone," Hunter replied. "And we had a report from one lookout saying that ten or twelve Stalkers are inbound from the west. Then the bombs began to fall. Now we're blind."

Ramsey felt an emptiness where his stomach should have been as he looked out the window into the tunnel beyond. He could hear small chunks of concrete hitting the roof and could see people running every which way as they sought shelter from the falling debris. What was it that Shakespeare had written? "Discretion is the better part of valor"? *Yes,* Ramsey thought to himself. *It sure as hell is.* He brought his eyes back to find that Hunter's were waiting. "The engine is running?"

"Yes, sir. Per your orders."

"And the charges are ready?"

Hunter nodded. "Ready and waiting."

"Okay," Ramsey replied. "Get all of the regulators onboard. You have five minutes."

"What about the workers, women, and children?"

"We don't have room," Ramsey said hollowly. "I wish we did. You have your orders. Execute them."

If Hunter disagreed with his employer's decision, there was no sign of it on his face. "Five minutes. Yes, sir." Then he was gone.

A blob of gray ash fell onto the front of Ramsey's snowy white shirt. He blew it off. The whole thing was unfortunate. *Very* unfortunate. Why, after months of missing it, had the stinks been able to zero in on Tunnel-Through? There was no way to know.

But that was what contingency plans were for. Would the mayor of Shipdown welcome him with open arms? Maybe, and maybe not. Not that it mattered so long as Olmey did what he was told.

The thought brought a grim smile to Ramsey's face as the train's whistle blew three times, regulators rushed to enter the passenger cars, and gunshots were heard as they turned to fire on any citizen who tried to follow them aboard. A woman appeared outside the window. Her fists made a thumping sound as they beat on the glass. Ramsey closed his eyes.

Capelli was surrounded by darkness. Thunder rolled in the distance, the earth shook beneath him, and his head hurt. Something told him that he should get up. But he couldn't remember why, and it was much easier to simply remain where he was. Then he felt something akin to wet sandpaper scrape across his face. The sensation was so annoying that he opened his eyes. And there, just inches away, was Rowdy's blood-encrusted snout, his breath fogging the air. The dog whined eagerly and licked Capelli's nose.

"Stop that," Capelli said, as he sat up. "Talk about bad breath! What have you been eating, anyway?"

Rowdy was in no way offended by the comment and continued to nuzzle Capelli as he struggled to his feet. Much to his surprise, the Attack Drone had survived the collision with the hill and, though more than a little battered, was hanging motionless ten feet away.

Capelli attempted to ignore the pain in his head as he made his way over to the machine. And just in time, too—a Stalker pilot spotted him and opened fire. Geysers of dirt flew up as Capelli jumped onto the motorcycle-style seat and opened the throttle.

Then he was off, with Rowdy running along behind. They were headed east, and as soon as he could, Capelli turned right. The curve of the hillside led him back towards the west and Tunnel-Through's southern entrance. Were the stinks aware of it? Capelli wanted to make sure they were.

But that plan went up in smoke as a series of carefully calculated explosions threw tons of rock aside and a massive locomotive nosed its way out of the tunnel and into the wan sunlight. The engine had a blocky appearance, was decorated with horizontal stripes of orange and black paint, and made a loud roaring sound. A sizable cowcatcher was sufficient to push medium-sized boulders out of the way as the train gathered speed. It didn't require a genius to figure out that Ramsey was trying to escape. And Capelli knew that if he was allowed to do so, the ex-judge would return.

So Capelli executed a broad, sweeping turn that would allow him to strafe the train from front to back. And judging from the storm of projectiles striking the Drone's shield, his approach had not gone unnoticed.

Capelli saw the engineer duck as projectiles bounced off the locomotive's steel flank. Windows shattered as the Drone approached the first passenger car and a regulator was thrown back into the interior. And so it went, until all of the cars had been attacked and Capelli was forced to arc away.

But the train was still rolling and, as if to emphasize that fact, the engineer blew the horn three times. The long, drawn-out shrieks were like screams of defiance as the behemoth continued to gather speed.

The overlapping explosions and the sudden appearance of the locomotive came as a complete surprise to Susan. As was the piloted Drone that rounded the east side of the hill to attack it. She assumed a Hybrid was at the controls until she saw Rowdy racing along behind the machine and realized what that meant. Somehow, somewhere, her husband had taken control of the Drone and was using it for his own purposes. The most important of which was to stop the escaping train.

So as a pair of crablike Stalkers minced forward, their weapons blazing, Susan knew what she had to do. The problem being that she was too low for the shot she needed to make. So she raised the lid, jumped down onto the ground, and closed it again. Then it was a simple matter to step up onto the bumper and climb onto the roof.

The Fareye felt light as a feather as she brought the rifle up to her shoulder. The locomotive had two horizontal windows. Both were very small. The engineer's head was no more than a dark blur beyond the dusty glass. But as the engine came towards her, Susan had to try. She squeezed the trigger, a hole appeared in the safety glass, and the target disappeared. The train began to slow. But would that be enough?

Ramsey swore a blue streak as he fired the Webley and the incoming projectiles tore his office apart. The Attack Drone was right outside. So close that he could see the man seated behind the translucent shield smiling. But that wasn't the worst of it. An explosion sounded and the passenger car jerked to a sudden halt.

The man on the Drone was forced to break off the attack as a half-dozen smaller machines swooped in to attack him. That gave Ramsey an opportunity to stand and reload.

Ramsey had just pushed the last bullet into place and closed the weapon when the door slammed open and Hunter appeared with Tilson at his elbow.

"The stinks blew the train in half," the regulator announced emotionlessly. "But some of the horses survived, and Thunder is waiting outside. We'll make a run for it."

It wasn't much as plans go—but something was better than nothing. So Ramsey followed the others onto the platform behind the passenger car. Two regulators were waiting on the ground with extra mounts.

"There's no horse for me," Tilson said plaintively. "What am I going to do?"

"Die," Ramsey said, as he shot Tilson in the chest. "Maybe that will shut you up."

Then, Ramsey swung his unwieldy body onto Thunder's hand-tooled saddle, and kicked the Clydesdale with both heels. That put the huge horse into motion as more Stalkers converged on the scene—and Hybrids rushed forward to prevent the fugitives from escaping.

But for a moment it seemed as if the four of them were untouchable as they followed the train tracks through a sleet of projectiles.

However, that was when Ramsey looked up to see the pile of smoking wreckage that had been the Attack Drone. And there, standing next to it, was a man and a dog. Ramsey was reaching for the sawed-off shotgun holstered to the right side of the saddle when the man raised a pistol and fired. Both of the regulators were snatched out of their saddles and thrown to the ground.

The shotgun didn't have much range. Ramsey knew that. So he held his fire as Hunter took a bullet in the chest, and was just about to pull the trigger, when a Chimeran missile corkscrewed in, hitting the ground fifty yards in front of him. It went off with a flash of light and a loud boom.

Thunder came to a sudden stop; Ramsey was thrown over the horse's head, and hit the ground hard. That knocked the wind out of him. But Ramsey knew he *had* to stand, *had* to run, and managed to push his body up off the ground. At that point he saw the man lying on the ground, clutching a bloody thigh. A woman was kneeling next to him. She had a rifle, which was butt-down on the ground. Probably because she thought he was dead.

The shotgun was gone, but the Webley was in its holster, and Ramsey pulled it. The .455-caliber pistol was up and ready to fire when a Chimeran bomb penetrated Tunnel-Through and went off. A series of secondary explosions shook the ground as rocks were thrown high into the air and the tunnel collapsed.

Having witnessed the destruction, Ramsey turned back just in time to see the man fire. Ramsey felt a sledgehammer strike his chest and fell onto his back. He was lying there, staring up at the gunmetal-gray sky, when the man appeared. His left arm was draped over the woman's shoulders and the pistol was pointed down at him. Why? Ramsey wondered to himself. *Why?* He coughed and felt something warm trickle down over his chin. It was difficult to speak. "Do I know you?"

"No," the man said. "You don't."

The gun produced a loud boom, but Ramsey didn't live long enough to hear it. Tunnel-Through was dead.

Haven, Oklahoma

Five days had passed since the Chimera had obliterated Tunnel-Through. It was nighttime, and Mr. and Mrs. Capelli were lying on the roof of Haven's five-and-dime, looking up at the stars from under three layers of blankets. It was a picnic of sorts—a celebration of the fact that they were still alive.

Ironically, it had been the citizens of Judge Ramsey's well-hidden community that saved their lives. Because as Tunnel-Through collapsed, and its citizens ran out into the open, the Chimera turned in on them. A terrible slaughter followed.

Capelli had only been able to escape the carnage by leaning on Susan and hobbling away from the railroad tracks. Then, after wiggling into the crawl space underneath a nearby railroad shack, they were able to hide until the Chimera left the area sixteen hours later.

The trek to Haven was long and painful. But Capelli didn't care. Not so long as he had Susan and Rowdy at his side. Now, after a good dinner, it was time to lie next to his wife and consider the future.

"We need a couple of bedrooms," Susan remarked. "One for the baby and one for us."

"Yeah," Capelli agreed reflectively. "That's going to take a whole lot of digging."

Susan smiled from inches away. "Do you have anything better to do?"

"Nope. I don't."

She snuggled up to him. "It feels good to be home."

Capelli was about to reply when what looked like lightning flashed along the southern horizon and the sound of thunder rolled across the land. Except that the sky was clear—that noise could not be thunder. Somewhere, down towards Oklahoma City, people were dying. *And other people are alive,* the voice put in. *Thanks to you. Well done, Sergeant Capelli. Well done.*